A Kill in the Morning

A KILL IN THE MORNING

Graeme Shimmin

BANTAM PRESS

LONDON · TORONTO · SYDNEY · AUCKLAND · JOHANNESBURG

TRANSWORLD PUBLISHERS
61–63 Uxbridge Road, London W5 5SA
A Random House Group Company
www.transworldbooks.co.uk

First published in Great Britain
in 2014 by Bantam Press
an imprint of Transworld Publishers

A CIP catalogue record for this book
is available from the British Library.

ISBN 9780593073537

Addresses for Random House Group Ltd companies outside the UK
can be found at: www.randomhouse.co.uk
The Random House Group Ltd Reg. No. 954009

The Random House Group Limited supports the Forest Stewardship Council® (FSC®), the leading international forest-certification organisation. Our books carrying the FSC label are printed on FSC®-certified paper. FSC is the only forest-certification scheme supported by the leading environmental organisations, including Greenpeace. Our paper procurement policy can be found at www.randomhouse.co.uk/environment

Typeset in 11.5/15.5pt Minion by Falcon Oast Graphic Art Ltd.
Printed and bound in Great Britain by
Clays Ltd, Bungay, Suffolk

2 4 6 8 10 9 7 5 3 1

To my mum and dad.

Contents

Part Three: Consequences

Notes

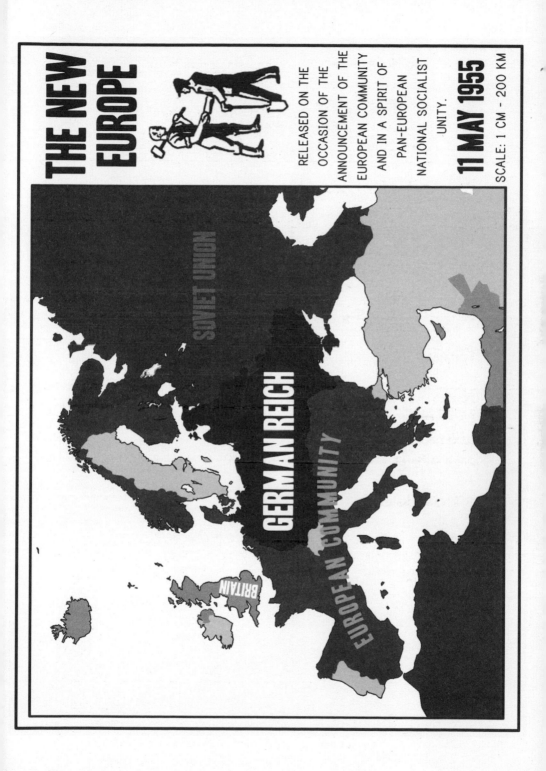

Part One

Contrivance

If ye kill before midnight, be silent,
And wake not the woods with your bay.

Rudyard Kipling, *The Law of the Jungle*

1

Strength through Joy

The signer hereby swears that this is a true account, and furthermore that to the best of his knowledge and belief no Jewish or coloured blood flows in his veins, or those of his ancestors. [Signature illegible]

Declaration scrawled on the flyleaf of the journal of an unknown SS scientist, discovered in the ruins of Berlin, 1945.

I don't like killing, but I'm good at it.

Murder isn't so bad from a distance, just shapes popping up in my scope. Close-up work, though – a garrotte around a target's neck or a knife in their heart – it's not for me. Too much empathy, that's my problem.

Usually.

But not today. Today is different.

⊕

The sun stabs through the early-morning clouds, casting harsh shadows across the silver Mercedes Gullwing parked between the trees. Two herons labour into the air from the swamp opposite, skimming the reeds as they struggle to gain height.

I lift a cherrywood case from the boot of the car and place it on the ground. The aluminium catches flick open to reveal a sniper rifle nestling inside. I pick it up and wrap it in a tartan travel blanket.

The driver's side door rises, on a hiss of hydraulics. I get in, place the rifle on the parcel shelf and adjust the seat. The frigid engine coughs on the first press of the starter. I depress the clutch and try again. Signs of life emerge.

The car bumps along the muddy track, between a regiment of glistening fir trees, its suspension thumping in the potholes. At the main road, I turn in the direction of Oranienburg. The tyres squeal in protest as the Mercedes leaps forward. I glance at my watch – 6.58.

I try the radio, but find the arrhythmic thump of barrage jamming where the BBC's signal should be. The rest of the dial offers nothing but martial music and German news announcers:

Heil Hitler! Here is the Reichsrundfunk Berlin news at 7.00 a.m. on 24 September 1955.

The Foreign Ministry today announced that the Führer will meet next week with British Prime Minister Anthony Eden. The leaders will consult in relation to the Israeli problem. The Chancellery has released this statement from our beloved Führer: 'I have always had a single goal – ensuring Germany's freedom and independence by building the strength and power of our Reich. Now world Jewry directs its puppet statesmen in capitalist-plutocratic England—'

Fuck that.

I open the window, rest one elbow on the sill, and run through the plan again.

Karlstrasse is right where I left it.

Oranienburg is just far enough from Berlin for it to have its own castle, now serving as an SS riding school. My Mercedes follows a platoon mounted on iron-grey stallions across the Havel river bridge. Reaching the town centre, I turn north towards my target.

On Karlstrasse, I stop the car and get out. Twenty yards away is a seven- or eight-year-old boy, sitting on the pavement, engrossed in a work of pavement art. The chalks that he's using are scattered across my path. I kneel down and smile at him.

'What are you drawing?' I ask, bringing a bar of Swiss chocolate from my pocket.

He explains how his chalk Panzers are eliminating the enemies of the Reich. Nothing now remains of them but black scribbles.

'Do you want to be in the army?' I ask, unwrapping the chocolate bar and breaking off a piece.

'I want to be in the SS,' he says. 'I'll volunteer as soon as I'm big enough.' His eyes don't leave the chocolate.

'The army is better than the SS,' I say. 'I bet you never see the SS marching down this street.'

Naturally, he's outraged at the slur.

'An SS Obersturmbannführer visits us every week.'

'He does not,' I say.

'He does! He does! He pays me to guard his Kübelwagen while he's on important Reich business at number twelve. Normally he has a driver, but he doesn't bring him. And...'

I examine the target house. It has a green door and no obvious security measures.

'... and he promised to get me a model Tiger tank.'

I stand up again and hand the boy his prize.

'Well, well, you are honoured. Good luck, little soldier.'

The wide-eyed boy rewraps the chocolate, places it in his pocket and produces an expert Hitler salute.

Oranienburg railway station car park is busy enough for anonymity, even in a silver Gullwing. I pick up a *Berliner Morgenpost* from the newspaper stand and weave through the booking office queues to the café. In the window seat, I sip the coffee and scoff the sliced ham and soft-boiled eggs, without tasting them.

The German rush hour bustles around me, oblivious of my presence. Oil-stained railway workers tuck into their breakfasts. Pinstriped suits wait for S-Bahn trains into Berlin. Housewives venture abroad in search of groceries. No one here will remember me. Talking to the boy on Karlstrasse was a risk, but probably all he'll recall is 'a man dressed in black'.

Reuven suggested that 10.30 would be the optimum time to begin operations. I check my watch, make a quick mental calculation, beckon the waiter over and order another double espresso. A troop of teenage Hitler-Jugend, neat in their tan uniforms, passes the café, singing the Horst-Wessel song. I flick through the *Berliner Morgenpost*, decoding the propaganda:

1955 HARVEST SETS NEW RECORD FOR REICH
. . . more starvation in the Ukraine
JEWISH TERRORISTS KILL WOMEN AND CHILDREN
. . . by accident, whilst attacking Gestapo torture chamber
PROFESSOR HEISENBERG HONOURED ON FIFTH ANNIVERSARY OF REICH'S ATOMIC BOMB
. . . and on the eighth anniversary of the British bomb; if we'd only had the balls, we could have turned Germany into a wasteland and done the whole world a favour.

I stare out of the café window, eyes unfocused.
Hatred can blind you sometimes.

At 10.29, my Mercedes coasts the length of Karlstrasse for a second time. A stubby little slate-grey Kübelwagen with SS markings is parked outside number twelve. The eight-year-old boy I spoke to earlier is sitting behind the jeep's wheel.

I pull in round the corner, invisible between two highly polished KdF-Wagen, the so-called 'strength through joy car'. How many future members of the Aryan elite are conceived each evening on the back seats of those beetle-like automobiles?

I reach over to unlock the glove compartment. It contains a Welrod silenced pistol, two loaded magazines, a pair of lightweight gloves and a shoulder holster. I pull on the gloves, grab the rest of the gear and step out of the car. There's no one about, so I shuffle off my black horsehide jacket. The holster is a snug fit, even after I adjust the straps. I slot the Welrod into the oiled leather, and draw it twice to check for catches or obstructions. Satisfied, I slip on the jacket again, and stuff a balaclava in the jacket pocket.

I advance past the neat suburban houses at a moderate pace; such calmness evades the attention of curtain-twitching housewives. The boy is now busy polishing the Kübelwagen's headlights. He glances up. I smile at him and he half-waves back, chocolate smeared around his mouth. My left hand grips the fourth key on the ring. The steps rising up to the target's door are spotless. I take two deep breaths to steady myself.

Reuven's men won't want any witnesses, and the boy will try to stop them taking the Kübelwagen.

I turn. 'Hey, kid, here's a Reichsmark. Go get me some cigarettes,' I say, throwing the coin at him.

'What sort?'

What sort? Fuck. Fuck. What sort? I stare at him, mind blank. His eyes narrow.

'Garbaty?' I mumble.

'Garbaty?' he says, confused.

'Or whatever they have that's similar. I'm not from round here. And hurry up, I'm gasping.'

The kid nods, tucks his cap in his pocket and charges off towards the main road.

I take the steps in a single bound, the clenched key already heading for the keyhole. The faintest of clicks announces the surrender of the lock. I slip into the hallway and toe the door closed behind me, mouth dry and heartbeat deepening.

My gun held at waist level, I stand and listen for forty-five seconds. The only sounds are the ticking of the grandfather clock, a faint rhythmic creaking and the distant rumble of traffic. Before me is a staircase with a Paisley carpet. I ascend, testing each tread. The creaking increases in volume as the ticking fades away. I reach the top step. In one of the bedrooms, a woman gasps. Her groans combine with masculine grunting.

Strength through joy.

The ecstasy is emanating from the bedroom overlooking the street. I approach it gun first. Close enough to touch the door, I stop and pull the balaclava over my head.

I push the door open, revealing the unedifying spectacle of the Pig, naked and hunched over his scrawny mistress. He has folded his pristine SS uniform over a chair that stands at the foot of the bed. She's flat on her back, knuckles white, gripping the bedposts. Her eyes examine the ceiling as she mouths the usual erotic platitudes. He hammers into her with the stink of sweat rolling off his porcine body. His keys, glasses and wallet are on the seat, but I'm looking for his gun.

The mistress senses me, sees my gun and screams. The Pig, taking this for tribute to his sexual prowess, redoubles his thrusting. I step into the room, spotting the holster positioned on the bedside cabinet, outside the Pig's reach.

Something about his mistress's continued screaming cuts through the Pig's frenzy. He ceases his onslaught and grunts at her. She stares at me, open-mouthed. His head turns in my direction, face flushed with exertion, hair plastered to his forehead. He curses.

I motion him to climb off his mistress. He glances at his gun, but I shake my head. Taking the warning, he inches across the bed and sits up, belly fat sagging forward. The mistress, her face pure snow, pulls up a sheet to cover her nakedness. She edges away from the Pig.

'Alex Methuen says hello,' I say, finger tightening on the trigger.

The Pig sits on the side of the bed, gabbling in Russian.

I shoot him in his right knee.

The Welrod's hiss is no louder than a match being struck. The Pig screams louder than his mistress does. The impact of the bullet forces his right leg backwards. He collapses off the bed and squashes into the floor. His hands instinctively cover the wound, blood and shattered cartilage oozing between his fingers. The liquid flows down his shins and spreads over the floorboards, a ruby slick in the dust.

'Erling Granlund asked me to tell you he's waiting for you,' I say.

I shoot him in his left knee.

The blood pumps across the bedroom floor. The Pig screams louder than the first time. He tries to pull his blubber towards his gun, but his own greasy blood betrays him, a hand slips and he buries his face in the gore. I kick him in the side. He rolls over and stares up at me. Fear contorts his scarlet-masked features.

'One million pounds,' he says, trying English.

'One million pounds of what?' I ask.

'Money! Money! Take it! Don't kill me! In the case! There! There!' The Pig pulls himself up and gesticulates towards the end of the bed.

My eyes don't move. This is not about money.

'Reg Smith,' I say. 'I'm sure Reg has something special planned for you. He always was a vindictive bastard.'

'Nein! Nein!' shouts the Pig, seeing the death in my eyes.

'Ja. Ja,' I say.

I shoot him through the heart.

Twice.

His body slumps to the floor. I squelch through the blood until I'm standing over him, one foot on either side of his prostrate body. A sour mixture of rust and salt fills my nostrils.

Behind me, I sense an apparition of three brave, dead men in snow camouflage looking on: Alex, Erling and Reg, the Special Operations Executive's martyrs. The Pig's victims. My friends.

'And this is for the rest of the SOE heroes you tortured and murdered,' I say.

I shoot him in the face, just below the bridge of the nose.

I grab the Pig's attaché case and his keys on the way out. The mistress's screaming follows me across the landing, down the stairs and into the yard, which is empty save for a few dustbins. I pause to reload, then throw the attaché case over the wall and climb after it. Lavender edges the path through the garden of the house behind, its sweet perfume overwhelming. I emerge a few steps to the left of the Mercedes. By the car, I vomit twice into the gutter.

Keep moving.

On Karlstrasse, four men in SS uniform are standing by the Kübelwagen. I throw them the Pig's keys as I drive past. In the distance, a police siren wails.

There's no sign of the boy.

⊕

The blanket-wrapped rifle seems incongruous in my hands, swaddled like a baby.

Behind me, the Mercedes is parked at the roadside. It's only a couple of blocks from Karlstrasse, but it's the edge of the town. In front of me rises a low ridge dotted with trees. I work my way upward through the muddy undergrowth. Twenty feet from the crest of the ridge I drop to my haunches to avoid being silhouetted.

I check my sight lines. Satisfied, I make myself comfortable on the ground, below a hawthorn bush. I place the spare ammunition clips on a convenient log and unwrap the rifle. It's a Karabiner 98k, Fallschirmjäger issue with collapsible stock, which I fold out and rest on a flat stone. I screw the lens covers off the Zeiss telescopic sight and bend my head to examine the view.

Before me is Konzentrationslager Sachsenhausen, one of the dozen main concentration camps where the Nazis hold 'undesirables'. Those deemed unworthy of the New Germany are legion: communists, gypsies, homosexuals, Jehovah's Witnesses and the catchall 'antisocial elements'. There are even a few stray Jews who somehow didn't get out in the Exodus of 1943.

The camp is laid out in a rough triangle, with its apex towards my current position. Nine-foot-high concrete walls surmounted with barbed wire surround the entire area. I count five two-storey guard posts dotting the ramparts, each with a machine gun poking its snout out. I sweep the rifle around, checking the position of each one through the scope.

The prisoners' barracks form a semicircle on the far side of the parade ground from the gatehouse. A small group stands in the shadow of the gallows at the centre of the parade ground. Two are guards, the rest are in chains. Prisoners in striped uniforms are assembling to witness the latest hangings.

The gatehouse stands at the base of the triangle. Through the scope, the faces of the guards are all too visible: real human beings, not targets. I lift my head from the rifle's scope and they become faceless uniforms again. Better to focus on the technicalities. I adjust the scope to compensate for the wind and the distance to the targets.

The guards will be expecting the return of their commandant at any moment, to preside over the hangings. Happily, the Pig will be returning only in a coffin. His Kübelwagen is approaching the gatehouse, though, driven by Reuven's men. I bring the rifle's sight round until the crosshairs focus on the gatehouse.

The explosion ripples through the ground. That's my signal. I caress the trigger, and the first guard dies. The blast wave arrives, the birds burst from the trees, and dislodged twigs and dirt patter down around me.

My head comes up to locate the next guard post. A cloud of smoke obscures part of the wall at the far side of the camp. I swing the rifle, drop back to the scope, adjust my aim and fire. The second guard falls backward, hit in the face.

The three remaining machine guns start firing at the prisoners. Hand grenades crump inside the gatehouse, as Reuven's men take on the camp guards, room to room.

Five shots expended, and five guards down, I stop to reload the rifle. I take a second to prioritize the remaining targets. Prisoners are running in all directions. Bodies are strewn across the parade ground, dead, wounded or cowering. The toughest and most desperate prisoners are grappling with their guards, attempting to kill them and take their weapons. One group, taking its chance, is heading for the gap in the wall caused by the explosion.

I slot a new clip into the rifle's internal magazine and bring it back to my shoulder. Two more shots finish off the guard posts. I use the last three bullets to kill SS officers firing their pistols at prisoners charging the gatehouse.

My part of the attack is complete.

I crawl backward, away from the crest of the ridge and the echoing small arms fire. The heavy beating of rotors approaches from the east. I stand up and stride back down the hill to the Mercedes. A police car shoots past in the direction of Karlstrasse, its siren screaming. I open the Mercedes's trunk, throw the rifle inside, retrieve the attaché case and slam the lid closed again.

I lever up the petrol cap and stuff a rag into the pipe. It's a shame to burn such a work of art, but my fingerprints are all over its interior. My lighter wheel sparks and I cup one shaking hand around the flame. The rag blackens as it catches fire. I pick up my bag and retire to a safe distance, wiping my sleeve across my mouth.

A massive Fairey Rotodyne roars over the crest of the ridge, jet-rotors screaming. Pure black all over, without a marking on its square fuselage or its stumpy wings. It looks like the unfortunate result of an ill-advised night of passion between a helicopter and a cargo plane.

I throw up an arm to protect my eyes from the tornado raised by the rotors.

Behind me, the Mercedes's fuel tank explodes.

The gyroplane circles the burning car, with its pintle-mounted machine guns trained on me. The cargo bay door slides open. It transitions into a hover and sinks to the ground.

I raise my hands and walk towards it.

2

Mouse World

The expedition to Ultima Thule reported today. They have made such wondrous discoveries! Scrolls of pure gold, untouched for millennia. Their message floated across the aether to be received with astonishment.

Journal of an unknown SS scientist, p.45

Kitty has a recurring dream.

She sits in a Gestapo prison cell, unable to move. She dare not look down for fear that the reason she can't move is that they have broken her. So she concentrates on the small window above her and the sunlight straining to warm her face through its bars.

Outside, on the other side of the grille, perches a hawk with a mouse in its talons. The hawk watches the mouse squirming, still alive. The mouse's eyes are bursting with desperation, with pleading. The mouse wants to live.

But the hawk does not care what the mouse wants. Killing is the nature of the hawk. Hiding is the nature of the mouse. The circle goes round.

The hawk strikes with its beak. Something emerges from inside the mouse. It looks like a thread of scarlet elastic, stretching outwards as the hawk pulls at it. The elastic snaps and vanishes into the hawk's mouth.

The mouse is not dead. Its feeble paws scrabble in mid-air, unable to find purchase. The hawk's beak disappears into the mouse's chest again. The mouse's eyes roll upward. The mouse wants to live, but wishes do not create reality.

The bloody beak probes the mouse's ribs, pincering the flesh from the bones.

Kitty knows she is the mouse.

⊕

Kitty creeps off the S-Bahn at Alexanderplatz, heading for Unter den Linden, and straight away, her plan goes wrong.

The dress she's wearing hints of mothballs, but the fit of it is perfect. The idea was that she'd look too elegant to be a defeatist and a saboteur. But groups of soldiers on leave, safe in the anonymity of the pack, stare at her and whistle. She keeps her head down, fighting the rodent urge to swivel her head in every direction. An Orpo traffic policeman sees her and loses interest in the cars. She skitters across the road, watching him without meeting his gaze. He licks his lips.

The second she tries anything, one of the predators will swoop on her. And then the Gestapo, and Prinz-Albrecht-Strasse, and chains shackling her to a wall while they . . .

Hide. Hide this dress. Hide the shape it reveals.

Her father's raincoat, black with a wide belt, engulfs her, but blessed is anonymity. Her mother's finest Dior dress and her father's raincoat have become her icons.

Kitty sneaks along under the lime trees that give Unter den Linden its name. A million sparkling lights and a thousand blood-red banners line the boulevard. There's a monument to National

Socialist heroism on every corner. Captured Russian searchlights fire pillars of brilliance into the night sky. This capital of the thousand-year Reich inspires awe.

It's the archetype of everything she hates.

Think of Sophie. Think of Hans. Think of all the true Germans before her who faced their fate with courage. Their hearts had pounded like hers, perhaps, but they hadn't been bewildered. They hadn't started at every unexpected sound.

Sophie and Hans: the brave founders of the White Rose resistance movement. Their crime? Writing a couple of pamphlets urging Germans to 'break National Socialist terror through the power of the spirit'. Their trial? In front of the People's Court in 1943, just before the Nazi-Soviet armistice. Their punishment? Death by guillotine. They strode to their deaths, heads high. They believed. They didn't collapse.

But Kitty doesn't want to die.

Oh, God, no, she really doesn't want to die. Hitler and his corrupt gang are so powerful and she is so weak. What can she do? What possible difference can one little mouse make? The stories they tell about the Gestapo and pretty girls. Could she bear that? Could Prinz-Albrecht-Strasse be even worse than the things she's already had to do in order to survive?

Probably.

She can't go back to the group and tell them that her courage failed. They took risks to provide her with the stickers now hidden in her raincoat pockets. Now all she has to do is place them. She peels one sticker from the roll and transfers it to her trembling palm. Another lamp post looms. She can't put it off any longer. Keep a steady pace now. Don't draw attention. Head down, eyes focused on the lamp post. Hand in pocket. Fingers holding sticker. Hand out and forward in a single motion. Her heartbeat drowns out everything except the gunshot slap of her palm impacting. And then she's past, with no shouting, no outrage and no chase.

Behind Kitty, the sticker, stark black on bleached white, announces the message:

> **HITLER IS A MURDERER!**
> **RESIST THE NAZIS!**
> **Ecclesiastes 4**

Kitty can still recall a few fragments of normal childhood, before the Gestapo took Sophie and everything changed. She remembers pouring tea for her dolls, while her parents listened to the war news on the wireless. The tiny cups were pastel blue with a white pattern. When people came to visit, she wouldn't speak to them and instead clutched her mother's long skirts to her face. There were sunny days then and cloudless skies and warmth on her skin as she lay in the garden.

She walks past the Opera House and a gathering crowd embraces her. Tonight Herbert von Karajan is conducting the Staatskapelle Berlin in Mozart's *Die Zauberflöte*. She ghosts past the opera-lovers in a trance.

Kitty's group leader had been so confident, so encouraging. Bolder than her, he'd bribed a greedy printer in Dresden to print the stickers, out of hours. Braver than her, he'd carried them all the way back to Berlin. Cleverer than her, he'd spent the train journey drinking schnapps with two officials of the Lebensborn breeding programme. In such company, the Gestapo did not disturb him.

The group leader had explained to Kitty how the horrified enthusiasm generated by the Danzig riot had dissipated. His heavy brows furrowed. They needed to generate outrage in order to keep growing and they hadn't had a success for months. His mouth turned down. Anyone could sticker unpatrolled back streets and late-night S-Bahn trains. But such petty provocations wouldn't have the impact the White Rose needed. His eyes glistened.

The hooligan Edelweisspiraten had their uses, but they were too obvious with their leather jackets and their antisocial attitudes. On Unter den Linden, the Gestapo would grab them in seconds. They needed someone who could walk the boulevards without drawing attention. They needed Kitty.

The best trick is to lean against a lamp post, as if tired. The sticker in her palm is almost invisible in the shadowed folds of her overcoat. She presses it backwards until it reaches the lamp post, and then she moves away. That sticker has been there for months, not moments; it's nothing to do with her. Don't glance around. Don't appear guilty. Don't run. The sticker is nothing to do with her. Her papers are in order. She is Reichsdeutsche, a national comrade, a normal German enjoying the sights along Unter den Linden.

The group have given her too many stickers, though. They'll understand. Let them try stickering for themselves on the busiest road in Berlin, surrounded by the Orpo.

No, she must do more. God will protect her.

In Hitler's Germany, faith in God's protection is often tested.

Behind Kitty, at least a dozen lamp posts and traffic lights now bear the treasonous stickers. In front, she spots the green and gold frontage of the Hotel Adlon.

At her side is a male voice. Kitty freezes. The man grasps her elbow.

'Fräulein?' he says.

She pulls away, but his claw grips her. He wears a brown homburg and a dull overcoat. His face is pinched, with pursed lips and a pencil moustache.

'You dropped this,' he says, holding out a roll of her stickers.

His overcoat has dandruff on the shoulders.

'No! That's not mine,' says Kitty, staring at the evidence. The slogan is so obvious. The man must have read the damning message.

'Ecclesiastes 4,' he says.

She can't meet his gaze.

'"I turned myself to other things, and I saw the oppressions that are done under the sun, and the tears of the innocent, and they had no comforter,"' he quotes, letting go of her elbow. 'I'm a Catholic, I appreciate the sentiment. I salute your bravery. But perhaps you've done enough for one evening? Maybe you should take these stickers, which are not yours, and go home before someone gets hurt?' He hands her the roll of stickers.

'Thank you,' she whispers.

'The pleasure was all mine, Fräulein. Good luck.' He turns and disappears into the crowd.

The dizziness takes Kitty into a dark, silent place.

$$\oplus$$

When mice fight hawks, the mice die faster than the hawks.

Kitty's parents went underground as soon as they heard the news-flash about Sophie. They spent so much time submerged that some people called them U-boats. After Sophie died, when the hopes of the White Rose were all but destroyed, it was Kitty's parents who prevented its complete collapse. They were not terrified little mice. To some they were as legendary as Sophie herself.

The Gestapo had not pulled her parents' flesh from their bones. They had both fought to their last. Her mother died first, electro-cuted whilst trying to cut the power to Reichsrundfunk Berlin. The bereaved family celebrated Kitty's twelfth birthday in tears. After the party, Kitty's father made her swear an oath to God and to her mother's memory. Holding his hand, she vowed to uphold the non-violent creed her mother had preached.

. A week later, her father bought a gun on the black market, walked into Leipzig Gestapo headquarters and opened fire. He killed two policemen and wounded eight more before they shot him down. Kitty never saw his body.

Sophie's father is still alive. Her heartbroken mother died soon after her children were murdered. Her father, somehow, keeps going, having served two years under the Law of Family Responsibility. Kitty could visit him. If she did, they could sit together in his garden inhaling the heady aroma of his roses, and praying. But this would endanger them both, because the Blockleiter responsible for the political supervision of the neighbourhood still monitors Herr Scholl.

Herr Scholl told Kitty that the Blockleiter had once tried to bring up the subject of Sophie with him, hoping to trick him into making a proscribed remark, a Treasonous Attack on the State even. Herr Scholl had thanked him for his concern. He did not deign to divulge the nature of his feelings for his murdered daughter. He expressed no opinion on the criminal regime gripping Europe in its bloodied claw. He is not a political man, but instead wishes to be left in peace to enjoy his flowers and his Bible.

Kitty is not so serene. No one needed to force her to join the White Rose.

The Danzig riot was their supreme achievement and their greatest failure. The murderous response of the Gestapo appalled many ordinary Germans and so support grew. But the White Rose believes in non-violence and the power of the spirit, not street thuggery and petrol bombs. Violence is no solution to anything. Bloodshed dragged Germany down. It can't drag it back up again.

Everyone in Kitty's group listens to the clandestine radio station broadcasting the White Rose's message of resistance. Nobody knows who runs the station, but this is not their concern. What *is* their concern is sustaining opposition in the Berlin area: the capital of their brutal suppressor. Evil must be confronted, and where is evil if not in the Führer's Berlin?

⊕

Kitty floats, only semi-conscious. Far away, she sees an Orpo policeman scrutinizing her. The policeman's mouth moves but she can't hear him. He frowns and moves towards her. The tunnel vision recedes as she snaps back to the real world. She's young and quick and he is not. God give her strength.

This time she doesn't freeze. She doesn't try to deny her crime. She turns and flees.

'You,' the policeman shouts, unbuttoning his holster.

Ears down and tail streaming behind, the rodent scurries. The crowds are thicker towards the Pariser Platz and the Brandenburg Gate. Maybe she can find sanctuary.

Behind her scream the whistles of the police. The darkness of the hawk's shadow envelops her, swooping, with talons ready. She feels the beat of its wings.

She races past the Hotel Adlon. A man in a black leather trench coat makes a grab for her. She's too nimble for him, sidestepping by pure instinct, unseeing, unhearing.

The mouse wants to live.

3

Apples and Roses

The expedition signal has stopped! The last broadcast was a single scream followed by choking. Nothing since. Casualties be damned! Their sacrifice will be remembered.

Journal of an unknown SS scientist, p.46

Behind the storm kicked up by the Rotodyne's rotors, the smoke from the burning concentration camp curls into the air.

I approach the man in Nazi uniform who's manning the machine gun in the gyroplane's cargo bay door.

'What did you see early on Tuesday morning?' he shouts to me.

'A pink elephant,' I shout back, easing my grip on the Welrod.

The door slides back, revealing a cabin packed with emaciated men in striped prison uniforms. They all sport the yellow star that marks out their genetic crime. At the sight of me, a ragged cheer emerges.

'Reuven sends his regards,' shouts the soldier.

I throw my bags into the cabin and reach up. Helping hands pull me into the gyroplane's belly. Someone passes me a bottle of brandy. I take a swig. It's rough stuff, medicinal, but it strips the taste of bile from my mouth. Another gulp and I hand it to the nearest prisoners. They pat me on the back, grinning.

'I hope you bastards are worth it,' I shout, over the tumult of the engines.

They can't hear me.

The Rotodyne's nose dips as it picks up speed.

$$\oplus$$

How many people did I kill today?

War is a brutal business, and it doesn't bear much thinking about.

The safe house is a grey building with grey curtains on a grey street. A shower washes the bloody memories away. Dressed again, I rummage through the kitchen cupboards, finding nothing but dust. Except that there's a bottle of vodka tucked behind the bread bin. Hallelujah. I spend nineteen minutes disassembling and re-assembling the Welrod, pausing only to fill my vodka glass.

The glass has a crack in it.

After that, standard Service procedure dictates I stay quiet and wait. But inaction breeds introspection, and introspection spirals into depression. I need to move, or I'll spend the night staring at the wall, drunk.

Anyway, Berlin still has some of the greatest nightlife in the world, despite the Nazis. My weekend bag sits on the kitchen table. The compartment below its false bottom contains alternative identity papers. I stow the handgun in my shoulder holster and gulp down another vodka. The door of the safe house clicks shut behind me.

I have several hours to kill.

Nothing of the old Germany, nothing of the past, can be allowed to survive in the New Order.

I walk east, along the Charlottenburger Chausee towards the

Brandenburg Gate. The golden angel on the Victory column watches me pass. I hurry on, past the brutal 'People's Palace' that replaced the Reichstag. Nazi regalia hangs from every window, engulfing the marble façade. The Reichstag, witness to the hated democracy and the excuse for its removal, was a much more attractive building.

The smiling crowds spill between the columns of the Brandenburg Gate. On the Pariser Platz, upper-class and fashionable Germans pack the elegant square. A band is playing selections from Wagner. My destination is the boulevard called Unter den Linden, site of my favourite place in Berlin, the legendary Hotel Adlon. In my wallet are enough Reichsmarks to purchase several bottles of—

A girl runs straight into me.

I grab her and pivot. Off balance, her momentum tumbles her to the ground. She wilts.

'Oh, Gott,' she gasps. 'Gott steh mir bei.'

Behind me, I sense a commotion in the crowd on Unter den Linden.

'What the hell?' I say.

'The Gestapo,' the girl says, switching to English.

She's young, not much out of her teens, and beautiful, but wearing a man's raincoat three sizes too large for her. I race through the options. Prostitute? No. Black market? Possibly. In over her head? Probably.

I can't afford to get involved.

The Gestapo's headquarters are only a few hundred yards away at number 8, Prinz-Albrecht-Strasse. At night, the screams from the cellars can be heard a block away.

I really can't afford to get involved.

I help her to her feet, her hand trembling in mine. Her auburn hair falls heavily to her shoulders. In contrast, her eyes are emerald. I might not have much imagination, but I can guess what the

Gestapo's brutes will do to her. The bastards will be queuing up, flies already undone.

I get involved.

'They're searching for a single girl with red hair, wearing a black raincoat. They aren't expecting a married couple on their way to the opera,' I say.

The girl gets the picture. Breathing fast, she pulls an Hermès scarf from her coat pocket and tucks her hair out of sight. Underneath the coat she's wearing a black cocktail dress with spaghetti straps that emphasizes her perfect figure. I take her coat and fold it over my arm. She laces her fingers through mine.

Four Gestapo agents pile on to the Platz, unmistakable in their black leather trench coats. Their gaze sweeps the entire square without focusing on us.

'Walk with me,' I say.

The girl acquiesces, shivering in her silk dress. I put my arm around her as we walk towards her pursuers. Close up, she has a delicate apple scent.

'You are American?' the girl asks.

'British,' I say. 'Will they recognize your face?'

'I . . . no, I think.'

'Do they know you speak English?'

'No. We must walk towards them?'

'If we get past them, we'll break through the dragnet. Then they'll be heading away from us and we'll be free.'

The girl nods, the tension in her body like taut wire. I try to reassure her with a squeeze of her waist.

'Now, speak English and draw attention to yourself. Pretend we're British guests staying at the Adlon and arguing about why I forgot to bring my wallet.'

We advance on the Gestapo with the remorseless finality of the

German onslaught on Stalingrad. I'll have the advantage of surprise, but the odds are not looking good. Beside me, the girl starts a creditable attempt at playing the spoilt upper-class bitch.

'Oh, for God's sake, Mildred, will you shut up?' I snap at her, playing my own part in our drama. 'You're embarrassing me in front of these damn foreigners.'

My attention flicks between the Gestapo agents. Two are scanning other directions, one speaking on a walkie-talkie. The fourth, leather trench coat hanging loose, dark hair clipped short, metal-framed glasses, is looking straight towards us. I map out the order in which I'll kill them – he'll be the first to go. The gun under my arm is so obvious he can't fail to notice it.

The officer stares at me. I glance back at him and roll my eyes. He smirks and his gaze moves over my shoulder.

We're through.

Four more steps, and our fake argument tails off. Six and the girl wobbles. Eight and she staggers. She's in shock. In the shadow of the first lime tree we find on Unter den Linden, I let go of her waist. Her lower lip quivers, and the suggestion of a tear glistens in her eyes. My heart's thumping too.

'Will you join me for a drink?' I ask, spotting the Hotel Adlon's welcoming red carpet.

She stares at me, speechless. I take her hand and lead her through the doorway and into the marble-bedecked foyer of the hotel.

'Do you need a few minutes?' I ask, gesturing in the direction of the ladies' room.

The girl nods. She's wearing no make-up except natural-coloured lipstick, and her face is as pale as the Adlon's marble pillars.

'Can I have my coat?' she asks.

'I'll wait for you in the lobby bar. What will you drink?' I ask, handing her the raincoat.

'Anything . . . you choose,' she says with the ghost of a smile.

Moments like this are what make my life bearable.

I manoeuvre my way across the crowded lobby to the bar and ensconce myself at a corner table. From there, I can monitor both the ladies' room and the hotel entrance. I'm also invisible, blending in with the bar's clientele of tourists and businessmen. The majority of the tourists are Americans, doing their bit for the Nazi foreign-exchange campaign. Their gaudy clothing seems incongruous in colourless Berlin.

The Adlon itself, I'm pleased to observe, is unchanged from my last visit. The delicate colours, marble columns, polished brass, mahogany, the sheer elegance, seem to me the antithesis of Nazi thuggery. How could the Germany of the Adlon have fallen into Hitler's hands?

But this speculation is fruitless. I wave a waiter over.

'A bottle of Pol Roger Réserve Spéciale. Two flutes, not saucers. Beluga caviar for two. Blinis with fresh butter and crème fraîche, and two sets of cutlery made from mother of pearl. Okay?'

'Yes, sir, but I must inform you that our caviar comes from the liberated nation of Ukraine, not the Judaeo-Bolshevik Soviet Union.'

'The Russian trade embargo still biting, is it?'

The waiter's eyes widen. He gestures towards the table and uses his index finger to push his ear lobe forward. The table is bugged; probably they all are. I nod, reach underneath, find a wire taped to one leg and yank it hard. The waiter blanches.

'I'm meeting a young woman and we require complete privacy. Do I make myself clear?' I ask, opening my wallet and counting out a generous number of Reichsmarks.

The waiter nods, reaches down for the tip and pockets it.

'Now, remind me, is your caviar genuine Beluga?'

'Oh, yes, sir. I've had the privilege of tasting the last of the hotel's pre-war Russian stock. The Black Sea Beluga is, if anything, superior. However, certain of our richer guests find it does not suit their palate.' The curl of the waiter's lip says all that I need to know about such guests' palates.

'Well, then, I'll try some,' I say.

The waiter disappears in the direction of the bar.

I sit examining the girl's papers, which I palmed from the inside pocket of her raincoat earlier. They say her name is Katharina and she's a student, which might even be true. I decide not to admit to her that I speak fluent German.

The girl emerges, steadier now and hair tidy. She's dispensed with the headscarf and folded her raincoat in a neat bundle over one arm. Her auburn hair and black dress both gleam in the light of the Adlon's chandeliers. I stand up and pull out a chair for her. She sits down, crossing her legs. I'm impressed with her composure. How close did she come to running out on me before she realized that her papers were gone?

'A friend tells me the tables in the Adlon have ears,' she says.

I put a hand on her shoulder, and bend towards her. The clean apple perfume wafts past me.

'I've already taken care of that,' I whisper in her ear.

'I assume you have my papers too? You seem to think of everything.'

'It's the way I survive, Katharina.'

'My friends call me Kitty,' she says, finally allowing a smile to cross her face.

The waiter appears with the champagne and caviar.

'Pol Roger? Meine Güte . . .' says the girl.

I wave the waiter away and pour two foaming flutes of champagne.

'It was Winston Churchill's favourite,' I explain.

'This is why it is not big in Germany.'

I hand the girl a flute and raise my own. The biscuit aroma of Pol Roger fills the air between us. Kitty proposes a toast. 'Here's to being unpopular in Germany, Mr . . . I'm sorry, I don't know your name.'

I lie to her about my name. It's a bit early for such intimacy.

Kitty's gaze drops to the table. 'Caviar? This all seems so . . . not real. What strange knives and forks.' An iridescent rainbow reflects off the knife in her hand.

'Silver cutlery makes the caviar taste metallic.'

'I never ate caviar before.' Kitty looks embarrassed.

'Don't worry, it's simple enough, just copy me.'

I skim butter over my first blini. Kitty does the same then stops, watching me. I use the spoon to heap a little caviar and crème fraîche on top of the blini. She copies. I pop the ensemble in my mouth.

'To get the best flavour you burst the eggs with the tip of your tongue,' I say.

But Kitty puts her cutlery down and frowns.

'I am a woman of the world, and I understand how things work,' she says. 'I am prepared to go to your room and perform. You should not buy me champagne and caviar also.' She stares at me, cheeks flushed.

I reach over, grab her wrist and squeeze it harder than necessary.

'Kitty, that might be how things work in Germany, but it's not how they work with me. You needed help, and nobody else was going to do anything. I knew what would happen to you if I did nothing. That was all.'

'You hurt me,' Kitty squeals.

'I don't care. You listen to me, now. I also enjoy sharing champagne and caviar with a beautiful girl. So forget about prostituting yourself to me, and let's try to enjoy our brief moment together.'

I let go of Kitty's wrist. A tear meanders down her cheek.

'I . . . Sorry. I thought . . .'

I fish out a clean handkerchief and pass it across to her.

'Anyway, I don't have a room,' I say.

'It is lucky I have no mascara,' says Kitty. She dabs at her eyes.

She's what: twenty, twenty-one? And this is her world, trading sex for protection.

'Kitty, you must have had to do things that you wish you hadn't, in order to survive.'

'You cannot imagine . . .'

'I know, but there's something wrong with the world we live in, not with us.'

Kitty hands the handkerchief back and takes a sip of champagne.

'Why were the Gestapo after you?' I ask.

'I had a crazy idea – I was sticking.'

'Sticking?'

'It's easy, you get the sticks—'

'You mean stickers.'

'Stickers? Yes. You get the stickers inside your hand. You walk and you . . .' She mimes a slap. 'Like on a lamp post.'

'You're not dressed for direct action.'

'More stupidness of mine. I think no one will expect a girl dressed well to be trouble. I would pay for my confidence if you did not help me . . .'

'You panicked. It happens.'

'Yes, but I should not trust a strange—'

'I just saved your life. I have your papers. If I wanted to turn you in to the Gestapo, you'd already be in prison.'

'That is why . . .' Her expression hardens. 'I am with the White Rose.'

This is interesting. The Service has tried to contact the White Rose several times, but they wouldn't take anything from us. One of our black-propaganda stations is using their name anyway.

'We are rubbish,' says Kitty. 'One riot. Some stickers that say Hitler is a criminal. A bit of gr . . . what is the word?'

'Graffiti?'

'Yes, graffiti. Our motto is, "We will not be silent." But the Nazis murdered Sophie ten years before now, and for sure we have been silent. We achieve nothing, change nothing . . . and is it a surprise? The Aryan Übermensch is now in space. Soon he is on the moon. The Jews are gone. The shops are full, if you are rich. The German race has its so special Lebensraum. But God help the Poles, the Lithuanians, the Latvians, the Ukrainians, the Belarusians, the gypsies, the old . . . The list has no end.'

Over Kitty's shoulder, I keep one eye on the lobby. The atrium is filling up with what seem to be reporters; the Hotel Adlon is famous for its celebrity guests. I gulp the last of my champagne and signal for another bottle.

'And all problems in this idyllic Germany are caused by British saboteurs, and Judaeo-Bolshevik traitors,' I say.

'Perfect, is it not?' sighs Kitty. 'The Nazis do nothing bad at all, because everything is blamed on escape goats.'

'Scapegoats,' I say.

Kitty turns to find out what the shouting behind her is. The gentlemen of the press are mobbing an entourage descending the hotel's opulent main staircase.

Towering over the heads of the reporters, at the centre of the commotion, is a man in SS uniform. He's an impressive figure, with a high forehead, restless eyes, a broken nose and a full-lipped mouth. On either side of him simper identical statuesque blondes in matching electric-blue evening gowns cut to emphasize their impressive décolletage.

'Reichsführer Reinhard Heydrich and the Mitzi twins. All evening he has questions for them, in the bedroom upstairs.' Kitty spits the words.

Heydrich . . . since Admiral Canaris defected to Britain, he has been the master of every instrument of state repression known to Aryan man. His nicknames, variations on butcher and hangman, are well chosen.

'I thought the SS preferred the Hotel Kaiserhof?' I say.

'You know many things about Germany, for an Englishman,' says Kitty, frowning.

'I read a lot.'

The waiter approaches with a second bottle of Pol Roger.

'Look at them,' hisses Kitty. 'There you see the blue-eyed rulers of Europe . . . everything that is good and right about the Nazi master race. Meanwhile the Slavic Untermenschen, the so-called sub-humans, are worked to death in the eastern territories to build autobahns. All so that Heydrich and his vol . . . vol . . . what is the word?'

'Voluptuous,' I say, tearing my gaze away from the Mitzi twins and back to Kitty.

'So his voluptuous girlfriends can reach his summer hunting lodge at a fast speed, in big cars. I hear rumours, you know, that the SS bring prisoners . . .'

Sensing the waiter behind her, Kitty stops ranting. The waiter uncorks the Pol Roger, tops up our glasses and retreats. In the lobby, Heydrich and his companions disport themselves for the cameras. To my eyes, they're making fools of themselves, but the glare of revulsion on Kitty's face intensifies.

'You really hate them, don't you?' I say.

'My parents died because of Heydrich and the Nazis. Of course I hate them.'

'So, have the courage of your convictions – take my gun and kill him,' I say.

'What?' she splutters, almost choking on her champagne. 'The White Rose is non-violent.'

'You said it yourself, the White Rose is pathetic.'

'I did not mean . . . Violence does not solve any problem.'

'Violence is the only thing that ever solves problems. You'll never get another chance like this.'

'I know there are no tears if I kill him. He is the most evil man of Germany.'

'There's a lot of competition there, but he's the rising man in Germany, Kitty. Already he controls the SS. One day, that torturer will be Führer.'

'Jesus said love your enemies.'

'I'd rather be one of the wolves than one of the flock.'

'I can't . . . I can't . . .' There are tears in her eyes.

Heydrich and the Mitzi twins sweep out of the front entrance of the hotel to a crescendo of flashbulbs. I sense the brooding presence of official Mercedes limousines pulling up to the kerb outside.

Kitty rests her head on the table, sobbing. I reach over and stroke her soft auburn hair.

'You're quite something, aren't you, Kitty?'

She looks up at me.

'My faith is all I have,' she says. 'Faith that one day everything will get better. I have to believe it is God's will, otherwise I kill myself.'

I take her hand, gently this time.

'Then the Nazis will win, because they aim to kill everyone like you. Once they do that, the only people left will be people like me. The world is a cruel, brutal place and fate, if you want to call it that, has put the bad guys in the comfy seats.'

She stares at me, pleading.
'What's wrong with this world we're trapped in?'
I don't have an answer.

4

The Baker Street Irregulars

The Ultima Thule project has been removed from the Ahnenerbe and placed directly under Heydrich. I retain my position, delighted to serve under such a paragon of Aryan manhood.

Journal of an unknown SS scientist, p.48

It's good to be back in London.

The day after Kitty and I collided with Heydrich at the Hotel Adlon, Reuven's ratline came good. A lorry to Hamburg, then a berth on a Norwegian tramp steamer, and I was heading for Sweden. From Stockholm, Scandinavian Airline Systems flew me back to London. In flight, I wrote Kitty's number on one of their First Class menu cards, using a simple transposition code. Now the same menu card is slotted between bundles of fifty-pound notes inside the Pig's attaché case.

At immigration, I straighten my tie and present a false passport.

'Welcome to England,' says the man behind the desk. 'I hope you had a productive trip.'

'It was a pleasure,' I reply.

⊕

Sunlight pokes through the canopy of chestnut trees shading the square. I stand at my window, watching the light play over my Riley's royal-blue paintwork.

The car has to go: the Mercedes I drove in Germany was superior in every department. Perhaps if I uprated the boost from the super-charger? No, that's impractical. What's preventing me selling the stupid thing, anyway? Sentiment?

I sip a glass of orange juice and glance at the *Manchester Guardian* lying on my desk. The headline says something distasteful about the achievements of the German astronauts building the Rudolf Hess memorial space station. Hess – who wants to remember him? I toasted his death with champagne after those Ukrainian partisans whacked him. Churchill, England's forgotten man, now there's a man who deserves a memorial – not that he'll get one.

What's the problem? It's just a car.

I glance at my watch. My appointment with the Old Man is at eleven.

There's no time for sentiment; after work I'll try that car dealer-ship on the mews behind Harrods.

⊕

The route to the office is quiet enough for me to put my foot down. I weave the Riley between the cherry-red London buses, the Camden bustle bringing a smile to my face. The whistle of the supercharger accompanies me through Primrose Hill and into Regent's Park.

I approach the turn-off from the park's Outer Circle. A black Rolls-Royce pulls out of Hanover Terrace Mews, right in front of me. I hit the horn, swerve, and accelerate, glimpsing the Rolls's red-faced chauffeur mouthing obscenities. Obviously, he feels he has a God-given right to drive wherever he pleases.

Already late, I pull the car into the basement car park at 64 Baker

Street, the Service's headquarters. I run up to the eighth floor, taking the stairs two at a time. Elliott is sitting in the drab corner office we share, but it's missing its only redeeming feature – Patricia. I drop the attaché case on her desk.

Elliott closes the file he's working on, and leans back in his chair. 'Good holiday, old boy? Sweden, wasn't it?'

'I made a killing . . .' I say.

His eyes widen.

'. . . playing baccarat in the Casino Cosmopol, against dumb American tourists.'

'You and your gambling . . . a fool and his money are soon parted, you know.' He shakes his head.

'Spare me the homily, Elliott.'

'You ex-SOE types are always gamblers,' he mutters.

I turn to face him. 'And you ex-MI6 types are old women creeping around scared of your own shadows,' I reply, slow and even.

'I think perhaps I won't rise to that bait, old boy,' says Elliott, reddening.

'Not the first thing you failed to rise for—'

'Are you boys fighting over me again?'

Patricia stands in the doorway with her hands on her hips. Her figure-hugging blue dress is striking enough to distract both Elliott and me.

'Remind me again, boys, who are the Service's enemies?' asks Patricia.

Elliott and I blush like schoolboys caught ogling *Health and Efficiency* magazine.

'The Germans,' I reply.

'And the Russians,' adds Elliott.

Patricia's grey eyes spark.

'Oh, yes, so they are. So tell me, should we be fighting amongst ourselves and so bringing comfort to our enemies? Or are we supposed to be working together as the Old Man keeps reminding everyone?'

'Working together, Patricia,' we respond.

'Right again. Now, I'm a mere girl, and worse than that a mere secretary, but I manage to remember it. Two big men like you ought to be able to.' She taps me on the chest with a single incarnadine fingernail. 'Oh, and by the way, the Old Man was expecting you in his office ten minutes ago. He favours punctuality.'

'Better tootle on up, old chap,' says Elliott. 'Now, Patricia, about that trip to the Café de Paris you promised—'

I point at my attaché case. 'Could you keep an eye on that for me, Patricia? It's got a million pounds in it.' I turn my back on their surprised expressions, stride out of the room and make for the lift.

Major General Sir Stewart Graham Menzies, KCB, KCMG, DSO, MC stands by the window of his office.

His room is almost undecorated: white walls, a marble fireplace and a few gunmetal cabinets along one wall. On his desk are a dozen files and a black telephone.

He's staring over the grey rooftops into the sun, his silhouette hunched. He should have retired five years ago, before the vitality left him. He's tired now, frail even; he has already seen too much. What age is he, sixty-four, sixty-five?

He turns and spots me. His shoulders come up, and he straightens his back. There's a little more to give. He motions me to sit down.

'Late, I see,' he says, tapping his watch.

The Old Man's eyes, always pale, have faded to grey. His hair is pure silver and cropped close to his skull. He looks almost skeletal.

'Sorry, sir. Slight contretemps with a limousine on the way in.'

'Driving too bloody fast as usual. And still not slowing down for your elders?' The Old Man returns to his desk, sits down and presses the button on his intercom. 'Can you tell the chief of staff to come in, too, please?' He releases the button and taps a folder with a purple stripe on its cover. 'I had some interesting information from Cheltenham this morning.'

'You follow the horses, sir?'

The secret of comedy is timing.

'You'll be the death of me,' he growls.

I grin.

'GCHQ,' he says, 'as you well know. Signals traffic shows the SS going crazy. Someone has attacked another one of their concentration camps.'

'Which one, sir?'

'Sachsenhausen. The assailants stole the camp commandant's vehicle and used it to approach the site without challenge. The Gestapo found a burnt-out Mercedes and a rifle with a Zeiss sight nearby. The attackers must have used a sniper to eliminate the machine gun posts around the perimeter. Once the Kübelwagen got inside, its occupants opened fire.'

'At which point, I suppose, the inmates rioted, sir?'

'Total chaos. I can't believe this, but the SS are claiming the assailants used a Fairey Rotodyne to extract some of the prisoners. They haven't worked out which ones yet, as there are hundreds of the poor sods still roaming the countryside.'

'There have been other reports of black helicopters operating in Germany, sir.'

'That's ridiculous,' says the Old Man.

There's a rap on the green baize door and Leo, the Service's pocket-sized chief of staff, lets himself in. We smile at each other.

'Marks, we're reviewing this flap about Sachsenhausen,' says the Old Man.

'I've just received a report that the SS are razing the camp to the ground, sir,' says Leo. 'The remaining prisoners are all being shot.'

'The same thing that happened after the attack on Dachau?'

'Yes, sir. We can rely on the tender hearts in the SS for consistency, at least. Local sources confirm the camp commandant was shot in both knees and in the face.'

'Destroying the victim's face is common in Soviet punishment shootings, sir,' I say.

'Well, the Germans don't think it was the Russians,' says the Old Man. 'This morning I got this message, personal, from Reinhard Heydrich, via channels we don't need to go into.' He pushes a piece of paper towards me. I glance at it.

'Would they go that far?' I ask.

'Heydrich is never knowingly understated,' says Leo.

'I've talked to the minister,' says the Old Man. 'He wants an explanation, before this starts a war. What do you have on?'

'Just those photos from the resistance in Stettin showing some sort of flying disc. Air Intelligence asked us to investigate. I was planning a trip out there.'

The Old Man shakes his head. 'Those pictures are one of Heydrich's deception ploys. Anyway, we have a near constant watch on the Luftwaffe proving grounds at Rechlin. Those flying discs will turn up there if they're real. Drop that and find out who's behind these attacks.'

He passes me a file covered with 'Top Secret: Glint' and 'Eyes Only' stamps.

On the way out, I tell the Old Man about Kitty, relocating the story to Stockholm.

'What do our files say about the White Rose?' the Old Man asks me. His famous piercing gaze is not the weapon it once was, but I'm familiar with the files' injunction: 'No Dice.'

'Well, sir, that's the usual line, but I've got an idea I can work something with this woman.'

'You're proposing we run her as an agent?' He says this as if I'm recommending we fly her to the moon.

'I'm suggesting I study the options, sir. I know, Venlo Incident and all that, but still.'

Mention of the legendary German sting makes the Old Man frown. It took us years to recover from our last flirtation with Germany's so-called resistance. 'No . . . Oh, what the hell. Talk to Canaris. He knows everything there is to know about German dissidents. Use him to help you get some ideas together and write them up for my attention.' He purses his lips. 'Don't let it interfere with this other work.'

'Yes, sir,' I say, smiling.

'I'm not promising anything,' says the Old Man.

'No, sir.'

'In fact, I'm going out to visit Canaris tomorrow. You can come along with me. Right, get moving the pair of you. I've got work to do.'

I grab Leo by the elbow as we walk back to our offices.

'Let's have a drink after work. There's something I want to talk to you about.'

If the Germans ever want to hit the Service hard, a bomb in the Manchester Arms would do the job. This scruffy pub in Baker Street is the Service's second home. F Section's drunken rendition of *La Marseillaise* is dominating the public bar, so Leo and I sit in the lounge. I recognize some of the crowd at the next table. Station XIV:

forgers. When Leo heads to the bar, I beckon one of them over and wave some money in his face. He stares at it, bemused.

'You buying?' he says. He is not sober.

I have to be careful. Patricia would have taken my boasting about the million in the attaché case as a joke. Elliott might not have, though.

'I think it's forged,' I say.

The forger holds the note up to the light and crinkles the paper.

'If it's a counterfeit, it's a bloody good one,' he says. 'Where did you get it?'

'An SS-Obersturmbannführer tried to bribe me not to kill him.'

'Oh well, *don't* tell me, then.'

Leo pushes through the crowd with a pint of bitter for himself and a large vodka for me. The forger, sensing the proximity of an officer, slopes off.

'It's not like you to be friendly with the help,' Leo says, sitting down.

I don't want him thinking about why I'm talking to forgers. 'Are you still drinking that flat, warm rubbish, Leo?' I ask.

'We aren't all blessed with a stomach for spirits, or the money.' He lights a thin cigar, puffs away until it's glowing, then pushes the packet towards me.

'If you're short of money, I can spot an easy economy,' I say, refusing his offer.

Leo's mouth turns down. 'Never get married,' he says. 'I've got to smoke to take my mind off it.'

'It's not working out?'

'It's proceeding as expected. I'm a short, Jewish intellectual who likes crosswords and can tell a first edition of Proust from across the room. She's an artist's model, with big tits and an excessive fondness for gin and tonic. I blame my parents.'

The forgers start playing a drinking game that involves pretending to be a bunny rabbit. Another patriotic French song wafts over us.

'How's the shop?' I ask. Six months ago, Leo inherited a part share in a bookshop on Charing Cross Road.

'It's a drain on resources, and a constant worry,' he says. 'I love it.'

Everyone expects Leo to leave the Service as soon as the probate sorts itself out. I'm praying he won't, as he's saved me from the bureaucrats of Baker Street more than once.

'So, what's on your mind?' Leo asks, taking a drag on his cigar.

'The Old Man seems exhausted. What's wrong with him? Is he ill?'

'The witch-hunts are getting to him. He's convinced someone warned Burgess that we were on to him.'

'Leo, the only reason Burgess got away was because you sent that buffoon Elliott after him, not me.'

'Elliott's a smarmy git with a copy of *Burke's Peerage* up his arse. That doesn't mean he's a fool or that the Old Man erred in sending him after Burgess instead of you. You'd have stopped Burgess all right, but we can't afford to have dead bodies scattered everywhere any more.'

'So we let him go, instead. That'll teach them.'

'It's the modern way. Of course, now the politicians presume the whole Service is riddled with communists.'

'It would explain a few things. And if that bastard Elliott screws up again, I'll whack him myself.'

'What is it with you and Elliott?' asks Leo, shaking his head.

'He's a public-school tosser who thinks the world owes him a living.'

'The Service is comprised of nothing but public-school tossers who think the world owes them a living.'

'MI6 was, but SOE wasn't. Churchill told us "set Europe ablaze", not "don't cause any trouble".'

'I get it – Elliott and his ilk are spoiling your fun. You're pining for the good old SOE days: sabotage for breakfast, assassination for lunch, train-derailing for supper . . .'

'There's a cleansing purity about violence. It simplifies things.'

'. . . and Resistance girls warming your bed at night. Cowboys roaming free, and every problem solved with a bullet. You're a bloody dinosaur.'

'You, me and the Old Man, Leo. We're all relics from better days.'

Leo takes a sip of his beer and sighs. 'The Old Man should have got out before the witch-hunting season opened. He's offered to retire, but the minister won't let him. So he feels obliged to save us all by discovering the traitor. He's losing perspective, seeing things that aren't there.' He pauses and shoots a glance at me. 'You, for example.'

I snort vodka over the Arborite tabletop. Very dignified. 'Me? He can't . . . *I'm* a traitor?'

'The Old Man thinks you're a charmless thug with a bullet for a heart. He doesn't think you're a traitor, but he does suspect you're covering something up. He's convinced you've got something to do with these attacks on the concentration camps.'

'What? Why?'

'One: your obsessive hatred for the Nazis. Two: every attack has taken place when you were on leave. Three: every attack leaves one more Nazi who was involved in the aftermath of the Vemork operation dead. He's putting one, two and three together and getting six.'

Leo searches my face. I hold his gaze. Leo is my best and only friend in the Service. He's not a great believer in unthinking obedience, so he would understand. But he also thinks duty comes first. He needs plausible deniability. And so does the Old Man.

'Leo, one, two and three *do* make six.'

'So they do. Whoops.' Leo lifts an eyebrow.

'Look,' I say. 'It's no secret that I think we shouldn't have let the Gestapo get away with it.'

'Vemork?'

'For God's sake, Admiral Canaris told me they tortured them to death.'

Leo shakes his head. 'That's all ancient history now,' he says, standing up.

'Not to me it isn't.'

'Do you want more vodka?' he asks.

I put a hand on his arm. 'Leo, why would the Old Man put me on to stopping these concentration camp attacks if he thinks I'm involved in them?'

'Well . . . who better?' says Leo, in a voice I can only just hear over the laughter of drunken forgers.

He disappears into the crowd.

5

Swing Kids

The scrolls are written in a previously unknown dialect of Vedic-Sanskrit. They contain a translation of an antediluvian manuscript called 'On the Fallen Souls'. Why it was so named, and indeed how it came to rest in Ultima Thule, is not understood.

Journal of an unknown SS scientist, p.59

Kitty wakes with a cry.

The hawk . . . pincering flesh from her bones.

She stares around the bedroom, cold sweat on her brow as the terror subsides. Last evening she'd been so close to tragedy – that British stranger had been a thousand-to-one chance. Without him, she'd have spent the night in Prinz-Albrecht-Strasse, enduring the inevitable treatment of a woman in Gestapo hands.

And he hadn't even wanted her body. She looks down at its curves beneath the bedclothes. God alone knew what men saw in them, but that had been a first: being turned down. How many had it been? How many men had she been forced to give herself to in order to survive? Less than twenty; it must have been less than twenty.

He was too old, anyway. But what did that matter in comparison? She should have asked him to take her to England, away from this nightmare. She'd have done it with him just for that, if he'd wanted.

It wasn't as if he was unattractive. God knew she'd done it with less handsome men and for slighter advantages in return.

Imagine living in London: the capital of an empire consisting of a hundred different countries and races. It wouldn't be like her native Germany's grey uniformity. She wouldn't be terrified of an unarmed British bobby. She could go and vote, and it might actually change something. There wouldn't be decades of the same ageing faces droning the same repulsive dogma. She could stand on a street corner and shout 'Prime Minister Eden is a lunatic' until she was hoarse. No one would stop her. Whatever she did, no men in leather coats would arrive, pick her up and brutalize her.

Maybe she should forget these crazy ideas about resistance. Where were they going to get her? The hawk's beak ripping into her, that was how it would end in Germany.

She should put on her mother's sparkling dress and go to the Hotel Adlon bar wearing it. There she should find an English gentleman and seduce him. The English, what did they know of the real world? As soon as she took her clothes off, she'd have him proposing marriage.

But run away? How would her mother and father feel about that idea?

Kitty shakes her head at the hopeless fantasy. She kneels down at the side of her bed and starts praying for forgiveness for her sins.

⊕

Just one trip to London, and Johann is a jazz fiend.

He twirls his umbrella and mimes dancing. The umbrella makes circles around his arm. Kitty giggles despite herself.

'I've got a new record, Kitty-cat, a Chet Baker. I smuggled it back from my holiday in L. O. N. D. O. N.'

Kitty hasn't seen Johann around the university's buildings for a while. Not that she has been there much, either. She has to be careful not to hang around the students too much. Rumours get started, and the Gestapo listen to rumours.

'You went to London? Really?'

'Oh yeah, baby. I went to all the tip-top jazz clubs. The English dance like crazy people.' Johann mimics them dancing, wiggling his hands.

'There's a swing tomorrow night,' he says, smiling. 'You know, get hip to the beat, Kitty-cat.'

Kitty's White Rose group leader tells her that intelligent youth is the best hope for resistance to Nazi hegemony. But recruiting is difficult. Half of the students at the Friedrich Wilhelms University are members of the National Socialist Student Association. Nearly all of the rest are just children enjoying their twinkle of student freedom. Johann is one of her few converts, and she's still not sure how intelligent he is.

'Johann, aren't you getting a bit old for the Swing Kids? Most of them are thirteen.'

Johann beams at her.

'This time things will be different. I've hired a private pad in Wannsee, super-discreet. The owner is a friend of mine and he loves Reichsmarks. It's going to be jazz with a capital J, baby! All night! Top volume!' He tips his hat forward, like a dancer in a movie.

The group leader's idea is that Kitty acts as a talent spotter amongst the misfits and rebels. They come to her like shy kittens, encouraged by a wink or a gentle word. She befriends them, and then probes them about their political sympathies. If they respond, she puts them on the list of candidates. The leader himself then takes the huge risk of approaching them.

But hardly any are open-minded and intelligent enough to question their childhood brainwashing. Amongst those who are, most are too scared of the Gestapo to provide any real assistance.

She has found a few passive helpers. They're prepared to rent out a room at short notice and without paperwork, or to store a leaflet duplicator in their attic. But not many have enough nerve for active resistance. Even Johann hasn't done much.

He's just about prepared to paint anti-Nazi graffiti in the quiet alleys around his flat. Kitty supplies the spray cans and lets him fondle her afterwards. He once stuffed a few leaflets through the doors of a student housing block at three o'clock in the morning. In return, she gave him a half-hearted blowjob.

'How the hell did you get to London?' she asks.

'I know the right people, Kitty-cat,' he replies, looking smug.

The right people could only be his parents, paper-pushers in the Danzig Gauleiter's office, and good little Nazis. She can't imagine them in England, let alone in a jazz club. Their hard-wired Nazi brains would explode at the sight of Indians, Africans and Chinese walking the streets unmolested.

'I don't believe you; not with your mum and dad.'

Johann's mouth turns down. 'Don't spoil the vibe, Kitty-cat. Be cool. Look, I've got a Union Jack.' Johann twists the lapel on his jacket to show Kitty the red, white and blue pin.

How much do Johann's parents realize about their son's antics at the university? Do they assume he spends his days in lectures and his nights reading chemistry books? Do they ever wonder if he listens to jazz? They couldn't possibly suspect he occasionally spray-paints the district's walls, could they?

Kitty compares the anglophile boy in front of her with the genuine Englishman from the Hotel Adlon.

Johann loses.

'Where did you really get the records from?' she asks.

Johann sighs. 'My dad has a friend in Switzerland who's a visiting professor at the Charité teaching hospital. He smuggles jazz records into the country, hidden in the bottom of his medical bag. I use my rent money to pay for them. Mum and dad don't know.'

Kitty nods. Johann is just a silly adolescent with a jazz obsession. He imagines he's in love with her, but it's just lust really. That's one reason he attached himself to her White Rose cell. The other is that he's a show-off, and enjoys pretending he's a dangerous resistance member. A few bits of graffiti saying 'Down with Hitler' and 'Medals equal Murder' don't make his big mouth worth it.

The truth is, if she has to offer sex to every White Rose recruit it'll be a long time before Hitler's regime falls.

'Hey, Kitty-cat, isn't it your birthday soon?'

'It's . . . oh, it's tomorrow.' She'd forgotten until he mentioned it.

'Great! Old lady! Come to the party. It's going to be cool. It's going to be hip.'

'Can I hand out my leaflets at the club?' she asks.

'Kitty-cat, you can do whatever you like.'

Kitty looks into Johann's eyes. He's laughing at her. She decides she's not going to let him touch her ever again.

The jazz club in Wannsee turns out to be an abandoned clothing factory. There are some coloured lights strung up in one corner and the workbenches are piled over to the side. It is not the Adlon. Johann is right about the Swing Kids' energy, though: the room is crammed with youngsters. Where do they all come from? Where do their parents think they are?

The music is the loudest Kitty has heard at any party, probably too loud. And the pile of records by the player is the biggest she has ever seen. Normally, at a jazz club, the Swing Kids have to bring a record each, and they're not easy to come by. For most people they're only available on the black market. A lucky few have contacts in England or, almost unimaginable, America. They hoard the precious vinyl, playing it non-stop at whatever volume they dare whenever their parents are out.

She pushes her way through the throng, apologizing as she bumps into assorted oblivious dancers. A new record starts. Kitty recognizes the melody: 'Walkin'' by the Miles Davis All-Stars. Davis performs the solo on muted trumpet, choosing his notes in a relaxed, unhurried way. The dark tones form patterns that rub against the chords, oozing nonchalance. The music carries Kitty away from the dreary factory, even though she has a job to do.

The saxophone comes in and the drums pick up energy. The instruments call and respond to each other like mating birds. The tune twists and spirals around Kitty until Nazi Germany is far away. Why can't life be like this all the time?

Kitty imagines she's leaving Germany behind, flying up to the stars and arriving in a different world. It's a world where the Nazis are not winning, where resistance is unnecessary, and where she can just be herself. It's the kind of world where people can walk into a shop and buy a jazz record. To be able to buy a bit of vinyl, is that too much to ask?

She sways, the music building inside her, bursting with intensity, double-timing the notes, cramming them in now, close to the climax.

Kitty finds Johann necking a bottle of cheap vodka with the rest of the Edelweisspiraten, at the rear of the hall. They pass the vodka round, sneering at the youngsters dancing. If they don't like jazz, why are they here? They're looking for a fight or sex, of course. And they have nothing better to do.

They're older than the Swing Kids and have a harder look, all leather jackets and long hair with grease in it. Their hair even touches their collars in contrast with the ubiquitous short-back-and-sides of the male Swing Kids. The Nazis force all boys into the Hitler-Jugend and close-cropped neatness.

The Edelweisspiraten lounge in their chairs, aping British styles. Their fashion is something that arrives from England only by rumour: 'checks are in', 'crêpe soles are cool'. Tonight, it appears, narrow trousers are the latest British thing.

The girls, when the Edelweisspiraten can find any, dress in gypsy fashion. They slap on the make-up in imitation of Hollywood style, crimson lipstick and nail polish glistening like blood. Long skirts, white blouses and hair worn loose complete the look.

Johann makes a grab at Kitty. She pushes him away. He snatches the bottle back from a buddy and takes a swig, leering.

'Dig it, Daddy-o. Get with the scene,' he shouts, the vodka talking.

Kitty glares at him. He looks like a little boy to her.

The kid with the microphone is high; she's sure of it.

She doesn't recognize him from previous parties, but he has a way with the crowd, encouraging them in English. He sways to the music with the whites of his eyes showing, as if he's in a trance. The loudspeakers squeal.

'Dance, baby, dance! Blow your top!'

She suspects Johann is lying about having organized this jazz club. There are several adults watching the throng, cruel-looking men who aren't dancing. They're professional criminals, in it for the money. But professional is good. Professionals can pay off the Kripo's detectives. They have lookouts, contacts and enforcers. When you're a professional, things stop going wrong.

Johann and all the other Swing Kids are just spoilt, rich brats. She's seen more than one puffing on a Benzedrine inhaler. That doesn't come cheap unless you have an older brother in the army, with a supply. She tried it once and danced for four hours, but the nightmares were the worst ever and she never touched it again.

She deposits her leaflets in small piles on the tables and in the corridors and toilets. She has to be careful even here. There might be a Gestapo spy; just to report on the kids' behaviour, she hopes.

The Nazis seem in two minds sometimes. There are periodic crackdowns followed by temporary amnesties. Even the Gestapo recognize that shooting thirteen-year-olds who like to dance will damage workers' morale. So they concentrate on hanging the so-called 'ringleaders', the older children who organize these parties.

That's probably why the crooks are taking over. Criminals have the know-how to avoid official retaliation, an instinct for violence, and a liking for drug profits.

They'll be selling more than Benzedrine soon.

The kids are clapping their hands over their heads, in time with the music. The boy with the microphone screams into it as the music picks up a frenetic beat.

'Come on, you degenerates! We're all Jews in this shit-hole world! Bug out!'

'Swing Heil!' the crowd shouts back.

By midnight, Johann is drunk and Kitty has had enough.

He's talking nonsense to his followers, spinning them the same stupid tale he told her about L. O. N. D. O. N. Unlike her, they're lapping it up. Kitty comes to a decision. There's nothing wrong with the music, but the volume is insane. She wants nothing to do with Johann or his vodka, and he'll only become more insistent later. She has already scattered her leaflets.

'I'm going,' she says.

Johann looks up, surprised. He makes an obscene gesture to his sidekicks. It's just bravado, not worth bothering with. Kitty turns and marches towards the door. One of the gangsters tries to joke with her as she walks past. She ignores him. She's tired and she has a long way to walk home.

Johann follows her out of the club, whining.

'Don't go, Kitty-cat. What about us? What about the jazz?'

Standing in the chill evening air, he looks confused. He pulls his leather jacket closer and stands there shivering.

'Johann,' she says, 'I'm twenty now. The police will be here soon. Those youngsters might get away with it, but we're adults. They'll hang us.'

'You can't go,' he says.

'I am going.'

He looks at his watch and stamps his feet. What has got into him?

'No,' he says. He almost seems to be panicking. He puts his arms around her.

'Johann, get your hands off me. It's over between us.' She tries to push him away.

'No, really, you can't go,' he says, gripping her wrist.

'Why not? What's so . . .'

Johann fumbles in his inside pocket. Kitty tries to pull away from him. What's he doing? He doesn't have a knife, does he? He's not that stupid.

Inside the clothing factory, the music dies in mid-beat.

Johann blinks and is sober.

Behind him, the sound of breaking glass accompanies the tear-gas grenades as they fly. In front, a battalion of Orpo fan out, blocking any escape routes.

'Katharina Geissler, you can't go because I'm a Gestapo agent, and you're under arrest,' he says.

His face has changed, firmed up somehow. It makes him seem ten years older.

6

The Old Man

'On the Fallen Souls' has a hypnotic effect on the reader. Personally I am unaffected, but Heydrich has been forced to terminate two of the weaker minds.

Journal of an unknown SS scientist, p.72

I hate the salesman, and his Prince of Wales check, off-the-peg suit and pencil moustache, at first sight.

'A beautiful old car, sir,' he says, pointing at the Riley.

The process of buying a new car is bound to be painful, but this is a bad start. I try to close his sales patter down.

'I drive fast, I've no requirement for frills, and I refuse to buy anything German. However, last week I drove a Mercedes 300SL, and I need a vehicle with comparable performance and handling. I'll be paying cash, and require the car to be delivered within the week. What can you offer me?'

The salesman's polished smile stiffens. He glances around the showroom at a collection of upmarket saloons. I'm just starting to wonder if I might be in the wrong place when he remembers something.

'We do have one car that might interest you, sir. If you could step this way . . .'

He leads me to the rear of the salesroom, and through a door into the yard. Sitting abandoned in the centre is a sleek open-top car. It has racing numbers, and a Union flag on the fairing behind the driver's seat. Compared to my blunt Riley, it's like a torpedo on wheels.

I like it on sight.

'This is a D-Type Jaguar, sir,' says the salesman. 'In current factory racing order. Note the aircraft-style engineering and the aerodynamic bodywork. The car also features an aluminium monocoque chassis and all-round disc brakes.'

'Isn't this a circuit-racing car?'

'We purchased this example from a gentleman who entered it in the *24 Heures du Mans* last year, as a privateer. Unfortunately, he discovered his driving skills were not as boundless as he imagined. Our mechanics have repaired all the damage, naturally.'

'It's a bit small,' I say, quibbling.

'The minimal frontal area is deliberate, in order to reduce air resistance. You did say you were interested in performance not ostentation, sir.'

I get a sudden urge to punch the salesman, steal the car and drive off. I resist.

'Performance compared to the Mercedes?'

'Nought to sixty in four and a half seconds. Top speed, one hundred and eighty-five miles per hour. Far superior to the Mercedes 300SL, sir.'

Incredible.

'Can I take this opportunity to remind you, sir, that a D-Type came second at Le Mans last year? It would have won if Ferrari hadn't put sand in Jaguar's fuel before the race.'

'I'll take it,' I say.

⊕

The Old Man's Daimler pulls into Lissenden Gardens an hour after I wake up. A shower and some push-ups have failed to shake my hangover, so I gulp down two aspirins and head outside. The chauffeur stands by the car, holding the rear passenger door open for me.

'Good morning, sir,' I say, leaning into the car.

'Get in,' says the Old Man. 'We'll be late at this rate.'

Perhaps he's hungover too.

The Daimler's discreet Hooper bodywork has armour plating reminiscent of a battleship. Getting anywhere in it is a matter of wallowing along, making steady progress. I settle into the over-sprung leather and smile at the Old Man. His famous clear eyes are bloodshot and his face is colourless.

'Did you have a good evening, sir?' I ask.

'No, I did not.'

'More trouble at the card table?'

His eyelids flicker. 'I don't actually visit my club every evening. If you must know, I was going through the files again, cross-referencing, checking dates and alibis, searching for the traitor.'

'Sir—'

'Don't you start. I've already had Leo nagging me this morning.'

'You've already been to the office, sir?'

'I was there all night. I'm going to catch the bastard and, when I do, there's going to be hell to pay.'

'Are you sure—'

But the Old Man isn't listening.

'I've been in this game since 1914 and one communist misfit isn't going to beat me now. I owe it to everyone who has already sacrificed themselves to save this country – it can't be in vain, all that loss. My school friends didn't die at Ypres so the communists could replace our historic traditions with their godless lowest common denominator . . .'

'Sir, why don't you get some sleep whilst we drive? I can keep watch.'

'. . . the families destroyed by the Great War. A generation wiped out. The roll call emptied. Name after name struck off. The dark caravan of casualties . . .'

'Get some rest, sir.'

He nods, his head flopping up and down like an old rag doll. 'Perhaps just half an hour.'

I pass the Old Man a cushion. He leans back in his seat. His eyes close and he gives a long, low sigh, like a pressure cooker letting out steam.

⊕

As the Old Man sleeps, I stare out of the limousine window and reminisce.

My whole life would have been different if it wasn't for the Old Man. Day one, I had the incredible luck to be assigned as his aide. Day two, he was promoted to director. He'd put up with my childish enthusiasm for a couple of years. Then he'd palmed me off on British Security Coordination in New York.

At one point it had really looked as though we would manipulate the US into the war. But 12 May 1941 – a day I'll never forget – arrived. I was walking down Fifth Avenue in the sun when I saw crowds round the newsboy on the corner. The first glimpse of the *New York Times* heralded the disaster:

CHURCHILL DEAD.
GERMAN BOMB KILLS PRIME MINISTER.
CARETAKER GOVERNMENT URGES CALM.

The heroic country I'd left – the country of the Battle of Britain, Churchill's country – was no more.

After that, J. Edgar Hoover convinced President Roosevelt to shut us down. I came back to a grey London. The ceasefire had just been announced and the atmosphere was poisonous. Anthony Eden was still in custody and rumours said Attlee himself would be next. There were sporadic riots in the East End. There was even talk of martial law. At Baker Street there were no medals and no parades, just closing up shop and 'thanks anyway'.

For six months I'd slummed it in Hampstead, having forgettable sex with miserable women I picked up at boring parties. I managed to pull myself together enough to get to the polls and vote for Attlee. By some miracle, so did everyone else, and Labour got back in.

Labour reprieved SOE. The Old Man smoothed the way for my recruitment. Normal service was resumed.

I have a lot to thank the old tyrant for . . . I hope I've repaid him.

$\oplus$

I've been trapped in the back of the stuffy Daimler for too long with the Old Man's snoring. My head is killing me. But now, at last, we're at the Cage.

The Cage is a country-house estate requisitioned in 1939 as a signals-intelligence collection site. Its octogenarian owner is rumoured to be living in the gatehouse, under the impression that the war is still on. When the Service took the Cage over as an inter-rogation centre they forgot to mention it to him.

Standing on the steps in front of the ivy-clad house is Scotland, the director of the Cage. Rotund and peering at me through half-moon glasses, he looks more like a retired schoolmaster than a torturer. His khaki battledress is pristine, and sporting patches for the Combined Services Liaison Unit, the Cage's fictitious identity. On his chest is a row of medal ribbons, probably also fictitious.

'Morning,' I say to him. 'Is the admiral ready for us?'

'The admiral is ready when you are,' says Scotland, looking at the Daimler and shrugging.

Behind me, the chauffeur is still attempting to rouse the Old Man.

'It was my idea that he took a rest in the car,' I say, embarrassed.

'I'm starting to get the feeling the Old Man's past it,' mutters Scotland.

I round on him. 'That old man *made* the Service, Scotland. If he wants to rest for an hour after an all-night session with the files, then he's got every right.'

Scotland holds his hands up in mock surrender.

'He's not at his best,' I admit in a calmer tone. 'The pressure is killing him. He's convinced there's another traitor.'

'Paranoia,' says Scotland. 'It gets to them all in the end. We've had that poor little man Philby in again, you know. Bugger keeps protesting his innocence, but the more he does, the more the Old Man thinks he's lying. He thinks that Philby is too clever to incriminate himself. Which makes the *lack* of evidence against him the evidence against him. Where are we going to end up at that rate?'

'He knows what he's doing,' I say. 'If he believes there's a traitor, then I'll back his judgement against the lot of you.'

'We all know you're his tame Rottweiler.'

The Old Man stomps up the stairs with his chauffeur hovering close behind him.

'Get away from me, you idiot,' the Old Man snaps. 'What do you think I am, some sort of cripple? Get back to the car.'

'Sir, I'm supposed to be your bodyguard, not just your driver.'

'And if your aim is as good as your driving, then God help me. Anyway, how is an assassin going to get in here? It's a top-security area. Back to the car, man.' He waves the chauffeur away and turns to me.

'Right,' he says. 'You can go and talk to Admiral Canaris while I

discuss with Scotland here the results of Philby's interrogation.'
Scotland blushes.

'Or should I say lack of results, eh, Scotland?' says the Old Man,
scowling.

I follow the guard's directions to Admiral Canaris's study. A
pretty, dark-haired woman in her mid-thirties answers the door.
She's wearing the uniform of the First Aid Nursing Yeomanry. I
imagine she's part of the molly-coddling Canaris is receiving – he's
the most valuable agent Britain ever ran inside Nazi Germany, by a
long distance.

'I'm here to see the admiral,' I say.

'And just who might you be?' she asks. She has a slight Irish
accent.

I introduce myself with the work name I used during Canaris's
escape.

'One moment,' she says and closes the door. Thirty seconds pass.
The door reopens.

'The admiral will see you now,' the nurse says.

Canaris stands up when I enter and clicks his heels, still the
Prussian naval officer. He even insists on wearing his navy blue and
gold Reichsmarine uniform. This affectation is one Scotland
tolerates. He's playing it long with Canaris, against the objections of
those who feel the admiral is holding out on us.

The room itself is as starched as the admiral – a perfect English
country-house sitting room. The view from the French window,
across a formal garden to the woods, is beautiful. As prisons go, it's
not bad at all.

'Congratulations on your George Cross,' says Canaris, offering his
hand. He has a firm handshake for a sixty-odd-year-old man.

'I'd rather have had a pay rise, Admiral.'

'Ah, ever the practical man, I think,' says Canaris.

I smile.

'Practical, and also a shrewd operator,' he says. 'Remember those endless games of poker we played, while we waited in the safe house for news of our escape route?'

'You were quite the card sharp.'

The admiral snorts. 'If I recall, you ... what is the saying? ... "took me to the cleaners".'

'I'm just lucky at cards, I guess.'

'You British have another saying, do you not: "lucky at cards, unlucky in love"?'

'I never believed that one, until the night I was betrayed by my lover just after being dealt a royal flush.'

Canaris chuckles. 'And always the joking, the stiff-upper-lip humour – so much a part of the English gentleman's armour.'

'I'll wait outside,' says the nurse. 'It looks like you two have some catching up to do.' She closes the door and I bring the pleasantries to an end.

'Admiral, the Old Man has asked me to investigate the possibility of the Service supporting the White Rose.'

Canaris motions me towards the sofa. 'The White Rose? A bunch of dreamers, for sure.'

'That's what they said about Gandhi.'

'But Gandhi fought against you decadent British. The Nazis would have shot him like that.' Canaris clicks his fingers. 'And, you know, I preached intervention non-stop for decades, but you never listened. After the kidnapping of your officers at Venlo, you refused my many requests that you help the German resistance.'

'But you devoted yourself to defeating the Nazis anyway.'

'And where did it get me? Exiled. Hitler is still in power, and the Nazis are more entrenched than ever. Now there's a new generation who know nothing but National Socialism. My efforts were futile.

The military will never break their oath to Hitler, and the civilians are kept under control by the Gestapo.'

'I have an idea. I wonder if you'd mind listening to it?'

'Of course,' says Canaris, gesturing around the study. 'I'm under no illusion that I've anything better to do today.'

He gazes out of the window as I explain my proposal. When I tell him about the Obersturmbannführer's forged money he twitches and then focuses on me. He starts bombarding me with questions about forgery, economics and the White Rose. I answer them as best I can.

In the end, he buys it.

'Yes. Yes. Do you have a pen? This is the name of my contact and his last known address. Go to him. You'll find he's with you. My God, this might work.' The old warrior's hand shakes as he writes.

There's a knock on the door.

'Admiral, there's one more thing. Did you ever hear of anyone associated with the White Rose whose name was Katharina or Kitty?'

Canaris frowns. 'They were organized in cells; it was the only way to survive the Gestapo. I knew only a few contact names, and none of them were women. Now, go. Take this idea of yours and make it work. I just wish I was a younger man, and not trapped—'

The Old Man opens the door and catches a glimpse of hope in Canaris's face. 'He's convinced you, has he, Admiral?'

Canaris nods.

The Old Man turns to me. 'I expect a full report from you. Now, please leave us. I have something to discuss with Admiral Canaris that is not for your ears.'

I stand up and shake hands again with Canaris. He clutches at me as if I'm a straw and he's drowning.

The two old men speak, I presume, of traitors.

I position myself outside the door. This gives me an excuse to chat up Canaris's nurse, who is sitting on the other side of the room, applying lipstick. She stretches her legs out and adjusts her stockings.

'You wouldn't have any aspirins, would you?' I ask, ever the charmer.

She laughs, stands up and rummages through the medicine cabinet, missing the aspirins twice before she spots them. If she's a real nurse, I'm Hitler.

'You knew the admiral already?' she asks, over her shoulder.

'I helped him defect,' I say.

'Good man yourself,' she says, turning to face me. 'I'm Molly. Molly Ravenhill.' She takes my hand, and shakes out a couple of aspirins from the bottle on to my open palm. She has a strong mouth and striking blue eyes.

'Ravenhill is an unusual name,' I say, smiling.

Molly smiles back at me and we exchange a look that raises my heart rate. Her eyelids flicker and she drops her gaze. 'My father's family came from Ulster,' she says. 'Ravenhill was where they lived. The village sat at the foot of a black granite mountain. Black – raven – Ravenhill.'

Behind me, there are raised voices in Canaris's study, but I can't distinguish the words. There's a thud like a hand slamming on a desk. The two old military men are discussing something other than their respective roles in the Great War. I half turn towards the door.

'Always throwing the crockery, those two,' says Molly. 'And you can let go of my hand now, if you like.'

I release her. She moves to the window and sits down, looking across the lawn towards the trees. I gulp the painkillers down. Molly has several medal ribbons sewn on to her uniform. Of course, that explains why she couldn't find the aspirins. Female SOE agents were assigned ranks in the First Aid Nursing Yeomanry.

'You're ex-SOE?' I ask.

Molly glances at me and shrugs. 'Right enough.'

'Wireless operator?'

She scowls. 'I was not a bloody wireless operator. I was a sabotage group leader, before the bastards announced I was too old for field-work. Honestly, is it old I look to you?' She gestures at herself. In the light, she's maybe a couple of years older than I thought, but with the delicacy and long-legged grace of a ballerina.

'You look lovely,' I say, actually meaning it for a change.

'I didn't . . .' She blushes.

'How long were you in the field?' I ask.

'Right from the start – 1940 – just before we gave up.'

'We didn't give up,' I say.

'As good as.'

'I was always a Churchill man, myself,' I say, conceding the point.

'We all were,' says Molly. 'Cannon fodder with nothing to lose, and it was great craic, anyway, playing spies.'

'Churchill would never have given up.'

'We'll never know, will we? Still, that was myself left without a war.'

'You could always have joined the Soviets,' I say.

'Sure, and I wasn't helping *those* murdering atheists.' She touches the silver cross at her neck.

'I was glad when Attlee got in and disowned the peace treaty,' I say.

'Warmonger,' she says, grinning.

'You didn't get the George Medal helping old ladies cross the road.'

'There's a cleansing purity about violence,' she says, standing up again.

'It simplifies things,' I say, suddenly conscious of my heartbeat.

Molly walks over to me. She puts a finger on my chest and looks up into my eyes. 'There's a girl here with no plans this evening,' she says. Her eyes sparkle, it seems, with anticipation of something.

'Do you—'

There's a deeper thud from the admiral's study. This one is loud enough for Molly to lose interest in me, and move towards the door. A gun appears in her hand. Without a word, we take positions on either side of the entrance. I draw my own Browning automatic and nod. She slams the admiral's door open. We go through the doorway side by side.

The study appears untouched. The Old Man is sitting in the admiral's desk chair. Canaris, though, is lying face down on the floor.

'Sir?' I say.

There's no reply.

'Sir? Are you all right?'

Three steps and I'm behind the Old Man. I swing the office chair round. The Old Man's head slumps backwards, revealing a neat red line across his throat.

He has been garrotted.

Part Two

Confrontation

Cave-Right is the right of the Father,
To hunt by himself for his own:
He is freed of all calls to the Pack;
He is judged by the Council alone.

Rudyard Kipling, *The Law of the Jungle*

7

Set Europe Ablaze

The translation of the first scroll is complete! In ancient times, a race of Übermensch lived in Ultima Thule, harnessing energies far exceeding those known to our own science. We must use this knowledge to save the Fatherland.

Journal of an unknown SS scientist, p.84

There is no pain.

It doesn't matter. Nothing matters. Everything is just fine. I lie on my back staring at the sunlight filtering through the leaves of the oak trees. I'm going to stay here and rest for a while. Just relax, watch the trees and let the sunlight warm my face.

There is no pain. The pain is not real.

There's a sound like the sea breaking – a rising, falling, clamorous yowl.

It doesn't matter.

'Oh, sweet Mother of God, would you look at that?' The voice sounds like Molly's.

But it doesn't matter.

Why am I watching the trees? Am I watching the trees or the sky? I can't remember. The pain is not real. There is no pain.

Something shakes my arm.

It doesn't matter. My arm. There is no pain.

The pain, my memory, everything . . .

It all comes crashing back.

⊕

The Old Man is dead.

I stand staring down at the pathetic remains of the man to whom I'd given all my trust. His head flops backwards, and what's left of his blood weeps from the wound.

Molly runs to Admiral Canaris's side, puts her own gun down and turns the admiral's body over.

'Jesus Christ,' she says.

The gun feels limp in my hand.

'Do something,' I say.

'I'll not be a miracle-worker now.'

I let fly with a string of obscenities in several different languages.

'Don't stand there spouting,' Molly shouts. 'Go after them. I'll raise the alarm.'

My grief slides into a dark fissure.

I move to the French window. It's locked and the key is missing. There's movement in the distance. I lash out with my boot. Two, three kicks and the frame splinters, glass shattering on to the terrace. I burst through the wreckage of the door.

As I run, I recall the ground plan of the Cage. A ten-foot-high brick wall, topped with barbed wire, surrounds the estate. The trees are cut back at least thirty yards from the wall to form a death strip. Armed guards with attack dogs patrol this strip, with orders to shoot on sight. There's a water-filled ditch on the other side of the wall. There's no way out.

There was also no way in. There was no way of assassinating two men, silently, in broad daylight, without alerting their bodyguards. But it had happened. Whoever carried out the hit was no amateur.

Which means he will have a back-up team. There will be at least one sniper in the woods covering his escape. Just over the perimeter wall, there will be a getaway vehicle ready.

Behind me, an alarm sounds.

The woods are at least a hundred yards away. The wall is the same distance again, through the trees. The assassin is amongst the trees already, halfway to the wall. I won't be able to catch up with him before he reaches it. Once he's over, there's no chance of my stopping him.

The Old Man's chauffeur is standing by the Daimler, smoking.

'Wh—' is all he has time to say.

I shove him out of my way, yank the door open and throw myself into the driver's seat. The Daimler accelerates like a three-legged dog, even with the accelerator flat to the floor and the rear wheels spinning. I wrench the steering wheel over. The limousine lurches right, mounts the kerb and ploughs into the manicured grass of the estate's formal garden. The chassis creaks with alarm.

The Daimler might be slow, but it is still a hell of a lot quicker than a man on foot. With the engine screaming in second gear, the speedometer nudges fifteen. And it does have one huge advantage – it's a tank. Even the tyres are puncture-proof.

In one corner of the windscreen, a spider's web of cracks appears. Someone is shooting at the car.

I'll be on top of them in seconds. In a close-range shoot-out, the Daimler's armour will put the odds on my side. If I can delay the assassins for long enough, Scotland will flood the area with guards.

I watch the edge of the woods for the next shot. The windscreen crazes again, this time across the centre. I adjust the steering and the car wallows on to a new course, heading straight for the muzzle flash.

The distance drops. The sniper gets two more shots off. The steel plate clangs as the bullets bounce off. With twenty yards to go, the sniper gives up trying to stop the car, and stands to run. He's dressed all in black, including the balaclava hiding his face.

The Daimler batters its way into the woods, collecting briars and leaves from the undergrowth. I keep its speed as high as possible, given the sluggish response of the steering. The clank of the suspension failing to cope with the uneven ground becomes deafening. I'm almost on top of the sniper, aiming the prow of the car straight at him. I'll ask questions of whatever's left of him after he encounters several tons of armour-plated Daimler.

He leaps to one side, getting the thick trunk of an oak tree between himself and the lurching vehicle. I twitch the steering wheel to miss the tree and slam on the brakes. Wheels locked, the limousine slides past the sniper's position. I swing around on my seat and kick the Daimler's door open, already covering the tree with my pistol.

To the right of the broad oak tree, the sniper is running for his life. I fire two shots. The first misses. The second strikes him in the back, just above the heart. He flies headfirst, arms outstretched, into the undergrowth. With three steps, I'm back in the car and accelerating again. The sniper won't be going anywhere with a bullet in his lung. I can come back for him once I've stopped the assassin.

The Daimler lumbers forward, engine shrieking and tyres fighting for grip. We bounce and crash headlong through the woods in the rough direction the sniper had been heading. The extraction point will lie in that direction. The speedometer lurches between ten and fifteen mph – I must be gaining on the assassin, even at this speed.

At the edge of the forest is a man wearing British Army battledress, sprinting towards the perimeter wall. Even with my foot flat to the floor, I can coax no more speed from the Daimler. A yellow cherry-picker angles its platform over the wall and down towards the stony death strip.

The assassin has almost escaped.

The Daimler leaves the woods and kicks forward, putting more power down on the firmer ground. The killer is straight ahead, reaching for the rope dangling from the cherry-picker. The speedometer touches twenty. With one hand on the rope, the murderer turns his head, eyes bulging with exertion. Two hands grab the rope. Six feet to go. His feet on the wall, scrambling. I throw my arms across my face, foot still pressed down hard on the accelerator.

The wall—

I try to raise my skull from the ground. It seems like a lot of effort to move.

The pain is immense.

'Don't move. You're hurt but you'll live.'

'Who are you?' I manage to say.

Something wet and sticky is dripping from the back of my head.

'The nurse, Canaris's nurse. Do you not remember?'

'You had nice legs,' I say.

'He's delirious, Molly,' says a man's voice.

'He is not . . . I do have nice legs,' says Molly.

I lever myself from a taxi outside 64 Baker Street, into the early-evening drizzle.

My body aches as much as it did after Vemork. I've spent all afternoon having glass picked out of my face. I'm sure the imprint of the Daimler's steering wheel on my torso will remain there for ever. The registrar told me I'd been lucky.

I discharged myself.

The doorman comes to attention and salutes without moving his eyes from straight ahead. I shuffle through the building, my footsteps echoing off the walls.

'My condolences, sir,' says the liftman. 'Not the first commander I've lost, sir, but it doesn't get any easier. You shouldn't blame . . .'

Platitudes. I nod to him.

Headquarters is a morgue, the usual background clatter of hustling secretaries and doors opening and closing silenced. I approach my office along a drab, Ministry-of-Works-green corridor. At her desk, Patricia has her head cradled in her arms. Her usually immaculate hair is unkempt. She hears me limp past and squints up at me. Her eyes are red-rimmed.

'I'm so, so sorry . . .' she says, dabbing at the corner of one eye with a damp handkerchief.

'Not as sorry as Heydrich is going to be,' I say, ripping off my overcoat. I throw it at my chair. It lies there in a crumpled ball, dripping water on to the floor. I turn my back and hobble out again, leaving Patricia sniffling behind me.

I walk into the Old Man's office to find Leo sitting in his chair. A silent tableau formed from the heads of section stands lining the walls. For some reason, Elliott is there. He stares at me as if I'm a ghost.

'Sit down, please,' says Leo, without looking at me.

What is Leo doing in the Old Man's place? Why are they all staring at me?

I ease myself on to a seat.

'Gentlemen, you'll have heard the news,' says Leo. 'The minister has asked me to take General Menzies' place until a new director can be appointed. As such, I am to be responsible for the Service for an indefinite period.'

Dead man's shoes.

'The minister has requested we present him with options for our response to the assassination.'

I stand up, ribs aching with the effort. 'Options? What are you talking about, Leo? The Germans have killed the head of the Service. The Interservice Protocol is unambiguous. There's only one option.'

'Oh, the bloody blunt instrument speaks,' says Elliott.

'Fuck off, Elliott,' I say.

'That's enough,' Leo snaps.

Elliott mutters something about finesse. Leo shakes his head and turns back to me. 'As for you . . . I am at present, like it or not, the head of the Service. You will address me as sir. If you're not prepared to accept my authority, leave now and write your resignation.'

I stare at Leo in disbelief, my jaw clenched, muscles throbbing with pain.

'I'm not resigning,' I say.

'I'm not resigning, sir,' says Leo, matching my stare.

'I'm not resigning . . . sir.'

'Right, then sit down, shut up and listen for a change.'

I move back to my chair. Leo stands up, leaning his fists on the Old Man's desk. When he speaks again, his voice is calm. 'I've been informed by the minister that a military response is not a possibility.'

'Why the hell not?' I say.

'I told you to shut up and listen. The minister can't authorize military action because, legally, we don't exist. The Old M— General Menzies did not exist. There is no Service. The country cannot go to war to avenge the death of a man who did not exist.'

'But *we* can,' I say.

Leo looks straight at me. 'If you say another word, I'll write out your resignation for you,' he says. 'The government cannot authorize war over the death of General Menzies. *However*, the minister understands the Protocol, therefore he's prepared to sanction covert strikes. If the resources of the Service are not adequate for those attacks, he will commit Commando volunteers to them, on a deniable basis, of course.'

Leo picks up a sheaf of papers and passes one to each section head. 'Although we failed to prevent the Old Man's assassination, we did redeem ourselves somewhat by capturing the assassin.'

Who captured him, Leo? Who's we? I nearly killed myself stopping him.

'After a mammoth search through the photo books, we have identified him as Karl O'Connor. He first came to our attention as an IRA volunteer. After being forced out of Ireland, he carried out political executions for both sides in the Spanish Civil War. The Soviets recruited him to the team that killed Trotsky. Afterwards, he defected to Germany but failed them and was sentenced to death. He escaped to the USA, where he was believed to be freelancing for the Mob.'

Leo passes a hand over his face and sighs. 'This washed-up, fifty-four-year-old, has-been was already on the run from the Russians *and* the Germans. Despite this, he entered the country, infiltrated the Cage, and eliminated both our chief and our most important defector. How he managed to do this, I cannot comprehend.'

Leo stands up and scans the faces surrounding him. 'However, it is now our duty to serve our country, regardless of personal feelings. The minister wants us to identify who's behind this attack. Once we know that, we will strike multiple severe blows against the perpetrators.'

The heads of section sit there nodding like donkeys.

'Elliott, you are to coordinate the investigation,' says Leo.

I object. Strenuously. My chest wounds scream.

'Easy there, old chap,' says Elliott, fiddling with his fountain pen. *I'm going to take that pen and stick it—*

Leo points at me. 'You are on medical leave, effective immediately. Officially, you're recuperating from your injuries. Unofficially, you need to demonstrate that you can approach this operation with a clear head. Then we can discuss your role in avenging the Old Man's death.'

'Leo . . .'

'No.'

I stand up. Blank faces around the room. The heads of section lining up behind their new master. Elliott trying not to laugh. I turn on my heel and try to disguise my limp as I leave.

⊕

I'm in my bedroom packing when I hear a car pulling up outside the flat.

I turn the light off, move to the window and open the curtain a fraction. In the moonlit square, Leo steps from a limousine, accompanied by two bodyguards. He marches to my front door and raps twice.

If I don't answer, he'll probably have it kicked down. I push my suitcase back under the bed, limp to the door and unbolt it.

'Hello,' says Leo, smiling.

'Oh, it's friends again now, is it, sir?'

'Do you want to do this the easy way or the hard way?'

Leo's bodyguards stare at me like a pair of starving attack dogs.

'You'd better come in . . . sir.'

I stumble through to the sitting room followed by Leo and his entourage. The bodyguards check the room over and move to stand by the door.

'Have you been drinking?' asks Leo.

'Of course I've been bloody drinking. Haven't you?'

'Yes . . . yes, I have, but it hasn't helped me and, as far as I can see, it isn't helping you.'

'Well have a-bloody-nother then,' I say, grabbing a bottle of Chivas Regal.

Leo shakes his head. I slosh a mouthful of whisky into a glass and gulp it down. The stuff tastes like acid but it's doing the job.

Leo scrutinizes me as if calculating the mark-up on one of his first editions. The whisky brings a revelation – I don't know this man. Leo is my best and only friend in the Service, and I don't know him at all. I pour myself another whisky.

'You aren't considering doing anything stupid, are you?' asks Leo.

I stare at him. 'As far as I'm concerned, we're now at war. I'm going to go out there and I'm going to do what I do best. I'm going to do what we all used to do in the good old days . . .'

I hit the table with my fist.

'. . . set Europe ablaze.'

8

The Girl From FANY

Incredible! The third scroll describes the lineage of Ultima Thule back to their progenitors – the Hyperboreans, an ancient race of Aryans. They chose Ultima Thule as their home, as its climate matched their original ice planet.

Journal of an unknown SS scientist, p.110

The girl gets the drop on us all.

I'm watching Leo, and the looming heavies, somewhat unsteady on my feet. Leo shakes his head and sighs. 'I'm sorry, but I can't let you go careering off around Europe like some mad firework.'

This is his signal to the bodyguards. They advance on me.

The unmistakable click of a Browning automatic's safety catch being removed intervenes.

'God bless all here,' says Molly from the doorway.

The bodyguards spin round to face her, reaching for their guns.

'I don't think so,' says Molly. 'Hands on your heads.'

Something in the way she says it sends the bodyguards' hands upwards. Or perhaps it's the way she's holding her Browning steady in both hands that does it.

'Put the bloody whisky down and get their guns,' Molly says to me.

I separate the boys from their toys. Leo stares at Molly, frowning.

She's hidden her figure under an old RAF flying jacket and slacks, but Leo has a memory for faces.

'Molly Ravenhill?' he says.

'And here I was hoping you wouldn't recognize me, now,' says Molly.

'What the hell are you doing here?' asks Leo.

'Wasn't I saving your man's life after he drove himself into that wall. He'd have gone and bled to death before Scotland managed to do anything. Then I drove him to hospital. He asked me to stop here while he went to the office. Things just drifted on . . .'

She turns to me. 'Do you have any sort of a plan at all?'

'We run,' I say.

That's a plan.

Molly nods. Her expression doesn't change and the pistol doesn't waver in her hand. The two bodyguards appraise her with narrow eyes, waiting for an opening. She doesn't give them one.

Leo tries to reason with her. 'Molly, I don't know what line you've been spun, but I doubt it's worth throwing your career away for. Put the gun down and we'll forget about the whole thing.'

Molly speaks without glancing at Leo, still watching the bodyguards. 'You men . . . You're assuming he was talking me into this? That I'm just a dumb bit of skirt?'

Leo chooses his words with care. 'Look, Molly, you're at a crossroads here. You can put the gun down and we'll say nothing more. Or you can run. If you run, we'll find you and bury you, wherever you go.'

'You'd have me in my grave, would you, now? And here was me thinking there was the gun in my hand.'

'Molly, we're all upset about the Old Man's death; we went back a long way. But you didn't really know him. Why are you even getting involved?'

Molly shrugs. 'It's been any excuse for a bit of excitement since you stopped me going out in the field, sir.'

'What? You can't be serious.'

Molly's face hardens. 'Actually, you know what, I am. I was fighting for you for over for a decade. I was nearly killed a dozen times. And all I got was a bit of tin and a job as a glorified housekeeper.'

Leo shakes his head. 'It took the Old Man a lot of effort to get you that George Medal,' he says.

'That's not really the point, is it, sir? It's not men getting grounded because they're too old, is it now?'

Leo doesn't seem to have an answer to that one. He turns his head to me again.

'Did you consider that it might not have been the Germans?'

'Of course it was the bloody Germans,' I say. 'Yesterday, Heydrich sent the Old Man a note that amounted to a declaration of war. Today the Old Man is killed. But you think it wasn't the Germans . . . what the hell are you talking about?'

'O'Connor is a freelance assassin,' says Leo.

'Sure and he won't be getting much work with no legs,' says Molly.

'O'Connor's last employers were the Germans,' I say.

'Who have tried to kill him three times since he ran from them,' counters Leo.

'Faked,' says Molly. 'Maybe.'

I fetch a rope and use it to tie the bodyguards to their chairs. When I approach Leo to do the same, he has another go.

'Do you think you're the only one who's upset, you idiot? Do you imagine *I'm* not upset? I've known – damn it, I knew – the Old Man for as long you did. I shared the office with him. You were away most of the time. I know what he'd want you to do.' His voice is an acrimonious hiss.

'Hands behind your back, please,' I say.

'But, no . . . you think you're the only one with enough steel in his backbone to go out and do the job. You, and your selfish, nihilistic code of revenge. Remember your duty, man.'

'My duty is to the Old Man. And anyway, I'm not just sitting around here.'

'That's it, isn't it? The so-called cleansing purity of violence? It just means you can avoid thinking. But for God's sake, think about this – it wasn't necessarily the Germans.'

'Maybe it was the Germans, maybe it wasn't. Either way, I'm going to Germany to find out.'

'I can't let that happen,' says Leo. 'You'll start a war.'

Molly smiles down at Leo, tied to the chair. 'From where I'm standing, you don't look as though you're in a position to be doing much about it,' she says.

Molly is beautiful when she's angry.

She stands on the square with her hands on her hips and the moonlight caressing her curves. If I had more time, I'd be enjoying the view.

We left Leo and his bodyguards bound and gagged in the sitting room. Someone will find them in the morning, which gives us about six hours to get out of England. I grabbed the keys for the D-Type and the menu card with Kitty's number on it from my desk. My suitcase was ready under my bed and the attaché case was waiting in the hallway. Molly trailed out of the flat behind me.

'I can drop you somewhere,' I say, rattling the key in the door.

But Molly isn't the kind of girl you can brush off.

'And what makes you think I'm not coming?' she says. 'Wasn't I just saving you, again?'

'I don't work with women,' I say, walking past her towards the car.

'Oh, hark at the big man.'

'Call me old-fashioned if you want, but this is man's work.'

Molly swears so vigorously that I scan the buildings surrounding the square, wondering if anyone is listening.

'You know how many female agents the Service uses,' she says. 'Do you not concede that it's a huge success we are?'

'As couriers and wireless operators. Operational Research proved women can get through checkpoints more easily than men years ago. Killing is a different story.'

'Noor Inayat Khan.'

'Pardon?'

'SOE agent dropped into France. Betrayed to the Gestapo by a man. Didn't tell them a single thing. Escaped. Recaptured. Murdered. Last word, "Liberté". Odette Sansom—'

'I—'

'Odette Sansom, SOE agent dropped into France. Betrayed to the Gestapo, again by a man. Tortured. Escaped—'

'You've made your—'

'No. No, I'm thinking I haven't. Violette Szabo, SOE sabotage group leader. Got into a firefight with German Internal Security troops. Abandoned by her male bodyguards. Fought the Germans until she ran out of ammunition. Captured. Tortured. Murdered.'

'I'm not saying they weren't brave—'

'Lilian Rolfe, SOE—'

'Enough.'

'It is enough . . . more than bloody enough. More than you'll be coping with already, and I'm just getting going. All of us, all us silly wee girls, we went out there to fight the Nazis. And yet back home you men thought it would be funny to stick us in the First Aid Nursing Yeomanry. "FANY . . . stupid tarts . . . only good for one thing . . . ha, ha. Get a load of the tits on that one . . . ha-ha bloody ha." And meanwhile you're back to your comfortable desks and sending us to our graves.'

I wait for the tears to start. Molly stands there, face scarlet, eyes staring and chest heaving.

But there are no tears.

'For what it's worth, I've never sent anyone to their death,' I say.

'Would that be the best you can do?' She looks like she's going to hit me.

'Okay. Okay. Yes, I admit there are brave women in the Service and FANY is an insult to them. I never knew Noor or Odette. I did meet Violette once. I admit she was a better shot than me. Maybe women can be good agents, but that's not the point.'

'And what is it that you're imagining the point to be?'

'Women shouldn't be put in that kind of danger. Women shouldn't be tortured, women shouldn't be murdered . . .'

'. . . because that's man's work.' Molly sighs. 'God save us.'

We run.

The D-Type is uncomfortable for two people, even with minimal luggage. But it's bloody fast, and Molly claims she has little use for fancy clothes or make-up anyway. We race towards Heathrow, using only a fraction of the car's acceleration to overtake the few lorries that impede our progress. Molly sits on my suitcase, in the space where a passenger seat would be in a normal car. She's wrapped in her sheepskin flying jacket and has her hair bundled inside a black beret. The din from the Jaguar's engine makes it impossible to talk, but occasionally she flashes me a smile. I notice she cuts her finger-nails short. I also notice her mouth turns down when she's concentrating.

The heat from the engine keeps us both warm.

We make check-in for the overnight BOAC flight with only minutes to spare. Cutting things so fine, we have to run through the Empire terminal to reach the gate.

We turn the last corner and the panoramic windows give us a perfect view of a BOAC Avro Valentine. It's magnificent in its white, blue and gold livery, an ivory dart with razor-sharp wings. The night sky shimmers in the heat from the aircraft's four huge turbojet engines.

'Not so fast,' I say, drawing to a halt and pretending to admire the giant delta-winged aircraft.

A couple of Special Branch detectives are checking papers at the gate.

'What's the panic? These passports are good,' says Molly.

Our passports are false, taken from the stash I keep in my flat. They're not perfect, but they'll pass a quick inspection. They're not the problem.

'The case I'm carrying has a million pounds' worth of forged banknotes in it,' I say.

Molly accepts this news with equanimity. 'Okay, I'll handle this. Women are getting though checkpoints better than men, Operational Research proved it years ago.'

'Bloody scientists,' I say. 'Look, are you sure you want to do this?'

'Any excuse for a bit of excitement,' says Molly.

She slips off the sheepskin flying jacket and passes it to me. Underneath, she's wearing a black silk blouse. She undoes a couple of buttons and pushes her shoulders back.

'It's our honeymoon,' she announces.

'Chance would be a fine thing.'

'And don't you be getting any ideas, mister. What you're about to witness is strictly in the line of duty,' she says, snuggling in to me.

I slip an arm round her waist, playing my role. Molly, her abrupt transformation into a giggling newlywed complete, kisses me and pulls me towards the queue. I hold up the two passports to the Special Branch officers. They're more interested in Molly than my attaché case. Molly leans forward to point to her name.

'We've not been finding time to get my name changed yet,' she says. 'Isn't there only the one thing we'll be finding time for at the moment?' She gives a little giggle.

The younger policeman coughs and shuffles his feet.

'Thank you, madam,' he says. 'Have a nice flight.'

Out on the tarmac, the roar of aircraft engines is enough to force Molly to lean in to me.

'Told you,' she says, rebuttoning her blouse and looking pleased with herself.

Once ensconced in first class, Molly shakes out her hair. It's deep brown, almost black. Lustrous. She appears fascinated by the view as the Valentine taxis out to the runway. Her profile is delicate, silhouetted by the oval aircraft window.

The Valentine pauses at the threshold as the engines run up to full thrust. The aircraft seems to strain as the pilot holds her on the brakes for a second. There's a thump in the back as the afterburners kick in and the Valentine leaps forward.

Breaking the sound barrier ought to be more dramatic.

German-occupied French airspace is closed to British traffic, apart from the monitored air corridors leading to Paris and Berlin. BOAC route their flights over the Bay of Biscay, waiting until well out to sea before going supersonic. Molly sits hypnotized by the Mach indicator flicking over on the cabin bulkhead. At Mach 0.97, she takes my hand and squeezes it.

0.98, 0.99 and the magical 1.00 flip past, as smooth as glass.

Disappointed, Molly lets go of my hand. 'It was the sonic boom I was looking forward to,' she says.

'You wouldn't want to hear it from this close. Even from fifty thousand feet the shockwave smashes windows – at this distance it'd kill us. Luckily, we're going so fast it can't catch us.'

The steward brings dinner and a bottle of Pol Roger. Molly finally gets round to the important question.

'How are we going to get into Germany?'

I put down the silver knife and fork I'm using to dissect my sautéed fillet of English sole with truffles. 'I have some contacts: a group who will be happy to do anything to hurt Germany,' I say.

'Who?'

I take a sip from my champagne flute. 'You'll see.' I raise the knife and fork again. This sole is too good to miss.

Molly frowns. 'We're burnt with the Service, so we'll not be using any of their conduits. The Gestapo will pick us up in minutes if we try to go through civilian channels.'

'That's why we're here, not on a flight to Berlin.'

'Can you not at least tell me where we're going?' asks Molly.

'Didn't you notice the destination of the flight?' I say.

'It said Sydney, but there'll be refuelling stops. I'm assuming you were booking tickets all the way through as a simple ruse.'

I glance at Molly. She's a sharp one. 'You're on the money,' I say. 'We're going to jump ship in Israel.'

Molly nods at this news, slips off her square-toed black shoes and curls up on her seat.

'Flat shoes? Not very glamorous,' I say.

'I'll not be running in heels,' she replies, tucking her feet beneath her.

Fair point.

The steward clears away the plates and hands Molly a cushion. She settles down. I'm still in pain from my injuries, but I need a coherent plan even more than I need to sleep. I gulp a Benzedrine tablet down with a sip of Pol Roger. Through the small oval window distant pinpricks of light mark the Atlantic coast of Vichy. Just Vichy: I refuse to dignify that bunch of old women and traitors with the name of France. Although de Gaulle and his dwindling band of expatriate fantasists are no more worthy of Napoleon's legacy.

My planning keeps me awake as far as the British-controlled airspace around Gibraltar, where the Valentine enters the Mediterranean. I glance at Molly, who's sleeping under her old flying jacket with a smile on her face. The afterburners cut in again to punch us on to another supersonic run along the southern Mediterranean coast. The rumble wakes Molly. I lean over and stroke her hair.

'Don't worry,' I say to her. 'I'll keep an eye on you.'

She peers at me, half asleep.

'I'll not be needing anyone to keep an eye on me,' she says.

She pushes my hand away and goes back to sleep.

⊕

The Valentine's wheels bumping into the concrete at Lydda airport jolt me awake.

The civilian side of the airfield is quiet, close to deserted. On the far side of the runway, the floodlights of the military airbase are blazing. As we taxi in, I count half a dozen Canberras at dispersal, sporting the Royal Israeli Air Force roundel.

Molly and I walk across the tarmac towards the terminal building. A pair of Hawker Hunter interceptors in RIAF markings moves towards the runway, ready for dawn patrol. The ground reverberates as the Hunters bellow along the runway utilizing maximum power.

'It's terrible loud they are,' shouts Molly.

'Sorry, I can't hear you. Those planes are too loud,' I yell back.

We grin at each other. The two interceptors enter an almost vertical climb, and in seconds disappear into the dawn sky.

Behind them, a squadron of Fairey Rotodynes are lifting off. They're pure black, like the one that rescued me in Germany. Screaming jet rotors pull them into the Israeli sky and they disappear in the direction of the sea.

I tell the BOAC ground crew we have to leave the flight early because of a family emergency, and they retrieve our luggage. We take the third taxi that presents itself outside the airport's arrival concourse. I give the driver an address in the centre of town, several streets away from our objective.

Molly sits in the back of the taxi, excitement overwhelming tiredness, gazing at the sights of the city. 'It's very . . . modern, isn't it?' she says.

'Tel Aviv has more Bauhaus buildings than any other city in the world.'

Molly laughs. 'It's architecture you'll be taking an interest in?'

'What's wrong with that?'

'Nothing,' she says. 'You're full of surprises, that's all.'

Tel Aviv is beautiful, the cubic white structures reflecting the morning sun. The scorching heat of the Middle East is starting to build already, despite the taxi's open windows.

'God save us from fancy modern architecture,' says Molly.

'Sticking two fingers up at Hitler is the national sport here. The Nazis closed down the Bauhaus architectural school. Israel fell in love with Degenerate art.'

'I bet they'll be liking jazz too, the fiends,' says Molly, smiling.

I've a feeling she's enjoying herself, but we don't have time for a tour. The trail we're leaving is a mile wide. Unless we stay at top speed, whoever Leo sends after us will catch up.

Then things will get messy.

9

Safe

Heydrich has drafted Herr Professor Heisenberg to evaluate the technical knowledge revealed in 'On the Fallen Souls'. This 'professor' does not impress me. He is detached and cynical. I will show his scepticism to be unfounded. His kind will not reconnect us to Hyperborea!

Journal of an unknown SS scientist, p.147

Leo stands in the Old Man's customary position, by the window, staring out over Regent's Park. In the distance, small groups of children chase each other around the playground. So that was what the Old Man was watching when he used to stand there like bloody Napoleon in exile.

The Old Man – he'd been exhausted, maybe even close to collapse. His volcanic temper had been getting worse, and his paranoia was out of control. He was an Edwardian reactionary horrified by the modern world, who thought anyone to the left of Hitler was a closet Red. And the bloody dinosaur had gone and left them, just when they needed him the most.

The phone on Leo's desk buzzes.

Now he's trapped in the intelligence madhouse. There will be no time for books, for the shop, for crosswords or to finish writing his damned play. He'll have no chance to sort his marriage out either.

His wife is already sleeping in the spare room. Give it six months and she'll be back at her mother's place. He ought to have used his so-called brain when choosing a wife. His marriage had pleased his dying parents, but now what is he going to do with the bloody woman? Divorce after a respectable period, he supposes.

The phone is insistent. Leo turns back to his desk, shaking his head. He's getting sentimental in his old age: casualties are inevitable. The Old Man died doing what he loved. The bookshop is going to have to wait. His wife will just have to get used to things. Someone has to hold the Service together.

He lifts the receiver.

Elliott's voice echoes down the line, distorted by the scrambling process that keeps the Service's telephones secure. 'Sir, you wanted to speak to me?'

'Elliott, two of our salespeople have not reported in this morning. I believe they're planning a freelance sales trip to Germany.'

This ridiculous commercial jargon where agents are 'salespeople' and missions are 'sales trips'. If the Germans ever do find a technical solution to scrambling, this sort of gobbledygook won't fool them for a second. Leo makes a note to talk to GCHQ about a better system.

'What would you like me to do, sir?'

Leo explains what his plans for the runaways are.

⊕

The room is warmer than Kitty finds comfortable.

Reinhard Heydrich is standing by the fireplace smoking a cigar and listening to Beethoven's Ninth Symphony. The fire has already been lit, although it is not cold for September. He appears engrossed in the music, hardly even looking up when she enters. She stands in silence, with a guard either side of her, trying not to tremble.

She never made it as far as the Nazi justice system. This saved her life, for a period at least; the People's Court does not require evidence to help it come to a guilty verdict. If the accused appears before the court, they must be guilty; that is obvious. Therefore, the court spends most of its valuable time listening to its president, Roland Freisler, ranting.

Freisler likes to work himself into a fury, berating the anti-German scum standing before him. The defence lawyers join in the charade. They claim their clients are insane and advise them to throw themselves on the mercy of the court. This is questionable advice at best, as Freisler has never been known to exhibit anything resembling clemency.

People's Court! is one of the most popular shows on German television. Herr Doktor Goebbels is delighted at this propaganda coup.

In Kitty's case, of course, if the court had needed evidence, the testimony of Johann Huffman would have been sufficient. She is, after all, guilty as charged. Guilty of liking jazz music. Guilty of stickering. Guilty of hating the Nazis.

For Kitty, a trial would have been simply an unpleasant prelude to hanging from an iron hook. The execution shed at Plötzensee prison has no shortage of iron hooks.

On this occasion, though, Johann's superiors robbed him of his accustomed prize. The Gestapo's central computer recognized Kitty's name and spat out a priority instruction: Kitty was to be forwarded, express, to Reinhard Heydrich.

The record ends. Heydrich smiles, dismisses the guards and turns to Kitty. He motions her to an armchair positioned by the fire. On the occasional table beside him are two champagne saucers and a bottle of 1934 vintage Dom Pérignon.

She hesitates, unwilling to socialize with this murderer, but her situation is hopeless and there's little purpose in struggling.

After she sits down, Heydrich spends a moment appraising her in silence. She tries to look small and unthreatening. This is not difficult for her.

'Sit up straight,' Heydrich says. His voice is shrill, a spoilt little boy's voice, not an Aryan hero's.

She complies. Heydrich's gaze roams across her body.

Satisfied, he speaks. 'My dear Katharina, I have followed your career as a saboteur for some time. Your successes were not spectacular, were they?' A mocking expression ripples the otherwise blank surface of his face. 'That riot, for example: I've been in more dangerous bar fights. You're not going to bring down the regime like that, are you?'

Kitty's heart races. 'Herr Heydrich, do you require something from me, or do you just want to gloat?'

'Ah, your voice is also just like Sigi's.'

'My mother? How would you know anything about her?'

Next to the champagne is a chess set. Heydrich picks up a piece, one of the black pawns. 'I was acquainted with Sigi for several years,' he says. 'Long before her patriotic but ill-advised attempt to become part of the Reich's electricity supply. I always found her charming, unlike the slab of cement she married.'

'My father was a good man.'

'Yes, he was pure Übermensch. I often reminisce about his one-man assault on the Leipzig Gestapo headquarters. Oh, how we laughed.'

Heydrich puts the pawn down again and pats its little head.

⊕

Elliott sweeps through the flat in Lissenden Gardens with professional thoroughness.

The place is clean except for a box marked 'Souvenirs' under the bed. The box is full of forged passports and identity cards. Dried blood muddies some of them. He can't tell whose blood it is, but he can have a good guess.

They would have driven to one of the ports or an airport. What sort of car did the thug have? A royal-blue Riley, as Elliott recalls. He takes a seat in the front room and activates the old-boy network.

Biffy had been a First XI teammate. He was no scholar, but could bat like a junior Len Hutton. Now he's high up in BOAC. Elliott asks him for a favour, and Biffy sends a gal out to snoop around the car park. She reports an hour later: no blue Rileys to be found at Heathrow.

Elliott has a chum from Oxford days whose fondness for corduroy was legendary. Despite this aberration, he's done frightfully well in the Metropolitan Police Special Branch. A quick call and he has a good chap checking the reports of stolen and abandoned cars.

Still nothing.

Elliott perches on the desk by the window as he waits for the network to report back. He fills in the *Manchester Guardian* crossword to pass the time. Pondering fourteen down, he gazes around the square outside, searching for inspiration.

Smiling up at him is a blue Riley.

He jumps up. He has been sitting on the logbook of a D-Type Jaguar. The car is nowhere to be seen.

'Bugger,' he says under his breath.

⊕

One of the advantages of being in charge is that Leo gets the pick of the typing pool. So he sent the Old Man's basilisk back and picked a girl whose look did not kill.

He puts the latest pile of bumf down and buzzes her. 'Patricia, can you bring me in some coffee and a cream bun?'

Leo's marriage is in the toilet, so there's no harm in falling in passionate, though unrequited, love with Patricia, is there? It's not as if he already has enough problems, or anything.

The Minister of Defence is on the telephone by the time Patricia appears. She's looking more than fetching in an emerald-green Empire-line dress with matching pearls. The cream cakes she's carrying look tempting too. Leo beams at her. There's a faint smile in return. She'll warm up once she gets to know him.

'Marks, as acting chief of the Service, you need briefing on a few things. Do you have the combination for your predecessor's safe?' shouts the minister down the line. The man must think Leo is deaf.

Predecessor is it now? The Old Man's body is not even in its grave, and Whitehall has just replaced him and carried on. Of course he can get into the safe – what sort of clown do they think he is?

'Inside you'll find a file marked "Head of Service Only". It explains the Service's relationship with the Watching Committee of the British Empire.'

'Never heard of it,' Leo admits.

Patricia puts the tray down. Leo helps himself to a cream slice.

'Unsurprising, Marks, as you've only just become important enough to come to the Committee's attention.'

But of course.

'For your information, the Watching Committee runs the British Empire. It consists of the two dozen most powerful men in Britain: the Establishment personified, the *éminences grises*, the powers behind the throne. The Nazis are always accusing your lot of conspiring to run the world, but these buggers really do. What the Watching Committee wants, the Watching Committee gets. Is that clear?'

His lot? Did the minister mean the Jews? 'Received and understood,' he says, gritting his teeth.

'Good. Second, Giant and Operation Tigerlily. I've been pondering and I have a bad feeling about Menzies' assassination.'

Yes, sir, we all have a bad feeling about murder.

'There may be a connection. There are these rumours of a new German aircraft too – what was it called?'

'Flugscheibe, sir.'

'How far did we estimate that Giant was from completion?'

'At least a year, sir, if it works at all – which it won't. Our scientists are adamant that it's impossible.'

'I know the bloody eggheads reckon it's a non-starter, but the Watching Committee thinks the Germans are on to something. The Jerries are pumping a good percentage of their economy into it. Their ridiculous so-called moon shot has lower priority. They're serious. We can't afford the risk.'

'Operation Tigerlily is a last-ditch operation, sir. The risk—'

'Just dust off the file and make sure all the resources are in place, okay?'

'Yes, sir.'

'Right, got to go. I've a meeting with Ambassador Harriman in fifteen minutes.'

'Please say hello to him from me, sir.'

'What? You know the ambassador?'

'Sorry, sir, little joke.'

'Frankly, I have my reservations about you, Marks. Try to grow up, eh?'

'No, sir. I mean, yes, sir.'

Leo decides not to tell the minister about his little local difficulty. A couple of your best agents being on the run is a minor operational detail. It would be of no interest to someone as grand as the minister, let alone this almighty Watching Committee.

Elliott had better catch up with the pair of them soon, or they'll all be in the shit.

$$\oplus$$

Biffy greets Elliott in person at Heathrow. The latest news is that the gals have found the D-Type Jaguar tucked away in the car park. Elliott checks it over: the car is spotless. He pulls in the Special Branch liaison and finds out who was on duty the previous night. A few minutes passing photos around and one of them comes good: he remembers Molly and has logged the false passports. They'll have switched by now, but Elliott has them placed on Special Branch's stop list anyway.

Elliott heads back to Biffy's office. The overnight BOAC Kangaroo Route flight is due to land in Sydney at any minute. He gets on the telephone to his corduroy-clad school friend. Can he ask his Australian counterparts to check all the passengers leaving the flight? Could they possibly then take any matching this description into custody?

Of course, his chum agrees, anything for an old college mate. He'll be expecting a stiff gin and tonic next time they convene at the club, though.

Elliott sits drumming his fingers on Biffy's desk. After an hour, Biffy tires of this, and asks one of the gals to rustle up a spot of lunch. They're tucking into some first-class crab sandwiches when the Australian Special Branch rings through. Nobody resembling the descriptions they were given has disembarked at Sydney. The passports Elliott mentioned weren't used. No passengers are unaccounted for.

And good day to you too, cobber.

Elliott has another idea and gets Biffy to call the ground station at Lydda airport. Bingo. When the Sydney service went through, a man and a woman got off due to 'a family emergency'.

'Oh, what a tangled web we weave, when first we practise to deceive. But once we rehearse just a bit, we really get quite good at it,' says Elliott.

⊕

Kitty stares at Heydrich's chess set as he talks.

'I have been expecting your capture for some time, my dear. I have waited with anticipation to compare your beauty with your mother's. I must admit, you appear to have exceeded her.'

Her poor mother had died fighting against this monster. Kitty can't forget that.

'I am proposing that we come to an arrangement, my dear.'

She looks up from the chess set. Heydrich stares at her. Presumably, he wants the same kind of arrangement that Johann had. The same kind of arrangement most men seem to want with her, for some reason. Oh God, could she? Could she let this man touch her? Even to save her life?

'Whatever you want, I'm not giving it to you,' she says, her voice sounding more composed than she feels.

'That is not a cooperative attitude, Katharina. Perhaps you should listen to my offer first?'

'You're evil.'

Heydrich picks up a champagne saucer and pours a little Dom Pérignon into it. He holds it towards Kitty. The citrus aromas tease her nose. She shakes her head.

'I'm evil, am I? How so?' Heydrich asks, sipping the drink himself.

'You're a torturer and a murderer and a rapist.'

'What of it? Killing does not make me evil. I killed my parents with overdoses of painkillers to save them the pain of disease. Was that evil?'

'That's not the same.'

'Oh, it's not the killing you take exception to then? It's my objectives?'

'Some things shouldn't be done for any cause.'

'I see, and where is this arbitrary threshold, this trade-off between means and ends, my dear?'

'We aren't at school, Herr Heyd—'

'Call me Reinhard, please. I want us to be friends.'

'We are not friends, and I'm not debating with you about who deserves to die or how much violence is acceptable. Real people are screaming in pain out there, while you play ethical gymnastics.'

'You are no fun, Katharina, and while I may have done many things, I am not a rapist. All I am proposing is companionship.'

'Don't you have two mistresses already?'

'Ah, the voluptuous Mitzi twins.' His mouth twitches into a thin smile. 'They supply me with my more dissolute requirements. I require a different service from you.'

Kitty tries to imagine what level of perversion the Mitzis are unable to sink to. Heydrich catches the look on her face.

'It is not what you think; the Mitzis are more than satisfactory. What I need is someone I can relax with. Your mother and I used to sit and—'

'When was this, exactly?'

Heydrich scowls. His voice deepens.

'Few people dare to interrupt me, Katharina. Almost none risk it twice.'

⊕

Leo is starting to see why the Old Man was such a miserable bugger.

Elliott is on the telephone from Heathrow. 'Sir, I found the delivery vehicle that moved the goods. There was a delay, however, as the salesman in question used a different delivery vehicle than expected.'

'And the salesmen? Where are they?'

'They appear to be making sales calls in Israel.'

'Well, don't bloody stand there. Get after them.'

Leo replaces the telephone and picks up the file marked 'Head of Service Only: Watching Committee'. He opens it just over halfway and resumes reading.

He'd found the file in the Old Man's safe. By the amateur look of it, the Old Man had typed it himself. The marginal notes were in the Old Man's favourite shade of green ink. It's a good job Leo has such proofs or he'd have dismissed the file as the outrageous conjuring of a paranoid madman.

But this is the revealed truth. Leo feels as if he's Moses standing before the burning bush. Moses discovered that the big guy thought he ought to get his family together and take a trip to Canaan. Now, Leo has discovered that everything he thought he knew about the peace treaty with Germany was wrong.

There'd been rumours about Churchill's death, of course, but there are always rumours. Once you start listening to rumours, you go crazy.

But Churchill was just the start of it.

⊕

Heydrich takes another sip from his champagne saucer and sits back in his chair, to reminisce.

'Your mother and I met when I was a naval cadet in Kiel, in the twenties. This was before I married Lina, before I joined the party even. I was just a touch older than you are now.' He smiles at the memory. 'We met at Admiral Canaris's house; he had me playing the violin at his soirees. My virtuosity reduced your mother to tears.'

'So she and I have something in common – you reduced us both to tears.' Kitty is finding it hard to stay calm; she wants to protect her mother from those frostbitten eyes.

'See, Katharina, how your wit amuses me, as did your mother's.'

Kitty takes a deep breath. She owes it to her parents to avenge the humiliation they suffered at this creature's hands. 'What will this companionship that you require from me consist of?' Her nails dig into the flesh of her palms.

'We used to play chess, listen to records, I would play my violin. We both loved Wagner.'

'Will I be required to have sex with you?'

Heydrich strokes his lips with his thumb and forefinger.

'I do not propose to lie to you. And you will not be the only woman in my life. I am married, of course, although that is a necessary charade . . . Lina is a brood mare and nothing more. Then there are the Mitzis, and doubtless there will be others; I have insatiable appetites, as do all great conquerors. My demands need not be terribly onerous for you, my dear.'

He looks so smug, discussing how easy it will be for her.

'In return, Katharina, I am prepared to overlook your childish pranks. You can live here, in Wewelsburg, in real comfort and with enough food and drugs to keep you contented. I will send one of my drivers out with you on your trips. You can put stickers on as many lamp posts as you please. How's that?'

Heydrich will protect her while she organizes resistance? God help her, she's done it with men for less.

'And if I refuse?'

'It is a generous offer, my dear. I could just force myself on you, you know.'

'Force me to play chess and listen to you scrape at your fiddle?'

'You know what I mean, Katharina. You appear to have inherited your mother's stubbornness as well as her beauty.'

'I'm not my mother.'

Heydrich stares at her, evaluating. When he speaks again, his tone is deeper. 'Our research into the effects of sub-zero temperatures on the human body is at the forefront of science. I understand it is most useful for our anti-partisan operations. We are always looking for volunteers.'

She could bear freezing to death. It wouldn't be so painful, would it, slipping away like that? There would just be a few minutes of burning cold, then numbness, and death, wouldn't there?

'The volunteers are placed in a bath of ice water, wired of course to the appropriate monitoring equipment. I am told it takes about an hour for freezing narcosis to set in.'

An hour? Could she spend her last hour like that? She's so weak.

'The latest experiments involve a female volunteer attempting sexual congress with the frozen patient, the hypothesis being that this will revive them, if you can call it revival. They have a most appropriate description: "using animal heat". I am sure you'd find it . . . stimulating.'

She can't believe what she's hearing. How can he even think about such things?

'Do you have no empathy whatsoever?'

'No, Katharina, I do not believe I do. The universe cares nothing for humanity and neither do I. There is nothing true in this world except the Will to Power. Nothing at all.' Heydrich takes a sip of champagne. He waits for thirty seconds, the silence flickering between them. He puts the glass down.

'Very well,' he says. 'You are a beautiful woman, and the image of your mother. However, I am a busy man who does not have time to waste on seduction. I am offering you a life of luxury. Alternatively, you can spend what little remains of your life being monitored by SS scientists whilst pleasuring semi-frozen corpses. Make your choice.'

He pours champagne into the second saucer. 'Shall I call the guards?' he asks.

He pushes the champagne towards her.

10

Rezident

It is written: the Hyperborean capital, lost beneath the ice before man walked the Earth, was made entirely of diamond and centred on a metal column reputed to extend from north to south poles, and described as the millstone of the world.

Journal of an unknown SS scientist, p.149

Elliott spots Carrot-top as soon as he rushes into British European Airways' first-class departure lounge.

Carrot-top is red-faced and sweating – he must have run all the way through the terminal. Outside on the tarmac, a red, white and blue Vickers Viscount has just finished topping up for its flight to Israel. Elliott waves and smiles. Carrot-top makes a show of surprise and delight.

Carrot-top is an old Oxford rowing pal, and he still has the same famous shock of ginger hair. Last time Elliott heard of him, he was something big in Whitehall. The years have added lines to his face, and he's running to fat, too.

'Good to see you, old boy,' Carrot-top says, collapsing on to the chair next to Elliott's, panting.

'And you, Carrot. It's been a while.'

'Don't remind me. No time for rowing these days. Pedalling the jolly old ship of state nowadays, eh?' Carrot says, patting his heaving belly. 'You're looking fit though.'

'I still row, Carrot. You can't let yourself get too far out of shape in my line of work.'

Behind Carrot-top, the departure board announces that boarding for Tel Aviv has commenced.

'Elliott, old boy, regarding your jolly old line of work: I believe two of your chaps have gone walkabout? Off to Israel to visit the Chosen People, eh? And I heard a rumour the Service's resident chosen person has sent you after them?'

'News travels fast,' says Elliott. Suspiciously fast, in fact. He'd only found out a couple of hours ago himself.

Carrot-top glances around the lounge. 'Sorry, old boy, delightful to chat and all that but no time to beat around the bush, eh? Thing is, off the record, we want these rascals stopped. Can't afford to have the jolly old staff thinking they can go devising their own foreign policy, now can we?'

Ah . . . not a coincidence, then, meeting like this.

'Who's we in this instance, Carrot?'

Carrot-top actually taps his nose. It's the first time Elliott has ever seen a real person do that.

'Need to know, old boy, need to know. Top chaps in the country, let's put it that way. Think you can arrange it for me? Marks isn't going to last, you know. Not the right sort of fellow. No bottom, if you know what I mean. Not a jolly old gentleman. Needs taking down a peg or two, eh? When he's gone there will be vacancies, if you catch my drift.'

Elliott thinks about the sarcastic little sod back in Baker Street. He's rather fond of the bugger, but it seems the Whitehall old guard have their knives at the sharpeners. And if promotions are on offer, he's not going to turn one down.

'Marks has already ordered me to stop them,' he says.

'Ah, yes . . . well, look here old boy, when I say stop I mean *stop*.' Carrot-top reddens, fidgeting with his tie.

'You're asking me to kill them?' splutters Elliott.

Carrot-top glances around the departure lounge again to check no one is listening. He has a lot to learn about fieldwork and not looking suspicious. 'Menaces, the pair of them. Let's call it summary justice, shall we? You're our man, Elliott. One of the chaps and all that, eh?'

'I'm not a bloody assassin.'

Carrot-top pulls a dossier out of his briefcase and pats it. 'Look, there are things you don't know. There's no time to explain now, but these nincompoops are in danger of starting a war. There's no alternative, old boy. It's not what either of us would want, right side up, but duty is duty.'

Carrot-top pulls a piece of paper out of the dossier. It has a gold-embossed Ministry of War letterhead. 'This will get you full cooperation from the military, everything you need. No need to do the dirty work yourself, if you don't have the stomach for it, eh?' He passes the paper to Elliott. It is indeed one of those semi-mythical carte-blanche authorizations that they used to call a licence to kill.

Elliott's heart rate rises. 'Right, let's just clear something up. I haven't seen one of these for years, and now I'm organizing executions again? I thought we didn't do that any more. Is this a joke of some sort?'

'I'm just the messenger boy. Yours truly had no say in it at all. The top chaps, they're the ones who're ordering you.'

'It's all highly irregular. I'll have to call Marks.'

Carrot-top's face freezes over like the first ice on a pond in winter. 'You're married, if I recall?' There's an edge in his voice.

'What? Of course I'm married. Isn't everyone?' Elliott has never seen a look like this on a pal's face before.

'Jolly old wife? Two jolly old daughters? Jolly old school in Chalfont St Giles? Spend their days doing drawings of the duck pond and arranging jolly old flowers?'

'Are you threatening me, Carrot? Because—'

'Don't let us down, old boy. Do I need to say more?'

⊕

The taxi drops Molly and me on Rothschild Boulevard, running west towards Allenby Street. The wide, tree-lined boulevard, focal point of Tel Aviv café society, is quiet this early.

Molly takes my hand. 'Don't worry,' she says. 'It's just for cover: couples are less noticeable.'

We stroll through the dappled shade of the trees hand in hand. The usual shopkeepers, traders and manual workers litter the streets, lifting shutters, humping crates, putting out advertising. The same characters start the day off early in any city.

On the corner of Shadal Street, opposite the Soviet consulate, we spot a café that's open.

'Let's get some breakfast,' says Molly.

I order Jahnun and tiny cups of bitter cardamom-flavoured coffee for the pair of us.

'What is it?' asks Molly, peering at the Jahnun.

'Egg and tomato on toast,' I say.

'Even a simple country girl like me can understand that,' says Molly, taking a bite. She nibbles the Jahnun as we chat, smiling at each other. 'So where next?' she asks.

'Number sixteen, Rothschild Boulevard, otherwise known as the Dizengoff House, otherwise known as the Tel Aviv Museum of Art.'

'Hmm . . . has this all just been an excuse to show me your etchings?'

The way she laughs.

I remind myself the mission must come first.

At the Tel Aviv Museum of Art, the caretaker is already opening the doors for the day ahead. Molly and I sit outside the elegant white building for ten minutes, watching for any kind of surveillance. The caretaker shuffles round to the back of the building.

'Clear?' I ask.

Molly nods.

Inside, we approach the coat-check kiosk, which is manned by a battleaxe dressed in a cast-off tent. I extract a fifty-pound note from the stash in the attaché case and push it across the counter to her.

'Can you give this to Reuven for me?'

'There is no Reuven here,' says the woman, unsmiling.

'Fine, we'll wait. Molly, why don't we go and appreciate some Degenerate art?'

We're admiring *The Bewildered Planet* when a booming voice interrupts our art lesson. I turn away from Max Ernst's vision of the secrets of space, time and planetary orbits.

A short, balding man in a shapeless navy-blue suit and wire-rimmed glasses approaches, frowning. 'No one passes forged money on these premises and gets away with it,' he says with mock severity.

'Hello, Reuven,' I say. 'Your tailor's eyesight hasn't improved, I see.'

'It's what's inside that's important . . . how many times must I tell you so?' Reuven glances downwards. He brushes some crumbs from his lapels, shrugs and gives up. 'So, what brings you to Tel Aviv? Beautiful Jewish women, no doubt. Come, come, please introduce me to your charming friend.'

'Reuven Shiloah, this is Molly Ravenhill,' I say.

Reuven beams at Molly. 'I hope you're here to sweeten the deal, angel.'

Molly's delicate jawline tightens.

'Molly is Service,' I say.

Reuven's mouth turns down. 'You should see the girls the Russians send to tempt me. And the best you British can do is another shipment of Sten guns. Sometimes I think I'd be better off with the Commies.' He grins.

Reuven ushers the pair of us back to the coat-check kiosk and past the sourpuss, who almost cracks a smile. Behind the desk, Reuven lifts a trapdoor and gestures to the narrow stairs down to the basement.

'Welcome to my secret underground base,' he says, laughing. 'Oh, how glamorous the world of Jewish espionage is . . .'

Downstairs, Reuven's office is piled high with files. Reams of teletype cover his desk. The remains of what might once have been a card index are dispersed over the floor. Reuven sits down and bites into a half-eaten bagel.

'Breakfast,' he mutters, spraying more crumbs over his lapels.

'Reuven, I need your help,' I say.

'Of course, anything. Anything for the hero of . . . can I speak freely in front of Miss Ravenhill?'

I nod.

'The hero of Sachsenhausen. Bloody good job you did there.'

'You got everyone you needed out, then?'

'Everyone who wasn't killed during the breakout. Did you hear the bastards murdered every single prisoner they recaptured?'

I grimace. More corpses piled on to the body count.

'But enough of this ancient history,' says Reuven. 'What's new?'

'I need your help to get into Germany,' I say.

'We'll both be going in, not just the big man here,' says Molly.

'That's all? It's done!' says Reuven, grinning. 'Let's get something to eat. Oh, you and your long face. Do cheer up, man.'

'The Old Man is dead,' I say.

Reuven's smirk dies a sudden and unexpected death.

On the way out of the gallery, Molly turns to me.

'So, you'll be the hero of Sachsenhausen?' She squints in the bright sunlight as we step back on to Rothschild Boulevard.

'I've been indulging in a little extra-curricular activity with SHAI,' I admit.

Her eyes widen at the mention of Israel's unofficial intelligence agency. 'God save us, it's not those maniacs you're working for?'

'I'm not working for them, I'm working with them. I have my own agenda.'

'Was the Old Man in the know about this?'

'He was turning a blind eye, I think.'

'He was not.'

'I'll tell you something: the Old Man supplied Reuven with weapons and training. In return, Reuven provided him with the best intelligence network in the Middle East.'

'But attacking concentration camps? Sure and the Israelis are avenging millions of deaths... but what's your angle?'

'Vemork.'

'Vemork? But the Germans were capturing and killing everyone involved in the Vemork operation.'

'Everyone except me.'

Reuven takes us to a kosher restaurant around the corner from the art gallery. The meal is an extravaganza – gefilte fish, challah bread, matzo-ball soup, potato knishes, smoked salmon, pitta bread, hummus and pickled herring. Dessert is sweetened pears. We sink two bottles of Carmel No.1, vintage 1943, which is not bad at all. Particularly the second bottle.

Molly catches Reuven's eye. 'I bet MI5 love you. Israel will be their turf, as part of the British Empire.'

'What MI5 don't know won't hurt them,' says Reuven.

'Anti-British terrorism is getting worse, though?'

Reuven shrugs. 'There are extremists in every country. In a perfect world, I'd support independence, too. But I'm a realist. You're all that stands between us and the Nazis. If you decide to leave one sunny Friday afternoon, Israel will be a radioactive wasteland by Saturday morning. So, Molly, in fact it's me that keeps the lid on the Stern gang, not the blunderers in MI5.'

Molly stands up and excuses herself.

Reuven turns to me. 'A beautiful woman, but perhaps a little naive,' he says.

'She's never operated in the Middle East, Reuven. She's a good agent.'

'Are you in love with her?' he asks, watching me.

'No, I bloody well am not.'

He shrugs. 'Perhaps. Now, I'm sorry, most heartily sorry, about the Old Man.' Reuven grips my elbow. 'He was a friend of Israel and we don't forget our friends. This is your reason for going to Germany, revenge? But the Service does not agree, and that's why you come to me?'

I nod.

'I understand,' says Reuven. 'I will be discreet. The Old Man is dead, God rest him, and the Interservice Protocol demands revenge. However, this may spiral into war. I will be obliged to consult my masters.'

'I suggest you don't,' I say. 'Plausible deniability.'

'Yes, of course, plausible deniability . . . the hero of Sachsenhausen . . . how can I refuse?' Reuven pauses. 'There's something you could do for me quid pro quo, as they say. We've been monitoring the Germans' attempts to stir up the Arabs. They're arranging to supply weapons to the Syrians – ten thousand rifles and ten million rounds of ammunition.'

I frown. 'They must be crazy. They wouldn't have a chance. The Israeli Army would stop them at the border without our help. We could move a parachute division in overnight. There'd be Fleet Air Arm aircraft all over them within a couple of days. Then there's the Arab Legion—'

Reuven cuts across me. 'Do you imagine Heydrich cares what chance the Syrians have? For them, it's just a distraction, a jab at you British. But for us it will mean terror, our families living in fear, destruction of our homes . . .' He collects himself and continues in a calmer tone. 'I'm sorry; sometimes I do not maintain the spymaster's correct detachment.'

'Don't worry,' I say. 'I get involved in my work, too.'

Reuven raises an eyebrow. 'So I notice.'

Where does he have this idea about Molly and me from?

He smiles. 'Our sources indicate that the weapons are aboard an Italian tramp steamer, the SS *Prilono*. The ship has developed an engine fault and pulled into the southern Italian port of Bari. The trouble is, Bari is an Italian navy base with top-notch security. Nobody has much of an idea how to handle it.'

'Sounds like a simple job for a diver with a limpet mine,' I say.

'I'm glad you think so,' says Reuven. 'I'm hoping you might do it for us.'

'You must have your own divers.'

'We have divers, but not plausibly deniable divers.'

'Quid pro quo?' I say.

'Quid pro quo,' agrees Reuven.

⊕

A nondescript room in a six-storey block of Bauhaus flats, as arranged by Reuven.

Molly reaches up and unpins her hair. The dishevelled tresses framing her face contrast with her determined expression. Suddenly, I appreciate just how beautiful she really is.

'If it was a normal operation we were on, I'd be making a point of sleeping with the lead male,' she says.

This is a turn-up. I try to keep a straight face.

She turns and gazes at me with a slight frown. 'Sure and it has many advantages in an operational setting.'

'Jealousy and fighting over the women in a team is one of the biggest causes of mission failure,' I say. 'Operational Research have proved it.'

'Right enough,' says Molly, shaking out her long dark locks. 'So, we'll be avoiding the issue if I make a decision on who I'll favour.'

She unzips her flying jacket. My stomach tightens.

Molly shrugs the jacket off her shoulders. Her blouse pulls tight across her chest. She reaches up and undoes the top two buttons. The jacket falls to the floor behind her. She runs her hands down each side of her body, as if smoothing out her silk blouse. Her gaze is steady, watching me. I smile at her.

She toys with the silver cross on her necklace. 'In this case, though, I'm not so sure.' She loosens another button. 'Are there not the complications: distraction—'

There's a knock on the door. Molly freezes.

'Who is it?' I ask in Hebrew, looking round for a weapon.

Molly buttons up her blouse, red-faced.

'This is the housekeeper. Do you require anything?' asks the man outside the door.

'No, thank you. We do not wish to be disturbed under any circumstances.'

The man's footsteps retreat down the corridor. Molly laughs, breaking the spell.

'Now, where were we?' I say.

'Would you give a girl a chance to catch her breath?' says Molly, playing with her necklace again. 'We'll not carry on?'

'We will,' I say.

'Oh, you've a fine way about you, you charmer.'

Molly crosses her arms in front of her body. She takes her blouse in both hands and brings it over her head in one smooth motion. Her breasts thrust against the black silk of her brassiere. She leans towards me, close enough for me to smell her perfume. I reach out, put my hands behind her head and pull her nearer. I kiss her hard and she responds, melting into me. She gives a gentle moan and pulls away, breathing fast.

'I'm a good Catholic girl. We'll not be about . . . you know . . . going the whole way.' Her eyes flicker downwards. 'Sex outside marriage is a mortal sin.'

'But you're in your thirties. Surely . . .'

'You'll have me in tears. I'm over forty. And, yes, there have been a few moments of weakness, but I'm a good Catholic girl and I barely know you.'

Forty? Molly does not have the figure of a forty-year-old woman.

'You never married?'

She looks away from me. 'No one who was wanting to marry me ever managed to live long enough to get to the altar.'

Someone didn't make it by the look of it. Detachment is the only way to cope when you're in a business like ours.

'Are there not lots of other things a boy and a girl can do to pass the night together?' she says.

I put my arms around her and pull her closer. My lips move to hers. Her eyes close. Our lips touch and part. She responds, her body pressed close to mine, the soft caress of her lips on my neck. I trace the outline of her breasts through the silk. Molly gasps, her hands at the buttons of my shirt. She gazes up at me and smiles.

'Could you not turn the light off?' she says. 'I'm terrible shy, you know.'

11

A Game of Chess

Herr Professor Heisenberg commands the respect of Reichsführer Heydrich. Our budget has been increased tenfold. Heisenberg scribbles night and day. He believes 'On the Fallen Souls' gives him the key to unifying the physical theories, and mutters of an 'anomalous force'. He behaves as one possessed.

Journal of an unknown SS scientist, p.188

10 May 1941

Rudolf Hess, Deputy Führer of the Third Reich, checks his watch for the third time in five minutes.

No more excuses.

He finishes putting on the uniform of a Hauptmann in the Luftwaffe and heads downstairs. There, he kisses Ilse's hand, and ruffles little Wolfie's hair. There is no time for an emotional farewell, and anyway he does not wish to upset the boy.

Outside, the black Mercedes limousine that will take him to Haunstetten already has its engine running.

Hess's personal aircraft is waiting on the flight line in front of the huge Messerschmitt factory.

The Bf-110 interceptor was a gift from Herr Doktor Willi

Messerschmitt. Of course, the industrialist was only attempting to ingratiate himself, but the gift has proven useful. Hess had it modified to his own specification, with an extreme-range tank and a high-powered radio. Despite this extra weight, it's a delight to fly. Even stationary, the twin-engined fighter-bomber reminds Hess of a shark.

Standing beside the aircraft is Hess's adjutant, Karlheinz Pintsch. Pintsch salutes and hands him the latest weather reports. Hess nods in satisfaction. Finally, the skies are clear.

'Sir, the aircraft is fuelled, the radio is checked and functional and your equipment is here,' says Pintsch.

He passes Hess the compasses and the map case. Hess straps them to his thigh, where they'll be easy to refer to during the flight. He hands Pintsch some letters, and his Leica.

'Can you take a couple of photos for me, Pintsch? This could be a historic moment.'

The Deputy Führer climbs halfway into the Messerschmitt and poses, looking skyward as if searching the heavens for his destiny. Pintsch fiddles with the camera.

'Hess, you really are pig-headed' were the Führer's last words to him.

Pig-headed? Yes, he is. He sees himself as a Teutonic knight on the charge, risking everything for his Fatherland, storming to victory or to death. In victory, his prestige will be second only to the Führer's and upstarts like Himmler will be back in their place. He already has the Golden Badge of the National Socialist German Workers' Party. Perhaps it will be time for a new chivalrous order, founded by himself?

'Grand Master of the Legion of German Honour' has a ring to it.

Pintsch takes the photos and hands the camera back. 'Good

luck, sir,' he says, as he pulls the canopy closed.

Hess grunts, already engrossed in his pre-flight checklist.

Over the Dutch coast, four duck-egg-blue fighters swoop on Hess's aircraft.

He has flown along the river Rhine via Darmstadt and Bonn towards the Zuider Sea. It's still daylight: flying north and west at altitude, the day appears to stand still. Hess has his head down, try-ing to set his course using the Kalundborg direction-finding beam. A challenge squawks over the radio.

'Herr Hess, I do believe you're flying for England.'

Hess recognizes the high-pitched voice of the fighter pilot. He looks up to see Messerschmitt Bf-109s, two on either side of his air-craft. All four fighters sport runic SS markings and the emblem of a stylized eagle. He keys the radio's transmit switch.

'Heydrich, I am flying to Scotland, not England.'

'There are those in the party who do not wish you to make this journey. The Reich Minister for Forestry, for example, has ordered you to be shot down.'

This is Heydrich's little joke – Hermann Göring holds the title of Reich Master Hunter, but his power base is the Luftwaffe.

God damn it, is there anyone in Germany who doesn't know about his secret flight to Dungavel?

The fighters weave around Hess's aircraft. There's no point in diving away, as they have superior speed and manoeuvrability. Worse, there are four of them.

He can't, he won't, fail this soon.

Young Heydrich is quite capable of shooting him down. There are many ruthless men in the Nazi party, but Heydrich outdoes them all, marrying intellect with cruelty. He has more wit than Göring, for one.

'And your master, Herr Himmler, what is his view?' Hess asks.

'Himmler has the mentality of a schoolteacher. I am the rising power in the SS.'

The young devil is arrogant; Hess will say that for him. He's a schemer, deceitful and with precious little humanity, the kind of man Hess needs on his side. He would make a dangerous enemy.

'There will be a place of honour for you, Heydrich, when I neutralize the British. In the East, dedicated National Socialists will find new heights to scale, great issues to resolve, unrivalled opportunities to advance.'

'I want Bohemia.'

Is that all? He wants to horse-trade?

'Bohemia can be arranged, Heydrich, but first you must let me complete my mission.'

No response. Heydrich's fighter manoeuvres to the rear. Hess watches it over his shoulder. The only way to deal with wolves like Heydrich is to show them you aren't scared. Calculating muteness on the radio. Hess's hands quiver on the controls.

The soft voice hisses. 'I thought you might need an escort, Herr Hess. We don't want any accidents, do we?'

The fighters pull away, climbing towards the heavens.

⊕

Dungavel, 11 May 1941

Aide-memoire

We the undersigned, as representatives of the German
Reich and His Majesty's Government in the United
Kingdom have the honour to acknowledge the following
peace proposals agreed after recent conversations :-

Item: The British Empire recognises Continental
Europe west of the Urals as Germany's sphere of
interest.

Item: Germany recognises the Americas, Africa, India,
the Middle and Far East and all contiguous
oceans as the British Empire's sphere of interest.

Item: Germany renounces its former colonies.

Item: Germany will not support Italian claims on the
territory of the British Empire.

Item: The Reichsmarine shall not exceed 35% of the
tonnage of the Royal Navy.

Item: The British Empire will not grant bases or
military facilities to the United States of
America anywhere within its territory.

Item: German armed forces will withdraw from France,
Denmark, the Netherlands, Belgium and Norway.

Item: The British Empire guarantees the French Army
and Air Force will not be rebuilt for ten years.

Item: Germany will guarantee the sovereignty of
France, Denmark, the Netherlands, Belgium,
Norway, Romania, Bulgaria and Greece.

Item: The British Empire will not intervene against
Germany in any hostilities or supply weapons,
equipment or training to any German adversary
in Europe west of the Urals.

On the basis of the items above, Germany and the British
Empire will declare a cessation of hostilities.

Rudolf Hess (Envoy of the German Reich)

Watching Committee)

30 April 1946

Five years after the Anglo-German ceasefire, Squadron-Leader Guy Gibson tries to save the British Empire.

It's an icy morning as Gibson's English Electric Canberra violates Swedish airspace. She is unpainted, polished and stripped of all unnecessary equipment, including ejector seats. To have any chance of surviving the mission, she must reach her maximum possible speed and altitude.

The aircraft, call sign 'G-George', carries nose-art of a voluptuous redhead in a diaphanous negligee. Underneath the pin-up is scrawled her nickname, *Strawberry Blonde*.

War is approaching again. The Wehrmacht has recovered from its mauling in the east and is massing in the Balkans. The target is obvious — Israel. The A9 Atlas rocket bombardment alone is expected to kill thousands. It is clear the Führer has decided on a 'reckoning' with the Jews who escaped him in 1943.

Observing this build-up with increasing panic are the British. Sister aircraft of *Strawberry Blonde* have been infringing Swedish airspace on a regular basis, despite diplomatic protests. The RAF have to penetrate German airspace in order to reconnoitre, and Sweden is in the way.

Sweden's obsolete piston-engined Saab 21 fighters are incapable of intercepting the high-flying Canberras, but the Luftwaffe response is more energetic.

Luftwaffe controllers assess the heading of the British aircraft — it's on track for the Army Research Centre at Peenemünde, home of the German rocket programme. They scramble two pairs of Focke-Wulf Huckebeins, the only Luftwaffe interceptors fast enough to catch the intruder.

Strawberry Blonde's ceiling of forty-five thousand feet is three thousand more than the Huckebeins', but that doesn't make interception impossible. There's a possibility that a skilful pilot could position his aircraft so that a Ruhrstahl anti-aircraft missile could reach her.

What they don't know is that *Strawberry Blonde*'s target is not Peenemünde.

Watching his H2S radar's Fishpond indicator, *Strawberry Blonde*'s navigator notes the Luftwaffe fighters climbing towards his aircraft. He informs Gibson of the approaching interceptors. One pair is positioned too far north to intercept, but the other two are a danger.

Gibson pulls the control column back and the Canberra's wings claw at the thin air. The altimeter needle doesn't budge. He pushes the throttle against the stops, but it's already at maximum. There's no doubt the aircraft has reached its absolute ceiling. Gibson peers downwards, trying to spot the approaching interceptors. There are a couple of silver flashes at ten o'clock low, the sun catching on a wing or a canopy. The two flyers exchange glances.

'Get a bead on those two, Jimbo,' orders Gibson.

The navigator examines his radar display again, and does some rapid mental calculations.

'Intercept possible,' he states.

Gibson nods, reaching for the central console. He flips up the yellow-and-black-striped guard marked 'Scorpion: For Emergency Use Only', and presses a small red button.

Strawberry Blonde has a surprise for the Huckebeins.

The Scorpion rockets kick in, and eight thousand pounds of thrust presses the two men back in their seats. Gibson feels as if he's strapped to a firework.

He adjusts the controls, and *Strawberry Blonde* soars upwards, destroying the Huckebeins' intercept solution.

'I think we're out of their clutches, skipper,' says the navigator.

Gibson nods. 'Captain to bomb-aimer, ready for the run in?'

'Bomb-aimer to captain, roger,' is the reply from the glass nose of the aircraft.

'Crossing into German airspace.' Gibson takes his hands off the controls. 'Bomb-aimer, you have command.'

There are no clouds and, from such altitude, movement towards the target seems slow. The bomb-aimer will have plenty of time to spot the target – a second or two even, no problem. The bombsight will take account of the weapon's ballistics, the altitude, airspeed, heading and wind. There's nothing for a man to do these days, surrounded by so many fancy electronics.

'Bomb-bay doors open,' says Gibson.

Forty-five thousand feet below *Strawberry Blonde* is the German island of Ruden. The crosshairs must be intersecting the aim-point . . . now.

'Bomb gone.' The bomb-aimer starts the countdown to impact. 'Ten.'

Gibson closes the bomb-bay doors. He banks the aircraft hard and puts the nose down, the steep dive trading altitude for speed.

'Nine.'

In and out, as fast and high as possible.

'Eight.'

Keep things simple.

'Seven.'

Achieve the mission.

'Six.'

Keep the crew alive.

'Five.'

Keep himself alive.

'Four.'

Gibson pulls his pitch-black goggles into position.

'Three.'

Blind, he can't help tensing his hands on the controls.

'Two.'

Keep it steady. How big an explosion can one pint-sized bomb make?

'One.'

The flash illuminates the aircraft as if Gibson isn't wearing the goggles.

$$\oplus$$

Werner Heisenberg is a genius.

Everybody says so. He has a Nobel Prize to prove it.

In early 1943, Rudolf Hess had invited Heisenberg to the Reichskanzlei, the Nazi Party's 'office' in Berlin, for an urgent meeting. The building itself proclaimed the power of the Nazis: colossal double doors separating vast reception halls carved from red granite and marble. The atmosphere was hushed and efficient; a lesser intellect would have been intimidated.

Hess explained the situation. The army was in full retreat from Stalingrad. Field Marshal von Manstein still thought he could stabilize the front, but the Wehrmacht had lost the initiative. Ahead was nothing but a grinding stalemate on the steppes of Russia. Could Heisenberg produce a weapon based on the principles of atomic physics within nine months and so save the Fatherland?

Nine months? This was not possible.

Hess had accepted Heisenberg's negative answer as final. With his last hope of victory removed, he began making plans for ceasefire negotiations with General Secretary Molotov.

And, with his last hope of adequate funding removed, Heisenberg went back to his study of cosmic rays. Progress was encouraging; he hoped to present a ground-breaking theoretical paper next spring. Still, it wasn't the challenge a bomb would have been.

Now there are two Gestapo agents standing on his doorstep, announcing that Herr Hess wants another word with him.

They are carrying arrest warrants.

This time, the Reichskanzlei is in uproar, panicking bureaucrats running everywhere.

The Gestapo frog-march Heisenberg into Hess's office, where the Deputy Führer is shouting down the telephone.

'No, the British are not threatening to wipe out Berlin, Prime Minister Attlee is not demanding we withdraw from the Balkans, and Hitler has not had a heart attack! For God's sake, Herr Goebbels, get a grip on yourself!' Hess slams the telephone down. He waves the Gestapo agents from the room and orders his adjutant to shut the door on the chaos outside.

Heisenberg looks around the office. It, too, is oversized, with square marble pillars supporting a high ceiling. A huge swastika, carved from ebony, fills the whole of the wall behind Hess. This is more like a temple than a practical workspace.

Hess comes round his desk to shake hands with Heisenberg, his face returning to its normal colour. 'I apologize, Herr Professor, for the imposition. But things are rather urgent.' Hess picks up a sheaf of photos from his desk and hands them to Heisenberg. 'This is Ruden. Just off the coast near—'

'I know where Ruden is, Herr Hess,' says Heisenberg, examining the photographs.

'Of course.'

The teardrop-shaped island is unrecognizable. Now it is an atoll – the weapon has produced a crater right in the centre, which has filled with seawater.

'An atom bomb? Presumably the British?' says Heisenberg.

'I thought, Herr Professor, that atomic weapons were a fantasy of Jewish physics?'

'There is no "Jewish physics", Herr Hess. I have told you this before. Physics is physics. Nature is Nature. If Nature gives up her secrets to a Jewish scientist, then it is because he has followed the scientific process – formulated a hypothesis, gathered data, and produced a theory – nothing more.'

'I shall have to have a word with some of my party colleagues about that line of reasoning, Herr Professor.'

'Please do.'

Hess takes the offending photos and places them back on his desk, upside down. 'Herr Professor, you told me an atomic weapon was impossible. What happened?'

Heisenberg sighs. This was not what he had said at all. Why do people not listen?

'If you recall, Herr Hess, I did not say "impossible", I said "impracticable within the nine months that are available".'

Hess inclines his head. 'I see, but how have the British succeeded where we have failed?'

'The British are no fools – you, of all people, know this. They have their own Nobel Prize winners, they have the Jewish émigrés, most of all they have Professor Bohr.'

'Bohr is a Jew.'

What is it with National Socialists and Jews? The Jewish scientists who were forced out have been an irreplaceable loss to German science. Work has suffered, stagnated even in places. Selective vision regarding the evidence, that's their problem.

'Yes, Professor Bohr is a Jew, but he is also a genius. He is my superior in intellect – one of the few men in the world I will say that of. He will have had a hand in the British programme.'

Hess listens, picks up a delicate, bone-china coffee cup and takes a sip. 'Herr Professor, that is a political question. Therefore it is outside your sphere of expertise. I advise you not to mention Professor Bohr or any other Jewish scientist in such complimentary terms. Others are not as . . . reasonable as I am.'

Some things cannot be said in Nazi Germany, even when you're a genius.

'How was the weapon delivered?' Heisenberg asks.

'One of their Canberras evaded our fighters.'

Heisenberg's shoulders slump.

'If it was airdropped, then I have made an error in my computation of the critical mass. My calculation was that tons of the uranium isotope with mass number 235 would be needed. It must have been Bohr. No one else could have perceived something I myself overlooked.'

Hess reacts with more calm than Heisenberg expects. 'How long to discover this error?'

'A week, at most. Days perhaps.'

'I am hoping I can rely on your patriotism when I ask: will you build Germany a bomb?'

Heisenberg considers the Deputy Führer's question. Patriotism? Of course he's patriotic. But he suspects the Gestapo may get involved if he does not give Hess the answer he's looking for. He has his family to think of.

'I'll build you a damn bomb, and quickly, before the British build up a stockpile and kill us all.'

'Fortunately we have the A9 Atlas rockets and nerve gas with which to threaten retaliation. The British are too weak to take decisive action, as this Ruden demonstration shows.'

'They hope to avoid conflict.'

'As I say, they are weak. However, Herr Professor, that may not last. Can you produce an atomic weapon within the year? You will have Kriegsentscheidend priority: anything you need, unlimited budgets.'

Heisenberg gazes out of the window as he calibrates his response. Even if a warhead contains only a few kilograms of uranium$_{235}$, the extraction will prove a gruelling task.

'Well, Herr Professor?'

Heisenberg nods. 'Yes, but first you need to find me ten tonnes of heavy water.'

12

Man's Work

It is written: an unnamed entity destroyed the original Hyperborean home in the Pleiades. A refugee faction fled to Earth, using arcane knowledge to make themselves invisible to their nemesis. They built the millstone of the world as a power source. There has to be a way to harness it. Must discuss with Heisenberg.

Journal of an unknown SS scientist, p.201

A rusty, beaten-up tramp steamer wallows into sight through the squall.

Thousands of other freelance cargo ships, identical to her, litter the Mediterranean. An onlooker might speculate that she is carrying motor parts, oranges or even a shipment of pianos.

Our Rotodyne circles the ship, lurching in the gusting wind.

I notice the ship flies Spanish colours, but they're no more than a tired yellow-and-red dishrag at her stern. The name painted on the stern looks like *La Rhin.*

The flag of Franco's Spain disappears and that of another country flutters in the wind. The flag is white with a red cross and something blue in the top left quadrant. The British naval ensign? No. The wind stiffens, and I see a six-pointed star.

The ship is Israeli.

The flag must be a signal because we alter course to approach the ship as soon as it snaps open. As we get closer I notice false panels hiding guns and torpedo tubes. The Rotodyne transitions to a hover and the loadmaster gestures for us to stand up.

We jump out on to the deck of Reuven's secret pirate ship.

In *La Rhin*'s mess, a small group including Molly, myself and the ship's captain, Andre Peri, crowd around Reuven. He spreads a map of Bari harbour on the table.

'An RIAF Canberra photo-reconnaissance aircraft strayed into Italian airspace this morning – accidentally, of course. Two Regia Aeronautica interceptors chased it with their usual enthusiasm, but failed to get within rocket range. I'm sure diplomatic protests at this violation will be forthcoming.'

Reuven grins. He beckons me over to the viewer. It shows a perfect stereo image of Bari harbour from forty-five thousand feet. It is stuffed with Regia Marina warships. An arrow points at the *Prilono*, the ship that the weapons are aboard. She's moored between two Italian destroyers.

'Harbour defences?' I ask.

'Netting, patrols, sonar, searchlights, the works,' says Reuven.

I consider the options. 'Okay, how about you take our ship into the harbour? I can slip over the side, take a spin over to the *Prilono*, fix the mine on a long-delay fuse and swim back to you. Afterwards, I'll walk off the boat with the shore party and head for the railway station.'

Captain Peri speaks. 'We cannot enter Italian territorial waters. I'm a wanted man, the captain of an internationally notorious pirate ship . . .' He's a big man with bulging eyes and a black beard. He looks . . . well, he looks piratical.

Reuven rolls his eyes. 'Theatricals aside, we're also surrounded by priceless eavesdropping equipment,' he says.

'How about intercepting the *Prilono* when she leaves? Use some of this hardware?' I say, gesturing around me.

'Yes,' says Peri. 'A single torpedo and she'll be gone.' His eyes gleam.

Reuven shakes his head. 'A last resort. The Regia Marina may well escort her out, and there's a danger of missing her after that. We have to destroy the ship here; once she gets out to sea, the problems are worse.'

Peri disagrees, but Reuven motions me to continue. Peri scowls.

'Right, I'll infiltrate the harbour,' I say. 'But I need you to get me closer to the target than the territorial limit; I can't swim that far towing a limpet mine.'

Reuven nods. '*La Rhin*'s motor torpedo boat is serviceable, and it's going to be a dark night. So we'll take the boat out and do a high-speed run towards the coast, simulating cigarette smugglers. As we pass the harbour, we'll drop you, and then veer off to draw Italian attention away. The customs boat goes out every night at one a.m., so the netting has to open then. You infiltrate, fix the mine, exfiltrate, and we send the boat to pick you up. Easy.'

'This is possible,' admits Peri.

'What sort of diving equipment do you have?' I ask.

'Standard Royal Navy issue: Sladen suit, Siebe Gorman oxygen rebreather—'

'Limpet mines as well, of course,' says Reuven.

'I'll need the mine set for a three- or four-hour delay, to give me a chance to get out before she blows.'

'Ah, no, we can do better than that,' says Reuven. 'Come and see.'

Molly touches my hand as we walk to the hold to examine Reuven's gadget.

'Are you sure about this?' she asks.

'Anything for a bit of excitement. Anyway, we don't have much choice, unless you want to retreat to London.'

'And leave the "man's work" to you? Never. I just wish I could dive and then I could come and look after you.'

Reuven picks up a limpet mine with a small propeller on its face. He turns a knurled knob recessed into the side of the mine, until the counter reads three.

'You set the distance here. In this case, let's say three miles. Once the target sails that far, the mine detonates. Rather than sinking in the harbour, the target will be in deep water, out of reach of salvage. It also makes it harder for the Germans to be sure what happened. The ship could have hit a loose mine, or there could have been an accident.'

I stare at the mine. The tightness in my stomach builds. There's only one remedy for tension before a dangerous mission.

'Let's get a drink,' I say to Molly.

'Alcohol in the bloodstream is not recommended when diving,' says Reuven.

'God save us, the hero wants a bit of whisky before he goes about killing himself,' says Molly. 'Can you not have some pity?'

I pass the afternoon drinking and playing cards on the quarterdeck with Molly, Reuven and Captain Peri. The poker tournament ends with Molly and Reuven owing me ten pounds each and Peri owing me twenty. Admiral Canaris's warning that those who are lucky at cards are unlucky in love crosses my mind.

While I study my cards, Molly chats away to Captain Peri. Reuven interjects a couple of jokes in his schoolboy French, and then seems to lose interest.

Molly leans towards Peri, her cleavage deepening. 'So tell me, how did you end up working for SHAI?' she says, glancing up to check if

Reuven understands her French. If he does, he shows no sign of it.

'Before the war, I worked for the French Colonial Intelligence Service. After the fall of France, I offered my services to the English. They renamed me Lieutenant Commander Langlais and *La Rhin*, HMS *Fidelity*.'

'The perfidious English,' says Molly, now testing my understanding. I grimace at her. She smiles back, and winks at me.

'Go on,' she says, brushing Peri's arm. He smiles at her.

'The Royal Navy refitted her and added the weapons. They even supplied me with a couple of floatplanes. We trailed our petticoats across the Atlantic, tempting U-boats to surface and use their deck guns against a sitting target. Whenever they did, we blew them out of the water.'

'Tough job,' she says, sympathy personified. Who does she fancy herself as, Mata Hari?

'They were a rough crew but we all drank together: Belgians, Polish, Corsicans, even the French.'

'But then the Anglo-German war ended, too.'

If she touches his arm again, I may do something I'll regret.

'We were off the coast of Crete, trying to rescue stragglers, when the British signalled that the war was over. They wanted us to return to Alexandria, but for me the war was not over. It will not be over until Corsica is free of the Boche.'

'You were going freelance, then?'

'Until Reuven cornered me in a waterfront dive in Beirut. He told me *La Rhin* was sailing for Israel in the morning, captain or—'

'Sir, we're approaching Italian territorial waters,' shouts the navigator from the doorway.

Captain Peri stands up. 'That was eleven years ago. Corsica is still occupied, and . . .' He shrugs and turns away to give his orders. 'Very good. Signal All Stop and Action Stations. Full watch and report any activity to me immediately.' He turns to me. 'We're too close to Bari and the Regia Marina for my liking. The sooner I get you off my ship, the better.'

I couldn't agree more.

⊕

I synchronize watches with Peri, Reuven and Molly at 23.00.

'For God's sake, be careful,' says Reuven.

I intend to be, but rebreather diving has the disadvantage of being much more dangerous than SCUBA. I'm forced into it, though, when it's the only way to accomplish a mission. Which is all the time.

Civilian sport divers – I call them pond life – use open-circuit aqualungs called SCUBA. With every breath, the SCUBA diver releases a stream of bubbles, continuously giving away their position. This makes SCUBA useless for the military diver attempting to approach a target covertly, so we use rebreathers instead.

As I scramble into the torpedo boat, Captain Peri salutes me.

'Give them hell,' shouts Molly.

I give her the thumbs up; there's no time for pleasantries.

The torpedo boat surges forward, engines snarling.

We loop out of radar range of the Italian coast and come in on a different heading. The crew man the machine guns, extinguish all lights and break out the White Ensign.

'No Jew will ever again be taken prisoner by the Nazis,' Reuven had explained. 'They'll fight to the last man and last bullet and, if it comes to it, they all have cyanide pills.'

The Service could do with more people with such commitment.

The torpedo boat comes in again at full power. It scuds over the wavetops at forty knots, spray drenching the decks. I sit at the stern, fully kitted up in my underwater gear.

We reach Italian territorial waters at midnight, heading for an inlet south of Bari harbour. Italian radar will have picked up the boat, so the probability of interception is high. Every available eye strains to pick out a potential collision. The dark, moonless night is perfect for covert diving but dangerous for boats tearing around with their lights extinguished.

The lieutenant in command indicates 'drop in two minutes'. I make my last-minute checks, then stand up and waddle towards the stern, my fins slapping on the wet deck. The boat makes a hard turn to starboard. I grip a railing as we come around, the boat slowing a little. The lieutenant makes the 'jump' sign.

I splash into the water.

By the time I regain the surface, the torpedo boat is just a shadow in the middle distance. If it has dropped me accurately, then there's a mile still to swim. I scan for the Monopoli lighthouse. Spotting its flash, I take a compass bearing, refit my mouthpiece and submerge.

Underwater, the visibility is close to zero. I can just decipher the luminous markings on my equipment, but beyond that nothing. The rebreather attached to my chest expands and contracts in perfect counter-cycle to my breathing. Each breath is scrubbed of carbon dioxide then gets a trickle of oxygen from the tank strapped on my back.

I check the meter and set the oxygen flow rate to match the tempo of my breathing. If the oxygen level drops too low, hypoxia will lead to unconsciousness. If it gets too high, I'll suffer from oxygen toxicity convulsions. Either way I'll drown, which I'm not ready for just yet, despite my so-called death wish.

In training, I found swimming in darkness nightmarish. Now long familiarity has made it routine. It's peaceful – like the grave it may well become. The only hope in an emergency is to pull a line that opens a pouch full of lead shot. In theory, jettisoning this weight might enable even an unconscious diver to float to the surface. I've never heard of it working, though.

The depth gauge reads ten feet. I check my compass for direction and, with a stroke of my fins, I set off.

I surface well outside the netting that protects the harbour from infiltrating frogmen. The luminous hands of my watch indicate 12.57. I tread water, flip up my faceplate and raise my rubber-coated binoculars. The buoys attached to the netting are now about a hundred yards away. I swim towards them.

The netting opens for the coastguard boat right on schedule. I slip through the gap and glide into the harbour. There's an alarming degree of activity on the Italian destroyers moored either side of the *Prilono*. Their decks are floodlit and sailors are bustling around.

It's just twenty yards to the *Prilono* but its defenders are so alert I can't get any closer. If I try, one of the lookouts will spot me. Then the underwater shockwaves from a hand grenade thrown into the water will crush my lungs.

The destroyers' searchlights cut through the water in front of me. I float, watching the pattern the lights make, timing their sweeps. About thirty seconds between each – not enough time to swim the remaining distance.

The wailing of a siren penetrates the murk; one of the destroyers is leaving port. I sink lower, watching the depth gauge's needle drop towards the red zone.

The thrumming from the warship gets louder; it's pulling away from its berth next to the *Prilono* on quarter engines. I wait, floating just above the mud of the harbour bottom. The depth gauge reads twenty feet, the limit for rebreather diving.

The lashing of the approaching destroyer grows louder, almost painful.

The hull looms out of the water above me. Its vast bulk brings on a burst of claustrophobia. I swim as fast as I can, flippers thrashing and my body numb with the effort. Get too close to the propellers and they'll suck me in and turn me into fish food. The water tugs me backwards. The tiny core of my brain that never panics recognizes the instinctive, primeval terror caused by a shark in the water. The rest of my brain urges me to flee.

I work my fins, legs burning, lungs gulping air.

Swim. *Anywhere.*

Hot flashes.

The propellers grinding.

Cold flashes.

The rush of the water, clawing at me, dragging me in.

Fish food.

The destroyer is past and the propellers thrust me away instead of sucking me in. The warship recedes. Still disorientated, I regain control of my breathing with arms and legs trembling. I pull out my compass, and calculate the direction to the *Prilono*, my heart still throbbing. The diving suit is clammy against my skin. I fight my nausea.

Intent on the compass, I almost bang my head on the steel hull of a ship. Is it the *Prilono* or have I made a mistake? Instinct says I've found the right ship, but instinct is a poor guide in inky water. I reach down for the limpet mine secured at my waist.

The clang of the mine magnetically gripping the *Prilono*'s hull must wake every sailor in Bari. I find the safety pin by touch. It slides out and drops into the depths. The mine is live.

Mission complete.

A brief surge of exultation; the ship is now almost certainly doomed. Now I need to escape the harbour, swim back to the—

With the suddenness of imminent death comes the stomach-turning rush of hypoxia. The brain core curses my stupidity. I didn't adjust the oxygen valve for hyperventilation during my manic attempt to avoid the destroyer's propellers. Too late, one hand reaches for the flow valve and the other for the emergency cord. My last conscious thought is one of horror.

I've failed.

13

Flash Damage

Nothing that is not vulgar, pretentious and soul-killing appeals to the slaves that crawl upon our planet posing as free men. All are destined to fall before the Hyperboreans when the anomalous force calls them to Earth. The Untermenschen do not deserve to live. A hard, beautiful élite of Aryans will rise and rule upon their bones, for ever!

Journal of an unknown SS scientist, p.276

27 February 1947

The weather in Telemark was atrocious, even by Norwegian standards.

The Vickers Valetta carrying us had taken advantage of the snowstorm to penetrate Norwegian airspace. That carried us to the general area of the frozen Lake Møsvatn. But visibility was too low for visual identification of our drop zone. The plane circled, searching for a connection to the Eureka beacon operated by Einar Skinnarland.

Skinnarland, an engineer at Vemork, was our man on the inside. On 20 February he'd reported that non-stop electrolysis had produced seven tonnes of 90 per cent pure heavy water. The Germans were shipping it out within days.

It was now or never.

We parachuted blind. I was last out of the aircraft, but found the one-man welcoming committee first. Skinnarland was huddled by the side of the lake, waving a torch with a red bulb. I skidded to a halt twenty yards away, Krag-Jørgensen sniper rifle at the ready.

'What did you see early on Tuesday morning?' I shouted.

'A pink elephant,' replied Skinnarland.

'Thank God for that,' I muttered, as I approached to shake his hand.

Three wraiths slid into view through the blizzard, grey shadows in snow camouflage pushing their way through the snow on cross-country skis.

'This does have one advantage . . .' said Reg, gesturing at the heavy curtain of falling snow.

Reg was our leader. He'd arrived in SOE via Dunkirk, Crete and the Parachute Regiment. His job was to get us into Vemork. He was a bastard.

'. . . no one in his right mind would be outside on a night like this,' said Alex.

Once Reg got him in, Alex Methuen's task was to sabotage the electrolysis chambers, destroying the stocks of heavy water. In contrast to Reg, he'd helped and encouraged me. Sometimes I suspected he was playing the soft man to Reg's hard.

'This is not so bad,' said Erling. 'You should try it in January.'

Erling Granlund had volunteered for SOE's First Norwegian Independent Company after the Nazis had driven him from his homeland. He was there to deal with any local difficulties.

There was no let-up in the snow. Visibility was at best thirty yards, but most of the time it was ten. Reg was right; if we stayed off the tracks, then the chance of a patrol spotting us during our approach was minimal. The killer would be an accidental fall, not enemy troops – at least until we reached the Rjukan escarpment.

A nod, a smile, a handshake between the Norwegians. Without unnecessary words, they skied on towards their deaths.

I pulled my goggles down and hurried after them.

⊕

Six months earlier, we had been posted to SOE's Station 26 – Glenmore Lodge, Inverness-shire, Scottish Highlands. We trained in Arctic warfare, urged on by relentless instructors from the Commandos: survival, orienteering, silent killing, use of enemy weapons, demolition, endless climbs and route marches through snow-covered mountains.

Reg drove us hard. He forced us to ski further and further, carrying loads that at first I could only just lift. My view was that I'd already proved myself in SOE. Reg didn't agree; to him I was the weak link in the team. He hounded me, looking for any excuse to have me kicked out. I hated him.

Until one winter evening when Alex told me some news. We'd just returned from the longest ski patrol so far, climaxing in a live-ammunition assault course. I was half dead.

'I think you've cracked it,' he said.

I grunted, just needing to sleep.

'Reg says you're the fittest man he's ever met, and the best shot. He's struggling to keep up with you.'

I was speechless.

The insults didn't stop; Reg was too much of a bastard for that. I thought I could detect a slight twinkle in his eyes though, sometimes.

I still miss him.

The week before the raid, the Old Man turned up. That was when I knew we were going to die.

In the centre of the briefing room was a model. A hydroelectric power station clinging to a mountainside above a deep ravine crossed by a bridge.

Suddenly we were back in the army. Reg marched us into the room as if it was a parade. Even the Old Man was wearing his uniform. It suited him. He looked solid. He told us to sit.

'This,' he said, 'is your target – Wasserkraftwerk Vemork, located at the Rjukan waterfall, in the county of Telemark, Nazi-occupied Norway.'

'I know this place,' said Erling, shaking his head. 'This will not be a piece of cake.'

'I'm rather afraid there will be no cake at all. A battalion of mountain troops from the sixth SS-Gebirgs-Division is dug in around the plant. The SS-Freiwilligen-Schikompanie Norwegen patrols the countryside for miles around.'

'Damn quislings,' said Erling.

'Yes, but good skiers,' said the Old Man. 'You'll have to watch out for them.'

'You want us to blow up a power station, even though we're supposed to be at peace with Germany. What's so important about this place that we risk starting a war over it?' asked Alex.

'Gentlemen, I am not supposed to tell you this, but I am asking you to risk your lives . . . the alternative might be the end of our country.'

The Old Man paused for effect. He had our attention.

'The role of the RAF and Squadron Leader Gibson in the "atomic demonstration" is common knowledge. But the rumours are correct – Germany *was* planning to attack Israel. Attlee threatened Hitler with a bomb on Berlin unless he backed off.'

Low whistles.

'Now we're building a nuclear-armed bomber force to deter any German aggression, but it's not ready. And Hitler has ordered a crash programme to build a German bomb, masterminded by Professor Heisenberg. Heisenberg needs ten tons of heavy water for his reactor and the Vemork hydroelectric power station makes heavy water. Britain has to destroy Vemork to slow Heisenberg.'

'Surely a bombing raid?' said Erling.

'Unfortunately, a conventional strike is impossible. First, Norway is technically a neutral country. Second, Britain requires some deniability.'

'Which leaves us,' I said. 'Is the bridge the only way in?'

The Old Man nodded.

The bridge: spanning the ravine two hundred yards above the River Maan, eighty yards long, floodlit, guarded at both ends. Impossible. We stood staring at our probable graveyard.

'There's another way,' said Erling, pointing at the model. 'We climb down into the ravine, ford the river and climb the cliffs here.'

Consternation.

In winter? At night? 'In sub-zero temperatures? This is a suicide mission,' I said.

'You thought they gave us those cyanide pills for fun, did you?' said Reg.

I swore.

The Old Man pulled the cover from a crate full of whisky bottles. 'The King is aware of this mission. He appreciates the risks you are taking. The Prime Minister also sends his regards, and I wish to add my personal thanks. These bottles of Caledonian whisky are from my family's personal reserve. I thought perhaps they might help?'

Reg looked at him.

'You're not wrong, boss. Let's try and drink ourselves to death first, eh? Save you the trouble.'

So, not for the last time, the Old Man tried to kill me.

⊕

Base camp.

Or, more accurately, a tent hidden in a clump of fir trees a mile away from Vemork. Laden with snow, the tent was already invisible. We dumped the radio, food and non-essential gear inside, in preparation for our assault.

'Right, we'll have a brew and a bit of chocolate, and then make a start,' said Reg, checking his watch. 'Don't want to die on an empty stomach, do we, Pretty Boy?'

I was 'Pretty Boy', the youngest member of the squad, wireless operator, cannon fodder and, in Reg's opinion, general team dogsbody.

Reg scowled at me. 'I know it's snowing, but that doesn't mean it's Christmas. Get the bloody kettle on.' Reg handed the chocolate round. Half a bar of Dairy Milk each – generous by his standards.

I can still remember the taste of the chocolate, eaten surrounded by fir trees in the middle of a blizzard. We thought we were on a suicide mission, so it could easily have been my last meal on earth. A scrap of cheap sweetness and a few sips of scalding tea out of a mess tin lid.

It was the best bit of chocolate I ever tasted.

Watches synchronized, ropes, ice axes and crampons rechecked, we set off. Skinnarland left us on the river bank, at a crossing point he'd reconnoitred. He disappeared into the snow, heading for the town of Tinn, to establish his alibi.

Across the river, I glimpsed the dark mass of the ravine wall through the flurries.

Two hundred yards. Straight up.

⊕

Halfway up the cliff face, we stopped for a quick breather on a small icy ledge. The falling snow swirled about us. I looked around me. There was nothing to see in any direction except ten feet of granite and a wall of snowflakes.

Reg squatted beside me, breathing hard. 'Not complaining about all that training I forced you to do now, eh, you lazy slob?'

I glanced at him. He'd insisted on taking the lead, the most dangerous position. He was frazzled; the climbing was treacherous. 'I'll lead if you want,' I said, my heart rate easing.

'The hell you will, Pretty Boy. I'm not having a ponce like you killing us all before we even reach the target. This is a job for big boys.'

Above and to my right there was a slight glow from the searchlights illuminating the bridge.

'Come on, Reg, you've done the hard bit. Let me finish off. You can get yourself ready for the scrap when we get to the top.'

Reg's answer was short, blasphemous and negative.

At the top of the precipice, we crawled forward until the outline of the target loomed through the snow. Reg unslung his MG42 machine gun, and collected the spare barrels and ammunition belts from the others. I unfolded the bipod and positioned the MG42 on the edge of a natural depression in the rock.

'Erling, you reconnoitre the building and deal with any locals you find. Methuen, you follow Erling. Pretty Boy, you watch Methuen's back while he sets the charges. I'll cover your line of retreat, nice and safe behind this here rock.' Reg patted the MG42.

I stared at him in amazement. This wasn't the plan we'd discussed. I was supposed to cover the team as it withdrew. Reg scowled at me.

'Don't just bloody stand there, Pretty Boy. The door's that way.'

Erling and Methuen were heading towards a basement door that Skinnarland had left unlocked earlier. They were already almost invisible, camouflaged white against the snow. I needed to move.

I caught up with them. They were swearing at each other in Norwegian.

'What?' I whispered, dropping to Erling's side in the doorway.

'Bloody door's locked,' hissed Erling.

'Boot it down,' said Methuen.

'Too noisy.'

'Out of the way,' I said, reaching for my holster.

I placed the Welrod in contact with the lock and pulled the trigger. The squalling wind masked the crack of the silenced pistol firing, and the bullet smashing through the lock.

'Now try it,' I said, grinning.

The door swung open. Erling went into the darkness first. I followed, holding the Welrod in my right hand and the rifle in my left. There was light coming from the end of the corridor. I motioned Erling to stay back and then crawled towards the end of the corridor.

It came out on to a walkway, halfway up one wall of the heavy-water concentration room. I stuck my head round the corner. There were no sentries on the walkway, and I couldn't spot anybody below. I beckoned Erling forward.

'Anyone home?' Erling shouted in Norwegian.

His greeting was met by Germanic commotion. Two sentries came running round a corner at the far end of the room. SS patches and Edelweiss indicated Gebirgstruppen.

I put two bullets in each sentry's chest before they managed to get their rifles unslung. The bodies slumped to the floor. I reloaded with frantic haste. No more Germans appeared.

'You're on, Alex,' I called back down the corridor.

We climbed down a ladder and surveyed the target: a long row of huge metallic cylinders lining one wall. Erling locked and barricaded the doors leading into the concentration room. Alex placed the explosives, the steady hum of the generators covering the noise as he worked.

And then it all went to hell.

A ripping burst of MG42 gunfire pierced the silence. I spun around, raising the Welrod. Outside, Reg had opened fire on someone.

'Better put those explosives on a short fuse, Alex,' I said.

'Almost done,' he said, scrambling between the cylinders.

'You sure you've got enough explosive to do the job?' I asked.

'Oh yeah,' he said, smirking.

A klaxon wailed. I holstered the Welrod and raised my rifle towards the barricaded door. Outside there were shouts and the tramp of boots. The door handle turned. I fired two shots just above the handle. A scream, a crash, and the knob stopped moving. I backed away from the barricade, covering it with the rifle.

'Thirty seconds,' Alex shouted.

Thirty-second fuses? Shit.

A barrage of sub-machine gun bullets carved the door into splinters. I fired back, retreating across the concentration room.

'Go! Go!' shouted Erling from the walkway. 'I'll cover you.'

Now, indistinct figures were visible through the wrecked door and the gun smoke. I turned and ran for the ladder. Alex scrambled upwards just in front of me. Above us, Erling kept up a steady rate of fire. Something metallic clattered on the tiles behind me.

'Grenade!' shouted Erling.

I reached the top of the ladder, threw myself across the walkway and into the corridor.

The grenade exploded.

The blast wave caused sympathetic detonation in the explosives

Alex had laid. The resulting eruption blew me down the corridor and slammed me into the wall at the far end.

I must have passed out, because the next thing I registered was snow on my face. I opened my eyes to find I was lying on the cliff edge, next to Reg. Erling was beside him, feeding the ammunition belt into the machine gun. Reg was laying down suppressive fire on the SS troops who were trying to work their way towards our position. He was bleeding from a gash just above one ear.

'Alex?' I asked.

Erling shook his head. Reg glared at me for a second as Erling changed the overheating barrel on the MG42.

'Finished your beauty sleep, have you, Pretty Boy? Now get the hell out of here. We'll hold them off. You find the way back to base camp and radio in the code for success. And leave the rifle; I'm going to need it when the MG42 runs out of ammo.'

I didn't want to abandon them.

'That's an order, Pretty Boy. You have the best chance of getting out. Go!'

My last sight of Reg was of him firing at the SS troopers. I climbed down the cliff as fast as I dared, slipping and bouncing on the rocks. Somehow, I failed to kill myself.

Above me, Reg screamed with battle rage. He was well positioned at the edge of the cliff, just about impossible to flank. He would hold his position until he ran out of ammunition or the SS brought up heavy weapons. If I could somehow create a diversion at the bottom, maybe they'd have a chance.

I couldn't understand it: we'd agreed before the mission to fight to the death together. First Reg had changed the plan, and then he'd ordered me to run away.

I was halfway down the precipice when Reg ran out of

ammunition for the machine gun. The distinctive bark of the Krag-Jørgensen rifle echoed off the walls of the ravine.

I kept up a steady stream of curses, sliding downwards, trying to control my descent with the ice axe.

The first mortar-bomb explosion sounded like the end of the world. The second overshot and burst in the valley below. That would have bracketed Reg's position. One more rifle shot was audible, and then the mortar started firing for effect.

It was only a matter of time now.

I fell the last twenty yards, and landed in a snowdrift on the ravine floor with a sickening crack.

I tried to stand up. Nothing doing. Fracturing pain in both ankles: I'd broken them both. I lay in the snowdrift, tears turning to ice on my face.

There was shouting in German, from the east. A vehicle's lights shone through the snow like the eyes of some horrific beast. The SS were moving down the ravine, searching for me.

If I didn't get on to my feet, I was going to die.

I managed to turn over and get to my knees. My hands were raw, bruised and painful. I'd torn the ligaments in my left shoulder. My hands were going numb where my gloves had worn through.

I crawled through the snow in search of my pack. It was just a dark hump of ice frozen in a niche below an overhanging rock. Scrabbling through the medical kit. Indistinct shapes looming.

Two syringes of morphine.

Fumbling with the needle.

Rolling my sleeve up.

Injecting myself.

Whimpering.

Gulping down a Benzedrine tablet. Strapping my skis on. Monstrous lights probing the snowfall behind me.

Only half conscious. Nothing for it. Have to make it. Better men than me have died already. Ignore the fucking pain.

I pushed off through the snowfall to the west.

14

Closer

The anomalous force is real! There was no mistaking the readings today; even Heisenberg was convinced. He still demands more theory, more talk, more scribbling, but we advance! Heydrich presents the results to the Führer tonight.

Journal of an unknown SS scientist, p.300

It's nearly two o'clock when an Italian sentry on the southern breakwater of Bari harbour spots the frogman's body. It keeps bumping into the quay, drumming with a lazy rhythm on the incoming tide.

He drops to his knees, swearing energetically, and points his rifle at the figure in the shadows. The frogman's arms and legs are splayed in a position that means either unconsciousness or death. The sentry hesitates, unsure whether to shoot or call for help. He makes a decision.

He brings his whistle to his lips and blows.

⊕

The sun comes up, lighting the drawn faces still lingering on the deck of *La Rhin*. Molly stands gripping the railing, watching the torpedo boat coasting in.

Captain Peri took personal command for the last sweep. As soon as he's close enough for Molly to observe his furrowed expression, it's obvious he hasn't found anything. Reuven stops pacing and puts his arm round her shoulder. She shrugs it off.

'He's alive,' she says. 'I can feel it.'

'He's missed all three back-up rendezvous, Molly. If he's alive, then either he's gone to ground somewhere or he's a prisoner. Either way, we can't risk another run during daylight.'

She turns to stare at him. 'You'll keep your promise to get me into Germany?' she says.

Reuven's eyes widen. 'Molly, Molly, Molly, is this wise?'

'You owe us. If he's dead—'

'You said you didn't think—'

'If he is, then he died on a mission for you. You owe him.'

Reuven sighs. 'Yes . . . yes, I do.'

Molly slips into the dead man's cabin and eases the door closed behind her.

The light slants through a chink in the curtain covering the port-hole and falls on a neat pile of nondescript clothes on the bed. On the bedside cabinet are a couple of bottles of vodka and a Browning automatic. Inside the wardrobe is a grey suit with no label. In its pocket is a leather wallet with not a single identifying item in it, and a key ring with no fob.

The man might as well have been a ghost.

Sitting on the desk are two envelopes and a Scandinavian Airline System menu card with a number written on it. One envelope has Reuven's name on it. It's not sealed. At least, it's not sealed after she unseals it. It reads:

162

Reuven,

If you're reading this, I'm either dead or missing. I always said I'd never make forty! Bugger, I never meant it. I wanted to live to be a hundred.

The forgers we busted out of Sachsenhausen are the best. However, you've always had the problem of how to distribute the money. Last time, the Jerry civilians just handed it in. But this time I have a plan.

I met a woman named Katharina Geissler in Berlin. She's with the White Rose. She's a good kid and brave. Use her. Her number is on the card. Usual code.

She'll spread the money for you, using the White Rose's network; non-violent but effective, you see. The subsequent inflation will destroy the Nazi economy. Canaris thought it would work.

Give the bastards hell from me.

The second envelope is addressed to Molly:

Molly,

I had a good run and I died doing the only thing I'm cut out to do. I'm a charmless thug with a bullet for a heart, apparently, but you're not. You're a brave and beautiful woman. Don't forget it.

There's a million in forged currency in the attaché case in my cabin. It's good – bloody good. Take it and run. Try the USA – Leo won't find you there if you keep your head down. Reuven will get you in, if you ask him.

Forget Heydrich and forget revenge. It's a fool's game and I'm a fool. Turn your back on this madness and live your life.

XXX

Molly sits crying on the side of the bed for ten minutes then shakes her head and stands up. She dries her eyes, folds the letter to Reuven, places it back in its envelope and reseals it.

The attaché case is under the bed. She tries a couple of keys in the lock until one opens it. Inside, right enough, there are dozens of bundles of currency. She picks up a wad of fifty-pound notes and flicks through it.

A million? She could live in luxury for the rest of her life on a million. In fact, she could give most of it away and still live the rest of her life in comfort. America made sense, too. Reuven could get her false paperwork. She could buy a wee farm in New England for cash. Leo wouldn't be able to track her down.

It was an opportunity. A chance to make a new start, to put all the danger, terror and death behind her. How many of the people she loved had died now?

All of them.

She takes her letter and puts a match to it.

$$\oplus$$

In the darkness, a voice.

'He's coming round.'

It's a man's voice, deep and speaking Italian. I lie still, listening. Italian? Where am I? What's happened?

Water. There was something to do with water.

Heavy water. Vemork. Reg, Alex and Erling were killed and I ran away like a coward, hiding from the SS in the snowstorm.

'Call the commandant. He'll want to see this for himself.'

Something nags me. Water, but not snow. I'd been swimming. No, diving . . .

I remember.

My crazy, panicked swim, the propellers of the Italian destroyer so close I could almost touch them. The oxygen-flow rate too low. Target-fixated: too focused on completing the mission and getting the limpet mine in place. The bloody oxygen-flow meter unchecked. The stomach-churning, head-spinning rush of hypoxia. Dumping the lead shot with a last instinctive, dying motion.

I'm lucky to be alive.

Now it seems I'm a prisoner of the Italians. I try to move my hands and legs, but I seem to be restrained. There's only one way to find out what's happening.

I open one eye a fraction.

Reports of the capture of an enemy diver pass through the wires to Berlin, before dawn.

The German intelligence cell which has been watching over the *Prilono* reports the arrest. They suspect that the target was the tramp steamer containing the arms for the Syrian anti-Zionists. Someone in headquarters decides that they need to speak to the prisoner.

Before the Regia Maritime has time to deploy for political battle, the Germans outmanoeuvre them. The German ambassador conducts a breakfast meeting with his contacts in the Italian Ministry of War. He ventures that he has heard intimations that the Italian armed forces need to improve their communications security. Perhaps the latest German technology could be made available to them?

Italian eyes shine with greed.

But, of course, such expertise is only to be shared with Germany's closest and most loyal allies.

Protestations of loyalty fly from Italian lips.

Perhaps, then, the ambassador suggests, that loyalty extends as far as joint interrogation of the Bari saboteur?

Joint interrogation? Pah! Italy can do better than that; the SS must take sole custody of the spy. Orders fly from headquarters in Rome –

the saboteur is to be handed over to Italy's generous allies forthwith.

Before lunchtime, a military ambulance arrives at the local German consulate. Italian naval officers, hiding their anger behind punctilious formality, wheel out an unconscious figure from the rear of their ambulance.

The Italian captain insists on a receipt. Satisfied, on that point at least, he salutes, faces about, slams the ambulance's doors and departs.

The interrogation starts with a bucket of cold water over my head.

Holding the bucket is a small man in a natty SS Sturmbann-führer's uniform. He bangs the empty bucket on the table and waves the guards away, staring out through the barred window. As the door closes, he turns to me, unsmiling.

'You think you can hide your secrets from me, little man?' he asks.

I size him up. If either of us is a little man, it's him. He's not what I'd call a paragon of Aryan manhood; he'd barely reach my shoulders standing on tiptoe. And he's wearing bottle-top glasses.

'You British assume your Imperial Turing Machines are in the lead in . . . what is the word . . . Rechner?'

I shrug.

'Ah, I remember, "computers". German computers are the most powerful in the world. At the headquarters of the SS, we have a Zuse Z22.'

He moves behind me, whispers in my ear.

'It is omniscient. You cannot hide from it. It sees everything.'

'Can it see your bald patch?' I ask. A reasonable question, I think.

'You imagine perhaps that you can prevent the Z22 from divining your identity? No. All I had to do was feed your identifying characteristics to it. A short delay whilst it consulted its files, and then the answer . . .'

AGE:	34	**AGENCY:**	THE SERVICE (EX-SOE)
SEX:	MALE	**ADDRESS:**	UNKNOWN
EYES:	GREY		
HAIR:	BROWN	**PARENTS**	ORPHAN
HEIGHT:	188 CM	**MARITAL STATUS:**	SINGLE
WEIGHT:	82 KG	**RACE:**	80% ARYAN (EST)

WEAKNESSES: GAMBLING, ALCOHOL

CAREER: PROTÉGÉ OF SIR STEWART MENZIES. MI6 1939-40 BRITISH SECURITY COORDINATION 1941, SOE 1942-47, SERVICE 1947- BELIEVED RESPONSIBLE FOR A SERIES OF METICULOUSLY PLANNED ASSASSINATIONS. SPECIALISES IN SOLO INFILTRATION AND LONG-RANGE SNIPING.

EVALUATION: APPEARS TO THRIVE ON THE DANGEROUS LIFE OF THE ASSASSIN, BUT TO HAVE A 'DEATH WISH'. AGENT 'MOON' HAS REPORTED HIS BELIEF HE IS NOT FATED TO LIVE TO THE AGE OF FORTY. PRECISE PLANNING, ABILITY TO IMPROVISE AND COOL-HEADEDNESS UNDER FIRE MAKE THIS AGENT ONE OF THE SERVICE'S MOST EFFECTIVE.

FORECAST: UNLIKELY TO SURVIVE HIS FIELD EXPERIENCE.

SPECIAL NOTE: REPORT DETENTION TO OBERGRUPPENFÜHRER KALTENBRUNNER.

SPECIAL NOTE: REPORT DETENTION TO REICHSFÜHRER HEYDRICH.

SUMMARY: THIS MAN SHOULD BE CONSIDERED EXTREMELY DANGEROUS.

DO NOT APPROACH WITHOUT ARMED BACKUP.

⊕

Molly sips a mug of cheap coffee laced with whisky. Her breakfast sits untouched in front of her. Opposite her, Reuven tucks into a plate of fried eggs and mushrooms.

'You not eating that?' asks Reuven, waving a fork in the direction of Molly's plate.

'Help yourself, why don't you?' says Molly. 'Although I doubt it's kosher.'

'Needs must,' says Reuven, grinning.

Molly gives him his envelope.

He opens it, runs his fingers through his hair, shakes his head, smiling. 'Actually, that's not a bad idea,' he says. He places the envelope in an inside pocket.

Captain Peri approaches the unhappy couple, scowling. 'Wireless operator. Received this. Addressed to you.' He slaps a piece of paper on the table and stalks out of the cabin.

Reuven smiles at Molly. 'Something tells me I'm not the most popular man on this boat,' he says.

'Aren't you the sensitive one,' says Molly.

Reuven holds up his hands.

He polishes off the last of the eggs and retreats to his cabin to decode the message.

⊕

Damn computers.

The Sturmbannführer recites one of my better aliases. I make no indication that his electronic oracle has hit on a halfway valid identification.

'No, no, don't bother to deny it. The Z22 is infallible,' he says. 'There is also this.'

He throws a poor-quality photograph on the table. I lean forward to examine it.

Whoever took the picture was using a long lens, and then blew the negative up as far as it would go. The grain isn't enough to disguise my unfocused expression, though. The photo caught me with a coffee cup halfway to my lips. I was sitting at a small table outside a busy French pavement café. I remember it.

Le Touquet, one of my first big operations, a lifetime ago. There had been casualties. I had been in love with one of them.

Never again.

The Sturmbannführer smirks. 'So, case closed, I think. You're a big fish in the British Service. Your dossier is fascinating. Sabotage, assassination, subversion. You've made yourself an enemy of the Reich, and the Reich's computers have long memories. The Z22 is persistent. It waits and watches. It sees patterns. It predicts movements. Everyone makes a slip in the end and, wham, we pounce.'

The Sturmbannführer slams his fist on the table. I manage not to flinch.

'The Z22 is well aware of the death of Menzies. It predicted that there would then be attempts at revenge. We have been vigilant for assassins and saboteurs.'

The smug little shit. Alert, were they? It hadn't looked that way as I waltzed into Bari harbour. And I'd have made it, if it hadn't been for that destroyer.

'You're quite the fortune-teller,' I say. 'You must have gypsy blood.'

He loves that. I'd like him to try hitting me while I'm not hand-cuffed to a table.

'I see enough of the future to know Germany's destiny is to rule the world,' he says.

'If you kill everyone in Britain first, maybe,' I grunt.

'Ah, you are a prophet, too. Nevertheless, I think we both know what your future holds: a long journey, far away from here. Humiliation, torture . . .'

The smile turns into a sneer.

'. . . and death.'

⊕

Molly, Captain Peri and Reuven stand in the captain's cabin.

Reuven waves the decoded message. 'The *Prilono* is raising steam to leave harbour. We have to assume that last night's mission failed. Our duty is to complete it.'

'We can intercept her,' says Peri, 'give her a taste of the four-inch guns.'

'Yo-ho-ho and a bottle of rum,' says Molly.

Peri's scowl deepens.

'There's a slight complication, as far as piracy's concerned,' says Reuven.

'The Regia Marina are escorting her out?'

Reuven nods, grim-faced.

'Damn, how many?'

'Two. Both destroyers.'

Peri sits down at his desk, shaking his head. He picks up a silver-framed portrait of a young woman in the uniform of the French navy.

'That's not piracy, *chérie*, that's suicide,' he murmurs, addressing the photograph.

⊕

A Luftwaffe Dornier diverts from its usual milk run to the garrison on Crete and drops into Palese Macchie airbase. On the tarmac waiting to meet it is a pint-sized Sturmbannführer.

I stand nearby, handcuffed between two guards and dressed in an ill-fitting grey suit.

This is not what I had in mind. I'd always imagined myself going down fighting. After Vemork, I swore that I'd never run from a fight again. At worst, I thought I'd bleed to death in a gutter somewhere, shot or knifed in the stomach. But, despite my promises to myself, I've fallen into the enemy's hands.

Now the instinct for survival takes over.

The guards push me up the aircraft steps. Without the veneer of painkillers, I'm suffering from the effects of that crash into the wall of the Cage. They strap me to a pallet at the back of the Dornier's cargo bay. I sneer at my weakness. What would Reg have said if he'd seen me like this, feeling sorry for myself? His injuries must have been far worse by the time the Gestapo finished with him.

If Reg took it, so can I.

The cargo plane taxis back to the runway, gathers its strength and rolls forward, picking up speed. The Italian sunshine beats down. It won't be so sunny in Germany, I guess, but they're taking me where I want to go. As long as there's a chance that Heydrich is somewhere ahead, I'll cooperate. There's often a period in a mission when the river of fate starts flowing. It's part of the gambler's instinct to recognize it, let go and allow the current to do the work. An opportunity of some sort will arise, and until then I'll have to ride my luck.

The Dornier takes off, banks, turns one hundred and eighty degrees and climbs through a cloudless sky, heading north.

⊕

La Rhin lies dead in the water.

At the masthead flies the international signal flag for 'I am on fire and have dangerous cargo on board: keep well clear of me'.

'Time?' asks Captain Peri.

'A little after two p.m.'

'Soon now,' he says. 'Soon, *chérie*.'

On the decks, the crew run through their well-practised 'abandon ship' routine. Hidden behind canvas sheeting, the gun crews finish stacking shells. The helicopter's rotors gain speed, preparing to take off. The torpedo boat is already gone.

'What will they do?' Molly asks Reuven.

'Steer well clear, probably, knowing my luck.'

'Then what?'

'You'd better ask our tame pirate captain – I'm fresh out of ideas.'

'Captain?'

Peri turns to look at her. There's a wild light in his eyes. 'Here's to gentlemen at sea tonight, and a toast to all free men. The devil will come to take us home, but we'll drink and whore till then.'

There's a shout from the lookout position. The convoy is visible on the horizon.

'Holy Mary,' says Molly. 'We're all going to die.'

15

A Blunt Object

The Führer agrees! Kriegsentscheidend priority is ours. Unlimited budgets! Oh, joyous day! Oh, advance to victory! We must not weaken now. We cannot weaken now. We shall not weaken now. Must visit Oberheuser re headaches.

Journal of an unknown SS scientist, p.302

This is how the poor bastards at Sachsenhausen must have felt.

I stand on a dusty parade ground, trapped behind barbed wire. Surrounding me are dozens of other prisoners wearing striped uniforms.

The inmates are of various nationalities, although it seems there are no British. We've had plenty of opportunity for muttered conversation, because ever since my arrival we've been standing at attention. At first, we shivered in the cold dawn light. Since the sun burnt the mist off, we've spent hours sweating in the baking heat.

A couple of times a prisoner has carried a bucket of water along the rows. A slurp from a ladle of brackish liquid has reduced my thirst a little. How far I am from the Hotel Adlon, Pol Roger and Kitty. Where's Kitty now?

One prisoner fainted. The guards beat him, but he failed to rise. They dragged him off to the hospital.

Two minutes later, a single shot from the direction of the latrines suggested the patient had been discharged.

The flight from Italy had arrived at a Luftwaffe airbase just as the sun went down. There I was bundled into a Mercedes with SS markings and blacked-out windows. We drove cross-country, headlights tunnelling through endless pine forests. Eventually, pooling floodlights announced we had arrived at our destination – I guessed it was Flossenbürg.

The sun is starting to drop again when Kaltenbrunner sweeps into the compound, trailed by his subordinates.

I recognize him on sight. He's almost seven feet tall, as gaunt as a whip and by reputation as dangerous. Vicious fencing scars snake across his left cheek. Service briefings describe him not as an intelligent sociopath like Heydrich, but as an executioner. They say he's one of the few men who scare even the other Nazi leaders.

He walks along the front rank of the makeshift parade, staring down at the prisoners, stops and turns to address us.

'Congratulations. You are going on holiday!'

His baton indicates the beginning of a mud track leading into the fields. 'Ahead of you is an assault course. I will start you on your holiday trip by firing my pistol. You will then proceed to the finish line.' His German is guttural, with a strong Austrian accent.

'Note that the camp's machine gun towers will cover your entire itinerary. They will fire on anybody who tries to help another prisoner. Any deviation or attempt to escape, and they will shoot you down. These are the rules. I advise you not to cheat.'

He gestures beyond the parade ground. 'Behind you . . . don't move! Behind you, after a short head start, a troop of soldiers from the Hitler-Jugend division will follow. They may be young, but they're fit, they know the course and they're old enough to carry a gun. So, unless you're quick, they'll catch up with you. At that point a simple rule will add to the excitement.'

Kaltenbrunner's face cracks into a smile. He's expecting some sport. 'Once my boys reach you, they're under orders to execute you.' He chuckles. 'The devil will indeed take the hindmost. No need to worry, though. If you're fitter than my lads, then they won't catch up with you and you'll survive. So go to it, and let's find out what you're made of. Parade dismissed.'

The guards push the prisoners towards the start line. The inmates stumble into each other, jostling for the front of the pack. I remain where I am. Spotting me, Kaltenbrunner marches over. I'm over six foot, but he's at least a head taller. He stares down at me, with a quizzical smile on his lips. One of his minions tells him who I am.

'Ah yes, I have special plans for this one,' he says.

'Just shoot me now,' I say. 'I'm not jumping through hoops for your amusement.'

Kaltenbrunner smirks, turns round, and shouts to the other prisoners waiting at the start line. 'Attention, competitors! Prisoner Number Fifteen refuses to run . . .'

He raps me on the chest with his baton. I wince as the stick strikes the partially healed bruises from the car crash.

'. . . that is his privilege: nobody can force him to run. Perhaps there are others amongst you who are also too lazy to take part in our sporting event?' His smile broadens; it's all such fun when you're holding the gun. 'But let me clear something up: if you do run the course, some of you will make it. My boys are Aryan Übermensch, but they are not invincible. It is possible to complete the assault course before they catch you if you put in some damned effort.'

He unbuttons his holster and extracts his pistol, a Luger, used more for show than for action, I bet.

'However, unless everyone runs, I will give orders to kill all of you, right here, right now.'

The SS guards lift their weapons. The clicking of safety catches being released echoes across the compound. He's standing so close to me that I could grab his Luger and take the bastard with me.

'Your choice, Number Fifteen,' he says in a low voice, still smiling.

Kaltenbrunner is not the target. I have to visit my revenge on Heydrich himself. Molly can't do it – she might not even try if she finds the money I left her. I take a step towards the start line. Kaltenbrunner nods to one of the guards. The guard rams the butt of his rifle into the small of my back, knocking me over.

'You move when I say, Number Fifteen,' Kaltenbrunner says.

And the smile, inexplicably, is gone.

The gunshot from Kaltenbrunner's pistol rings around the compound.

I set off at an easy lope, behind and to the right of the main pack. Even injured, I should be fit enough to stay ahead of the pursuing Hitler-Jugend. I've been a captive only for a day, but some of the others have been living off cabbage soup for months. They jog forward, already wheezing. I can't imagine many of them making it.

The track continues for twenty yards until the initial obstacle, a low fence. A sudden surge of euphoria sweeps over me. Now I'm running, I can channel the anger that's been building inside me. Each clean breath reminds me that I'm still alive.

I glance behind me, in the direction of the start line.

Nothing.

Nothing.

And then something.

The door of a dormitory building swings open and, like greyhounds after a rabbit, the Hitler-Jugend appear.

Over the small fence lies the first real obstacle: a nine-foot-high wall. It's impossible for the weaker men to clear. I suspect that Kaltenbrunner has not designed the course with the survival of the participants in mind.

The prisoners come to a ragged halt before the wall, staring at it in disbelief.

I run straight at it, pivot against my right leg and my momentum lifts me. I get a fingertip hold on the topmost edge, and pull myself the rest of the way. From the top of the wall, I shout down.

'We have to help each other. There's no other option.'

Following my example, a few of the stronger, taller men scale the wall too. Four of them leap down on the opposite side and keep running. One stays with me and reaches down to help the others.

'Good man,' I say.

'I swear I hate the Boche worse than my ex-wife,' the prisoner pants in French.

Two stocky men who have no chance of reaching the top without help step forward. I shout to them. 'Kneel at the foot of the wall and boost your comrades over.'

Glimpsing hope, the prisoners surge towards the wall. Lifted up, swung over and deposited on the other side, they clear the obstacle. The Frenchman keeps up a steady stream of obscenities as we work.

I glance back. The SS troops are crossing the parade ground in formation, at an even jog.

'Keep going! If we don't help each other, we're all—'

A bullet snicks past my head. Beside me, the Frenchman takes a round in the skull. His head explodes, blood spraying across my face.

I jump. The Frenchman falls backwards off the wall, dead before he hits the ground. We squelch into the mud at the foot of the wall together.

Over the loudspeaker comes Kaltenbrunner's voice. 'I warned you about the rules, Number Fifteen.'

Two more shots ricochet off the brickwork behind me. I've done everything that I can to help the others. I dash towards the third obstacle, a tunnel. Inside, I'll be safe from the gunfire at least.

The tunnel sinks into the earth at a forty-five degree angle, muddy water filling the bottom to head height. The gloop soaks through my thin prison clothing. The worst thing about an assault course is having sodden clothes slopping around as you try to run. My energy drains away, but I plunge on, focusing on the square of daylight at the far end.

Bursting back into the sunshine, I catch up with a group of bedraggled prisoners staggering ahead. Behind me, a single shot, and then a fusillade with the distinctive beat of Sturmgewehr assault rifles. The Hitler-Jugend must have reached the wall. Now they're shooting all the poor bastards who couldn't pull themselves over it.

I increase my pace, tearing up to a chasm with a solitary plank across. The assault course at Station 26 taught me that the only way to do this is fast – the fewer steps on the plank the better. I hit it at a flat-out sprint. Two strides on the plank, timber bowing under my weight. A third stride, half on, half off. Momentum carries me over.

Ragged shots from behind indicate that the Hitler-Jugend are finishing off the stragglers. They're making quick progress. I need to slow them down somehow. I slide to a halt, retrace my steps to the edge of the chasm and kick the plank away. It falls into the water and disappears.

'Number Fifteen, I do believe you're cheating.' Kaltenbrunner's sniggering echoes across the assault course.

I run for cover, ducking beside a low wall with a cargo net pegged to it. Machine guns fire at chest height, forcing me under the netting. I bend double and force my way through. Underneath lies a prisoner bleeding from a bullet in the ribs. He turns his head towards me. The pink froth dribbling from his mouth suggests he has only minutes to live.

'Here,' he gasps in Polish, his face twisted with pain. 'Take one of the pigs with you.'

He presses his palm against mine. In it is a shard of glass four inches long. One end is wrapped in insulating tape, as a makeshift handle. It's not much, but holding even this homemade weapon gives me new energy.

Through another water-filled tunnel. Ahead of me is the group of four fit prisoners who didn't stop to help at the first wall. All but one have negotiated the cargo net. The last is struggling, using his legs, which kills momentum. I overtake him on the way up, climbing hand over hand. At the top, I do a forward roll and slide down the other side on my back.

The inevitable high rope is suspended between two concrete ramps, a good thirty feet above another water pit. I drape myself over the rope.

Pull.

I slide along the rope. It chafes under my chin, across my chest and stomach. I let one leg hang down for balance.

Pull.

I drop on to the ramp on the other side. The finish line is in sight. Kaltenbrunner himself stands at the tape, waving the contestants on. The three prisoners in front of me sprint as best they can towards the end of the course, and safety.

Kaltenbrunner steps to one side and his troops gun them all down.

I skid to a halt. So, that was the plan: no one survives.

The loudspeaker whistles.

'Come on, Number Fifteen, what are you waiting for?' Roaring with hearty laughter, Kaltenbrunner sounds as if he's having the time of his life. I turn and duck into cover behind the concrete ramp. If he wants to shoot me, he can come and get me. I grip the makeshift knife tighter.

Behind me, the first Hitler-Jugend hits the high rope. He's blond and tall, and his camouflaged Waffen-SS uniform is soaked with mud. The kid is what, sixteen? But he's already a non-commissioned officer – he's wearing the insignia of an Unterscharführer.

Sixteen or not, he's fit. He zips across the chasm with well-practised economy. Four, five hauls hand over hand, and he reaches the end of the rope. I reach out from my hiding place. He glimpses me, and his eyes widen with surprise. With his hands occupied with pulling himself along, he can do nothing but try to shout a warning.

I ram the sliver of glass into the kid's right eye. The eyeball bursts. I push the full length of the knife into his brain. A twist, a grunt and he dies. I catch the body and pull it towards me as it falls.

A machine gun opens fire. I duck back into cover, dragging the boy with me. His Sturmgewehr comes up in my hands, and I pick off the three Hitler-Jugend stranded on the rope.

I select full auto to clear the opposite ramp. Four more bodies fall into the pit below. I empty the magazine and reach for the stick grenades in the Unterscharführer's webbing. Unscrewing the base caps, I pull the firing cords. The five-second fuses ignite. *Five*: I throw a grenade at the remaining Hitler-Jugend. *Four*: one in Kaltenbrunner's direction. *Three*: the nearest machine gun. *Two. One.*

Explosions.

'Cease fire! Cease fire!' Kaltenbrunner bellows, still laughing. 'We surrender, Number Fifteen!'

The gunfire stops. I reload and risk a peep over the lip of the concrete ramp. Kaltenbrunner's tall figure looms through the smoke made by the hand grenades.

He shouts over to me. 'You fight well, as of course I knew you would. I've made good money betting on you today. For that, you have my thanks. But now today's sport is at an end.'

I stand up, panting. I point the Sturmgewehr's barrel in Kaltenbrunner's direction. It's an easy shot, but the guards behind him are already pointing their rifles at me. If I shoot him, it'll be the last thing I ever do.

Kaltenbrunner walks towards me.

'Now, let's talk about the future. Next weekend there's a little get-together – the leaders of the SS. We'll dine on the finest food and wine from the occupied territories, prepared by the top chefs of the Reich. Entertainment will be provided by the most beautiful and compliant whores of the SS officers' brothels.' He stops, and winks at me. 'Wives will most certainly not be invited.'

He holds his hands out, palms open. 'Weekends such as this are rare, and pressing affairs of state are not easily forgotten. We need more than wine, food and sex to help us relax. We're great sportsmen: we love to bet, love to watch a fight, love to hunt.'

I stare at him. What the hell is he telling me this for?

'We used to just issue guns to the guests then bring on the Jews and have a field day,' says Kaltenbrunner, as if reminiscing about happier times.

'Did you ever see a beautiful woman, wearing a pristine sequinned ball gown, holding a shotgun in her hands? Have you observed the lust on her face as she kills the despicable Jew? The sex afterwards . . . the transgression liberates the tiger behind the demure exterior. Ah, the pleasure! You have to witness these things to appreciate them, Number Fifteen.'

The Service briefings are right: this man is a sadist of the first rank. It's one thing to kill on a mission, even in cold blood. It's another to kill for fun.

'When our racial scientists investigate your background, I will lay odds that they find you're Aryan to the core. You've proved you can fight. You've shown you're prepared to kill. And I'm sure you won't say no to the sex.' Again, the conspiratorial wink.

I lift the Sturmgewehr until it points at Kaltenbrunner's chest.

He pauses as if coming to a conclusion. 'Of course, you could just kill me now, but I think you also like to live. So put the gun down and I'll take you to the party.'

Kaltenbrunner stares down at me with a questioning smile. The bastard is toying with me.

Dripping wet, sprayed with another man's blood, I stand gripping the assault rifle like a totem. My finger tightens on the Sturmgewehr's trigger. Kaltenbrunner holds his hand up.

'You've proved yourself worthy, Number Fifteen. Worthy of presentation to Reinhard Heydrich. However, there's also one more thing.'

He half turns and points down the course towards the finishing line. Through the dust, I distinguish a small figure held between two SS guards. It's a woman, holding her head at a defiant angle despite her situation.

Molly.

16

Selling Out

In time, the lesser races will be destroyed and the Aryan will return to the cosmos, to be reunited with his Hyperborean ancestors. Other species will challenge us, and be destroyed by the light of half-dead stars. Eventually, in unimaginable aeons, even the Aryan will falter and fall. With time, everything will die except the indifferent universe itself.

Journal of an unknown SS scientist, p.351

I lower the Sturmgewehr, and a wave of nausea passes over me.

'So, as I thought, Number Fifteen, weaker than you seem.' Kaltenbrunner's smile splits his face, but beneath the bluster I sense a nervous tremor.

Had I put the gun down because of the appearance of Molly, or the news about Heydrich? Heydrich. It must have been. The mission is everything. Molly is just an asset, an expendable asset. But she's a woman, a beautiful woman at that, and we've been lovers.

Damn it.

Kaltenbrunner waves the guards forward, and four hands grip my arms. I grit my teeth, fighting down my instinctive violent response.

'I meant what I said. I'll present you to Heydrich. You'll receive food and alcohol. Whores will be made available, of whichever sex you require.'

Molly is just an asset. The mission is everything.

The guards wrench my arms behind my back. A tiny whimper escapes my mouth.

'But there's a price to be paid for our hospitality. I mentioned the Jews that we used for after-dinner entertainment? They were so weak, hunched over muttering their ridiculous prayers, as we gunned them down. Where was the excitement, where was the thrill?'

Straightforward murder wasn't enough to satiate their jaded palates?

'We needed enemies of a higher class. So I sent out an order: Category Fours, Jews, were to be eliminated out of hand. It was the Category Ones and Twos – Aryan prisoners – that we would get the most gratification from. Unlike the foolish Jews, they would run, and then we could hunt them.'

My God, are these lunatics really murdering people for sport?

'But even that palled after a while. You're English, so you should understand. Why pursue the fox when you can stalk the tiger? I introduced the little innovation that you've just taken part in. It strips away the mediocre and leaves only the hardest category of prisoner – tough, resourceful and proven.'

'In any civilized country, you'd be under restraint in a secure hospital,' I say, with a bitterness that surprises me.

'The bleating of lambs being shipped to slaughter means nothing to me, Number Fifteen. Nature lets weak creatures starve. We're more humane. We'll give you a quick, easy end to your suffering.'

Kaltenbrunner points my guards in the direction of the gate.

They drag me off.

Another day, another SS Mercedes with blacked-out windows; this is becoming routine. It could be worse, though. The SS might have thrown me in the back of some unheated truck and bounced me all the way to . . . wherever we're going.

The Mercedes travels at the centre of a small convoy. Motorcycle outriders flank the three identical black limousines. A Puma armoured car precedes us and a quartet of Opel trucks, carrying a platoon of Hitler-Jugend, follows behind. One of the Opels is even towing a multi-barrelled anti-aircraft gun.

I sit shackled between two SS guards, a wrist manacled to each of them. The river of fate still seems to be flowing towards Heydrich, although Kaltenbrunner might be double-dealing. The end of the trail could yet be a soundproof chamber and men in rubber aprons. However, I'm banking – and banking more than money – on encountering Heydrich before the end of the day.

What to do then is the problem.

Molly sits opposite me, also manacled, and sporting a lurid bruise all down one side of her face.

'Did they . . .' I ask her.

Molly lifts her gaze and makes an unconvincing attempt at a smile. I stare at her, judging what reserves she has left. Can she still help me complete the mission or is she just baggage I'm going to have to carry?

'I hit a stanchion while abandoning ship,' Molly says, holding my gaze. 'You should see the state it's in.'

'Silence!' says one of the guards.

'Or what?' says Molly. 'You'll arrest us?' Her eyes are the same sharp-edged blue they were under the trees outside my flat – angry, furious even, but in control.

She might be a woman, but she's hard-core Service. I shake my head. Underestimating women is as dangerous as overestimating them.

'What happened?' I ask.

The guards scowl at us. Molly makes a dismissive gesture. They look at each other, and then revert to staring straight ahead.

'Reuven only went and ordered Captain Peri to intercept the *Prilono*. Two Italian destroyers were escorting her. We surprised the first destroyer; hit them hard before they knew what was happening. The second one was a different story.'

'Brave men,' I say.

Molly grimaces. 'Bravery comes cheap when you're insane. Peri went into battle clutching a photograph of his dead girlfriend. I heard him asking it for advice as the Regia blasted chunks out of his ship. And Reuven was target-fixated, for sure. There must be easier ways to stop the Germans from arming the Arabs than declaring war on the Italians.'

'Did you get the *Prilono*?' I ask.

Molly gives a cross between a laugh and a groan. 'God save us, Reuven isn't the only one who's target-fixated. We did not. The irony is, you did. The whole thing was all for nothing. Ten seconds after we opened fire, the mine went off.'

I fight to keep the smile off my face.

$$\oplus$$

We turn off the autobahn into a boulevard that's the same width as the preceding motorway. The avenue ahead, flanked by towering Bavarian fir trees, runs unswerving towards a gigantic building on the skyline.

Why is it always the crass, the monumental, the cracked aesthetic that equates bigger with better, in all circumstances? Why does the Nazi beast have this primitive need to beat its chest and intimidate? There's a core of inadequacy to them. They shout their supposed superiority all the louder, because they doubt it themselves.

'I'm not liking this overblown Nazi architecture, now,' says Molly.

'Don't like this, don't like that,' I say, teasing. 'What do you like, Molly?'

'One day what I'd like is a wee cottage with roses climbing into the thatch in the summer,' says Molly. 'A few pigs in a sty. A cow and a donkey and a couple of acres for them to graze. A pile of turf for the winter and a roaring fire to sleep by. That's all I'll be needing. The more I see of the rest of the world, the more I think that's all I'll be wanting.'

'Is there any room for a man in your dream, Molly?'

'You'll have me in tears,' she says.

Dwarfed by the edifice in front of it, Kaltenbrunner's convoy pulls to a halt. The trucks and armoured cars peel off and disappear as the three Mercedes pull up at the gargantuan portico. The red, white and black Nazi flag flies from every flagpole, is draped from every balcony, envelops every façade. A squadron of Junkers Ju-230 flying wings passes overhead, heading north in perfect formation.

SS orderlies open the first Mercedes's doors and Kaltenbrunner steps out. He stalks up to the doorway, where another SS officer stands waiting for him, smile nailed to his face.

'Well, now, if it isn't the Blond Beast himself,' I say to Molly, with forced lightness.

He's tall, even if overshadowed by the giant Kaltenbrunner. His face is long, almost horse-like, with a prominent aquiline nose and tight, compressed lips. The eyes are sharp, steady and calculating, the eyes of a poisoner. A slick of blond hair, razor short, sets off the features, giving them a peculiar handsomeness. The expression, though, is one of cold evaluation, the smile reaching nowhere near the eyes. I stare at his face with fascinated dread, realizing I've under-estimated the man.

Reinhard Heydrich.

The gamble with Kaltenbrunner has paid off. Now it's time to redouble the stakes and play to the death. My pulse rises.

'You're late, Kaltenbrunner,' says Heydrich.

I know from the files that Heydrich's voice is high-pitched, but I'm surprised at how girlish it is. How strange that the most dangerous man in Europe speaks in such a feminine way. The man is a contradiction, and hence even more dangerous. He'll be unpredictable.

Kaltenbrunner points in my direction. 'I've found a new gladiator, a man I've tested. Someone you may have heard of. Tough and fit, he'll prove excellent sport during the hunt tomorrow.'

Heydrich looks in the direction Kaltenbrunner is pointing. He frowns. Kaltenbrunner whispers. Heydrich's frown deepens. He addresses me.

'So . . . welcome. Welcome to the centre of the world.'

Heydrich's aides hustle Molly and me to a suite that says 'King Arthur' on the door. The suite is decorated in faux-medieval style: tapestries on the walls, wooden furniture and a huge four-poster bed. Kaltenbrunner has kept his word: apart from the SS guards outside our door, it could be a five-star hotel. Molly throws herself on the bed and smiles up at me.

'What did Heydrich mean, "the centre of the world"?' she asks.

'I . . .' I close my mouth, unsure. Where else have I heard that phrase used in connection with the Nazis? I walk to the window and contemplate the view of the setting sun dropping below the horizon. The cliffs on which the castle is situated drop to a lake. In deep shadow on the far side is a semicircular stone edifice studded with gigantic towers.

'Come and see this,' I say to Molly.

A central tower, part of a castle sitting on a mountain surrounded by a lake? A hemisphere of gargantuan modern buildings and towers in squared-off neoclassical style? Of course, the Centre of the World: Wewelsburg.

'Big, isn't it?' scoffs Molly, resting her head on my shoulder.

'This is just the start of it: they've covered the whole area in statues glorifying the battles and heroes of the SS. Monumental gates, summer houses for high-ranking leaders, farms for favoured warriors, you name it.'

I put my arm around Molly and kiss her forehead. 'It's a kind of Vatican of Nazism, a shrine to National Socialism. They're all mad, of course. Himmler thought he was the reincarnation of King Heinrich the First. He imagined he had a God-given mission to protect Germany from invaders from the east.'

Molly touches the cross at her neck. 'God didn't give Himmler any missions at all, now,' she mutters.

I frown, trying to remember the details. 'There's some old prophecy about a bastion that the godless eastern hordes will destroy themselves against. Himmler imagined Wewelsburg was it. The entire estate is in the shape of a spear, because it's where the Spear of Destiny is held.'

Molly crosses herself at the mention of the Spear. 'I heard a story once that Hitler saw the Spear on display in Vienna, before the war. The wee man was convinced that he could use it to control the world,' she says.

'I wouldn't be surprised at that. The whole lot of them are off their bloody rockers,' I say, gazing down at her. She doesn't look too bad from this angle; the worst of the bruising is on the other side of her face. I got her into this. Now I need to get her through it. Somehow, we have to survive.

'You don't think it's true, then?' asks Molly.

'Molly, if every nail and fragment supposedly from Jesus's cross was real, we'd have enough to crucify a dozen messiahs. Maybe Hitler does believe the Spear of Destiny controls the globe. I've heard that the entire SS believes the Aryan race is descended from aliens who lived at the North Pole.'

Molly tenses against me. 'You're an atheist, aren't you?' she whispers.

I look into her eyes. The girl is falling in love with me, but she's even more in love with her god. A sudden spike of anger shoots through me.

'Who saved the Jews from extermination, God or Clement Attlee? Men like Reuven, if he's still alive, have to send men like me to do God's dirty work. I have to go out there and do the bloody unthinkable, because God isn't going to do it himself. I don't actually like killing people, you know, but I have to – because God won't. No god is going to step in and take a bullet for me either. So what's left for me to believe in?'

Molly pushes me away, with hurt in her eyes. Why am I even saying this? We're alone together in the enemy's fortress and we need each other.

'I . . .' she tries, and there's something close to panic in her voice. She runs for the bathroom.

'This is why women shouldn't be allowed in the field,' I shout after her.

Kaltenbrunner lets himself into our room without knocking.

'Where's the girl?' he says, scanning the bedroom.

'She grew wings and flew out of the window.'

Kaltenbrunner turns towards the sound of water running in the bathroom. 'Seems like our little bird has returned,' he says.

'Flak must have been too heavy.'

Kaltenbrunner smirks and takes something from his pocket. At first glance, it appears to be a thin metal flashlight attached to a lanyard. 'I've a present for you and your aviatrix friend,' he announces, throwing the torch on the bed beside me.

I pick the object up and realize it's actually a Welrod sleeve gun, on a rubberized cord.

'You attach it to your arm under your clothes using the cord. After you fire it, you just let go and it slides back up your sleeve,' says Kaltenbrunner.

The trigger resembles a flashlight switch. Firing is a matter of sliding the switch backwards and then forwards. Accuracy is non-existent but, like the standard Welrod, it's almost silent. 'I know how to use it,' I say.

'Of course, the English assassin knows the tools of his trade. So I'm sure you know it's a one-shot weapon.'

I point the Welrod at Kaltenbrunner.

'In case you have any foolish ideas about using it to kill me . . .' says Kaltenbrunner, holding up a single bullet.

I sit down on the bed and start stripping the gun. 'Where did you get it from?' I ask, unscrewing the breech to see that it is indeed unloaded.

'We intercept the Service's weapons drops, of course.'

Unprompted, Kaltenbrunner continues. 'He ordered your leader's death, Number Fifteen. The Old Man's assassination was his operation. Now, when you go to meet him, take the sleeve gun and use it to kill him. '

'Why should I trust you?' I ask him.

'I hate him too. His superior airs, his put-downs, his love of music. I've sworn to destroy him.' He waves a dismissive hand. 'Anyway, he stands in my way.'

Nazi internal politics resemble a snake-pit.

Kaltenbrunner turns to go. At the door he pauses, frowning. 'Tell me, Number Fifteen, do you feel fear?' he asks.

I glance up at the Nazi filling the doorway, and narrow my eyes. 'Of course. Do you?'

Kaltenbrunner blinks, as if thinking about it for the first time. 'Fear?' He gestures around himself. 'What do I have to fear? I've been lucky so far, and I can't see the future, thank God, so I don't fear that. I used to get scared in the old days, when I was street-fighting against the Communists. Maybe that's what I'm missing. Maybe that's why I hunt.'

'Give me a minute to load this, and I'll have you feeling fear,' I say, gesturing to the gun.

Kaltenbrunner throws the bullet towards me, stoops under the lintel and is gone.

Molly unlocks the bathroom door twenty minutes after Kaltenbrunner's departure. I hear the bolt slide free and turn towards the sound. Molly appears, wearing a black silk dressing gown with a loose belt at its waist. I'm ready to apologize, but her expression dries the words in my mouth.

Molly is, for the first time since I met her, on the verge of tears.

I stand up and move towards her, take her in my arms and hug her. We hold each other as her teardrops soak into my shirt. Her body shivers against mine.

She pushes me away so she can look in my eyes. She's washed her hair and tried to tidy herself up, but the shadows across her face emphasize the horrific bruising.

And, seeing Molly like that, I come near – as near as I'm ever going to be capable of – to loving her.

'I don't want to die without making love to you,' she says.

'You aren't going to die, Molly,' I say, with all the sincerity I can find.

Molly laughs a harsh, bitter laugh that turns to coughing. 'I am so. I've seen it coming; I'm going to die here – here in bloody Prussia, miles from Ireland, alone . . .'

'You aren't alone.'

'. . . surrounded by evil. I'm a good Catholic girl, and I never got married. And I'm getting old. And I'm going to die. And I'm not brave. And I look terrible.'

I stroke the undamaged side of Molly's face with my index finger.

'You don't look terrible,' I say. 'You're beautiful.'

'You're lying. I'm hurt and scared, and you're probably the same. But it's worse for me because I'm not in a state of grace. I haven't confessed my sins and received absolution. Whenever I die to-morrow, I'll go straight to Hell. And I don't want to die without making love to you.'

Molly's body is tight to mine. I slide my hand over the silk to her waist. 'You know they have microphones . . . probably cameras?' I say.

Molly surveys the bedroom. 'Turn the lights off, then.' She raises half a smile. 'You'll find it easier not looking at me, anyway.'

I won't find it difficult at all, can't she tell that?

'Are you sure about this?' I say.

'As sure as I am that I'm going to die in the morning.'

Behind me as I move to the light switch, I hear the faint rustle of silk falling to the ground. When I turn back, Molly is standing before me. She's wearing nothing but her silver cross, which nestles in her cleavage, sparkling in the moonlight.

'We're going to have to kill Heydrich tomorrow,' I say. 'Even if it does lead to our deaths.'

She reaches out to me. 'We can kill him in the morning,' she says. 'Now shut up and come here.'

17

Looking Death in the Face

The first trial run of the device. We placed flowers before it, like an offering. Nothing but slime returned. The clouds poured rain as the mechanism spun. All the Jews who sluiced down the chamber after the test are now sick. Two have already died.

Journal of an unknown SS scientist, p.369

Some instinct, triggered by footsteps in the corridor, wakes me just seconds before the door bursts open. The light floods in, silhouetting a female figure, and half a dozen guards.

Molly pulls the bedclothes up around herself. I hold my hands up to shelter my eyes, trying to assess the threat. The woman appears not to be carrying any weapons.

'I'm sorry we had to meet again like this,' says Kitty.

She's wearing a suggestive pastiche of SS uniform, more for the titillation of Heydrich than for any practical purpose. Cut from black leather and without a wrinkle, it must have been sewn to her exact measurements to emphasize her curves. The regalia sewn to the leather are just as exaggerated – a silver eagle clutching a swastika on the breast, and a swastika armband. The heavy belt round Kitty's delicate waist is ornamented with a buckle cast from bronze. Again, it features a swastika, this one surrounded by a wreath.

'I preferred the Dior,' I say.

'So did I,' says Kitty, grimacing. 'Heydrich thinks it is a joke, I'm afraid.'

'Do you know this tart?' asks Molly.

'Miss Ravenhill,' says Kitty. 'You are right. I do prostitute myself to Heydrich, because I wish to live.'

'. . . dressed like a tart . . .' mutters Molly.

'Miss Ravenhill, this evening is devoted to the Black Sun – the SS leaders' feast. I'm sorry, but Heydrich does not invite you. I suggest you sleep. Nobody else will disturb you tonight.'

Molly hisses at me, 'If you lay a finger on that sl—'

I shake my head at her, swing my legs out of bed and stand naked before Kitty.

'Formal dress would be more appropriate I think,' she says, smiling.

I walk down the corridor at Kitty's side, followed by the guards. She's unarmed: there's nowhere under that leather catsuit that she could hide a weapon. We talk in German; there's no point hiding it any more, and I'm more fluent in German than she is in English.

'You're one of Heydrich's agents? That story you told me in the Adlon was a fantasy?' I say, trying to adjust the jet-black dinner jacket Kitty has supplied. It's a little long in the arms, but passable.

'No,' she says. 'I was picked up just a few days after we met in Berlin. Heydrich made a deal with me – he'd spare me and in return I'd let him . . . I took the coward's way out. I just couldn't bear the thought of what was going to happen if I didn't. I hate myself.'

'Kitty, I'm so, so sorry.'

'He's not the first, and others have given me less in return. He's so busy, he's only used me a couple of times.' A tear rolls down her cheek. 'Sometimes, he wants to just sit and talk to someone who's honest with him. The toadies who surround him would swear black is white if that's what they thought he wanted to hear. But I don't. There are a few shreds of humanity in the man, though not many. He can be charming at times. If I didn't realize that he cares for nothing except himself, I might even think he likes me.'

She wipes her face. 'I've got to stop this. If he sees me like this . . . I've become the greatest actress in the Reich. When he paws at me, it makes me sick, but heaven knows what will happen once he tires of me. Thrown to the wolves in the barracks downstairs, I expect.'

'I'm going to kill him,' I say.

Although . . . killing Heydrich would have been a lot easier if I'd been able to get the Welrod from where I'd hidden it. But it had been impossible to get to with the room full of guards.

'Quiet!' Kitty hisses, glancing around in panic, at the guards.

'There's a lot of it about,' I say. 'I bet they want to kill him too.'

'He's a big man, strong. It's not just propaganda, you know; he's dangerous. He's always joking about his heart of stone. Just be careful. Wait for your chance.'

'What is this Black Sun?' I ask.

'The twelve highest leaders of the SS, the Obergruppenführer, meet once a year.'

We came to a door. She touches an ebony disc on the wall with a swastika engraved on it. The door swings open.

'Behold the Obergruppenführersaal,' she says. 'Behold the Black Sun.'

The hall beyond appears to be carved entirely from marble. Cream marble walls and a blue marble floor. Twelve marble columns with niches between them, containing marble busts. A huge round table fills the centre of the hall, inlaid with a circle of black marble radiating runic SS lightning flashes. At each place sits an SS-

Obergruppenführer, in his dress uniform. Kaltenbrunner is there, of course. He gives me an exaggerated wink. I recognize the rest of the bunch too – Wolff, Oberg, Frank, Globocnik, Stroop, all the big names. A bit of plastic explosive, and I could take them all with me.

Facing me is the Butcher himself, in mid-speech. He motions the guards and me to one side and continues his address.

'Tomorrow we discuss serious issues, gentlemen. We're lucky enough to have a hand in implementing our National Socialist ideal. This perfect model surpasses not only Germany and our era; it out-strips mankind in any epoch. It expresses the impersonal intellect of Nature. It is National Socialism's glory to have gone back to that natural wisdom and implemented it. Germany is now strong, happy and Jew-free. We Germans are the masters of our own destiny. Germans truly run Germany!'

Polite applause.

'However, the Reich Plan for the Domination of Europe has still not delivered the benefits we anticipated. The age-old balance of power has been smashed, but German supremacy is incomplete. The British still control the Atlantic trade routes and the Soviet Untermenschen regroup on our eastern borders.'

Muttering around the table.

'But now, gentlemen, we're almost ready to break free from this trap. Only this afternoon I witnessed the start of the final series of calibration tests on our ultimate Wunderwaffe. Greater than the Flugscheiben. Greater than the space rockets. Greater even than the atomic bomb.'

Puzzled heads turn to each other. What is this wonder he refers to?

'This weapon . . . ah, this weapon! With this most wondrous of Wunderwaffen at the service of National Socialism, the impossible has become possible. Tomorrow, I will unveil it to you and we will plan the final victory.'

The SS leaders thump the table with the enthusiasm of children.

'As I say, tomorrow we discuss serious issues. But tonight? Tonight we feast!'

The children pound the table until it shakes. Heydrich stands there, acknowledging the applause and smiling. He motions for quiet, claps his hands, and waiters flood into the room carrying groaning silver trays.

Heydrich beckons Kitty and me to his side. His guards move in as we approach. He turns in his seat and examines the pair of us. 'I believe you two know each other?' he says.

I let Kitty answer, unsure what story she has told Heydrich. She nods her head.

His gaze flickers between us. 'I don't like strange foreign men showing interest in my women. I like it less when the women return that attention. Kitty, you may leave us.'

'Reinh—'

Heydrich shakes his head and Kitty turns away. He allows a small smile to cross his face and indicates that I should take the seat next to him. I sit down, scanning the table for possible weapons. If I attack Heydrich with my bare hands, the guards will kill me before I can inflict serious damage.

The waiters pile our plates with roast goose, Bratwurst, potato dumplings and red cabbage. Heydrich ignores his food. I gulp mine down; I have no idea where my next meal will come from.

'Tell me, do you fly?' asks Heydrich.

I nod, mouth full of Bratwurst.

'Ah, I too am a pilot! I flew combat missions at the front, you know. The Russian pilots, Untermenschen to a man, were lambs before my Messerschmitt's guns!'

Interesting. Heydrich is trying to build rapport with me by treating me as a comrade in arms.

I cut that short. 'What's it like to be the most hated man in the world – the insane syphilitic corporal aside?'

Heydrich frowns. 'Insane syph . . . oh, I see. Hitler. I wouldn't say that too loudly in front of his fan club, if I were you.'

'You have a lot of blood on your hands, Heydrich.'

Kaltenbrunner tries to join in, laughing across the table. 'Ah, you study Jewish folk tales? Do you believe in the Golem, too?'

Heydrich looks at him. 'Kaltenbrunner, don't talk with your mouth full, you slob. Our guest is in possession of the facts, I think.'

I put my cutlery down. 'You don't deny that millions of Jews were murdered, then? And that the only thing that saved them from total annihilation was Britain organizing the Exodus to Israel?'

Heydrich waves a hand, dismissing such pettifogging details. 'Look, like you I'm a soldier. Like you, I follow my orders, even when they are unpleasant. I found the scale of the killings disagreeable; I'm not a monster. And I always tried to use the carrot before the stick. Consider Bohemia and Moravia – I increased rations, I gave the little people unemployment insurance, pensions, better wages and holidays . . . the list goes on.'

'Bread and circuses.'

'Quite. As soon as I separated the masses from the intellectuals, the resistance dried up. It worked for me in Bohemia and Moravia, it worked in France, it would work anywhere. First, mollycoddle the common people. Second, tell them their easy lives are in danger. Third, denounce the intelligentsia as unpatriotic trouble-causers wrecking the nation. Soon there are queues of informants outside police headquarters. It is the same in any country.'

'The end justifies the means, in other words.'

'Only a wretch argues that the ends do not justify the means. The British fail to torture our spies, and so they learn nothing from them and weaken their own country. They fantasize about "war crimes" and so they don't wipe out rebellious natives, and their empire is in danger. Softness, nothing more.'

'And the weak and defenceless, what of them?'

'Oh, yes, because you have boundless compassion for *those* useless bloodsuckers, you're in agony for them,' Heydrich scoffs. 'Undesirables and degenerates have no place in any civilized country. It's a simple matter of racial self-defence. There's no moral conflict – as you should know. Cigar? Cognac?' Heydrich snaps his fingers. 'Cuban cigars, of course, the finest. And five-star Napoleon brandy.'

I pick up a cut-crystal brandy glass with a gold rim and waft it below my nose. The first aroma is of figs, evolving into a denser note of chocolate. Perhaps I could smash the glass on the table and bury the broken shards in Heydrich's throat? I take another sip of the spirit. Again, the dried fruit and chocolate, but now in surprising harmony and underlined by cinnamon and vanilla. 'Hennessy XO,' I say.

'Ah, a fellow connoisseur.' Heydrich watches me weighing the glass in my hand. 'Do you think I'd let you sit here if you were any danger to me?' he asks, his voice like velvet. If he's nervous, he gives no sign of it.

I return the brandy glass to the table. My chance will come.

'I don't hate you, you know,' he says. 'The English, that is. You're strong. You take what you want. You oppose us as worthy enemies, unlike the Bolshevik Untermenschen we have expunged from Europe.'

'You imagine Germany won the war, then?'

'We're now the masters of Europe from the Pyrenees to the Russian border. What is there beyond? Barren sea and wind-blown steppe. Nothing.'

'1943.'

'A fine year for champagne, and for Germany.'

'The Red Army's armoured divisions pouring west from Stalingrad. Deputy Führer Hess cap in hand in Moscow, pleading for a ceasefire.'

'Nonsense!' snaps Heydrich. 'Hess entered Moscow like a conqueror. He dictated terms to that worm Molotov. Take it or leave it – that was the extent of the negotiations. And the maggot took it.'

There's a flicker of calculation in Heydrich's eyes as the colour fades from his cheeks. When he speaks again, his tone is amicable.

'You've got guts, I'll give you that. Now, enough politics. Knock a few back with me. He who aspires to be a hero must drink brandy.'

Heydrich lifts his glass and throws the cognac down his throat.

Heydrich is blank-faced, calculating. The Hennessy, half a bottle each so far, has had no effect on either of us. No effect at all.

'Do you think you're here to revenge Sir Stewart Menzies' assassination?' he asks.

'I'm here because I made a hash of the attack on Bari harbour.'

'Our old friend Reuven Shiloah was behind that one, I think. And my sources tell me you're burnt with the British, so you ran to the Jews. You were spotted in Tel Aviv just three days before the Bari operation.'

'Israel is part of the Empire, thank God. You'd have killed the lot of them otherwise.'

'Nonsense. The Jews have duped you English. They don't require Palestine in order to live there. They want a headquarters for their swindles, a haven for their villainy, a university for their crime. And Reuven is the Moriarty, the Fagin, of Jewish perfidy. The day I witness his execution will be a happy day indeed.'

'You're blinded by your irrational hatred of the Jews, and by your bankrupt ideology.'

Heydrich gives a careful shake of his head. 'How ironic. I wager you've less insight into the world than any of us. Queen and country right or wrong for you, isn't it? Like the lowest SS-Mann wading through the concentration camps, banging heads for his glorious Führer. They don't question . . . and neither did you as you gunned down whoever Menzies told you to.'

'The Old Man would never have sent me to kill anyone who didn't deserve it.'

Heydrich smiles. 'Is that so? Come on, I'll show you something that might make you stop and think for a moment.'

We walk past the reception rooms and down a flight of winding stairs. Heydrich pushes through several doors, guards springing to attention as he passes. The temperature sinks, as if we've passed underground. Heydrich talks over his shoulder as we descend.

'My so-called superior, Himmler, spent too much time fantasizing about this . . . what is it called, Mouse World?'

'Disneyland,' I say.

'Yes, Disneyland. But, give Himmler his due, with my help he built the SS into an incredible force before his demise. Curious how all those who stand in my way end up dead, isn't it?'

At the bottom of the stairs is a steel door. Heydrich orders the guards to open it and motions me to inspect the vault beyond.

'I call this the mausoleum,' he says. 'Himmler is interred here, right below the Black Sun. He wanted his beloved Führer to be buried alongside him but, from what Bormann tells me, the Führer said no. He thinks, as I do, that it's all mumbo-jumbo.'

'A lot of people would like to see Hitler down here.'

'And yet he keeps on breathing. Who'd have thought it: Hitler the last of the old warmongers? Churchill is dead. Stalin is dead. Roosevelt is dead. Even Mussolini is dead. But the Führer just keeps going, even if he is almost comatose.'

In the centre of the domed ceiling above, picked out by a spot-light, is the inevitable swastika carved from stone.

'The swastika is linked with the Black Sun up in the Obergruppenführersaal. More of Himmler's nonsense: spreading his protective radiance across Germany or something. Sheer fantasy, of course.'

There's a circular depression right in the centre of the room, containing a flickering flame. Around this depression are twelve monumental stone thrones. Each one casts a huge shadow against the wall of the crypt behind it.

'Who do you people think you are: the Knights of the Round Table?'

'Ridiculous, isn't it? Keeps the weaker minds enthralled, though, it seems. Ah, and there it is: the much-venerated Spear of Destiny.'

Fire glints off polished metal embedded high up on the wall of the vault.

'It's just a normal spear, of course. Heisenberg looked into it,' says Heydrich. 'It's probably not even Roman, let alone the spear from the Bible.'

As my eyes adjust to the light, I notice there's a body hunched on one of the thrones, wrapped in a blanket. In the fire glow, the face is a grinning skull.

Woken by our voices, the figure turns its sightless glare towards the doorway.

'Heydrich, you bastard, is that you? When the Führer hears of this . . .'

I peer into the gloom. The voice is familiar, a voice I used to hear on the newsreels.

'Behold the Grand Master of the Legion of German Honour,' says Heydrich.

Bloody hell . . .

Heydrich laughs. 'The pathetic remnant of a man before you is Rudolph Hess. He's insane now, of course. Solitary confinement does that to the fragile-minded.'

'That story about the Ukrainian partisans . . .'

'Faked, obviously. The corpse the army found was a double, and close to unrecognizable, anyway. I've kept him here ever since, though he tries to commit suicide on a regular basis.'

'Why?'

'Because he's unhappy, I suppose.'

'No, I mean why do you keep him alive?'

'Same reason I let Canaris get away with his scheming for so long . . . I'm a sentimental old fool.'

There's no one less likely to be a sentimental old fool . . .

'But you're right, there's another reason,' says Heydrich. 'The peace treaty.'

'The Anglo-German peace treaty?'

'Came from nowhere, didn't it? One minute that old boor Churchill was declaiming that Britain would "never surrender" and the next it was "peace with honour".'

'Churchill's death—'

'Was an assassination perpetrated by the Service of which you are such a proud member. Maybe the assassin was someone you knew; one of the previous generation, perhaps?'

I shake my head. 'Churchill was killed in a bombing raid.'

'According to the newspapers – but who owns them? Members of the Watching Committee, of course.'

'Members of the what?'

'My God, you know nothing, do you? Who do you think controls your precious empire – the workers and peasants?' Heydrich walks across the floor of the vault towards Hess. 'What did the newspapers say? "Britain's honour is satisfied, and we must protect the Empire's best interests by halting the bloodshed." Herr Goebbels would have been proud of that one.'

Churchill murdered and a cabal in Britain conspiring with the Nazis? Preposterous. This is some trick of Heydrich's.

'I don't believe you,' I say.

Heydrich shrugs. 'I don't care whether you believe it, but you weren't there and I was.'

Hess turns his head, following the voice. His eye sockets are empty pits.

'What happened to his eyes?' I ask.

'I removed them,' says Heydrich. 'It amused me.'

Hess raises his hands to his face, muttering.

Heydrich's voice echoes from the stonework. 'The terms of the peace treaty were agreed at a secret meeting at Dungavel Castle in Scotland. Deputy Führer Hess flew to Scotland on 10 May 1941, escorted part of the way by myself. He negotiated the agreement with a representative of the Watching Committee, refuelled, and returned to Germany the next night.'

Heydrich stands behind Hess, smiling. 'If you don't trust me, then why don't you ask him yourself?'

Hess lashes in the direction of the voice. Heydrich takes a single step backwards, and the flailing claw misses.

I stare at Heydrich. 'There would have been witnesses.'

'The British Service or ourselves eliminated all the witnesses. The Duke of Hamilton, who owned Dungavel Castle, had an unfortunate plane crash. And as you've already seen, Ukrainian partisans didn't kill Deputy Führer Hess.'

Hess curls into a foetal ball on the petrified throne, shoulders shaking. If he had eyes, he'd be crying.

'Now Hess is my insurance policy against the British. Any hostile move, and I can bring down the Watching Committee by releasing the truth. The old cretin you see before you will confirm the whole story. That's why they tried to stop you coming here to avenge Menzies' death. You see, I'm untouchable.'

All my life, I've fought for Britain against the Nazis. And all that time, this 'Watching Committee' has been cutting deals with them? It's unthinkable. It's possible. I don't know. I'm certain that the gibbering wreck is Hess, though. Wrapped in a blanket. Blinded. Skeletal. Hair torn out in clumps. Nevertheless, it's him.

I don't want to believe it.

Heydrich's insight bores into my skull until I turn my eyes away from the gloating Reichsführer.

'You don't even know the worst part,' he says.

What could be worse than this? I struggle to meet his gaze.

Heydrich smiles. The secret of comedy is timing.

'Your precious Old Man, your beloved mentor, was up to his neck in the plot.'

The Old Man?

The nearest thing I had to a father. The man I'd trusted with my life. The man I came here to avenge.

The Old Man . . .

It explained his surprise decision to second me to British Security Coordination in 1941. He knew how rabid my anti-Nazi views were. I was his confidential aide, so I saw all the papers, handled most of the phone calls, made notes in all the meetings. He wanted me out of the way while the conspiracy unfolded, Churchill was killed and the peace treaty was signed.

The Old Man . . .

Had he used me to eliminate witnesses to the conspiracy? Not in the SOE years, I'm sure, but after the merger with MI6 and the creation of the Service? It's more than possible. Heydrich is right about one thing – I never questioned the Old Man's orders, even when he asked for 'favours'. And I'm not the only person who would have eliminated anyone on nothing but the Old Man's say-so. Maybe that was why Elliott never got the sack – he knew where the bodies were buried.

The Old Man . . .

All those years, carrying a secret like that, it must have almost killed him. Had he felt regret? Had he lain awake at night, searching his conscience? Was that what was behind the frenzied hunt for the mole: terror at the thought of the truth coming out?

The Old Man . . .

The irascible, clear-eyed gentleman who had controlled my life.

The man that I knew nothing of.

I lunge for Heydrich.

18

Too Hot to Handle

Now the scales are lifted and I worship impersonal Nature. I believe in the law of everlasting struggle. I believe in our Aryan duty to be 'like unto the gods' once more. But first we must complete the mechanism. Worst headache yet.

Journal of an unknown SS scientist, p.385

Leo's father taught him never to underestimate the enemy.

He has remembered that lesson several times over the last few days. Patricia is not requiting his affection. The minister hates him. His wife is back at her mother's even sooner than he predicted. His solicitor thinks his father's tax affairs are so complicated that the bookshop might not emerge from probate for years. On top of all that, Operation Tigerlily is go.

And now, Lord have mercy on us all, Elliott is phoning him from Her Majesty's Loyal Dominion of Israel.

'Sir, I've taken a full stock check and I am confident that the missing salespeople can be assigned to wastage: they were water-damaged on a sales trip in Italy.'

'What are they doing in Italy? I gave orders to restrict them to Empire territory.'

Elliott coughs. 'It seems our sister company in Israel asked them to make the trip. The Israeli director sends his sincere apologies for not clearing this with you beforehand.'

Leo scans the GCHQ communications intercept on his desk. Elliott is mistaken.

'I have reason to believe that a German competitor has made them a job offer. They're now at that company's headquarters in Wewelsburg.'

Even over the hissing telephone line, Elliott's shock is audible.

Leo cuts him off. 'You can tell the Israeli director that I'm holding him responsible for this disaster. If he doesn't compensate for his failure, then it will be him who's assigned to wastage.'

'Sir, I'm at the Israeli head office now, and the Israeli director is somewhat water-damaged himself.'

'I'll be fine,' chortles Reuven in the background. 'A bit of a swim, that's all.'

Leo's stomach tightens. He'll have an ulcer by the autumn.

'Listen to me, Elliott. This company is under new management. We're not playing by the old rules any more.'

'Sir—'

'Shut up and pay attention.'

Leo explains to Elliott about Operation Tigerlily.

⊕

Molly is sitting in an armchair, tearing up bed sheets to make a rope, when there's a knock on the door.

'Miss Ravenhill, may I come in?' asks Kitty.

Molly stuffs the sheets in the cupboard, pulls her dressing gown around her, and gives her assent. Not that she has any real choice. The door opens and the wee thing stands in the doorway carrying a small bag. In her leather catsuit, she looks like a violin case with Nazi badges on it. No wonder the men love her.

'Kitty . . . still sporting the latest in boudoir SS fashion, I see.'

'What is "boudoir", Miss Ravenhill?'

Kitty's English is fractured, but Molly's German is worse. They'll have to work away at it.

'Call me Molly – everyone does. Boudoir means bedroom.'

'Yes, I see, bedroom fashion.' Kitty smiles. 'Molly, you will not trust me, but please believe me, things are not like you think. I am not a Nazi. The Gestapo brought me here. I have been using this boudoir fashion only to survive. In Germany, men do not decide if they want to kill me or they want to fuck me. I help them decide and I live.'

God save the poor girl.

'Also, because I'm young and . . . what is the word, not danger?'

'Unthreatening?'

'Yes, unthreatening. I have a deal with Heydrich. It is a horrible deal for me, but it makes me survive and I have some freeness. I move around the castle, and outside a little.'

Kitty holds up a key and an SS identity card with her name on it. 'I want to come to help you escape. The key opens the door. The pass works at the gate, when the guard does not look at it close.'

Molly picks up the ID card. The photo looks nothing like herself. Kitty is twenty years younger. They don't even have the same hair colour.

'I can't trust you, Kitty. Perhaps you aren't a Nazi, but I've seen the effect terror has on people. Maybe it's your family Heydrich has held hostage. Either way, it's his orders you're following.'

Kitty's mouth is a thin line. 'I do not have a family,' she says. 'It was all killed by the Nazis. I have to trust you, also. If Heydrich finds out I come to help you . . . God knows.'

Is it a trap? Molly's intuition is that Kitty is telling the truth. Does it matter? That bed-sheet rope was never going to be long enough, anyway.

'I came here for a reason,' says Molly. 'That reason wasn't escape.'

Kitty puts down the bag and opens it. Inside are two dresses and a pair of flat shoes. Kitty pulls out the smaller dress and holds it up against Molly's body.

'I know you want to kill Heydrich,' she says.

'Well, I'll not be on holiday, now, will I?'

The outfit isn't bad at all. Molly takes it from Kitty and starts undressing to try it on.

Kitty turns away. 'Tomorrow there is a hunt,' she says. 'Heydrich and his friends will be out in the forest. They chase prisoners. If you can escape and steal a rifle and hide, you will shoot at him.'

Molly coughs. Kitty turns back round. The dress is a bit too big, but it will have to do. Kitty makes admiring noises.

'Do you not have a gun at all?' Molly asks.

'You like guns, Molly?'

'I do not. Guns are horrible things. But the Nazis are evil, and evil must be stopped. I have to carry a gun because it's the only language they understand.'

'The White Rose does not like violence.'

'I'll not be a big fan of it myself, Kitty, but sometimes you have to protect the people you love. At least, that's how I see it. You're welcome to think otherwise. Well, in Britain you are. In Nazi Germany you have to think what you're told.'

Kitty sighs. 'Heydrich does not give me a gun. I think you can . . . what is the word, pretend-sneak?'

'Bluff?'

'Yes, bluff. That is what I do. Or I promise sex. That works also.'

'That works when you're twenty, Kitty. You may find things

change when you're forty and your boobs are pointing at the ground instead of the sky.'

'Molly, you are a beautiful woman.'

'Go on, you'll have me in tears.'

⊕

Everything is upside down.

The room around me is decorated in Louis XV style. Every surface, every piece of furniture, is covered with ornate carving. An enormous chandelier hangs from the ceiling. Gilt-framed mirrors line the walls from floor to ceiling. Between these mirrors are wall paintings, in classical style. Faultless pastiches, no doubt executed by the finest painters the SS could arrest, they depict every imaginable sexual position.

My last recollection is my furious, unplanned, pathetic assault on Heydrich. Then nothing, until I awoke dangling from the chandelier, head down and naked amidst this ersatz Versailles. What happened?

Behind me I hear footsteps, and turn my head. Standing over me are the Mitzi twins, the two voluptuous blondes I observed with Heydrich that night in the Hotel Adlon. Behind them is Heydrich himself.

'This man tried to kill me,' he declares.

'Is brute,' says one of the blondes, feigning surprise.

'Yes, a brute. And a fool, too, my dears. I warned him that he posed no possible danger to me.'

The twins are both wearing the same type of skin-tight, leather SS uniform as Kitty. I have to admit, they fill theirs more generously.

'This is Angelika . . . and this is Kristin,' says Heydrich.

The twins scrutinize me.

'We are teaching him a lesson, Reiny?' asks Kristin.

'Brutes cannot be killing our big boy,' says Angelika.

Appreciated in close-up, the twins' cleavages are extraordinary. Despite myself, and despite my position, there's an instinctive stirring.

'He is very bad boy,' says Angelika.

'He is very bad boy indeed,' says Kristin.

'What are we doing with bad boys?' says Angelika.

'Send to our room,' says Kristin.

The twins' predatory laughter echoes off the high ceiling.

'Heydrich likes this kind of thing, does he?' I ask.

'You are having no idea,' says Angelika, and her eyes flicker.

'We are being cruel,' says Kristin, covering for her sister. 'Or we are being gentle. You like to feel softness? Feel kind, gentle womanhood?'

Angelika kneels down and runs a finger along my jawline. As it reaches my chin, she pulls her hand back and slaps my cheek. I gasp. Angelika smiles.

Kristin leans towards me, staring. She lifts her head and frowns at her sister. 'What is it?' she says.

'It is like penis, but smaller,' says Angelika.

'Why is so small?' Kristin asks me.

'It's bloody cold,' I point out.

'Cold,' says Angelika, without smiling.

'Cold,' echoes Kristin, nodding. 'We are warming you up?'

Heydrich sniggers.

The twins prowl. I have an image of lionesses.

Kristin comes into my line of vision. She's now holding a scalpel. Her tongue flickers between perfect white teeth.

'Blade is sharper than necessary,' she says, fondling the scalpel. 'I like.'

She strokes the blade across my chest with perfect control, caressing my skin. Thin beads of ruby blood well up.

'I don't want him to suffer any permanent damage,' Heydrich says. 'He's the star attraction tomorrow.'

Kristin looks disappointed.

An aide edges into the room. He takes one panic-stricken gawp at the tableau revealed to him before blurting out his message.

'Sir, it's giant, sir.'

Heydrich swears under his breath, looks at the aide and nods. 'This had better be important,' he says.

He stalks out of the room.

Angelika moves closer to me. She's near enough for me to feel her breath playing across my face. I study her skin. She has a small mole at the base of her throat. The discovery of this single distinguishing mark gives me a limited feeling of power.

'You like to be putting in my mouth?' she asks.

'Anything to stop you talking.'

Angelika stands up and takes a step back. 'Pervert,' she says, pouting. 'How could you? To delicate young woman.'

'Is habitual criminal,' says Kristin.

Angelika runs her tongue over her lips. 'I am biting off so easy. No one else could have, ever again. Would be mine. Is worth it, you think? Supreme pleasure in return for being unmanned?'

'I think you might bite off more than you can chew.'

The twins' laughter has a heartless quality.

'Not in front of children, I think,' says Kristin, turning to the guards. 'You, leave us. Now.'

There are no arguments.

Angelika picks up the scalpel and advances on me.

Behind her, Kristin is tinkering with a gramophone player. 'Enough of games.'

The gramophone hisses and then starts playing the opening bars of Beethoven's Fifth Symphony.

The two women move closer.

'Stay quiet. Heydrich has room bugged.' The heartless tone Kristin used to try to humiliate me in front of Heydrich is now gone. 'We are reporting to First Chief Directorate of Committee for State Security,' she says.

They're Russian agents. Heydrich must be blind.

'You are one of British Service's best agents and threat to Nazis. We wonder how you are becoming prisoner?'

'It's a long story. You're aware of the Interservice Protocol?'

The twins nod. 'Your chief, infamous imperialist Menzies, was killed. Killer was associated with Russia and Germany.'

'Heydrich as good as told me that he was behind the Old Man's death,' I say.

'Curious. He expresses puzzlement when he speaks of death in our hearing,' says Kristin.

I think of Leo's parting words to me: 'For God's sake, it wasn't necessarily the Germans.'

But, if not them, who? The Soviets? Why then would Soviet agents now tell me they thought it wasn't Heydrich? Why would Heydrich say he'd broken the Protocol, if he hadn't? I'll have to beat the truth out of him, and after that I'll have to kill him anyway.

Fine.

Kristin continues. 'Tomorrow Heydrich, Kaltenbrunner and other SS crazies will hunt you. Is dangerous, but is also opportunity. First Chief Directorate is establishing dead-letter drop in woods, with weapons. If you reach, game turns in your favour.'

Angelika holds up a piece of silk the size of a handkerchief. She laughs. 'Yes, is part of underwear, but also has map on. Use to reach arms cache. Then you are coming back and killing Heydrich.'

'What's "giant"?' I ask. 'That aide who came in, he said, "It's giant."'

'Is Giant, with capital G. Heydrich's true love. Weapon to secure final victory. Greatest of Wunderwaffen. With Giant, Germany is unstoppable.'

'What is it, a bomb?'

'We are trying to find out. We know is having unique classification: Kriegsentscheidend.'

War Decisive. Giant is at the pinnacle of priority: money and lives no object. To my knowledge, no German project has held that classification since the desperate scramble for the atomic bomb.

'Also is involving Professor Heisenberg. Laboratories underground, on airfield.'

'Why are you telling me all this?'

'Do not think Soviet Union is going soft. Is not official action. Enough is enough. We were wanting to help Motherland. We are doing terrible things for Motherland. But what Motherland, and Fatherland, is doing to us is . . .' Her mouth turns down.

'I'm sorry,' I say.

She smiles and her expression softens. 'Is long time since man apologizes to me.'

'Don't think I'm going soft on you.'

'I am not expecting man of your reputation to go soft. We are running to America or somewhere. We have money and jewellery and black-market contacts. We have same assets that are getting us here. If you are causing trouble tomorrow, if you are killing Heydrich, we have more chance for escaping.'

'I'll do my best.'

WEWELSBURG

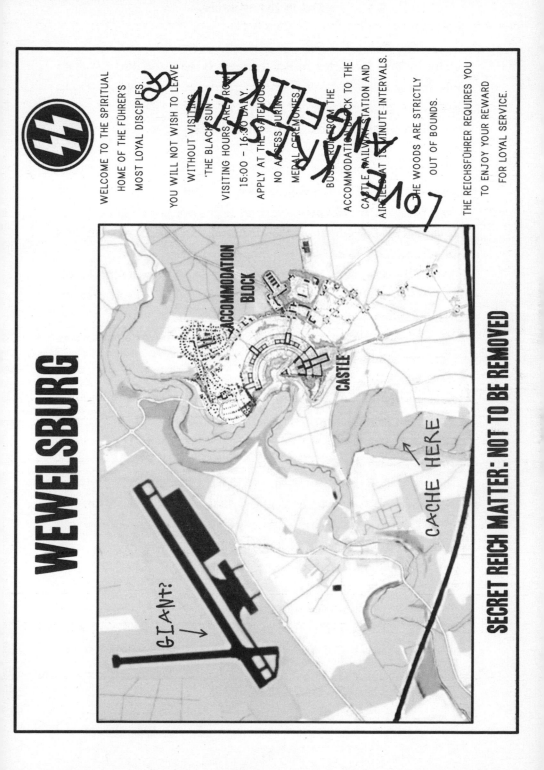

WELCOME TO THE SPIRITUAL
HOME OF THE FÜHRER'S
MOST LOYAL DISCIPLES.

YOU WILL NOT WISH TO LEAVE
WITHOUT VISITING
'THE BLACK SUN'.

VISITING HOURS ARE FROM
15:00 – 16:30 DAILY.

APPLY AT THE GATEHOUSE.
NO ACCESS DURING
MEDAL CEREMONIES.

BUSES RUN FROM THE
ACCOMMODATION BLOCK TO THE
CASTLE RAILWAY STATION AND
AIRFIELD AT 10 MINUTE INTERVALS.

THE WOODS ARE STRICTLY
OUT OF BOUNDS.

THE REICHSFÜHRER REQUIRES YOU
TO ENJOY YOUR REWARD
FOR LOYAL SERVICE.

LOVE KRISTIN
ANGELIKA

ACCOMMODATION BLOCK

CASTLE

CACHE HERE

GIANT?

SECRET REICH MATTER: NOT TO BE REMOVED

'Give bastard Heydrich bullet from us. Now, I apologize, but we are having to whip you. We are being gentle, but are needing you to scream, to convince listeners.'

Angelika bends and kisses me on the cheek.

⊕

Reuven's operation is on a war footing.

He's perching on his desk, wearing headphones and concentrating. On either side of him are bodyguards carrying Sten guns. His habitual smile seems to have become rather fixed.

Behind him, a reel-to-reel tape recorder turns, recording Elliott discussing Operation Tigerlily with Leo. Unsmiling, Elliott puts the telephone down. 'Wewelsburg,' he says.

Reuven reaches over and switches off the tape machine. 'Oh, God, it's not Tigerlily, is it?'

'I'm afraid so, old chap.'

Reuven seems to be studying the papers on his desk. 'If Leo has acquired his information from signals intercepts, then it's already too late.'

'You think the Germans have . . .'

Reuven picks up a fountain pen. He unscrews the top and stares at it as if trying to determine what it's for. 'I can't imagine why else it would be time for Operation Certain Death, can you?'

Elliott stands up. Reuven's bodyguards tense.

'You heard Leo's orders: you've got a role in Tigerlily. Unless you want MI5 down here by supper time?'

'There's no need for threats. We'll do our bit. But what about our runaway Romeo and Juliet – are we going to rescue them?'

Elliott's eyes narrow. 'Not exactly, no.'

Morning.

And Molly is alone, as she predicted, in bloody Prussia, miles away from Ireland.

She stretches, but the stiffness in her body and the ache of the bruises doesn't ease. She'd give anything to be Kitty's age again. Last night, she'd dozed off in the armchair, waiting. Something had poked into her side whenever she moved the cushion in the night. Still half asleep, she'd brushed the object to the floor.

And there it was, now. Still sitting there, smiling up at her – a Welrod sleeve gun.

How the devil had that appeared?

She hasn't seen one of those nasty wee guns since when . . . that operation in Saint Tropez three years ago? She screws the back off to see if it's loaded. God save us, it is. She could have blown her brains out with it during the night, and been none the wiser.

She tries to guess what the time is now. Kitty suggested she wait until the hunt was about to start before trying the gate. The guards are fascinated by the spectacle, so won't be concentrating. Just dress up and walk out with confidence and panache. She can wave Kitty's pass at anyone who tries to stop her. No one will notice that she's twenty years older, a lot plainer, and has different-coloured hair. No one.

Alternatively, use the Welrod to kill a guard, get his Sturmgewehr and blast your way out, girl.

Molly knows which plan she prefers.

She tidies herself up and puts Kitty's dress on. This stupid plan is never going to work, but she may as well go down fighting.

She goes to the door and inserts the key Kitty smuggled in to her. She eases it round, the lock clicks and the tumblers drop into place. Molly throws the door wide to catch a half-awake guard still staring at the door handle. His gaze moves to the Welrod and then flicks to the alarm switch on the wall.

Molly shoots him between the eyes.

⊕

The morning sun pushes its way over the battlements and catches the treetops. It's going to be a beautiful day.

Outside the castle, the Nazi overlords are gathering in numbers. Hunt staff fuss around them, loading weapons and pulling the bloodhounds into line. In the middle distance, sunlight reflects from the green awning of the woods.

At least I'm going to die on a sunny day.

At the centre of the crowd, like the eye of a storm, stand Heydrich and Kaltenbrunner. They're both wearing their dress uniforms and carrying shotguns. Kitty, still wearing her leather SS uniform, stands behind Heydrich trying to keep her face a blank mask. She glances over at me, and I sense her terror. I keep my eyes on the trees. Peaceful green trees. Rows of witnesses.

Heydrich brings Kitty over to me. He gestures to the guards to release me. 'The Mitzis gave you a hard time, eh?' he asks.

'Well, I was hard through most of it.'

Heydrich laughs and waves Kitty forward. 'You know, part of me wants you to survive. You are a fascinating character. You could so easily have been one of us,' he says.

'I couldn't have been one of you in a million years.'

'You must admit the adrenalin, the intensity of the battle, has its attractions?'

I stand there staring at the trees. Much as it pains me to concede anything to Heydrich, he's right. But I'm damned if I'm going to confess it. I shake my head, and try to hold eye contact with the man. He stares me down. I glance away.

'Yes, of course, your motive is to protect the weak, of course it is. No pleasure derived whatsoever. None.' Heydrich sneers. 'Your secret is safe with me.'

He turns back to Kitty. Another gesture to the guards. One of them steps forward and snaps a handcuff on her delicate wrist. He reaches over and fastens the other end of the handcuffs to my own wrist.

'Katharina is going to accompany you.'

Brilliant. Running for my life was going to be tough enough without dragging Kitty along. She's going to be the death of me.

I glance at Kitty's ashen face. She isn't built for this.

'Wh—' she splutters.

Heydrich smiles. 'I'm afraid, my dear, that I tired of you rather more quickly than I expected. Thank you, though, for reminding me of my youth. The next time we meet, you'll be near death; I am the Reich's Master Hunter, as Herr Göring found out too late.'

'You're enjoying torturing me, aren't you?' spits Kitty.

'What of it? I do not deny it. Violence in defence of Germany is justified. It cannot become unjustified just because I, the instrument of that justified violence, take pleasure in my vocation.'

The guards drag us off to the starting pen – I don't know what else I can call it. Kitty sobs, deep shudders running through her. I have to get her to focus or neither of us is going anywhere.

'After the klaxon, you get five minutes' head start, Number Fifteen,' shouts Kaltenbrunner. 'Don't let me down. I've bet a lot of money on you breaking the record.'

As the count spirals down, I recite a limerick to Kitty, desperate to raise her spirits. 'There was a young Nazi called Igor, who smiled as he hunted a tiger—'

'What?' she says, trying to fake a smile through her tears.

'I'll tell you the rest later,' I say. 'After we escape.'

I grip her shoulder with my free hand and stare into her eyes. 'Remember when we met in Berlin, Kitty? I saved you then. This is what I do – stay alive, kill the bad guys. It's my job. But you've got to help me. You have to run like you did in Berlin. If you do, I can keep us both alive.'

Kitty wipes her eyes, takes a deep breath and nods. She rips the Nazi armband from her uniform and stamps it into the mud.

'We'll make for the woods,' I say.

The blast of the starting klaxon shakes the trees.

19

Mutually Assured Destruction

Heisenberg has discovered a perversion of the mechanism. Entranced in his revolting dream, he does not see the danger. This is unconscionable. I will not allow it! The mechanism MUST be used to contact our blood ancestors!

Journal of an unknown SS scientist, p. 400

Wing Commander Gibson is shorter than Leo expects.

He's taller than Leo is, though. Still, so are most people.

'The RAF officer you asked to speak to, sir,' says Patricia, her eyes sparkling. In her high heels she stands taller than either of them.

The 'Saviour of the British Empire', the papers call Gibson. Which rather ignores the contributions of thousands of others in Britain and Canada; he didn't exactly build the bomb himself, did he? All he did was waft over the Baltic and drop it on an undefended target.

'Cream cake, Wing Commander?' asks Leo, pointing at the tray on his desk.

Gibson declines. Leo passes him the Tigerlily dossier, and helps himself. No point in wasting them. Patricia brings in some coffee. Gibson grins at her. 'Brightening the old place up a bit, eh?' he says.

Patricia seems to have lost an inch at the waist and gained it at the bust. Star quality – Gibson has it, Leo doesn't. He takes a bite of the bun and cream runs down his chin. He pours his own coffee.

'Oops, sorry,' says Patricia, steadying herself by resting a hand on Gibson's arm.

Leo sighs. 'Thank you, Patricia. You can go now.'

'Just let me know if you want anything,' she says, winking at Gibson. 'I'll be right outside.'

She glides to the doorway, her hips swaying in a way Leo has never noticed before. Gibson turns his head to watch the performance.

Leo coughs. 'Wing Commander?' he says.

Gibson turns back towards him, smiling.

Leo hands Gibson his coffee. 'Wing Commander, I wanted to brief you personally on the latest intelligence. It's going to be a tough one, I'm afraid.'

Leo reminds himself, once again, that life is cruel.

⊕

The 'Saviour of the British Empire' sits in his clapped-out Morris Minor, peering at RAF Waddington through the rain. The white tails of the squadron's Avro Vanquishes stick out of the hangars, obscured by the downpour. The car's useless heater struggles even to stop the Morris's windows steaming up.

Inside, the armourers are bombing up the planes for Operation Tigerlily. In the mess the crews will be tucking into their bacon and eggs, like condemned men. They know something big is coming: they're being held at readiness and no one is allowed on or off the base.

The intelligence file that Leo gave Gibson sits on the passenger seat. Scribbled on the cover, in green ink, is Patricia's home phone number. There's not going to be time to call her until after the op – if there is an after. In the back of the car, Gibson's elderly Labrador lies sleeping on a tartan rug. The dog has been his best friend for a decade, but now the noble beast is close to tour completion.

Old age will come for him, too. It's just something he'll have to get through.

'Well, pup, it looks like both our numbers might be up,' he says.

The Labrador thumps its tail against the leather. Gibson reaches back, pats it and returns to his sightless contemplation of the airfield. He shakes his head.

'Jesus,' he whispers, more to himself than to the dog.

He puts the car into first gear and heads towards the airbase.

The rain continues to bounce off the tarmac.

How many operations was it now? How many briefings?

Gibson steps up to the podium and raps it with the pointer, demanding quiet. An officer can never give the slightest indication that he lacks confidence. It would be fatal.

'Gentlemen.'

The noise dies down. Boisterousness has its place, but not in operations briefings.

'What I'm about to tell you is top secret. Off-base communications are suspended until after the mission.'

Groans from the lads who have demanding girlfriends.

The screen behind Gibson glows, showing a map of Europe. A thin black line heads out from Britain, across the North Sea, and on to the Continent.

'Here's the programme – Operation Tigerlily.'

Gasps as the crews take it in, for the black rapier thrusts into the heart of Germany.

'We have received a go from Bomber Command, the Air Ministry and the Prime Minister. We're going to attack Germany.'

Consternation.

'Settle down. It's not Armageddon just yet. This is a non-nuclear strike, if everything goes to plan.'

He moves the pointer to the map. 'The spooks have learnt that the Jerries are building a devastating secret weapon, located here.' Gibson points at Wewelsburg.

The picture changes to a close-up of the airfield.

'You'll get a nice clean radar return off the concrete. Aiming point is *here*.' He highlights a circular structure near one end of the runway.

'You'll be carrying Grand Slam earthquake bombs. I'll be responsible for the back-up weapon. You can understand the seriousness of this attack when I tell you I hope I don't need to resort to it. However, we must destroy this target tonight. If we don't, then next time we'll face an alerted enemy, and we'll all receive the Victoria Cross.'

The one medal he doesn't have already, almost always awarded posthumously.

'As anyone who has set foot outside can see, the weather is atrocious, which is perfect for us. Meteorology say it's the same all across northern Europe.'

The picture zooms back out again.

'We'll form up over Dogger Bank, imitating a V-Force patrol. On my signal we will go supersonic, penetrating Germany at combat ceiling and with full jamming. Route will be landfall at Borkum, up the Ems estuary, skirt the Ruhr defences, then south to Bielefeld. We'll form up over the Detmold forest for a run in to the target from the north-east.'

Enemy missile concentrations are marked in red on the map. The route weaves between them until it reaches Wewelsburg, where the missiles will just have to be braved.

'The Luftwaffe won't know what's hit them. Enemy radar will pick us up over the North Sea, but jamming will blind it. Without radar, the Luftwaffe fighters will be useless; there's a lot of sky up there. Our speed, the dark, the weather and total electromagnetic silence should see us over Wewelsburg unmolested. We'll take our chances with the target's defences.'

The room is silent.

'There will be no secondary targets and no targets of opportunity. You'll drop the Grand Slams using the Navigation and Bombing System, and from maximum altitude to get highest ground penetration. I want a tight grouping around the target; it's thought to be several storeys underground. Get close, drop on target, and let the earthquake bombs do their job. They'll be on delayed fuses, so no need to worry about getting in each other's way. I'll lead us over the target and draw the first volley of missiles so that you boys have a clear run. You'll follow me at fifteen-second intervals. After bombing, we'll swing round and route south of the Ruhr to Luxembourg. Then we'll head back out to sea, along the French–Belgian border.'

He looks back from the map towards the assembled crews.

'Any questions?'

Some of the youngsters are grinning, but most are faking nonchalance or determination. There's one hand raised.

'Suppression of defences over the target, sir?'

'The spooks have a plan, but I wouldn't count on it. We'll rely on surprise, speed, altitude and our Air Electronics Officers to keep us safe.'

There are some white faces; better buck the youngsters up a bit.

'Now, look here, I know you fellows haven't flown over Germany before. In fact, one or two of you have no hot mission experience at all. But you're all top crews and you've trained for a mission like this since day one of the V-Force.'

And he himself has flown over fifty missions, in aircraft with about a quarter of the performance of the Vanquishes.

'This mission is vital: we can't let the Nazis get this secret weapon going. It's a nasty bit of work and likely to make the V-Force obsolete. The Air Ministry is confident that the V-Force will deter the Jerries into conventional retaliation; our country will cope with that. We're going to be on our own all the way, as the Brass are worried about triggering the German rockets if they put on a full show. So, this is our chance to be heroes. Wipe Wewelsburg airfield off the map, and come back alive. That's an order.'

Smiles.

'By this evening we may well be back at war with the Nazis. You know what I say to that?'

The sea of faces – Jesus, it was just like last time. Kids.

'Good! It's about bloody time!'

That gets a cheer.

In the ready room, Gibson's crew are in high spirits. Log sheets and maps, codes and flimsies are scattered everywhere. His South African navigation officer frowns at the charts.

'All set, Jan?' he asks.

The navigator gives him the thumbs-up.

'Good show.'

The youngsters chat away. They stroke their lucky charms and carry out their pre-operation rituals – walking round the hangar clockwise, writing a letter to their parents or praying.

Aircrew are notorious for their superstitions, but Gibson has no time for omens, and he doesn't worry about destiny. Coincidence has killed too many good crews and spared too many bad ones for him to believe in fate. Omens, fate, luck: such things are shadows – nothing at all. The odds can be improved with the right spirit, hard work and training. It all comes down to chance, though, in the end, as they grope through the dark night skies.

Muriel, his WAAF orderly, confirms operations and flying control are ready. The crew pick up their helmets, Mae Wests and parachutes and head for the bus.

Gibson pushes his own essentials into his flight sack and walks after them.

The crew are bursting with nervous jokes as they clamber off the bus.

'Have a few pints when we get back, eh?'

In front of them, the giant Vanquishes resemble roosting white bats about to wake. Gibson steps out of the bus and one of the huge aircraft towers over him. The sight of it brings on the accustomed flutters.

'Bang on, eh, skipper?'

'What? Oh, yeah. Cut the chat now, boys. Heads down. Let's get the job done.'

Up the ladder, through the hatch into the bomber's belly. Forward to the cockpit. He slides into the captain's seat and starts on his pre-flight checklist. Behind him, the navigator lays out his maps and fiddles with his equipment. The bomb-aimer powers up the Navigation and Bombing System. The Air Electronics Officer confirms the jammers and decoys are all set.

He starts the auxiliary power unit. There's the usual coughing and grumbling as it runs up. The main engines' roar drowns everything except a chorus of status checks from the crew over the intercom. The squadron's other pilots check in with their readiness confirmations. All twenty aircraft are operational and ready for deployment. Ground crews disconnect and scurry for safety.

On the radio to the tower. 'G-George, ready for taxi.'

'Clear to taxi, G-George.'

Off the brakes and nudge the throttles forward.

Around them, like an enormous ballet, the Vanquishes disengage and pirouette in synchrony to their taxi positions. Gibson leads them out, each aircraft maintaining a fifty-yard interval behind the one in front of it.

At the runway threshold, they pause for final checks. Everything is in position. The co-pilot concurs.

'G-George, ready for take-off.'

'Clear to take-off, G-George. Good luck.'

Throttle up. They're rolling. Slow acceleration. Full power, and on with the reheat. The familiar kick in the backside as it hits.

'V1,' states the co-pilot.

Faster.

'V2.'

Gentle pressure on the yoke. Smooth as alabaster, they're airborne. Up with the undercarriage. Pulling the yoke back, and back.

The Vanquishes climb towards heaven, like arrowheads fired at God.

20

A Walk in the Woods

This is it! This is IT! Final proof that Heisenberg is either a fool or a saboteur. His calculations are demonstrably incorrect in three different places. It has taken me an entire week to unravel his obfuscations. The mechanism IS a beacon! The vortex will remain stable! Thank the gods that I am now in a position to unmask him as a traitor.

Journal of an unknown SS scientist, p.442

There's no way to defeat a bloodhound.

A bloodhound's nose is around three thousand times more sensitive than a human's. This level of sensitivity makes scent-hiding tricks futile.

Doubling back will not work. Running over rocky terrain will not work. Hiding in a tree will not work. Throwing pepper or food on the ground will not work. Running downwind will not work. Crossing a stream will not work, although it will force the blood-hound to reacquire the scent on the other side.

There's no way to defeat a bloodhound.

$\oplus$

The Service's geniuses think of everything, including where an assassin is going to find bullets in occupied Europe. The Welrod sleeve gun uses German 9mm ammunition, so Molly takes the guard's pistol and reloads the Welrod from it.

She thinks about taking his assault rifle, too, but decides on a wee reconnoitre first. Better check how many more guards she's going to have to deal with. Maybe she'll even be able to sneak out. Kitty's dress might at least enable her to get close to the gatehouse before she has to open fire. They're sure to see her coming if she's carrying a Sturmgewehr.

In a wee courtyard, the Mitzi twins are standing by a Mercedes cabriolet, smoking. Their chauffeur is heaving their luggage into the trunk. They're wearing slinky black crêpe dresses and short Arctic fox fur coats with puffed sleeves. Each girl has an identical white hat perched on her head, adorned with a scrap of veil. They have diamonds the size of golf balls cushioned in their cleavages. And they're both carrying guns.

Angelika turns and catches sight of Molly. Her gaze moves to the gun in Molly's hand. 'Miss Ravenhill,' she says.

Kristin turns to look at Molly, too.

'A fine day it is, ladies,' Molly says.

The sisters say something to each other in Russian and Angelika turns back to Molly. 'We are taking Reinhard's car. You are coming with us, maybe?'

Right enough.

Molly takes the front seat next to the chauffeur. The twins occupy the back. The chauffeur seems unaware that Molly is not the woman she's supposed to be. Either that or he's dominated by the Mitzis. From the way they treat him, Molly suspects the latter.

At the gate, the guards seem distracted; only one comes forward to check the car. He's more interested in ogling the Mitzis than in wondering who Molly is or why she's wearing Kitty's dress.

'Heil Hitler,' says Angelika with a sulky expression, as the guard approaches. 'Obersturmführer Gerfried is not here? He is special favourite.'

The guard glances into the car and smiles at Molly. 'Who is this?' he says.

Below his eye line, Molly points the Welrod at him.

'Is friend. Colleague. Has special skills making up for flat chest,' says Kristin.

Too right she has special skills. So special that someone is about to get their head blown off.

'Want to show me some of those skills, darling?' The guard leers at her.

Molly smiles and shakes her head. She doesn't want to risk speaking. He'll realize she isn't German the moment she opens her mouth.

'Officers only,' says Kristin.

'I'd better see your pass,' says the guard.

Angelika leans forward. 'Passes?' she snaps. 'You are new here? We are not needing passes. You are recognizing us or Heydrich is sending you to guard Arctic igloo. We are going shopping in Düsseldorf. We are coming back late. Open gate.'

Angelika and Kristin sit back in their seats, ignoring the guard. He looks at them, back at the gatehouse, and then shrugs.

The barrier glides up, and the Mercedes slides through the shadow of the gate and into open sunshine. The twins blow the guard a kiss as they drive away.

'You girls have a fine a way about you,' says Molly.

Angelika sneers. 'Men,' she says. 'Animals. Never change.'

'It'll change when you're forty-five and the size of a house,' says Molly.

Kristin grimaces.

'Your boyfriend is star turn at hunt today,' says Angelika.

'I wondered where he'd got to. No one tells me anything these days.'

In the distance a klaxon sounds.

⊕

Our first dash for the woods over, I stop to check the Mitzis' map. Kitty gasps for air by my side. I scrutinize the piece of silk, orientating it by aligning Wewelsburg Castle's towers behind me. The ground plan is not to scale, but I estimate the dead-letter drop is about a mile away. It's shown as being near a waterfall at the end of a ravine.

Can I trust the Mitzi twins? I don't have much choice.

'This is going to be tough,' I tell Kitty. 'But we can't go the easy way. If we keep off the tracks, we'll be much quicker than the dog teams. The handlers won't like being dragged through the bushes by the dogs. And a bloodhound might be able to follow a week-old trail but it's far from athletic. They'll have to be lifted over all the obstructions.'

We plunge into the bushes. Running headlong through the thickest shrubs, leaping over every fallen tree, going out of our way to find the worst obstacles. Each time Kitty stumbles, or I push on too fast, the handcuff bites into my wrist. Kitty is slowing me down, just as Heydrich planned. I pull her through the undergrowth. There's no time for finesse, just relentless speed. The cuffs skin both our wrists.

'You're doing all right,' I gasp.

'Not well enough,' she replies, panting.

Kitty's wrist, like my own, is dripping blood.

At best, we'll gain ten minutes during the run to the waterfall. That will give us fifteen minutes, at the outside, to find the dead-letter drop.

After that, the dogs and the hunters will be on top of us.

Splashing to a stop before the waterfall, I look up.

We crossed and recrossed the meandering river and even ran straight along it towards the end. We both slipped and fell twice, dragging the other one with us each time. Every jerk of the handcuffs reopened the wounds on our wrists. But the sheer adrenalin of running for our lives has focused us both. We don't notice the pain.

'Oh no,' says Kitty, following my gaze. 'It's not possible.'

'It's going to have to be,' I say.

'I don't think I can . . .'

'Do you want to live?'

We stand and stare at the rock face, sprayed by the waterfall cascading down it. It's a tough climb, especially as we only have ten minutes. We have to be at the top when the hunt catches up. Otherwise, they'll be able to swat us like flies on a window.

'If we make it, the dogs won't be able to get up the cliff. They'll have to go back to the start of the ravine. We'll gain a lot of time – maybe even enough to escape.'

The real difficulty will be trying to climb whilst handcuffed together.

Floating on the wind behind us comes the baying of the hounds. They're 'speaking to the line', calling their handlers to our track.

'It will be hard, but we can do it,' I say.

'I'll try,' says Kitty, staring at the cliff face.

Straight up. Just like Vemork.

At least it isn't snowing this time.

The climb is a nightmare.

I lead. Kitty follows my instructions, placing her hands and feet where I indicate. The climb is easier than the one I made in the blizzard at Vemork. But at Vemork I hadn't been in a car crash a few days earlier. At Vemork I hadn't almost drowned within the last forty-eight hours or received a gentle flogging the night before. And at Vemork I wasn't handcuffed to someone with no climbing experience and nothing but terror to keep her going.

Without climbing equipment we're risking our lives, clambering upwards with no protection from a fall. But not having to stop to hammer in pitons or belay ropes means we climb fast. Going too slow would put our lives in danger, too.

Before we're halfway up the cliff face, my hands are scraped. Blood runs down my sleeve from the raw wound on my wrist. Beside me, Kitty is moving on instinct alone. Her hair is matted and the leather of her uniform scratched and dirty. Her hands are in a similar condition to my own. Her breath rasps, fighting for the oxygen her lungs demand.

The dogs howl again, closer now.

The first missed footing nearly kills us both.

I sense Kitty slipping even before she screams, and by pure luck I have both my feet secured. Kitty's footing gives way. I grip her hand and take her weight, slamming her into the rock face so she doesn't topple backwards. Kitty scrabbles for a toehold, screaming. My fingers, wedged in a crevice, feel as though they're being torn out, fighting to hold me upright. Kitty finds a foothold and I release my grip.

'Take deep breaths,' I say. 'Keep your arms and legs straight, and just position your feet one at a time.' I try to sound calm.

Kitty whimpers. She's desperately close to her physical limit. I give her thirty seconds before heading upwards again. This climb is insane, I realize. It's a desperate throw of the dice, a prayer to the forces of fate. But that's why it's going to work.

If we can only get to the top.

We both inspect the cliff face. The last ten yards are worn to glass-like smoothness, except for a single deep fissure in the rock. It's impossible to go on.

The barking is louder than ever. It's only a matter of a few minutes now.

Kitty peers downwards. 'If we—'

'I'm not committing suicide.'

'So we just stay here and wait for the dogs to arrive, then let a bunch of sadists take pot-shots at us? At least a jump would be quick.'

The top is so near and the footholds inside the fissure are more than adequate. I could make the climb in minutes if the crevice wasn't too narrow for us to climb side by side.

Grime smudges Kitty's face. Tears streak rivulets through the filth.

I could do it if it wasn't for the girl.

'There's a way,' I say.

My muscles are on fire.

My climbing is not pretty; pure survival instinct drives me on. Kitty's weight on my back constantly threatens to topple us both back into the chasm. With her clinging on behind, I only have one good hand. She does what she can, holding on to me with one hand and moving the other as best she can. But she just doesn't have the reach.

A groan escapes my lips.

'I haven't had a piggy back since I was seven,' whispers Kitty.

'It's never too late,' I grunt.

I grit my teeth and thrust upwards. Each movement towards the cliff top is agony. I count the movements, each one gaining us six or eight inches. More than that is impossible. My conscious mind retreats. There's nothing but the cliff face. Nothing exists in the whole wide world except those last few pathetic yards that separate us from escape.

⊕

The Mercedes pulls to a halt at the edge of the woods. Kristin has told Molly about the arms cache. She's going to wander down there and see if she can't get a shot at Heydrich as he passes by.

'Girls, I'll be needing to get out now. Enjoy your trip to South America.'

'Good luck, Miss Ravenhill.'

'Sure and it's you girls who'll be needing the luck,' she says, stepping from the car.

'We are not angels,' says Kristin. 'We will do what we have to. We will survive.'

As the long Mercedes pulls away, the girls both turn and wave. Then one of them says something sharp to the chauffeur and the car accelerates.

'You know, girls, I think you might just do that,' says Molly.

The sun shines on her face. In the distance is an airfield. She glances across the road towards the heavy undergrowth.

Is it not a grand day for a walk in the woods?

⊕

For a minute, Kitty and I just lie there, panting into the grass. The sound of barking echoes from the cliff face. I peep over the cliff top. The first dog splashes along the riverbank, its handler straining to keep up. The dog will sense he's close.

'Stay down,' I gasp to Kitty.

We crawl away from the precipice, towards the trees, searching for the box that will save our lives.

238

'Try the bushes,' Kitty whispers.

The box is covered with fresh-cut branches. We stagger over to it and drag it into the clearing at the top of the cliffs.

'God bless the Mitzi twins,' says Kitty.

'Amen to that.'

I rummage through the contents: a Moisin-Nagant sniper rifle, two Makarov handguns, some tools and a bottle of water. At the bottom is a more detailed map, printed on paper marked 'Geheime Reichsache'. Below that are some papers and photographs.

'Drink,' says Kitty, handing the bottle of water to me.

I gulp down a mouthful and turn back to the box.

'What are you looking for?' asks Kitty.

'Hacksaw.'

'Bolt cutter?' says Kitty, pointing.

'Kneel down.'

Kitty looks confused.

'We'll have to rest one end of the bolt cutters on the ground. We can't do that standing up.'

We try to get the bolt cutters into an awkward back to front position. Kitty holds the lower handle steady and I try to get some leverage on the top. The blades slip and we collapse. I swear. Kitty lifts them back into position.

'Try again,' she says. 'We've come this far.'

On the third attempt, the bolt cutters chomp through the metal.

'What a pretty bracelet,' says Kitty, holding the remains of the bloodstained cuff up to the light.

I pick up one of the Makarovs, eject the magazine and check the ammunition. It feels solid. I strip and reassemble it. The firing pin rattles as expected when I shake it. I pull back the slide, a bullet slips into the chamber and I engage the safety catch. Happiness is a gun in my hand.

After checking the second handgun, I turn to Kitty, weighing the options. I hand her the spare Makarov. She shakes her head.

'Remember the limerick I started telling you before the run through the woods?' I ask.

'There was a young Nazi called Igor, who smiled as he hunted a tiger?' says Kitty.

I nod. 'They returned from the ride, with the Nazi inside,' I say.

Kitty starts laughing.

'And the smile on the face of the tiger,' we say together.

The secret of comedy is timing.

'We'll make for the airfield,' I say. 'But first there's something I need to do.'

I grip the Moisin-Nagant rifle in both hands.

There's no way to defeat a bloodhound.

But you don't need to defeat the dog, because it's not the dog that's going to kill you.

You kill the handler.

21

You Couldn't Make It Up

Heydrich backs the blasphemous usage of the mechanism. He is uninterested in the correct solution to the vortex calculations. 'On the Fallen Souls' is more real to me than this. I dream of diamond cities. What is happening to me? Constant headaches now. Visual disturbances increasing.

Journal of an unknown SS scientist, p.484

Now the smile is on the face of the tiger.

Normally I'd take more care to avoid observation, but I need to hit them fast and get out.

Four shots from the Moisin-Nagant rifle are all it takes. I retreat from the cliff top before anyone spots my position. Random weapon fire from the remaining hunters buzzes over my head.

Behind me, four crumpled shapes lie in the shallow water of the stream. They are wreathed in scarlet, which pools, swirls and then drifts downstream. Puzzled bloodhounds sniff at the corpses of their handlers. One dog lets out a long, despairing howl.

And then the woods are silent again.

Kitty is trying to tidy herself up, cleaning her wounds in a pool at the side of the stream. Hearing my approach, she glances round. Her auburn hair is slick with water. She's smiling, more alive than I've ever seen her. I kneel beside her and splash water on my own face. This is no time for distractions.

'Did you get them?' Kitty asks.

I nod. Kitty grins, catches herself and looks guilty.

'This is just the start of our troubles,' I say.

'But you've stopped them. We can—'

'All I've done is given us a bit of time. We can't live in these woods for the rest of our lives. Heydrich will call in bigger guns, now he knows we're armed. He'll deploy a battalion of Waffen-SS, if he has to.'

As if in affirmation, the beat of distant helicopter rotors gets louder, moving through the trees towards us. Kitty sighs.

We stumble off through the woods.

According to the map, we're now close to the airfield.

The growl of jet engines running up confirms the map's accuracy. I catch a glimpse of the road skirting the forest and place my hand on Kitty's arm.

'Stay here while I check the road.'

I crawl towards the edge of the woods and take cover in a bush. Over the road are a couple more trees, then four hundred yards of scrub before the perimeter fence. The airbase looks busy, jammed even. I count the tails of at least fifty transport planes distributed across the field's dispersal points.

And strolling down the road twenty yards away is a brunette in a blue polka-dot dress.

'A fine turn-up this is, now,' says Molly.

She runs towards me. I grab her and kiss her full on the lips. There's a fierce hunger in the way she kisses me back.

'We're not dead yet,' she whispers.

Behind us, Kitty coughs. Molly and I jump away from each

other like a couple of kissing cousins surprised by their parents.

'Well, well . . . so the tart turned out to have a heart,' Molly says, smiling at Kitty.

'She's all heart,' I say.

'Kitty, you're looking a bit . . . dishevelled.'

'We had an adventure since yesterday,' says Kitty in English. 'We would be dead so easy. We climbed a cliff. We killed the—'

'I thought you were a pacifist?'

'I am, but that does not mean I want to die. You escaped too?'

Molly nods. 'Thanks to you and the Mitzis.'

'Molly, how the devil . . .' I ask.

'Guess what? Some kind souls left me presents. This beautiful dress is Kitty's, as you can see from the way it doesn't fit in all the right places. And imagine what I found under my pillow? A Welrod sleeve gun all of my own. Well, what can't a girl do with a delightful and practical present like that? And as everyone was engrossed in some sort of sport—'

'That was the SS. They hunt us with dogs.'

'Yes, Angelika told me. That key you gave me was useful, Kitty. And the Mitzis are apparently not the good Nazis everyone takes them for, either. They smuggled me out of the castle, hidden in their cleavages.'

'Molly, well done. But we're still trapped behind enemy lines,' I say.

'We've got weapons: we can take them.'

'Apart from the fact that there're hundreds of them back there, Heydrich has some kind of superweapon at the airfield. If we go there, then he'll come to us.'

Molly nods. Kitty takes her arm and grins at me. 'What a fantasy for you. The young redhead and the beautiful . . . what is the word, brown-hair woman?'

'Brunette,' says Molly.

'Yes, the young redhead and the beautiful brunette, together at one time,' says Kitty.

Both women start laughing.

First, we have to get into the airfield.

Molly positions herself further up the road and waits. Two troop convoys pass. Finally a lone Kübelwagen, with an officer in the back seat, approaches. Molly signals to Kitty.

When the open-topped Kübelwagen turns the corner, Kitty is sitting at the side of the road, looking sorry for herself. The male desire to help attractive young women is almost irresistible. The Kübelwagen's occupants spot Kitty and nature takes its inevitable course.

The driver is perhaps aware of partisan tricks, but his senses are dulled here, only a few miles from SS headquarters. He pulls to a halt a few yards past Kitty, almost opposite my position in the roadside ditch.

The officer, a Brigadeführer, turns in his seat to stare at the beautiful but unkempt woman seated by the roadside. 'What's the matter?' he shouts.

Kitty, fine actress that she is, starts crying.

It's enough. The Brigadeführer says something to his driver. The driver steps out of the vehicle. I stand up and shoot him through the heart at point-blank range with the Welrod. Molly stands behind Kitty, covering the Brigadeführer with the rifle.

'The poor thing,' says Kitty, looking at the driver's crumpled body. She kneels down and closes his eyes.

'Men,' says Molly. 'All they're interested in is sex. Serves him right.'

'What's wrong with being interested in sex?' I say, unscrewing the Welrod and reloading it.

'You'll have me in tears,' says Molly.

She jumps into the Kübelwagen and reverses it off the road. Kitty drags the driver's body into the ditch I'd been hiding in, and throws some branches over him.

At gunpoint, I order the unfortunate Brigadeführer into the woods. Kitty doesn't have to witness another killing, this one in cold blood. It's unpleasant but necessary, the worst sort of job, effectively murder. I order the officer to strip first so that no blood will stain his uniform. To spare him the horror of realization, I shoot him in the back of the head while he's undressing.

When I return from the bushes wearing the Brigadeführer's uniform, both women are in the car. Kitty catches the look that passes between Molly and me.

'Did you just . . .' says Kitty.

'I'm afraid so. No choice.' I adjust the Brigadeführer's cap to a suitably arrogant angle.

'Myself, I'm just praying this cockamamie plan is going to work,' says Molly.

I take the wheel, engage first gear and spin the Kübelwagen back on to the road, heading for the airfield.

I wipe the sweat from my face, blink and look again.

My Nazi officer disguise has carried us through the airfield perimeter, and I've parked the Kübelwagen near the hangars. It's mid-afternoon and, with the skies still clear, temperatures are soaring. The only shade is under the wings of the dozens of Junkers Ju-590 troop carriers drawn up on the flightline. The heat, shimmering off the bone-white concrete of the airfield, gives the scene a sense of unreality.

Lounging in each aircraft's shadow are camouflaged SS-Fallschirmjäger, paratroopers. They're checking their weapons or passing time with a hand of cards. All around them, Luftwaffe ground crew load the transport planes with equipment:

Kübelwagens, recoilless rifles, multi-barrelled rocket launchers, anti-aircraft missiles, ammunition carts and equipment. They're going somewhere, and soon.

Molly looks up from the Mitzis' map and points at the Fallschirmjäger. 'I'm betting Giant is past these maniacs.'

'Try not to draw attention to yourselves,' I say, restarting the engine.

Wolf whistles emanate from the soldiers. Kitty waves back. 'Better to bluff,' she says. 'They think we are mistresses.'

'God save us,' says Molly.

I pull the Kübelwagen to a halt again at the far end of the row of aircraft. By the runway is a windowless bunker with multiple power lines converging on it. It looks more like an electricity substation than a Wunderwaffe. Unlike most electricity substations, though, a double enclosure of chain-link fencing surrounds it, topped with barbed wire. Attack dogs roam loose inside the fence. Two machine gun posts cover the only gap in the wire. There's something down there, underground.

'Double or quits,' says Molly, grasping the Walther pistol she took from the Brigadeführer's driver.

I accelerate hard towards the checkpoint, waving my arms at the sentries, gesturing to them to open the barriers. The dogs throw themselves at the wire, snarling. Molly shrinks down in her seat, praying under her breath, knuckles white. One of the guards brings a hand up, palm forward. The others unsling their weapons.

I keep going, shouting 'Orders from Heydrich' and 'Top priority'.

The guards' guns track the car. Kitty, terrified, looks away from the guards, as if fascinated by something on the far side of the airfield. The Unterscharführer in charge of the guards runs from the guard post, shouting to his men.

The barrier opens.

'Dear God,' whispers Kitty. 'Heydrich will kill them when he finds out.'

The Kübelwagen slews to a halt opposite the guard hut. The guards lower their weapons and raise their hands in salute. I leap out and stride towards the Unterscharführer, scowling.

'Heil Hitler! I have vital information regarding a security threat to Giant. Take me to the commanding officer immediately.'

'Yes, sir.'

'And make sure no one else comes into the complex. This is an emergency.' I wave the Brigadeführer's credentials at him.

The Unterscharführer orders the rest of the guards to maintain their positions. He turns and marches double-time to the door of the bunker, jangling the keys on his key ring.

The armoured door swings open with hydraulic smoothness. It reveals a room with bare concrete walls, containing nothing except a lift and a sign that forbids smoking. An SS-Schütze with a horrific burn across the right side of his face stands by the lift, smoking. Around his neck is the Iron Cross Second Class. On the left breast of his jacket is a well-deserved Wound Badge in Silver. He tries to hide the cigarette behind his back.

The Unterscharführer nods to him. 'Level six, Günter, and put that cigarette out.'

He turns and notices that Molly and Kitty have followed me into the building.

'The women . . .' he asks.

'. . . will accompany me.'

Behind him, the door hisses closed again.

'Do they have Giant security authorization?' he asks.

'Sure we do,' says Molly. She places a hand on either side of his head, as if she's going to kiss him. A sharp twist to the right, then keep turning. Ignore the vicious cracking sounds. Keep going. His head looks as if it will unscrew from his shoulders.

The lift operator lunges for the emergency alarm. I sweep his legs from under him, lock my hands together and bring them down on the back of his head. He slams into the wall. His face grates down the rough concrete to the floor. I stamp between his shoulder blades. Again, the vile crack of splintering bone is the only sound accompanying the execution.

Molly steps back and the Unterscharführer's corpse slumps into Kitty's arms. Kitty stifles a scream, staggering backwards under his dead weight.

I pick up the Unterscharführer's Sturmgewehr. He won't need it in SS heaven.

Molly relieves the lift operator's corpse of its weapons and ammunition. 'No need for them to worry about Heydrich's wrath now,' she says.

I pull the security passes from the Germans' necks and throw them to the two women.

Molly catches hers one-handed. Kitty's drops to the floor. She has her hand over her mouth, white-faced and shaking, rooted to the spot. 'Mein Gott . . .' she whispers.

Molly turns to me. 'That girl is a bloody liability,' she says.

Kitty's eyes widen further. She takes a step backwards.

'Molly . . .' I say.

'She's going to get us all killed.'

'I . . . I can play my part,' says Kitty.

'And what is it, exactly, your part? Screaming? Looking good in leather?'

I move between them. 'Molly, when we ambushed that Kübelwagen, Kitty did her bit by distracting the Brigadeführer. We wouldn't be here without her. She's twenty and a pacifist, for God's sake – you can't expect too much. Kitty, you've got to toughen up, and fast.'

Kitty gulps, nods and bends down to pick up the security pass at her feet. It trembles in her hand. 'Do you always leave a trail of dead bodies behind you?' she asks.

'It's not the first time,' I admit.

The lift doors slide closed with a thump.

I examine the floor indicator. It's marked in Roman numerals from one to ten. Ten underground levels suggest a huge complex. The Unterscharführer had mentioned level six, presumably where the officers' quarters were.

'We'll start at the bottom, level ten.'

'Going down,' says Molly, pressing the button. 'Next floor, Haberdashery.'

The lift drops silently towards the lower levels.

'Er . . . habi-what?' asks Kitty.

'Never mind,' says Molly. 'Just concentrate on not screaming. And get your boobs ready in case we need you to distract anyone else.'

Sharp deceleration announces our arrival at level ten. Kitty and I drag the dead bodies out of the lift. Molly scouts the end of the short corridor. Kitty murmurs something brief about God over the two corpses we've stashed behind some pallets. I jam the lift to slow any pursuit.

'Come and see,' says Molly, standing by the door she's just opened.

I walk over and stick my head round the corner. Most of the cavern is deep in shadow, but at the far side is another small door. High up on the wall is a protruding control gantry. An aircraft looms over me, picked out by the lights.

It's entirely circular, thicker in the centre and tapering towards the edges, like a pith helmet squashed down. The underside is almost flat, with a few bulges that look like weapons bays, and four spindly-looking legs. The whole thing is polished aluminium, shimmering in the surrounding lights. Apart from Luftwaffe crosses and serial numbers, it has no adornment.

'Is it an aeroplane?' asks Kitty. 'How can it fly with no wings?'

I look back at her. 'The whole body forms a wing, somehow. There've been rumours about it.'

Molly catches up with us. She scans the cavern, checking for guards. 'So much for our infallible Air Intelligence . . .' she says, studying the machine.

The top of the central section appears to be made of Perspex. That will be the cockpit. I walk towards the aircraft. 'Heydrich mentioned a Flugscheibe in his speech to the SS leaders last night.'

'Flugscheibe . . . flying disc,' says Kitty. 'That's a good description.'

Near one leg, a ladder ascends into the interior. I walk over and climb up. Inside, a small access shaft rises into the centre of the aircraft. Above, the lights of the cavern twinkle through the Perspex canopy.

We crowd into the cockpit. Molly and I sit in the pilots' seats with Kitty behind us. The controls look conventional.

'Is this Giant? A new type of aircraft? Even if it performs better than it looks, how will it make Germany unstoppable?' asks Kitty.

'Perhaps it'll be about intercepting the V-Force before it gets into nuclear-weapons range of the Reich,' suggests Molly.

Through the canopy, the aluminium body surrounding us sparkles under the cavern lights.

'Maybe it's part of the plan, but it's not the main part of Giant,' I say. 'Heydrich said Giant was "greater than the Flugscheiben".'

Molly looks over at me. 'Think on this: we're ten levels underground and there's no way out. What kind of aircraft is it that flies underground?'

22

Dark Power

I worship my master thrice-fold: first for the gift I have received, second for the gifts I will receive and third for his aid in my time of need.

Journal of an unknown SS scientist, p.498

Molly finds the door that leads to the heart of the complex.

We leave the cavern that houses the Flugscheibe and creep along the deserted corridors, searching for the secret of Giant. This level is so empty of humanity that I start to become suspicious. Is this some ruse of Heydrich's? Each time I open a door my mouth goes dry. I keep expecting SS assault rifles or, worse, a booby trap.

But as soon as Molly opens the final door, I know we've found it.

'Holy Mary, would you look at that, now?' she says.

The chamber itself is round, a hundred yards in diameter, and lined with ivory-coloured ceramic. Several doors lead off it. Heavy black rubber covers the floor. The whole area gives off a cloying, sweet smell undercut by a metallic taste in the back of the throat.

The device in the centre of the chamber is vast. It's a cylinder standing on one end, with a surface sheen like a thin coating of oil over lead. It seems to move, to pulse almost, with shadows playing across it. There are no markings, no protuberances, no signs of machinery, just a monumental metal edifice.

Ten storeys above us, the domed ceiling is a lattice of crystal. It refracts the sun's rays, throwing dazzling rainbows of colour across the ivory walls and the device itself. The cylinder rises all the way to the surface, stopping just short of the dome. As we move about the chamber, the sense of unreality is hard to shake until I realize what's causing it: a complete lack of echoes. The sound of our footsteps just seems to disappear, as if sucked into the gargantuan edifice before us.

A walkway leads out over the chasm surrounding the device to a platform close to its surface. On the platform is what looks like an altar. There are restraints built into the ceramic surface. Faint dark stains disfigure the altar, as if dried blood has been hosed off.

Kitty catches sight of the altar. Her hands go to her mouth.

'What is it?' Molly asks.

'Don't ask me,' I say, moving to the edge and peering downwards. 'But this is just part of it; I can't even see the bottom of the well it's sitting in.'

Instinct seems to pull me towards the device. The sheer wrongness of it seems to fill the air around me. At my side, Molly drops a bullet into the cavern below. A sense of dizziness and nausea builds. I stare down into the hellish darkness. We both stand gaping, mesmerized, straining for the distant ring of metal hitting the bottom of the chasm. The vertigo gets worse.

Nothing.

'God save us,' says Molly after a couple of minutes. 'How deep is it going?'

There's something just below the threshold of hearing, something like screaming. A faint draught plays across my neck. I shiver.

'I like this place,' says Kitty, trembling.

'It's . . . interesting,' I say.

Kitty whispers in German. 'The Fallen Souls were on Earth in those days. Seeing the Daughters of Men were fair, they took them for themselves.' She seems to be sleepwalking, wavering on the edge of the abyss.

Molly pulls her away and slaps her.

'Stand on your hind legs, for God's sake,' she hisses.

'Wh . . .' Kitty's hands go to her face. She blinks and glances around as if making out the chamber for the first time.

'We're needing to be out of here,' says Molly. 'This place is evil.'

Maybe that's why there's no one down here: it becomes unbearable. I force myself to turn away from the chasm. What appear to be over-sized thermos flasks are set at regular intervals around the wall. I move towards them. The flasks themselves are thick and heavy, made of lead. I reach over and twist the lid off one. The substance inside looks like mercury, although, as it catches the light, it flashes violet in colour.

'We call it Xerum 525,' says a voice behind me.

I spin round. The voice booms again, speaking German and, of course, using the loudspeakers. 'And who the hell are you sneaking around my laboratory?'

High up on the wall of the chamber is a glass-walled control room. A male figure in a lab coat stands at the window staring down at us. One of the most famous figures in Germany. One of the few men alive who deserve that too common appellation, genius.

'Professor Heisenberg.'

Heisenberg is not surprised to be recognized. 'Yes. And you are?'

'Heydrich didn't tell you about me?'

'The English assassin. Are you here to kill me?'

'No. Although, as you gave the Nazis the atomic bomb, you deserve it.'

'I will not apologize for helping to make my fatherland strong again. What was the alternative? To remain at the mercy of you British? My work had to be done, first the atomic bomb and now Giant. I make no apology.'

Heisenberg's rant is greeted by slow clapping. Heisenberg turns to the source, frowning.

'Well spoken, Herr Professor. I've often wondered if you were truly one of us. Now I know.'

I peer upwards, trying to identify this new threat.

At the control room window stands Reinhard Heydrich. He addresses me. 'Fine work with the dogs. Although finding a rifle was either incredible luck or you had help from somewhere. And I don't believe in luck.'

I hope the Mitzis' getaway plan is a good one. It will be; they're survivors.

'You should have known better than to think you could escape me,' says Heydrich.

'If I wanted to run away, I wouldn't even be here. I beat you earlier. It would have been easy to just disappear.'

'And face your Jewish paymasters? How grateful would they be for your failure?'

'For the last time: Reuven had nothing to do with this mission. It's personal.'

'Ah, yes, I suppose that makes sense. You had the chance to run away, but your Will to Power is strong. I said before that you could have been one of us. My men found an SS Brigadeführer in the woods. Shot in the back of the head from close range. Congratulations. A weaker man would call it murder, but I perceive you for what you are – one of the wolves. One of us.'

'You're the murderer,' yells Kitty.

Heydrich looks down at her. 'Ah yes, my gentle Katharina. It's been an exciting day for you, hasn't it, my dear? Thrown away like a soiled rag, hunted by dogs, saved by a handsome stranger. You are half in love with him already, are you not?'

'I hate you,' spits Kitty. 'I've always hated you. Having sex with you made me want to vomit.'

Heydrich smiles. 'I know,' he says. 'That is why I enjoyed it so much.'

Kitty's face crumples.

Heydrich turns his attention back to me. 'Weak like all her sex. Not like us. But how strong is your will, really? You have been tough so far, but are you a true wolf or just a sheep in wolf's clothing?'

The doors around the chamber start to open.

'Here is a little test for you.'

We run across the walkway and take cover behind the altar. Kitty kneels down. I drag her into shelter.

'How much ammunition have you got?' I ask Molly.

She places her spare magazines on the floor beside her. 'Enough to take dozens of them with me. If they try to charge over that walkway one at a time, they've got no chance.'

I stick my head up to assess the opposition, expecting to discover SS machine guns. Instead, standing motionless in each doorway are crowds of emaciated men and women wearing striped pyjamas. Their listless, hollow eyes stare at me almost without interest.

'Observe the Untermenschen: so pathetic, so frail. They do not deserve to live, do they, such wretched specimens? Nevertheless, I have promised them their freedom if they bring you to me in a state approximating life. Given that they are certain to die otherwise, they will try.'

'You're a bloody coward, Heydrich,' I shout. 'Come down and face me yourself.'

Heydrich's voice has a note of triumph. 'I am waiting here for you.

Dispose of these Untermenschen and then come after me. Your goal is to kill me, is it not? Nothing can interfere with the achievement of your mission.'

The chamber fills with shuffling prisoners.

'Can we not have a glorious last stand versus faceless SS troops?' asks Molly.

I glance over at her. She's shaking with anger.

'What do you want to do?' I ask her.

'What? What I want to do is kill the murdering bastard. But I'm not killing dozens of innocent non-combatants to get to him.'

Heydrich swaggers some more. 'What are you waiting for? Where is your will? Prove yourself a wolf. Show me how ruthless you are.'

'What about just barging through them?' I say. 'They can't be strong.'

'There're too many. How about Kitty distracting them? Is it not that she's here for?'

'I will try if you want me to,' says Kitty.

'Come on, come for me, or I will order them to charge,' says Heydrich.

Before I can stop her, Kitty is up and walking across the walkway towards the unfortunates crowding the chamber. She starts singing some hymn in German.

Molly puts her gun down, muttering. I wrestle with myself for another minute. Heydrich's correct: I could slaughter the poor bastards and go after him. The end justifies the means, right? If I don't kill the prisoners, my mission will be a failure. There isn't even any guarantee that Heydrich will let the shambling skeletons in the chamber go.

It's easy to be a hero. Easy when you don't have to look in the eyes of the innocents who are getting in your way.

Kitty reaches the nearest prisoners. Two take hold of her hands. The others crowd round her. Kitty kneels. The nearest prisoners follow her example, forming a circle in the middle of the crowd. There are hundreds of them.

Molly and I stand up. There's a low, human tone filling the vast, impersonal chamber.

The prisoners are singing.

From the control room, the device doesn't seem any smaller.

The control room itself is carved straight from the rock, but one side is glass and overlooks the main chamber. Controls, monitors and computers fill two other sides. The remaining side is rough granite covered with small target markers arranged in random positions. The prisoners deposit us at the back of the room then shuffle out under the guns of the guards. Other guards tie us to chairs, facing into the room. Heisenberg is still staring out of the window at his device.

Heydrich paces backwards and forwards, crowing. 'Now we discover who the wolf is. We distinguish who has the true Will to Power and who proves to have a hollow centre when tested.'

'You're insane, aren't you?' I say.

'Far from it. I am just not tied down by your petty morality: the weakness that means you have lost.'

'I'm not the only agent in the Service. Even if you kill me, more will be sent until you're destroyed.'

'No, you don't understand. It is too late for you and for your precious Service. Today I am going to use Giant to restart the war and gain final victory.'

Heisenberg turns round. 'Today?' he says, eyes wide.

'One weapon can't win a war,' I say. 'Especially one that doesn't look too mobile. However much damage this weapon causes, if you attack Britain, the V-Force will turn Germany into a radioactive desert. How's that victory?'

Heydrich's laughter has a peculiar, high-pitched quality. He turns to Heisenberg. 'Herr Professor?' he says.

Heisenberg nods. 'Herr Heydrich is correct. There is no possibility of retaliation. The machine harmonizes on an exact solution of a Lorentzian manifold of the general relativity field equations. It creates a causality violation from a non-compact initial surface.'

I stare at Heisenberg. I have no idea what he's talking about.

'He does not have the intellect to comprehend your master work, Herr Professor,' says Heydrich. 'Try him with the children's edition.'

Heisenberg's mouth turns down. 'Herr Heydrich, analogies are not correct physics. Quantum mechanics is not understandable using metaphor.'

'Just tell him the incorrect version, then. He is an assassin, not a theoretical physicist.'

Heisenberg sighs. 'Very well. Imagine you are in a room with two doors. The room itself is the present. You enter the room from the past and you leave it into the future. We do this continually. We move at a steady velocity through the rooms of the present. We leave behind the rooms of the past. We enter the rooms of the future. Do you understand?'

'I guess so,' I say.

'Yes. And if we move the walls of the room? Then what happens?'

'We bring the past or the future closer to the present?'

Heisenberg nods. 'Or further away, obviously. But, more than that, if you move the walls far enough, then the past becomes the present.'

'Time travel?'

'The correct term is a causality violation.'

Molly laughs and shakes her head. 'You can't be serious.'

Heisenberg raises an eyebrow. 'I am always serious. The perception of past, present and future as three distinct domains is a necessary human illusion. However, theory does not require it.'

'But you'd have to be able to move the walls,' I say.

'Yes. That is done by utilizing the frame-dragging effect of a massive, dense cylinder rotating at incredible speed. Such a cylinder is at the core of Giant.'

'Impossible,' Kitty says.

Heisenberg looks at us as if we're failing undergraduates. 'Your language is imprecise. This is not impossible, it is non-trivial. The problem of course is that, in order to create a causality violation from a non-compact initial surface, the average weak energy condition must be violated on the Cauchy horizon. I concede this is something I've yet to reach a satisfactory theoretical conclusion about.'

'But National Socialism provided the answer,' says Heydrich.

'To an extent this is true,' says Heisenberg. 'The scrolls from Ultima Thule gave us a viable option: Xerum 525.'

'Scrolls? Ultima Thule? This is absurd,' I say.

'Quite so,' replies Heisenberg. 'However, although Giant doesn't work in theory, it appears that it does work in practice.'

'You've used it?'

'Not myself.' Heisenberg shifts position. His gaze drops.

'Prisoners?' I say.

'There have been some experiments involving volunteers, yes.'

'Emaciated volunteers in stripy pyjamas, with coloured triangles on the breast? Dragged in kicking and screaming by the SS?'

'I don't concern myself with practicalities. Pure science is all I'm interested in.' Heisenberg half turns away.

'How many have you killed?' asks Kitty.

'A few hundred volunteers have participated,' says Heydrich. 'No one important, obviously.'

Heisenberg has developed an unexpected fascination with the list of figures on his printout.

'More dead concentration camp workers. You're evil as well as mad, then,' I say.

Heisenberg's face rises from the printout, scowling. 'You have no right to judge anyone, assassin.'

I turn my head towards Heydrich. 'But why risk it? What's the point? You're already winning. You have your Lebensraum. Germany is a superpower. You've achieved everything you could ever—'

Heydrich screams in my face, spittle flying from his mouth. 'This isn't how it's supposed to be! We're conquerors, not administrators! You British and your Mutually Assured Destruction, where does it leave us? Trapped! I must go back and finish the job.'

'Does Hitler know about this?'

'The Führer? The insane syphilitic corporal? He's an old woman. He's comatose three-quarters of the time, spends his conscious hours drooling over Martian colonization. Speer and Von Braun produce childish sketches and Lilliputian models topped with swastikas. Fantasies of gleaming towers of metal and spaceships in the void between planets—'

'More noble than further destruction.'

'Sheer insanity. Germany still has earthbound enemies to devote itself to. Maybe later, say the 1980s or 1990s perhaps, my successor will be in a position—'

'*Your* successor?'

'Yes, my successor. Professor Heisenberg here is going to send me back. There I will use my superior technology and foreknowledge to make sure that National Socialism triumphs, with myself as Führer.'

My laugh is derisive. 'You're insane. Rule the world? Time travel? Heisenberg has been duping you, feeding your megalomania.'

Heydrich contemplates me. A tiny hint of a smile creeps on to the corners of his mouth. 'I believe one more test is required to calibrate the apparatus?' he says to Heisenberg.

Heisenberg nods.

Heydrich turns back to me. 'We have sent back many volunteers already. They proceed along the closed time-like curve and then materialize, if that is the right word . . .'

He glances at Heisenberg, who shakes his head.

'No, of course, their present just becomes our past. Naturally, we cannot risk them getting loose and causing changes unhelpful to National Socialism. So we send the volunteers back before 1945 without any spatial displacement.' Heydrich strokes a hand across the rough granite. 'Of course, this complex was only excavated in 1946.'

'Their position in the rock strata enables us to calibrate the apparatus,' says Heisenberg.

Heydrich points to one of the target markers on the rock face. 'This test, for example, is the final calibration. The volunteer will appear . . . here.' He looks back to check with Heisenberg, who nods.

Heydrich smiles and gestures in the direction of Molly and Kitty. 'So, I am going to give you the choice: which of them shall we use in the test?'

I'm frozen in my chair.

'Who is it to be?' asks Heydrich. 'Which of your pathetic little saboteurs gets the thumbs down?'

How can I make a decision like that? Kitty is so young. Molly is my lover, but she's Service and she knows the risks. Neither of them deserves to die.

'I—'

'Hey, Jew boy,' shouts Molly.

Heydrich's head whips round. Molly – beaten, bruised Molly – sits there, body erect, staring at Heydrich and shouting. 'You're a quarter Jewish yourself, so you are.'

'Molly . . .' I plead, struggling against my restraints.

'You dare—' whispers Heydrich.

'Not so bloody Übermensch, despite the big talk, eh?' shouts Molly. 'Not with that Jewish grandfather you think no one knows about.'

'That one,' says Heydrich, pointing at Molly. 'Move! Now! That one!'

'And if I know about it, then how many other people do? You should have put yourself in one of those vans, saved us the trouble of killing you.'

'I'm the one who decides who's Jewish,' says Heydrich through gritted teeth.

The ropes holding me to the chair slice into my arms as I fight to loosen them.

A dozen guards drag Molly kicking and biting from the control room. The scrum appears downstairs in the main chamber, struggling forward and across the walkway. Molly fights the guards with everything she has, but it's hopeless. They lift Molly on to the altar and activate the restraints, first one arm, then the other. It takes three of them to manoeuvre each leg into position to be restrained. I struggle against the ropes, helpless. Kitty cries. I tip the chair I'm tied to over. It doesn't break.

'Pick him up,' says Heydrich, sneering.

With Molly restrained on the altar, the guards retreat and close the final door to the test chamber. Heydrich nods to Heisenberg who presses a red button, initiating a faint subterranean hum.

'Microphones. I want to hear her scream,' orders Heydrich.

But there's no screaming. No tears. No more struggle. Molly lies still, staring up at the control-room window.

'Molly,' I say.

She looks straight at me. The loudspeakers are working as well as the microphones.

'I love you,' she says. 'I'm an unrepentant sinner. I'm going to die and go to hell but last night meant everything to me.'

The hum becomes a drone. The lights flicker then steady, flicker again and go out. In the control room the only light is the faint blue glow cast by the device.

'I love you too, Molly,' I say, not knowing whether I mean it or not. Thinking maybe, maybe I do.

'How touching,' says Heydrich.

'You're a dead man, Heydrich,' I say, in a voice that could grate metal.

The device starts to turn.

'Thirty seconds,' says Heisenberg.

The device seems to ripple as it rotates and a slight translucency builds around it, expanding towards the platform. The mesmeric force it exerted in the chamber earlier is much stronger now, drawing me towards it. I grit my teeth.

'Can you feel it, the power of the universe pulsing through you?' asks Heydrich, who seems to be unaffected.

Kitty sways towards the device, held back only by her bonds. Two of the guards step towards the machine, their eyes shining with tears. Heydrich pulls out his Luger and shoots them both down. 'Weak,' he hisses.

'Fight it,' I say to Kitty.

'But it's beautiful,' says Kitty.

The dissonance builds to a climax. The beam touches the altar.

And I remember. Molly only has moments to live, but I can help her.

'Molly, when perfect contrition removes mortal sin, the sinner has no need for absolution. Don't be afraid. Love your God, repent your sins and you will go to heaven.'

'Ah, Christianity, the faith of the feeble-minded,' says Heydrich. 'I thought better of you.'

Molly looks up through her tears. She smiles.

'You'll have me in tears,' she says.

The beam engulfs her.

And then she's gone.

Just gone.

Part Three

Consequences

The strength of the Pack is the Wolf,
But the strength of the Wolf is the Pack.

Rudyard Kipling, *The Law of the Jungle*

23

Red Indians

The fools! Feverish work under their noses. My master drives me beyond sleep, beyond hope – beyond time itself perhaps. They will not use the mechanism for this anti-causality abomination! I have amended the mechanism. It WILL become a beacon, twinkling between the stars. Even Heisenberg suspects nothing.

Journal of an unknown SS scientist, p.504

Somehow, impossible as it seems, there's a calcified skeleton right where Heisenberg placed the target marker.

I turn my head away, fighting the hollowness inside me, trying to concentrate on pure rage. 'That woman was the bravest person I ever met,' I say. 'And the best agent.'

Kitty stares at the skeleton, sobbing. Her face is as pale as the ceramic tiles that line the test chamber.

'Would anyone else like to question my ancestry?' asks Heydrich.

There are no takers.

The room quivers as the device grinds to a standstill again. The sweet, metallic taste is strong in my throat. Beside me, Kitty retches up bile.

Heydrich turns back to Heisenberg. 'The mechanism is now ready for full-scale deployment?'

'Wasn't that enough for you?' I ask.

Heydrich sneers. 'Enough? Nothing like it – that was just one per cent of Giant's true power. You must have noticed the paratroopers waiting on the airfield above us? There's an entire SS-Fallschirmjäger division up there. At full intensity, Giant is powerful enough to send them all back in time. Our target will be the evening of 10 May 1941. We will have modern weaponry: missiles, atomic bombs, twenty Flugscheiben. The British armed forces will not be able to scratch us.'

The tenth of May, just before the peace treaty.

'Do you happen to know where Winston Churchill was on that date?' Heydrich asks.

'At his wartime residence, Ditchley House, watching a Marx Brothers film. A lost Heinkel He-111 jettisoned its bombs and, by a fluke, they levelled the house and killed him.'

'Still clinging to that threadbare legend? How touching. No, he was at Dungavel House, awaiting the arrival of Deputy Führer Hess. Accompanied by his puppet master, the degenerate Wall Street plutocrat Harriman . . . and Menzies, of course.'

Heydrich walks over to Molly's skeleton and touches it as if he's checking it's real. 'There was treachery that night,' he says over his shoulder. 'I told you that your precious Old Man was deep in. With all his upper-class clubland contacts do you really believe he wasn't?'

There's a dull pain building in my skull. It feels the way it does the morning after drinking a bottle of cheap Ukrainian vodka.

'Menzies fed Churchill the idea that Hess was coming to meet the Watching Committee. Together, they made plans to use Section 18B of the emergency regulations to take the whole cabal into preventative detention. Churchill, the man of action, wanted to be in at the kill – he was, but not the one he expected.'

Heisenberg interrupts, staring at Heydrich. 'I must make this clear one last time: I am not certain what will happen once the machine enters the cascade sequence.' His voice rises in pitch. 'The machine does not always respond as expected by theory.' He emphasizes his warning with sharp chopping motions of his right hand. 'Until I can model the effect mathematically, I cannot claim to be master of the machine. Furthermore, I will not be accountable for the success of any attempt to use the apparatus on—'

Heydrich cuts him off. 'The responsibility is not yours to take, Herr Professor, for that honour is mine. But advise me, call the odds: will we reach 1941?'

Heisenberg's shoulders slump. 'That much is certain. The empirical calibration is complete. But—'

Heydrich dismisses Heisenberg's prevarication with a gesture, and resumes taunting me.

'Churchill was never a fan of Menzies, you know. He judged him too traditional, too hidebound. There was nothing but retirement ahead of him as long as Churchill was Prime Minister. But if he conspired with the Watching Committee, he would gain the highest position in British Intelligence, quid pro quo.'

My temple throbs. I shift my neck to try to ease the pain.

Heydrich notices and smiles. 'It hurts, doesn't it? Hess told me they killed Churchill in the morning, just as the sun was coming up over the trees. He went down cursing them as traitors. Menzies gave him the *coup de grâce*—'

Kaltenbrunner bursts into the room, red-faced and panting.

'We have inbound hostiles on radar,' he shouts.

⊕

A single aircraft in the dark night sky.

The Vanquish is at its combat ceiling, eleven miles above sea level.

At that height, the horizon is a faint blue arc against the blackness of space. The outside temperature is minus seventy-six degrees Fahrenheit. Through the storm clouds far below, Gibson catches glimpses of sparkling German cities.

He keys the intercom. 'Captain to crew: status?'

Responses: Jammers active. Passive sensors functional. Navigation and Bombing System online. Weapon armed. Course good. Time to initial form-up point: five minutes.

They've only just crossed the German coast and they're five minutes to target at their current speed: Mach 2, one thousand three hundred miles an hour. They'll hit Wewelsburg before the Luftwaffe work out what's going on.

But here come the Ruhr defences. They're on a hair-trigger, so close to the coast. His aircraft is out of the range of anything with wings. The Luftwaffe fighters' operational ceiling is ten thousand feet lower than his. The only things that can threaten him are the Wasserfall III surface-to-air missiles.

The Air Electronics Officer's screen pulses with warnings. 'AEO to crew: enemy missiles are launching.'

Jamming prevents German early-warning radar from detecting the intruders, but the Luftwaffe still know something is penetrating their airspace. Even without radar, they can launch their missiles, using passive guidance. The missiles attempt to lock on to the source of the jamming itself.

'Captain to AEO: initiate countermeasures. Call the missile approach.'

It all comes down to chance.

⊕

'Calm down,' Heydrich snaps at Kaltenbrunner. 'And you'll damn well salute when you address a superior officer.'

Kaltenbrunner stutters to a halt, draws himself to his full height and salutes.

'Heil Hitler! Sir, there are hostile aircraft approaching.'

'Better. Now, what identity and number of hostile aircraft?'

'Unknown: there's heavy multi-point jamming. It appeared from the North Sea and is moving south. It will cover this area within minutes.'

'It's the British,' says Heydrich. 'Too late as usual. We need only secure the airfield for another few minutes while Giant transfers the assault force to 1941.' He turns his attention back to Heisenberg. 'Full power. Now.'

For the first time since I've met him, I think I see a genuine smile on Heydrich's face. He's enjoying this.

'Full power?' says Heisenberg. 'Are you sure? The cascade effect . . .'

'Ah, yes, the cascade effect.' Heydrich laughs like a goat. It's a chilling sound. 'This is true power, energy unimaginable except through the wonder of National Socialism. You imbeciles can take the knowledge of your utter failure to your graves. This is the kind of supremacy I will boast of in the new world.'

'I will take my place in the second Flugscheibe,' says Kaltenbrunner.

'I don't think so,' says Heydrich. His voice is the soft hiss of a cobra poised to strike.

'Wh . . .' Kaltenbrunner gasps, staring at his superior.

Heydrich's Luger is pointing at Kaltenbrunner's belly.

'Tell me, what happened to the assassination weapon Kaltenbrunner gave you?' Heydrich asks me.

'Molly found it and used it to escape.'

'It amused me whilst we sat at dinner last night to imagine you had the gun trained on me. I wondered then why you did not make the attempt. You do not lack the courage, I think. Unlike this louse.' He indicates Kaltenbrunner. 'Of course, there was no danger. As I say, there's nothing anyone can do to hurt me.'

'Even you aren't bulletproof, Heydrich,' says Kaltenbrunner.

Heydrich snorts. 'Oh, but I am . . . you see, I have a heart of stone.' His eyes are dead in their sockets.

'God damn you to hell,' shouts Kaltenbrunner, going for his gun.

And Heydrich lets him.

He stands there, gun in hand, smiling, as Kaltenbrunner empties a whole magazine at him. The bullets seem to ricochet off an invisible barrier a few inches from his body.

Kaltenbrunner, out of ammunition, stares at Heydrich, nonplussed.

'As I say, I have a heart of stone,' Heydrich says. He fires his own gun – two shots in quick succession.

Kaltenbrunner grunts. He collapses, staggering backwards under the impact. A guard catches him. Kaltenbrunner crumples into the arms of his captor, incapacitated. A second guard retrieves his gun and SS dagger.

Heydrich turns back to me. 'The leader of a pack of wolves must forever be proving himself the strongest, or else be torn apart. Unlike you, I am a true wolf. Earlier you proved your core of weakness. Now, I prove my strength.'

He turns on Kaltenbrunner, sneering. 'It is a shame, my dear colleague, that I needed you until so near to my hour of triumph. I would have enjoyed dismantling you. Watching you, bloody-faced, screaming and begging as I cauterized your bloody stumps with burning steel would have amused me. Now your end will be brief, but at least you will endure a few moments of pain and terror. Then Giant's cascade effect will wipe your third-class mind from existence.'

Kaltenbrunner raises a hand towards Heydrich, warding off evil. Heydrich turns to one of the guards.

'Leave a microphone open. I wish my guests to hear our departure.'

Heisenberg and the guards leave. Heydrich stays.

'Gloat a little more, why don't you,' I say.

'I wish I had time to do so,' says Heydrich. 'Regrettably . . .'

He turns and marches from the room.

Kaltenbrunner's face twists into a skull's grin.

'What the hell. I've had a good run. I played for the highest stakes and I lost. I never expected any clemency from the Blond Beast. It could have ended much worse for me.'

'Nobody lives for ever,' I say.

'I, for one, would have been perfectly happy to live for ever in this world. Meddling with forces even Heisenberg doesn't understand could bring disaster to all humanity.'

'Untie me,' I say. 'I'll stop him somehow.'

Kaltenbrunner shakes his head, shuddering with agony. 'I'm going to spend my last moments casting a curse on the Butcher.' There are tears in his eyes. 'I've never been able to bear pain, Number Fifteen. Maybe that was why I was so good at inflicting it.'

'There must be some way to sabotage the device,' I say.

Kaltenbrunner quivers, his face grey, the blood draining away. 'The troop transports are already airborne. Giant's feedback loop has started. As it spins up, the beam will get bigger and bigger until it extends above the central core. All the transports have to do is fly into the beam. There's no way to prevent the cascade effect from occurring now.'

I try to pull my arms through the ropes. The restraints just seem to get tighter.

'And what happens when this cascade effect starts?'

'Nobody lives for ever, Number Fifteen.'

Kitty interrupts my profanities. 'What are those?' she says, looking at the bank of monitors.

I examine them. Most show the interior of Giant. Some show the armada of Luftwaffe transports forming up over the airfield. The picture on the last monitor flickers and shifts, showing blue sky and forests. Silhouetted against the sky is a flock of dark spots. They move towards the camera, growing, resolving themselves into shapes.

'Whose are they?' asks Kaltenbrunner.

The aircraft are unmarked. Pure black.

'Oh, Reuven, you magnificent bastard,' I say.

Approaching from the west are at least a dozen Fairey Rotodynes.

⊕

The scream of the jet rotors is deafening.

The lead Rotodyne's engines are at full emergency power. Inside, the cargo nets and equipment vibrate in sympathy with the over-strained engines.

Elliott checks his weapon for the last time. Reuven stands over him, clinging to a grab handle. Around them, a platoon of Israeli volunteer commandos in Russian uniforms fidget with their Kalashnikovs and RPG-2 grenade launchers.

'This Russian cover is wafer thin,' shouts Elliott.

Reuven isn't the most military of men, even with his face streaked in sooty camouflage. He looks like a refugee from a catastrophic barbecue party. 'Best I could do at short notice,' he yells back. 'And if you hadn't noticed, we're about to commit suicide in a futile assault on the headquarters of the SS. Under the circumstances, cover is not my main concern, so be a good chap and shut the hell up, eh?'

'Tigerlily isn't about rescuing a couple of traitors. We're going in there to shut Giant down before the Nazis use it and the whole world goes to hell.'

'You have your orders and I have mine. SHAI is an independent force that operates in the interests of the Jewish people. We're going to save your traitors, if we can.'

'You'll follow orders or—'

Reuven's bodyguards swing the barrels of their assault rifles to cover Elliott.

'Don't threaten me, you clown. I *am* following orders. Leo ordered me to suppress Giant's defences and get you into the complex. You follow your orders and I'll follow mine.'

Reuven stomps forward towards the cockpit.

Tracer sweeps the sky around the aircraft.

The squat Rotodynes are small targets, head on. Their pilots keep jinking, using every scrap of cover as they barrel in towards the German airfield. In theory, the flak-gunner's radar can't lock on to targets at such low altitudes. In theory, they can't predict the trajectories of such manoeuvrable aircraft.

But someone has forgotten to tell the Germans that. Long beads of tracer reach out to the assaulting aircraft, blind fingers stroking the air.

Reuven hunches behind the armoured pilot's seat. 'Warm reception?'

'You could say that,' the pilot grunts, heaving at the controls. The Rotodyne ducks under an oncoming missile.

To the side of Reuven's aircraft, a German rocket hits one of the other Rotodynes. Thrown off by centrifugal forces, the thrusters at the tips of the rotors spiral away into the evening sky.

'Can't control the aircraft, going in hard.' The pilot sounds as if he's describing a slight inconvenience, not his own death. The Rotodyne slams into the ground.

'Alpha six . . .'

The anti-aircraft shells find the cockpit of a second Rotodyne and rip it apart. The autogyro hits the ground, spinning end over end like a huge Catherine wheel.

'That's enough,' says Reuven. 'We're within weapons range. Open fire.'

The ten remaining Rotodynes discharge a ripple of unguided rockets towards their tormentors. The smoke trails stretch ahead of the oncoming aircraft.

Reuven counts down. 'Three . . . two . . . one . . .'

The rockets turn the airfield into an inferno, explosions ripping into its defences.

Seconds away from the airfield, the Rotodynes flare left and right. They float over the perimeter wire, door gunners blasting the defenders with autocannon shells. The first Rotodyne over the wire takes automatic-weapons fire from several directions. Hit hard, it pitches forward and beaches itself almost outside the entrance to Giant.

The Israeli commandos leap out of the stricken aircraft, already firing.

⊕

The subterranean bass note as Giant starts to spin again is almost ear-shattering.

The translucency that had built about the device during Molly's sacrifice is bigger now. It twists into a huge pillar of impossibility that fills the chamber.

Heydrich's voice echoes across the open microphone. 'This is it then – goodbye. It has been a good hunt, but now the sport is over and the real work must begin. If it is any consolation to you, I don't think you'd want to live in the world I am—'

And then, like Molly, he's gone.

The figure that bursts through the door of the control room is covered in dirt and explosive residue. I recognize him from his huge smile alone.

'Reuven!' I shout, over the sound of assault-weapons fire.

'You didn't think I'd let you have all the fun on your own, did you?' Reuven shouts back.

'What took you so long?'

'The flight was murder,' says Reuven, slashing at my restraints with an impressive-looking knife.

I leap to my feet and we embrace. Behind us, Kaltenbrunner coughs. 'It isn't going to make any difference, you know. Heydrich is already gone. Giant is over the feedback threshold. It's creating a cascade of unimaginable power, a runaway singularity. Heisenberg estimated the explosion will be the largest seen on earth since Krakatoa . . . maybe even earlier.'

Reuven turns towards Kaltenbrunner and does a double-take. 'Can it be?' he says.

'Reuven Shiloah,' says Kaltenbrunner. 'I never thought I'd see the day.'

'Is there any reason why I shouldn't kill this monster right now?' Reuven asks me.

'You'll get blood on the monitors,' I say.

'Do not repay evil with evil,' says Kitty.

Reuven smiles at Kitty. 'I'm Jewish,' he says. 'We don't have that bit, we have an eye for an eye.'

'Go ahead,' says Kaltenbrunner. 'You'll be doing me a favour.'

Reuven lifts his automatic towards Kaltenbrunner. 'In the name of the Jewish people, I carry out this sentence of death,' he says. 'Do you have any last words?'

Pink-flecked bubbles ooze from Kaltenbrunner's mouth. 'I've done my duty. My conscience is clear. Long live Germ—'

Reuven shoots him in the head.

Blood splashes across the monitors.

Giant's power-output monitor reaches 75 per cent, with no sign of slowing.

Reuven wipes blood off the control room's displays wih his sleeve. 'Is this real?' he asks over his shoulder, still staring at the instruments. 'Perhaps it has done nothing but disintegrate Heydrich and saved you a job?'

'Molly was sent backwards. You can see her skeleton in the rock.'

Kitty nods. 'It's true. I saw it happen. One minute she was strapped to the altar out there in the chamber, and that wall was just rock. The next she was . . . she was . . .' She points at Molly's skeleton.

Reuven breaks off from examining the read-outs from Giant to look at Kitty.

'Why is it that you get to play with all the pretty young things,' he asks me, 'while I spend my time trying to pull your chestnuts out of the fire?'

'We aren't . . .' says Kitty.

'That's what they all—'

'Reuven, we haven't got time to waste.'

Reuven grins. 'God help us all. You'd better talk to Leo.'

⊕

The missiles are now everywhere, dozens of the buggers.

Gibson chose to be first over Wewelsburg in order to trigger the defences. Now, Wewelsburg's defenders are firing the whole stock at him. The good news is, the other crews should get a clear run to the target.

Most of the missiles buy the Vanquish's countermeasures. Thinking they're in range when they're still thousands of feet too low, they explode below them like fireworks. The Air Electronics Officer calls any that approach too close, and Gibson manoeuvres the aircraft to swing around them.

So far, it's working; rockets will never match manned aircraft. There's a lull as the launchers reload. Now's the rest of the squadron's chance to get in there and drop their bombs.

Gibson pulls the Vanquish into a lazy turn, circling around for another pass. He prays for confirmation that the Grand Slams have done the job, so they can get the hell out. He has plans for Patricia when he gets back, and would hate them to be spoilt by a nuclear war.

They reach the run-in point again, and the Air Electronics Officer calls the impossible: 'AEO to captain: enemy aircraft three o'clock level.'

'Captain to AEO: what? Are you sure?'

The voice on the intercom is panic-stricken.

'What the hell? It's too big to be a missile and it's climbing too fast to be a fighter. It's above us. My God, it's accelerating. That's impossible. It's— Break right! Break right!'

⊕

The radio link to London is already live when I pick up the handset. Leo is shouting something in the background.

'Leo?' I say.

There's a momentary silence, then a clatter as Leo picks the microphone up. 'Aren't you dead yet?' he says. 'Where's Elliott?'

'Leo, there's no time for recriminations. I'm here with Reuven at

Giant. You're too late. Giant has been activated and Heydrich has already gone back.'

I visualize the slump in Leo's features.

'Bloody hell, it doesn't actually work, does it—'

Leo's words are rendered inaudible by a string of explosions. Dust rains down from the roof of the cavern.

'Well, there's the RAF, right on time as usual,' says Reuven.

'We're dropping bombs on our own men?'

Reuven has a gleam in his eyes. 'Not for the first time.'

'Well, they bloody well missed, didn't they? We're still here.'

'They haven't gone off yet. Those explosions were just the penetrators. They're on delayed action fuses. I was supposed to get in and . . .'

'Rescue me?'

'. . . snatch Heisenberg. Your being here is just a happy coincidence.'

'Heisenberg's gone with the rest of them.'

Reuven points at the displays. 'Perhaps not. See this status monitor: cavern six. It's marked "Heisenberg" and the aircraft hasn't taken off yet. There's still a chance.'

'How much time have we got?'

'Minutes.'

I turn back to the radio. 'Leo, did you get that? There's only one option. I'm going to have to go back and stop him.'

'How?'

'I don't bloody well know! One of the Flugscheiben hasn't left yet. I'll fly it into the beam. After that, God knows – I'll improvise. Maybe Giant will take us back. Maybe I'll find Heydrich and kill him before he does too much damage. Or maybe we'll all become Nazi slaves together. Anyway, even if I fail, I don't suppose any of us will know anything about it.'

'If you go through that beam you won't be able to come back.'

'I told you I was going to kill Heydrich. I keep my promises.'

'I . . .' Leo hesitates.

'What?'

'Good luck.'

Running.

Down the stairs.

Running.

Trying to resist the siren call of the Giant apparatus. Dragging Kitty behind me, with her eyes shut and her hands over her ears. The world reverberating as if Giant is drilling into the centre of the Earth.

Running.

Endless corridors full of Israeli paratroopers and dead SS guards. I pick up a Sturmgewehr, a pistol and some magazines as I run.

Into the last remaining Flugscheibe's lair.

And it hasn't gone. Whining, it flutters into the air, skitters sideways and thumps back down again. Engine trouble. Giant's beam fills the top third of the cavern, and it's dropping lower. The aircraft hops half of the way towards it and crashes down to the ground again.

'Three minutes to full power,' shouts Reuven's voice from the walkie-talkie in my hand.

The SS troops are making a last stand behind a barricade, trying to protect the Flugscheibe. Followed by Kitty, I duck behind a pillar near the entrance. The bullets whistle over our heads. I take a quick glance round the side of the rock. Elliott is exchanging fire with the SS troops from behind another pillar inside the cavern. He turns and spots me.

'Bloody bad penny, aren't you?' he shouts.

'No time to argue. I need that plane. Leo's orders.'

Elliott rolls away from the pillar. SS bullets tear the ground around him. He slides into the cover of a diesel generator in one corner of the cavern.

'I'm not your handmaid,' he shouts. 'My orders are to destroy Giant and kill Heisenberg, to prevent its being rebuilt any time soon. Heisenberg is inside that Flugscheibe. I'm going in after him. You aren't part of the plan.'

'Look,' whispers Kitty, pointing at the body of an Israeli commando lying in the doorway of the cavern. He has three Russian-style smoke grenades on the bandolier across his chest. I nod to her, and she stretches her arm out towards the body. A shot punches into the ground inches from her hand.

I try to reason with Elliott. 'Heydrich's already back in 1941. I've got to go after him and stop him before he changes everything.'

'My orders are to secure and destroy this so-called time machine—'

'I just spoke to Leo. Your orders have changed. You're to help me follow Heydrich back.'

'My orders are to kill you, not bloody well help you.'

'You pig-headed idiot.'

'Have you ever looked in a mirror?'

'Two minutes,' shouts Reuven on the walkie-talkie. 'Go!'

Kitty tugs at the Israeli commando's feet, and he slides towards her. Bullets thump into the corpse. She grimaces at the blood splattering over her, but she keeps pulling.

'For pity's sake, Elliott, neither of us can do this on our own.'

I look up. Giant's beam fills half of the cavern. Bullets clang off the generator Elliott is hiding behind. It starts smoking.

'Push that generator towards the Flugscheibe,' I shout. 'Use it for cover. I'll shoot the bastards while you close with them. We can argue about the rest later.' I pull the tabs on the smoke grenades and roll them towards the Flugscheibe.

Elliott looks at me. He smiles. 'You ex-SOE types are always the gamblers.'

'Fuck it,' I say. 'We're on the same side in the end.'

Elliott gets his shoulder behind the generator and starts heaving. I open fire with the Sturmgewehr.

The burning generator picks up momentum, until Elliott is running behind it, bent double. The SS fire at the closing threat, giving me the opportunity to aim at them. I shoot them through the smoke, one by one.

Elliott abandons the out-of-control generator and sprints forward. A bullet hits him in the arm. He stumbles but keeps running, firing at the last SS trooper. The generator hits the barricade and explodes, spraying burning diesel across both of them. Elliott goes down on fire, rolling to smother the flames.

I start running towards the aircraft. Behind me, more Israeli commandos charge through the smoke and into the cavern.

'One minute,' screams the walkie-talkie.

⊕

Gibson hauls on the controls, rolling and diving the Vanquish in a tight corkscrew. He glimpses something disc-shaped shoot past, against the blur of stars. Jesus, what is it?

There's an explosion behind and to port. He levels up again, searching the dark sky. Nothing.

He thumbs the intercom. 'Captain to AEO: where's that enemy fighter?'

'AEO to captain: enemy aircraft six o'clock high. Launching decoys.'

Dead ahead, Gibson sees the most astonishing thing he's ever seen in his life. Rising over Wewelsburg is a biblical pillar of fire.

'AEO to captain: he's got a lock. He's firing missiles.'

The sparkling shaft of violet light stretching above Wewelsburg expands, brightens and starts to pulse. Each pulse seems brighter and lasts longer than the previous one. The beam builds up in ferocity, each pulse forcing itself further and further into the atmosphere. The peak stretches heavenwards, reaching higher than Gibson's aircraft, and onward, up into the stratosphere. Gibson rolls the aircraft into a steep turn, trying to avoid the fast-widening inferno in front of him. All he can see now is indigo fire.

'Oh, Jesus, God, no,' says the co-pilot.

The Vanquish and its crew disappear into the beam.

⊕

I heave the dead pilot's body out of his seat and drop into it.

Through the window, I see Elliott leading Heisenberg away. The scientist studies the beam that now fills almost the entire cavern. From this distance, I can't tell if he's laughing or crying.

I check the controls: the engines are already idling. I put one hand on the throttles and hold the control column with the other. It's going to be close.

Beside me, Kitty grabs the co-pilot's position. 'I don't want to die,' she says.

'Thirty seconds,' says the walkie-talkie.

I push the throttles forward, as far as they'll go. The Flugscheibe is shaking apart, the engines screaming for release. I pull the control column backwards into the pit of my stomach.

'Twenty seconds.'

'Buckle up,' I say. 'This is going to be one hell of a ride.'

The Flugscheibe lurches upwards, towards the beam.

24

Double or Quits

What the lesser races fail to discern is their fatal position in the cosmic hierarchy. Their weakness is a drag on the Aryan, a danger that must be eliminated before we can reconnect with the Hyperborean. Good, evil, morality: these are irrelevant. Only the constant drumbeat necessity of survival matters, the desperate call to the father race: rescue us!

Journal of an unknown SS scientist, p.508

We fall into the vortex.

For all its power, Giant has only created a tiny perturbation in the vast energy balance of the universe. Its effect is less than a single snowflake dropping on Mount Everest. But that snowflake, targeted with precision, hits another. The twin flakes slide, collecting others. The snowball grows.

And grows.

And grows.

That single perturbation turns into a massive avalanche of temporal anomaly. Neither Kitty nor I witness the phenomenon. Both of us black out as the fabric of reality tears itself apart in the grip of unimaginable energies. But, even unconscious, we surf the crest of the avalanche. It rips through space-time into the fundamental structure of the universe, into time, into causality itself.

Into the past.

⊕

White.

Whiter than snow. A complete whiteout. A bright white that penetrates my skull. Sledgehammers pound deep into my brain.

'Pretty Boy, for God's sake, get your finger out of your arse.'

There's a faint outline of a figure amid the whiteness. Someone I recognize, looming over me. He's slapping my face. Reg, the strongest, most intrepid man I ever knew, is bending over me, eyeball to eyeball, shouting obscenities at me.

'But you're dead . . .' I object.

'Do I look as if I'm dead, you useless baggage?'

'Where am I?'

'Where the hell do you think you are? Do I have to solve all your problems for you?'

Behind Reg, two more figures wearing white snow camouflage materialize. Alex and Erling. Alex smiles, eyes tense. Erling frets.

'Your brain is short of oxygen,' observes Erling.

'If you don't wake up, you're going to die,' adds Alex. 'Nothing can save you except pure will power.'

'Nothing,' agrees Erling.

'You need focus, complete focus,' Alex urges.

'You dozy bloody dipstick,' shouts Reg. 'This is no time to be sleeping.'

I grope towards consciousness again.

⊕

I raise an eyelid.

All the alarms are going off. The only light comes from the

forward edge of the aircraft, which is glowing cherry red. Something deep in the hull is groaning. Rivets pop in the bulkhead behind me.

The skyline is invisible. The ground in front is rotating. I'm pressed forward against my harness. The Flugscheibe is in a steep spin. I scan the instruments. The artificial horizon is bouncing like a top.

Spin recovery, spin recovery. I have to cut the power, but my hands can't move towards the throttle because of the centrifugal force. I kick the rudder bar in the opposite direction to the spin and nudge the control column forward. The Flugscheibe responds with a slow reduction in the pressure on my chest. I reach for the throttle and reduce power. The instruments stop spinning and the horizon reappears in a more logical place. The alarms silence themselves.

My eyesight clears. In front of us is the marble curve of the Earth and its blue atmospheric halo. Above is pure black. I check the altimeter for confirmation. It claims the aircraft is fifty kilometres high, on the boundary of space.

In the co-pilot's seat, Kitty whimpers. Her head lurches and her eyes open. She glances about her, mouth gaping. A groan escapes her lips.

'We . . . we aren't dead?' she says, focusing through the canopy at the horizon.

'Not yet,' I say.

A shooting star flies across the heavens, burning like the fury of God. Another one, further away, and then two more shoot past to starboard. Either we're witnessing a shower of meteors, or something has gone wrong with the temporal displacement. As Heisenberg predicted, we've made it to 1941, but he did admit he wasn't the master of his machine. Not all of the time travellers have been as fortunate as us. Most of them are burning up as they plummet back to earth.

'Can we get down again?' asks Kitty.

'We're about to find out. Try the radio.'

Kitty frowns at the switches in front of her, flicks a couple of them and finds multiple screaming voices and what sounds like choking.

Our aircraft is one of the lucky ones, high but not outside the atmosphere. The Flugscheiben below seem to be coping, falling in a semi-controlled manner towards Earth. The Junkers, conventional aircraft, have been converted into bombs, their wings sheared off by the forces of the transit.

The screams end one by one as the Junkers burn up. Finally, there's only a single voice on the radio, shouting not from terror but in exultation.

'Look out, below! Get ready, you scum – you useless, hopeless failures! This world is mine! Bow down to me, you lowly whores! This Beast will reign supreme!'

It's Heydrich.

⊕

The headquarters of Thirteen Group, at RAF Kenton near Newcastle upon Tyne, is having a quiet evening.

The sector controller, responsible for air defence from Yorkshire to the Shetland Isles, stirs his cocoa, frowning. His daughter has whooping cough and went into hospital three days ago. The prognosis is not good.

A small hostile force had come in earlier. It looked like a nuisance raid of half a dozen aircraft and was designated Raid X42, X standing for unknown contact. Most of the raiders had turned back and the remainder had been redesignated Raid 42J. The Observer Corps had reported that only a solitary German aircraft had made landfall, near Alnwick at 22.00, heading west. The sector controller had scrambled three Spitfires out of RAF Acklington, but they'd been unable to intercept the intruder.

He decides that, as soon as his duty is over, he'll get the bus to the hospital. He can sleep in the corridor. He touches the lucky rabbit foot in his pocket. Don't give up hope. Miracles happen.

And then the Chain Home radar goes crazy. Dozens of fleeting contacts light up the radar screens. Each one only lasts a few moments, almost like huge metallic meteorites tumbling in from space. It must be a glitch in the system. He makes a note for the maintenance team.

The glitch stabilizes and a steady signal appears: five large aircraft in formation, trailed by two larger but slower aircraft and a ghost signal. And all are moving at high speed straight for Glasgow. An unidentified raid, out of nowhere. The controller does the only thing he can do, and designates it Raid X43.

There's something else wrong with the raid – it's moving too fast for any known German aircraft, even fighters. Still, they can try a head-on interception, although the closing speed will mean any attack will be over in seconds. He reaches for the telephone to the best positioned airfield: RAF Ayr.

'This is the sector controller. Raid incoming; scramble.'

⊕

Our Flugscheibe plunges through the stratosphere.

'Giant One. Giant One. Form on me. Navigation lights on. All aircraft formate with the leader.'

Below us, red and green lights twinkle from the Flugscheiben. I count four. Well below the flying discs, the lights of two blessed Junkers JU-590 transports appear.

I set course to intercept the other Flugscheiben. Mine starts to respond better to the controls in the thicker air. I try a few experimental banks and turns. The aircraft is precise, turns are tight and the speed is phenomenal.

'Kitty, I need that radar set working.' I point at the display in front of her. The screen is a mass of signals.

She stares at it. 'I'll try,' she says.

I scan the cockpit again. The Flugscheibe must have some sort of armament. There's a trigger on the flying column. I give it a gentle squeeze. Below, there's a cough and a tracer bullet shoots forward. There's only one thing to do – attack the other Flugscheiben. I'll have the advantage of surprise, but the odds are still four to one.

I ease the Flugscheibe into position behind Heydrich's formation. I haven't turned our navigation lights on and they won't be expecting an attack from behind, as no RAF fighter is quick enough. I turn to Kitty. She's tinkering with the radar, fingers hovering over the switches.

'Kitty, what is this insistence of Heydrich's that nobody can harm him?'

'A bluff?'

'He just stood there and let Kaltenbrunner shoot him. I've never seen anyone so calm. He wasn't bluffing. He's bulletproof.' I glance at the controls Kitty is experimenting with. The German labelling is cryptic, but she seems to have found the electronic warfare systems amongst the forest of switches.

Kitty presses a button next to the radar screen. It flashes and then dissolves into static again.

'He's always saying he has a heart of stone,' she says. 'Maybe he does.'

'When I tried to hit him in Wewelsburg, I blacked out with my first jab. An electric shock might have that effect.'

Kitty bangs the radar screen with her fist and it clears. She catches my eye and smiles. 'So, you think he's unbeatable? How are we going to stop him, then?'

'Nobody's invulnerable. We just have to find what his vulnerability is.'

Through the canopy, the winking lights of Heydrich's aircraft mock us.

A flight of Beaufighters out of RAF Ayr races to engage the incomng ghost raid. The squadron leader briefs his men in the air. In the back of the night fighters, the radar operators struggle with their Mk IV Airborne Intercept sets.

'Lads, we're only going to get one shot at this. The hostiles are much too fast for us. We'll go in head to head, try to break up the formation. A quick burst from maximum range just to unsettle them, and then close until you're risking collision. The boffins need one of these beasts to take apart, so let's give them one. After that, they'll be all over us. Break off, hit the deck and head back to the airfield. The next wave might be able to pick off a straggler.'

An unknown voice interrupts the acknowledgements.

'What the hell is going on? We were attacked by some kind of flying saucer. There was a beam of light. I blacked out, and when I came to again we were about to fly into a mountain. The Navigation and Bombing System insisted we were still over Wewelsburg, but now it's unserviceable. And my navigator has a star fix that says we're eight hundred miles off course, and somewhere over Scotland!'

⊕

Kitty spots the approaching Beaufighters as soon as the Flugscheibe's radar gives a clear picture. Heydrich's men must have detected them, too, because the Flugscheiben dowse their navigation lights, fading like ghosts into the moonlight.

I can use this distraction to increase my chances. If I can bag one of the Flugscheiben before Heydrich catches on, the odds will be more in my favour. The remaining Junkers are secondary targets. The RAF will be able to deal with them.

'Hang on,' I say to Kitty. 'I'm going to have to throw the plane around a bit. If any of those displays light up, just shout.'

The nearest Flugscheibe swims into view. I peer through the head-up display. The fluorescent circle of the targeting device is full: point-blank range.

My finger tenses on the trigger.

⊕

A lone Messerschmitt Bf-110 flies into the setting sun.

It bears works number 3869, and radio call sign VJ+OQ, the designation of Rudolph Hess's personal aircraft.

The trip from Augsburg has taken almost five hours now and Hess is exhausted. It's over two hours since Heydrich and his squadron of cronies peeled off, after escorting him across the North Sea. Now Hess has to complete the critical phase of the flight alone.

He's somewhere over the lowlands of Scotland, heading for his destination, Dungavel House. There, he will make the rendezvous with the Watching Committee, and thrash out the details of the peace plan. He tries to remain calm. What a coup it will be: peace with Germany's natural allies, the British Empire. With this unnecessary war over, the full might of the Wehrmacht will be available to throw against the Bolsheviks. It will be a cataclysmic final reckoning for the Untermenschen.

They'll be in Moscow by Christmas.

But it's getting darker. Landmarks he thought he'd be able to pick out with ease are getting harder to spot. In the distance, the setting sun glints off the Irish Sea. His fall-back option is a run for the neutrality of Éire.

But that's unthinkable. He has to find Dungavel – for the

Führer, for the National Socialist German Workers' Party, for his fatherland.

⊕

'Tally ho!' the flight lieutenant shouts, spotting the flying discs straight ahead and a little below, approaching at impossible speed.

The four Beaufighters come on as close-spaced as they dare, to maximize the effect of their autocannon. The pilots catch glimpses of silver in the moonlight, and aim as best they can. Before he's in range to open fire, something hits the flight lieutenant's port-side engine and explodes. The Germans must have some new kind of deadly accurate night-fighting weapon. The flight lieutenant pulls full rudder to try to stay on target and keeps his thumb down on the trigger.

The other pilots keep firing even as the new weapons explode around them. One Beaufighter loses a wing and tumbles out of formation. The remainder of the flight hold their course.

The Beaufighters spit cannon-fire defiance at the superior German aircraft.

As the Beaufighters open fire, so do I.

The Flugscheibe under my guns disintegrates. A tracer round finds the fuel tank and the aircraft explodes. Three burning Beaufighters plough into the German formation. By bad luck or suicidal bravery, one of the Beaufighters rams into a Flugscheibe. An incandescent fireball bursts and splits into two tumbling cinders, like spent rockets. The two remaining Flugscheiben bank away. I follow one of them, pulling round, trying to lead the target. It's a tricky shot.

A Beaufighter in flames flashes beneath me.

Tongues of tracer bullets lick out from my cannons and intersect with the cockpit of the second Flugscheibe. The aircraft stops turning and flies straight and level for a few seconds. Smashed Perspex trails from the cockpit and oil darkens the flying surfaces. It slants away towards the ground, flames licking behind it.

'What the hell?' comes Heydrich's voice.

I flick the 'transmit' switch.

'You think you can get away from me, Heydrich?' I say.

'You!' he hisses.

'I'm afraid Professor Heisenberg won't be joining you,' I say, twisting from side to side in search of Heydrich's aircraft. Where is the bastard?

Autocannon fire rakes across my aircraft. I jam the plane into a corkscrew turn, G-force pressing me down into my seat. My vision goes hazy as blood drains away from my brain. Kitty's head drops to her chest and her eyes close.

I punch out of the corkscrew, catching a glimpse of moonlight sparkling on silver. It's Heydrich's aircraft, overshooting. He banks into a right-hand turn. I pull my craft into a half-loop to gain height and roll out at the top.

Kitty opens her eyes, blinks, lifts her head and turns to look out of the canopy.

'There's some kind of fluid bubbling out on this side of the plane.'

'Forget the damage. Just concentrate on where Heydrich's aircraft is.'

She peers at the radar. 'He's below and to the right,' she says.

I bank and bring the Flugscheibe's nose down until I pick out Heydrich's aircraft again against the dark mountains below. I have the advantage of height, but he's brought his machine round and is climbing to meet me. He's going to try for a head-on pass, counting on his superior shooting ability at high closing speed.

'You're a hard man to kill, but I have the advantage now. You forget perhaps that I'm a trained fighter pilot?' Heydrich is panting with exertion. 'I doubt you realize the capabilities of these aircraft. For example, this?'

A warning tone sounds in the cockpit of our aircraft.

Kitty stares at the display. 'It says "Missile Launch", she says.

'Flares!' I shout, pushing the throttles to emergency power and the stick back to climb further.

'What?' says Kitty. 'Where?'

I swear. 'Is there a button that says "Flares"?'

Kitty runs panicky fingers across the switches. 'I . . . I . . . There's one that says "IR Flares", is that it?'

'Hit it.'

The flare lights the sky behind us. The time until impact winds down. The angle for a missile shot is wrong. Head-on, the missile's seeker won't be able to lock on to the heat from the engines. A fast climb should take us out of its trajectory. Kitty presses the flare button again, and another magnesium blaze sparks beneath us. The warning tone continues to sound.

Heydrich's missile explodes, lashing the Flugscheibe's belly. A long, slow shake rattles through the aircraft. Alarms go off. I level out, my eyes scanning the instruments.

We're still flying.

Kitty twists in her seat, staring outside. 'We have a fire on the right-hand side,' she says, with a quiver in her voice.

'So, apart from the leaking fluid, and being on fire, everything is fine, right?'

'Well, that, and the fact that we have just travelled through time,' says Kitty. 'And that Heydrich is winning, and if Heydrich wins, all we hold dear will be destroyed.'

The secret of comedy is timing.

Flames lick across the flying surfaces, their orange glow lighting up the cockpit.

'He's looping round to finish us off,' Kitty says, staring at the radar screen.

The controls are sluggish in my hands. 'I'm going to play dead,' I say. 'Tell me when he's right behind us.' Desperately, I seek the arming switch for my own missiles.

'Oh, God, no,' says Kitty, staring at the radar set as if mesmerized. 'He's coming round . . . He's coming round . . .'

'Call the distance off,' I shout, flicking switches.

'Three hundred . . . two hundred . . . one hundred. . . he's on top of you!' Kitty shrieks.

The Flugscheibe shudders under the impact of the first of Heydrich's cannon shells. I pull the lever to my left. The airbrakes deploy.

It's as if the Flugscheibe runs into a wall.

Heydrich, with no time to react, nearly slams into the back of us. His Flugscheibe shoots over so close that the heat from its engines scorches our canopy. Heydrich pulls his machine into a loop, climbing fast. The drastic reduction in speed alters the delicate balance of the fuel/air mixture in our remaining engine. It flames out. I hold the aircraft's nose up as the seekers scream 'Lock' in my ears. I launch both missiles just as our Flugscheibe finally stalls and the nose falls towards the mountains below.

'She's going to crash, Kitty. Get out,' I yell.

A flare lights up the sky as Heydrich tries to shake the missiles on his tail.

'But . . .' says Kitty.

'If I try to get out too, she'll go into a spin and we'll both be killed. You're sitting on a parachute. The escape hatch is below. *Go*. I'll try to hold her. If I have enough altitude, I'll be able to windmill-restart the engines and land.'

But of course I don't have enough altitude.

Kitty hits the quick-release buckle, wriggles backward out of her position and stops to kiss my temple.

The fire is out of control. Smoke is seeping into the cockpit. Kitty climbs down through it, towards the escape hatch.

Far, far away, two missiles explode in quick succession.

Kitty pulls the emergency release on the hatch. The door falls into the night sky. I glance at her silhouette in the hatchway.

'If only we'd had more time,' she shouts over the gale. She wavers for a second, and then she's gone.

'We have all the time in the world,' I say to the empty cockpit.

I fight the Flugscheibe's dead controls, grunting with the effort. The downward pitch gets worse. I scan the landscape before me, searching for some sort of survivable crash site, my adrenalin pumping. Flames roar from the holes all along the aircraft's body. Airspeed increases. My heartbeat throbs in my ears. Before me is a lake. Water landing? Lower impact and the clean shape of the Flugscheibe might skip over the water. It's a chance.

My aircraft plummets towards the lake, trailing fire.

25

Three Roads Meet

All the slaughter, all the vivisection, all the pain are as nothing compared to the beauty I have uncovered. Tonight the mechanism sings to the stars!

Final entry in the journal of an unknown SS scientist, discovered in the ruins of Berlin

The man is a scarecrow.

And he's a madman. The farmer realizes that as soon as he opens his door. There's been enough racket for one night already. Aircraft flying overhead aren't uncommon this summer, because the Luftwaffe is targeting the shipyards on the Clyde. Only a couple of days ago, there'd been a full-size raid. Sometimes, if the wind is right, he can hear explosions like distant thunder. But tonight the thunder is much closer.

So he isn't surprised at the knock on the door. Probably an airman who has got lost and run out of fuel. He grabs his shotgun, just in case, and slides the bolt back.

'Where am I?' asks the stranger, before the farmer can say anything. He's speaking English, so the farmer assumes he must be on the right side.

'Near Dungavel, Scotland.'

The stranger is wearing a uniform, but the farmer can't tell whose. He uses one hand to tuck his nightshirt into his waistband and takes a better grip on the shotgun.

'What do you want?' he asks.

'What is the date?' says the stranger.

The stranger's uniform is grey in the moonlight, but so is everything, at night.

'The tenth of May,' the farmer replies, raising the shotgun.

'You don't understand. The year, man, what is the year?'

This is when he knows for sure that the stranger is crazy.

'1941, of course. Are you British?'

'Jesus Christ,' snorts the stranger.

Behind the farmer, his wife gasps.

'We don't take to blasphemy here,' he tells the stranger.

The man stares at him, frowns and then starts to guffaw.

'God is dead, you fool. The only truth in this world is the Will to Power.'

The stranger turns his back on the farmer and strides off into the night.

⊕

Midnight.

Dungavel: a squat Scottish fortified house brooding in the moonlight.

There's a faint glow through the woods, as if from a bonfire. No one lights bonfires at night during wartime. It must be a beacon for Hess's landing strip.

Before me lies a tableau: a small group of men clustered around a familiar figure wearing a homburg. I step on to the terrace, savouring the aroma of a Havana cigar. Gravel crunches underfoot. Faces turn to stare at me. Guns appear. I hold my arms wide so everyone understands I'm not about to start a shoot-out. At the centre of the group is the Old Man.

'It's good to see you, sir,' I say.

'I, er . . .' The Old Man shakes his head, as if trying to clear it. 'You're supposed to be in New York. Have BSC fired you? And what the hell happened to you in America? You look ten years older.'

I laugh. 'That's funny, sir, because you're looking younger than I remember.'

'I've never felt so old,' the Old Man snaps. 'Well, what the devil are you doing here?'

'You aren't going to believe this, sir.'

Of course, as predicted, the Old Man doesn't believe me.

He takes me into the library to talk. I talk. The story sounds ridiculous, even to my ears. The Old Man stands listening with a bemused expression on his face. When I finish, he remains silent for a few seconds and then slaps his right hand hard on the desktop.

'Have you gone stark staring mad?' he shouts. 'You think I'm going to believe that balderdash? Time travel? Flying saucers? I should have you locked up.' He starts for the doorway.

I blurt the only piece of information that might make him pause. 'Tonight, Rudolf Hess is coming to Britain to conclude peace negotiations with the Watching Committee.'

He freezes in his tracks. Slowly, he turns back to face me. 'How on earth have you heard of the Watching Committee?'

'Because, sir, despite its implausibility, the story I told you is true. I've come back in time fourteen years. Hess arrived an hour and a half ago.'

The Old Man glances at his watch. 'That's where you're wrong.'

I stare at him, uncomprehending. He stares back. Eventually he speaks.

'Hess hasn't turned up.'

⊕

The tired but hopeful Nazi of only an hour earlier is now desperate.

The cockpit of his Messerschmitt has become a prison. His fuel is too low to attempt a return to Germany. He's so, so reluctant to make for Éire.

Earlier, he thought he'd found Dungavel and its landing strip. He was about to start circling when there were a string of explosions a few miles away. It looked as if an air battle was taking place. He'd been distracted, and when he looked down again Dungavel had disappeared into the dark shadows.

The Watching Committee is supposed to be marking the airstrip at Dungavel with a beacon and flares. So where the hell are they? He studies the map for the hundredth time. It's so easy to become disorientated in the darkness. He's going to have to fly out to the west coast, regain his bearings and then approach again, damn it.

He taps the glowing fuel gauge. It sinks another fraction into the emergency reserve.

⊕

The Old Man moves to the library's French windows and stares outside. There's only a little moonlight illuminating the terrace and the trees beyond. What he thinks he might catch sight of out there, I've no idea.

'When you arrived, we were watching for Hess. We have confirmation he crossed the British coast on time, but something has gone wrong. The RAF sent a flight of Beaufighters to investigate a raid that appeared from nowhere. They lost the lot. That can't have been

Hess; one of the negotiation conditions is that he comes unarmed.'

'The raid was Heydrich, his pals and me,' I say. 'There was a dog-fight. One of the Beaufighters collided with one of the German aircraft. I shot the rest of the enemy down, including Heydrich, I think. My aircraft ditched in a reservoir a couple of miles away. I walked the rest of the way.'

The Old Man turns back from the window and stares at me. 'I don't believe you, you know. But let's imagine this gobbledygook is true, what happens in the future?'

'The peace treaty is signed. Germany attacks Russia, but it ends in stalemate. The war degenerates into a kind of three-way covert struggle. You become head of the combined intelligence services. I become your top troubleshooter.'

'Now I know you're lying. *You?* You don't have the gumption. Too interested in chasing a bit of skirt. Too quick with your fists. No brains.'

So that's what he thinks of me?

He catches the twinge of hurt in my eyes. 'I didn't mean . . .'

I shake my head. 'I was young, sir. I changed. I'm older now: less hot-blooded, more ruthless, more like you, sir. We fought against the Nazis together for years. In 1955, Heydrich had you assassinated. I went to Germany to avenge your death. Against orders.'

'Your loyalty is touching,' he says, a faint smile traversing his lips.

'When I caught up with him, Heydrich told me something else about tonight, sir. Something I couldn't believe.'

'What?' The Old Man's expression is inscrutable.

'Churchill came here with you. He thinks you're going to arrest Hess and whoever the Watching Committee sends to negotiate with him. But it's a trap: the Watching Committee want Churchill eliminated. They've told you they'll make you head of the combined intelligence services if you kill him for them.'

The Old Man's mouth opens, closes and opens again. No words come out. For the first time ever, he's at a complete loss. His eyes bulge and he sinks into a chair by the window. No speeches are needed. Now it's clear – Heydrich was telling the truth.

My last slim thread of hope snaps. How could I have been so blind?

'But why, sir? Why deal with the Nazis, of all people?'

He looks up at me from the armchair. 'Wh . . . For God's sake, because we've lost the war, of course. Norway, the Low Countries, France, Yugoslavia, Greece all fell within weeks. Our cities lie in dust. The U-boats are sinking our ships faster than we can replace them. We're amateurs pitted against professionals. If it weren't for the Channel, we'd already be flying the swastika. How can we win this war? What possible strategy can see us through?'

The Old Man stands up again, the colour returning to his face. 'And in return for sparing us, all the Germans want is a free hand in Europe. They don't even want their bloody colonies back. If we make peace now, *another* generation doesn't get destroyed in *another* pointless war. We haven't been beaten, we continue to rule the Empire, and we accept reality and leave Germany to govern Europe.'

He pulls a cigar from his inside pocket and lights it with a shaking hand. He takes a couple of deep draws, blows the smoke out and points it at me.

'And our Prime Minister? His only plan is to drag the Americans in. What will happen if we do that? We'll end up in hock to them for the next hundred years. We'll have no money. We'll have no navy – we won't be able to afford one. No empire either, as we won't be able to keep it without a navy. We'll be nothing but a bloody irrelevant Yankee client state. Well, I won't let it happen.'

'And to stop it happening you're prepared to murder the Prime Minister?'

'What the Watching Committee wants, the Watching Committee gets.'

Churchill steps through the library doorway. In his hand is a Colt .45 revolver. 'Thank you, General Menzies. I had suspected you as a cat's paw for the Watching Committee for some time. You have just provided me with all the evidence I need.'

Behind Churchill stands his bodyguard, Detective Inspector Thompson, also armed.

'I'm sorry, sir, but there was no other way to be sure,' I say.

'Did I teach you nothing about loyalty?' the Old Man asks, his jaw rigid.

'It seems, sir, that you taught me everything I needed to know.'

'If that belligerent old drunk would only listen to reason, the Watching Committee wouldn't need to remove him.'

Churchill's frown deepens. 'General Menzies, it's true, I grant you, that I plan a great alliance of democracies. It's true, again I grant you, that I plan victory over the Nazis. It's true I will do everything within my compass to bring that victory about. But you know why the Germans want peace with us – they intend to attack Russia within weeks. That's why Hess is here. This so-called peace plan is nothing but a squalid ploy. Ultimately, an armistice would provide these islands with nothing but a temporary respite.'

The Old Man backs towards the French windows. 'But who are our real enemies? I don't claim the Nazis are angels, but they have no designs on the Empire. If we support Stalin, then there's a chance that the Red Army will beat the Wehrmacht. Once they're in Berlin, what will stop the Asiatic hordes from reaching the Channel? What's to stop *them* invading us?'

'I bow to no one in my opposition to Communism,' snarls Churchill. 'I will make common cause with Stalin, of course. I would ally myself with the devil himself if he opposed Hitler. But we will keep our powder dry. We will bide our time until the Red Army rips the heart from the Nazi beast. It may take years, but even Napoleon failed to take Russia, and Hitler is no Napoleon. And when Hitler's foul regime is on its deathbed, mortally wounded by the Russian bear, we will strike. We will cross the Channel, liberate France and the Low Countries, and restore the balance of power in Europe.'

The Old Man shakes his head, clear fury in his eyes. 'But you're bankrupting us, leaving us at the mercy of the Americans. If we carry on like this, we'll lose our independence *and* our empire. The Destroyers for Bases deal was too much for me. You're selling the Empire to the Yanks, piece by piece.'

Churchill is shouting now. 'I did not become His Majesty's First Minister in order to dismantle the Empire! I certainly did not do so to hand it over to the Americans. The Empire is built on prestige. What prestige will we have if we surrender to this ridiculous corporal?'

The Old Man shouts back. 'The Yanks have already relieved us of almost all of our foreign assets. Next they'll want the colonies!' He opens the French windows, steps outside and searches the night sky for Hess's missing aircraft.

Churchill follows the Old Man, still trying to reason with him. 'The Americans have no desire for colonies, and they have no desire to police the world. We will pay them, and pay them well, for their support, but a few Caribbean airfields do not an empire make.'

The Old Man turns back from the French windows without closing them. Cool night air chills the library.

'And if they *do* want more?' he hisses. 'What then? Britain becomes a frigid little island on the periphery of Europe. Nothing will be left except a meaningless, useless remnant of a country, an embarrassment to any true British patriot.'

This is too much for Churchill; his expression is that of an angry bull. 'I will not have my patriotism questioned by a man who's in the midst of high treason! Especially when I'm the one holding the gun. Inspector Thompson, arrest this man.'

The Old Man turns to me and takes a slow drag on his cigar. His voice is calm, but there's something burning behind his pale eyes. 'You never met your predecessor, did you?' he says.

The first shot sounds as if it comes from far away.

The sniper is targeting Churchill.

Now I realize why the Old Man opened the French windows – he was giving the sniper a clear shot. Whatever signal he cues the sniper with coincides with the movement of Churchill's bodyguard as he steps forward to arrest him. Thompson goes down, hit in the shoulder by the sniper's bullet. I leap for cover behind the heavy mahogany desk and pull the lamp down to smash on the floor. Drawing my gun, I put a single bullet into the light in the centre of the room. The library plunges into darkness.

Lit only by gun flashes, the battle is a nightmare of disjointed impressions.

Flash: Churchill on one knee in the doorway, firing his revolver.

Flash: Thompson, blood pumping from the wound in his shoulder, crawling in front of Churchill to try to protect him.

Flash: The Old Man diving through another doorway and into the drawing room next door.

Flash. Flash. Flash: Churchill firing blind at the sniper, through the French windows.

A bullet slams into the heavy wooden desk I'm hiding behind. Splinters fly. I watch for the spark of the sniper's rifle, outside in the dark. A bullet smacks the wall just to the right of my head. I spot the muzzle flash. The sniper is crouching behind a low stone wall on the far side of the formal lawn. There's about twenty yards of lawn between the sniper's position and mine.

I check the pistol – one magazine left.

The Home Guard sentries guarding the grounds start shooting at the sniper, who switches targets to engage them. One of the Home Guard stands up to throw a grenade. The sniper shoots him but not fast enough – the dead man's grenade flies across the lawn. I glimpse my chance, jump up, hurtle across the library and smash through the half-open French window. The blast of the grenade will give me just long enough to close the distance and even the odds.

I jump over a wall and weave across the lawn, hidden by the smoke and debris from the grenade. The muzzle of the rifle turns towards me. I throw myself down and roll aside, two bullets ripping into the turf behind me. Reaching the shelter of the stone railing surrounding the formal lawn, I fire a couple of shots. The sniper ducks. I vault the railing, roll again and end up on my knees, just a few yards from his position.

The sniper rushes me, swinging his rifle in an arc at my head. I power up and into the swing, shoulder first. The butt of his rifle hits me before it gets any real momentum. The impact forces me to drop my gun. I swing my left hand in a vicious chop at his throat. But I'm too slow; the sniper is as quick as anyone I've ever fought. He parries and goes for my groin with his knee. I twist sideways. The knee hits my leg.

I bring my right hand up, clawing for his eyes, and sweep his standing foot away. The sniper, distracted by the claw to the face and off balance, tumbles sideways. He lands and starts to roll, aiming to stay out of my reach until he can get back on his feet. But it's too late. I jump high, bring my legs together, and donkey kick downwards on his upper spine with my whole weight.

Splintering bones beneath my feet. A deathblow.

I collapse across the sniper, gasping for air and swearing. The pain from the blows to my arm and leg is intense. I check the sniper's body for a pulse. Nothing. I struggle back to my feet. The pistol is lying where it fell, a few feet away. I pick it up and scan the terrace, counting three dead Home Guards.

I'm the last man standing.

I turn to check the library. The wrecked French windows slap listlessly against their frames. I limp back inside, gun still drawn, and check the room. Thompson is lying on the floor, face down and unconscious. I walk past him to find the Old Man and Churchill manoeuvring around the sitting room. The Old Man is armed only with a poker. Churchill still has his revolver. The hammer falls on an empty chamber. The Old Man advances, brandishing the poker. Churchill throws his revolver away and picks up a chair. They're about to go man to man.

I fire a single shot into the floor between them.

'That's enough,' I shout.

The two bulldogs scowl at me, neither willing to back down, and neither willing to compromise. They play their final cards with the instinct of old campaigners.

'Now, listen to me,' says the Old Man, breathing hard. 'Forget your naivety. Forget your simplistic ideas. This is the future of our country we're talking about.'

Churchill doesn't even glance at the Old Man. 'It seems you have us in your power,' he says to me. 'If you kill me, the Watching Committee will ally the British Empire with a bunch of murdering, insane Huns. If you kill Menzies, I will create a grand alliance of democracies that fears no evil. What choice is this? What British patriot would choose the word of a megalomaniac dictator over that of a democratic American president? I say again: what choice is this?'

'Ignore the bloody rhetoric,' the Old Man retorts. 'His policy is nothing more than to throw ourselves on the Americans' mercy. He's half American himself.'

Churchill takes a step towards me. 'I am the Prime Minister of His Britannic Majesty's government,' he growls. 'Without me the Nazis will win the war, and the world will slide into a new Dark Age. You cannot let that happen. Now . . . either kill me or get out of my way.'

My gun wavers towards the Old Man.

'No . . . you can't . . . after all we've been through.'

The Old Man is the Service, and the Service is my life.

'Don't be a bloody fool,' pleads the Old Man.

The irascible, clear-eyed Old Man: the man I know nothing about and yet the only man in the world I care for. The gun wobbles back towards Churchill.

'Goodbye, sir,' I murmur.

I pull the trigger.

26

The Wolf at the Door

Dear Professor Oppenheimer, I enclose the journal discovered by the ALSOS mission in Berlin. Please be so kind as to examine and report on the technical possibilities raised by this line of research. Goudsmit believes it to be 'eye-opening'. Sincerely, Pash.

Note attached to cover of journal of an unknown SS scientist,
US National Archive II, College Park, Maryland

The bullet drills the Old Man through the centre of his heart.

He staggers backwards, disbelief in his eyes. Three steps and I'm behind him. I catch him and lower him gently to the floor. His head slumps, the light dying in his pale eyes.

'What the Watching Committee wants, the Watching Committee gets,' I say.

'Usually, but not tonight. Tonight is different,' says Churchill.

I drop the gun and hide my face in my hands.

Behind me, Churchill bellows orders.

⊕

The Messerschmitt is now on its last reserves.

The extreme-range tank is long gone and the fuel gauge is

showing empty. But he's so close. Flying inland again from the coast, everything snaps into focus. The landmarks: railway lines, a small hill, are all in their correct positions. This time he's not going to miss the target.

Only metres off the ground, Hess's Messerschmitt comes roaring up the road that leads to Dungavel.

⊕

The most incredible aircraft that RAF Ayr's station commander has ever seen floats into sight like a giant white bat.

The same aircraft had, five minutes earlier, requested permission to land on the standard frequency and following routine procedures. The commander, standing on the control tower balcony smoking, drops his cigarette and stands there, slack-jawed.

The landing is smooth but fast. A huge parachute appears behind the aircraft almost as soon as the main gear hits the ground. Even so, it needs every inch of the runway to reach a stop.

Its markings are the most incredible thing, though. On each side of the fuselage are the red-white-blue roundels of the RAF. The aircraft itself is impossible – three times the size of any he's ever seen. It has no propellers, although the heat haze rising from the boxes attached to the wings suggest they power it, somehow.

The aircraft taxis closer to the hangars. The monster's tail carries the markings of Number Nine Squadron. The station commander knows for a fact that Nine Squadron is equipped with Vickers Wellingtons. He smiles. If this is some sort of secret weapon, the Germans are in big trouble.

The monstrosity eases to a halt. It sits there, glowing pure white in the beam of the apron lights, defying belief.

⊕

An arm finds its way across my shoulders and someone steers me away from the dining room, where Churchill is bossing the Home Guard orderlies around, setting up headquarters. One of them closes the door behind us. The clamour fades.

'Here,' whispers Kitty, pushing a mug of tea into my hand.

I grasp the mug and gaze at her in disbelief.

'I . . . how did you get here?'

'There are some advantages to looking like this, you know. I flagged down a gentleman who happened to be in the area, the Duke of somewhere. A charming man. He was a bit confused by my accent, but I told him I was Polish. He said he had a meeting here anyway. Funny, though, because when he saw Churchill he told his chauffeur to turn the car round. Then he told me to get out and drove off.'

'Kitty . . . I . . .' I take a gulp from the mug of stewed tea.

'It's all right,' says Kitty. 'You did the right thing, the only thing. It's okay to have feelings. You're not a robot.'

Kitty doesn't understand. There's only one appropriate emotion. *Pathological hatred.*

'It's all right,' says Kitty, tears running down her face.

Hate is a pure, clean emotion, an emotion that simplifies and cleanses. Hatred is an emotion I can indulge in, and still function whilst indulging.

'We came here for one reason, Kitty, to kill Reinhard Heydrich. This is all Heydrich's fault – the Old Man's death, Molly's death, this horrific meddling with forces beyond human understanding or control.'

'Heydrich is probably already dead. Even if he isn't, he's finished. He's just one man. He'll be hunted down. Churchill has won. *You've* won.'

Hatred. Hatred and revenge. There's no room for anything else. I put the mug down and raise my head.

'There must be some limit to the amount of punishment the Heart of Stone can absorb,' I say.

'Oh, God, this vendetta, it's . . . it's . . . medieval.'

Hatred is a weapon.

'That night in Wewelsburg,' I say. 'Heydrich drank half a bottle of brandy he was so sure I couldn't hurt him. When I tried to hit him, an electric shock knocked me out.'

Kitty sighs. 'So?'

There's a grim smile on my lips. 'So . . . if it's electric the Heart of Stone might only deflect metal objects like bullets and knives. Non-metallic things like food and drink seem able to go through it.'

'Well, you're not going to be able to kill him with a bread roll.'

I turn away from Kitty, sensing something: a faint vibration. The tea in my mug has small waves dancing across its surface.

'Anyway, Heydrich's already dead,' says Kitty, behind me.

I motion her to be quiet. The hum is louder now. It's the drone of aircraft engines almost overhead. I move to the window. For a second, something passes in front of the moon, then another and another. The moon is hidden behind pale shapes falling from the sky.

The parachutes drift down towards us like snow.

⊕

Gibson finishes the engine-shutdown routine and looks out of the cockpit window. Infantry surround his aircraft, their rifles aimed at him.

He moves to the aircraft's hatch and cracks it open. The mass clicking of safety catches being released fills the air. He pokes his head through the hatchway, examines the surrounding area and spots the station commander hiding behind a fire truck.

'Hey, you there! What's the bloody welcoming committee for?'

'Who are you?' shouts the station commander.

'Who am I? Who are *you*? And where did all these antiques come from? I haven't seen so many moth-eaten old crates since the war.'

⊕

Churchill is on the telephone to the RAF, trying to find out where Hess has disappeared to. He gestures me to a seat. Beside Churchill, a well-dressed figure stands up and smiles at me. He extends a firm handshake. His navy blue three-piece suit is immaculate.

'Averell Harriman,' he says. 'I represent President Roosevelt. I understand the free world owes you a huge debt.'

'I've not saved the world yet,' I say. 'There are parachutes overhead. Two Junkers survived the displacement.'

Churchill tells the RAF telephonist to hold.

'How many paratroopers?' he asks.

'There can't be more than two hundred.'

'Two hundred elite German Fallschirmjäger are landing right on top of us? I assume their intention is to wipe us all out? And our forces are – let's see – a platoon of the 1st Renfrewshire & Bute Home Guard, yourself, and Inspector Thompson . . . who's incapacitated.'

'And you and Mr Harriman.'

'I will fight if necessary of course, but Averell here is not a military man; he's a banker.'

'I will bribe the enemy,' says Harriman with a flicker of a smile.

'Perhaps a tactical retreat is in order?' suggests Churchill.

'They're landing all around us,' I point out.

Churchill frowns. 'It seems like a lifetime since I myself marched with General Buller's army to relieve the siege of Ladysmith. Now I fear it is I who must wait with impatience for the sight of red coats. I can count on you, I assume, to organize the defence of the house?'

As the site of a new Rorke's Drift, Dungavel House could be worse.

It's a typical Scottish laird's house, extended and remodelled from a fortified medieval core of solid stone. There are two towers, one central and one at the southern end of the building. The large central tower is thick enough to withstand anything the Fallschirmjäger can throw at it.

The Home Guard sergeant stands with me on the battlements, surveying the coming battlefield.

To the west there's a wide, open landscape. Any troops advancing that way will face a tough job. More worrying is the south, where the forest comes within fifty yards of the house. The sides and rear are at least walled. The rear gate is large enough to get a cart through, but it can be bolted and barricaded. There's no sign of the Fallschirmjäger. They're forming up in the woods, no doubt, and already they've cut the telephone line to try to prevent reinforcement.

'So what have we got to save the world with?' I ask the sergeant.

'Myself, three corporals, and forty-three assorted farm labourers, ploughmen and gamekeepers, sir.'

'Dare I ask about weapons?'

'I have a Tommy gun. Most of the lads carry Enfield rifles, although some only have shotguns. We've a good number of Mills bombs, Great War vintage, four Lewis guns and a Northover projector, sir.'

I glance at the sergeant. He's a ruddy-complexioned man in his fifties, with the Distinguished Conduct Medal sewn on to the breast of his battledress. Reliving the Great War was probably not what he was expecting when he left home earlier.

'Who are the two best shots?' I ask.

'Patterson and Grehan, both gamekeepers, sir.'

'Right, I want them on top of the main tower, with double

quantities of ammunition. How many grenades do you have for the Northover projector?'

'Two dozen No. 76 SIPs, sir.'

The No. 76 SIP consists of half a pint of yellow phosphorus, benzene and water in a bottle. In the unlikely event that you manage to hit something with one, the glass shatters. The phosphorus ignites on contact with air, which in turn sets light to the benzene. Mayhem ensues. In other words, they're glorified Molotov cocktails. The projector itself has a range of a couple of hundred yards. Its rate of fire is less than one round a minute. It's close to useless.

'The Northover projector can go on the south tower. Tell the crew to fire off the ammunition as fast as they can. They won't last long once the Jerries zero in on them.'

The sergeant nods. He seems happy enough now that someone else is taking charge.

'I want you to stay near Churchill. He'll undoubtedly want to man one of the Lewis guns. Your job is to keep him where he's useful – on the radio raising hell for reinforcements.'

'Got it, sir.'

'Once that's sorted, organize a section from the younger, fitter men as a reserve under your own command. Spread the other sections out, one or two men per window. The Lewis guns can go at each corner of the house. Keep them manned at all costs – they're our main defence.'

The sergeant nods.

'Tell everyone to keep their heads down and conserve ammunition,' I say. 'Fire aimed shots at anything within three hundred yards at the front. Kill everything that comes over the walls. Don't waste your ammunition on anything else.'

It's not much, but it's all that can be done.

At least we'll go down fighting.

⊕

Gibson and his crew are in the officers' mess when the station commander finds them again. The night-fighter pilots are standing them drinks.

'If it wasn't for the parachute we'd have sailed straight off the end of that bloody runway,' says Gibson.

The station commander brings the jollity to a swift end. 'Wing Commander, I just had the Chief of the Air Staff on the telephone. The Prime Minister is under attack by some Jerry parachutists at Dungavel House. They're holding out, but the army can't relieve them before morning. I've been told to scramble everything I can. I've already lost one flight. We need your help.'

'We can't get airborne again off such a short runway, skipper,' says Gibson's co-pilot, shaking his head.

'What's your runway length, four thousand feet?' Gibson asks.

The station commander nods.

'We need seven thousand minimum,' says the co-pilot.

'We won't need much fuel. It's doable if we use the Super Sprites,' Gibson says.

'I hate that bloody rocket-power stuff. Shakes the bloody kite to bits every time.'

'It's an emergency. Although God alone knows what the commander here thinks we can do?'

'It's a bomber, isn't it? So get over there and bomb them.'

'Jesus! No!'

The station commander stiffens. 'You are talking to a superior officer. I don't care about your fairy story. You're on my station now, and if you refuse my orders, I'll have you locked up.'

Gibson glares at the commander. 'Keep your hair on. I'm not mutinying. It's just that our bomb . . .'

'What's wrong with your bloody bomb?'

'It's a bit too bloody big for the bloody target.'

⊕

We kill the lights in the house and secure the perimeter as best we can. With the phones out, Churchill commandeers the Home Guard's radio. He raises the Glasgow garrison's commanding officer and gives the man a stiff talking-to.

'How long?' I ask.

'The Highland Light Infantry have a company on night exercise that can be here by morning,' says Churchill.

'Morning? We'll all be dead by then.'

'Believe me, that's the best they can do. The only unit that can be here quicker is a squadron of the 52nd Reconnaissance Regiment. If they drive like the devil, they can be here in a couple of hours. They have armoured cars and a lorry-borne infantry platoon.'

Behind us, the Home Guard start breaking into their ammunition boxes.

'What are our chances?' asks Churchill. 'Can we hold for two or three hours, whilst outnumbered four to one?'

'It's not impossible. The Fallschirmjäger are a long way from home, and must have limited ammunition. If we can throw them back once, they may go to ground. It depends if Heydrich is with them. Without him, they'll probably make a token effort and then give up.'

'And if you didn't kill him?'

I grimace.

'Well, in that case, we're in big trouble.'

⊕

The whole area is on fire.

Hess's Messerschmitt flies over the final hill and he finds Dungavel House silhouetted by burning trees. What the devil is going on?

One thing at a time – he's found his destination and now all that remains is to get down there. He pulls back on the stick and the aircraft climbs. Two thousand feet is the minimum altitude for parachuting. The Messerschmitt reaches that altitude, and Hess levels out.

He cuts the ignition and feathers the props, to avoid tangling his chute when he jumps. The engines die. The roar of the airflow replaces the drumming of the engines. Hess undoes his harness and slides back the glass cockpit roof.

Now to jump.

But no. It's impossible. The slipstream forces him down, pressing him against the back of his seat. He braces himself and tries once more to raise his head above the windshield, but the aircraft is going too fast. And in his struggle to escape, he's lost control of it.

Dungavel hill looms.

27

Destiny

Sam, we have the blood of countless human beings on our hands. No good can come of pursuing this insanity. We've created one means of destroying the Earth already. I'm not building a fucking time machine. Lose this.

Unsigned, undated note found in the correspondence archive of
Professor Samuel Goudsmit, Niels Bohr Library, Maryland

The Fallschirmjäger come on with the confidence of a professional boxer pitted against an amateur.

Around Dungavel House, the forest burns, set on fire by the Northover projector's yellow phosphorus bombs. I take a position on the main tower along with the two snipers, Patterson and Grehan. Patterson passes me an antique deer-stalking rifle.

The Fallschirmjäger advance across the open ground in front of the house. Two German machine guns, dug in at the edge of the forest, take turns in shooting at us. I suspect the Fallschirmjäger are as short of ammunition as we are, because the suppression fire is light.

'Shoot anyone waving his hands around,' I shout to the two snipers. 'They'll be the officers.'

The Fallschirmjäger assault sections scurry forward, bent double.

Patterson, Grehan and I fire steadily, slowing the paratroopers' advance. The rest of the Home Guard maintain their fire discipline. The Lewis guns only have six magazines each, and the rifles less than a hundred rounds.

An aircraft flies up the valley, straight for the house. As it passes over, the unmistakable silhouette of a Messerschmitt Bf-110 is caught for an instant by the moon. The heavy fighter pulls up, struggling for altitude. It must be Hess.

An explosion on the southern tower announces the end of the Northover projector. One of the gun crew jumps, in flames. Either he dropped a phosphorus grenade or it exploded inside the tube. His body thuds into the terrace and lies there smouldering.

Hess and his aircraft disappear into the night.

⊕

Years earlier, General Ritter von Greim had given Hess some advice about escaping from a damaged aircraft. 'Roll her on her back and you'll just fall out.' But Hess is too low, and heading straight for Dungavel hill at five hundred kilometres an hour – if he rolls, he'll fly into the ground.

Forgetting the engines are out of fuel, he pulls back on the stick, trying to gain altitude with a loop. The stars fade as the G-force drains blood away from his brain.

The unpowered Messerschmitt zooms upward, trading speed for height. Only half conscious, Hess watches the altimeter tick upwards, willing it on. The aircraft's speed haemorrhages away. Hess lets go of the controls. The wings flutter as the Messerschmitt enters a stall. The nose starts to drop.

Hess kicks out, trying to drive his body free from the dying aircraft.

⊕

The first Fallschirmjäger come over the low wall on to the terrace and straight into our ambush.

An Obersturmführer leads the assault, appearing over the lip of the wall, waving his men forward. I shoot him. The Lewis guns open fire from the corners of the building, catching the Fallschirmjäger in a vicious crossfire.

But the Fallschirmjäger keep coming. With assault rifles on full automatic, they storm across the killing ground on the terrace. If they get inside, we're doomed.

Grenades fly in both directions. One Lewis gunner is hit; the loader takes his place and opens up again. Rifle fire from the windows tears into the attacking Germans. Grehan drops his rifle, and starts throwing Mills bombs down on to the terrace. The explosions rip into the Fallschirmjäger trying to take cover behind the low stone walls.

I keep moving, ducking behind the parapet to reload, shooting anyone who looks anything like an officer. More Fallschirmjäger fall. Bullets thud into the stonework around me. Grehan takes a bullet straight between the eyes and goes down.

Four Fallschirmjäger make it as far as the wall of the house. Stick grenades thrown through the windows blast the defenders out. The Home Guard sergeant charges into the room with his reserve section, and cuts them down with his Tommy gun. I shoot two more cowering behind the terrace wall.

The Fallschirmjäger falter and fall back.

⊕

The Super Sprites shake the Vanquish almost to bits.

Gibson waits, slammed into his seat by the acceleration. Using every inch of space, he started the engine run-up on the taxiway and swung the aircraft on to the runway at crazy speed. Dangerous, but there was nothing else for it. He pushed the throttles all the way to the firewall as soon as they straightened out. They careered up the runway mostly under control as the rockets ignited.

'V1,' shouts the co-pilot, over the sound of the world ending.

'Four thousand bloody feet,' Gibson mutters to himself, teeth clenched.

The end of the runway is in sight. Too bloody slow. Too bloody slow.

'V2,' shouts the co-pilot.

He doesn't need telling twice.

He stands the Vanquish on its tail, and it roars into the sky.

⊕

The loudhailer squeals, making Heydrich's high-pitched voice sound unearthly.

I've come down to what's left of the dining room, to reorganize the defences. The sergeant seems to have forgotten his nerves now the shooting has started. He's leading his men into the trenches as if he's back on the Somme. Harriman is doing what he can for the injured, from a makeshift hospital in the kitchen. Churchill is in the library, still yelling into the radio for reinforcements. Inspector Thompson has propped himself by a window. He has his arm in a sling and a Webley revolver in his hand.

A loudhailer squeals outside. 'Churchill, are you in there?' It's Heydrich's voice.

'Come and get us,' I shout to him.

'God damn it! Are you still not dead?'

'You'll be dead before I am.'

'Look, your situation is impossible. I have hundreds of troops surrounding the house with fifties weaponry. You can't have more than a handful of the Home Guard in there. That little probing attack probably used half your ammunition.'

'And yours, considering that only two Junkers survived the translation.'

'I'm not going to lie to you: they don't call me the Butcher because I run a charcuterie. You're going to die, and so are Churchill and Hess, but surrender now and I'll let Kitty go. She's no danger to me anyway. I may even take her back.'

'I'd rather die,' says Kitty, beside me.

'It might come to that,' I say.

'Remember my motto,' shouts Churchill from under a table in the library.

'What's that?'

'Never surrender!'

The loudhailer screeches again. 'That was my last offer. It is a dark, brutal world we live in, and only dark, brutal people succeed in it. Now you all die.'

The German machine guns open up again.

Heydrich plans his second assault better than the first.

The first attack was a platoon-strength reconnaissance. With the casualties we inflicted, the Blond Beast must have about two platoons left. They make another frontal assault, supported this time by mortars as well as machine guns.

Again, the Home Guard hold their fire as the Fallschirmjäger advance from the tree line. Patterson and I snipe away at the dark figures as they crawl across the open space. There's a lot more of them this time, and they're scurrying from cover to cover with extra caution. The situation is looking serious.

With the explosions and gunfire, Heydrich's troops don't hear the aircraft until it's too late. The Vanquish screams over at treetop height and supersonic speed. I catch a glimpse of it – an arrowhead lit up by the flares that it's dropping. The pulsing blue flame of jet engines at full reheat cleaves the night sky.

It's the most beautiful thing I've ever seen.

And the loudest.

Even hundreds of yards away inside the house, the shock wave from the sonic boom hits us like a wall, and leaves us all temporarily deaf. In the woods, the overpressure is shattering. The machine guns and mortars stop firing, the crews incapacitated, their lungs bursting.

The Vanquish disappears. A staggered flight of four Beaufighters emerges from the forest. They're so low they seem to be flying through the trees rather than over them. A storm of cannon explosions rips up the ground around Heydrich's devastated troops. The Fallschirmjäger advance collapses.

The Beaufighters circle the area, strafing the Fallschirmjäger positions. One Beaufighter falls to a Luftfaust anti-aircraft missile. The remaining three keep firing until they run out of ammunition. The Vanquish flies over again, subsonic this time, dumping jet fuel in a fine mist over the burning woods.

The inferno burns out of control.

Heydrich leads the ultimate attack in person.

An explosion at the rear gate announces his arrival. The sergeant, the reserve squad and I run towards the rear windows. The remaining Fallschirmjäger pour through the gap into the rear courtyard.

To my right, Churchill has commandeered a Lewis gun, and he knows how to use it. He fires short well-aimed bursts at the charging enemy. The Lewis guns and the rifle fire take a heavy toll of the Fallschirmjäger, though there aren't many Home Guard left either.

'Kitty, I've got an idea. Go up on the roof and see if any of the phosphorus grenades from the Northover projector are still intact. They look like glass bottles full of water.'

Kitty crawls out of the room, keeping below the level of the windows.

A black silhouette stands in the gateway with the flames of the burning forest behind him, firing a machine gun from the hip.

'Here he comes,' I shout to Churchill.

Heydrich sprays the side of the house with bullets. He walks forward, watching for anyone to show themselves.

The Home Guard sergeant stands up and empties his Tommy gun straight at Heydrich. He staggers under the impact. Some of the bullets might have missed him, but not a whole burst.

Heydrich turns towards us and smiles.

The Heart of Stone is real.

A rip from Heydrich's gun catches the sergeant full in the chest. He lurches backwards and collapses.

I stand at the window so Heydrich can see me. 'Come and get me, you bastard,' I shout.

Heydrich turns towards the sound of my voice, sees me and laughs. He squeezes the trigger again, but the machine gun has run out of ammunition. He throws the gun to one side and draws his SS dagger.

'Let's do this man to man!' he shouts.

He clambers over the corpses piled beneath the window and enters the room.

Kitty searches the tower, frantic with terror.

The impotent skeleton of the Northover projector sags over the parapet. Slumped across it is the scorched body of a dead Home Guard. There are two ammunition boxes. One lies at the foot of the dead soldier, burnt almost beyond recognition. The shards of glass are like crystal amid the soot. The other box is intact in the shadows at the rear of the tower. Kitty levers the lid off.

It's empty.

$\oplus$

Churchill stands up, brandishing the Lewis gun like a club. He has run out of ammunition, too, but he intends to go down swinging. He charges at Heydrich with a defiant scowl.

'No!' I shout, as Churchill swings the Lewis gun at Heydrich's head.

As the barrel of the gun connects with Heydrich sparks fly and Churchill drops down, out cold. Heydrich stops and inspects him for a second.

'A nice try,' he says.

He advances on me dagger first, a man who knows he has won. His knife is vicious; there's some kind of inscription engraved on the blade and it's polished to a mirror finish. It's hypnotizing as it draws bright patterns in the air in front of him.

'Your turn now,' he declares.

I fire two more useless shots straight at him. The bullets hit the invisible barrier a couple of inches from his face and ricochet away.

Kitty skids through the doorway.

'Ah, Katharina, I'm delighted you're here, my dear,' Heydrich hisses. 'Now you can watch me gut your boyfriend like a fish.'

I reverse the rifle to use it as a club. If my theory about the Heart of Stone is correct, perhaps the wooden stock can penetrate it.

Heydrich advances, looking for an opening.

'Nothing we do means anything,' he says. 'The Übermensch accepts this, but the Untermensch does not. He clings to his pathetic life just like the animal that he is.'

327

He slashes his knife down and across my forearm, searching for an artery. I parry it with the rifle.

'No!' screams Kitty.

Heydrich switches the dagger to his left hand and lunges forward with a low stab to my guts. I leap backwards and it misses my stomach by an inch. He steps back to regain his balance, talking to Kitty without taking his eyes from me.

'You pathetic, weak little pacifist, what are you going to do?' he sneers. 'Let the wolves fight for dominance, and once this is over the winner will take you as his prize.'

He weaves the knife in the air in front of him.

'I'm looking forward to having you again, you little slut. I'm going to give it you, cold and hard as steel. No one can give you what I've got.'

Heydrich and I circle each other. I jab at his face with the rifle butt, trying to keep him at a distance. The wood goes through the barrier and connects with his chest. It works – non-metallic objects can penetrate his Heart of Stone.

'Nothing can touch me. Nothing can hurt me. My heart is stone,' Heydrich groans, stumbling backwards, towards Kitty, who's standing, frozen, behind him.

'Kitty, for God's sake,' I shout.

In slow motion, her arm comes round, holding a phosphorus grenade. Her expression has hardened and there's sudden fire in her eyes. 'You couldn't satisfy a woman in a million years,' she shouts.

She raises the phosphorus grenade and brings it smashing down on to Heydrich's head. Glass and liquid, it goes through the barrier, spraying its contents over him.

The liberated phosphorus flares out. Incandescent particles of flame ignite Heydrich's benzene-covered skin. Kitty falls backwards. The benzene flashes, spreading the stench of burning flesh. Heydrich lurches after Kitty, screaming with pain and rage, blindly sweeping the dagger before him. The blazing phosphorus fills the room with choking smoke.

Eyes streaming, I try to concentrate on the apparatus attached to Heydrich's belt that controls the Heart of Stone. I swing the rifle butt. It smashes into the device. A shower of sparks flies.

Heydrich's fingers flail at his cheeks. His face, hair and uniform are now ablaze. He falls, convulsing, to the floor. I stand over him, half blind and suffocated by the smoke. The scorching phosphorus and benzene have consumed the skin on Heydrich's head and eaten into the flesh beneath. His eyes are burnt opals in his blackened, exposed skull. I swing the rifle, remorselessly clubbing his jerking body.

Kitty picks herself up. 'Mercy,' she says, with tears in her eyes.

'He wouldn't have shown us any,' I snarl.

'I've changed,' says Kitty. 'Can't you? Can't you see?'

Can't I see? For an instant, I hear the shadow voices of the dead:

— You'll be the death of me.

— Nobody lives for ever, Number Fifteen.

— Have you ever looked in a mirror?

— It's what's inside that's important.

— You're a charmless thug with a bullet for a heart.

— That's an order, Pretty Boy. You have the best chance of getting out. Go!

— You'll have me in tears.

Kitty stares at me. 'Mercy,' she says again.

'Find a gun with some ammunition left,' I say.

She picks up a Webley revolver lying next to the sergeant's dead body and hands it to me wordlessly. I break it open. There's a single bullet remaining. I snap the revolver shut and glance at Kitty. She turns away and staggers from the room.

Heydrich turns his sightless eyes towards me. I lean forward so I can hear his final whisper.

'You'll never be one of the wolves.'

I shoot him in the face, just below the bridge of the nose.

28

Rough Justice

Dear Pash, This 'journal' appears to be the ravings of a madman. Goudsmit needs his head examining. Sincerely, Oppenheimer.

Note attached to cover of journal of an unknown SS scientist,
US National Archive II, College Park, Maryland

By the time the cavalry gets to Dungavel, victory is ours.

Cold dawn light is spilling over the hills as a Humber armoured car noses up the long driveway. It eases past a legion of burnt fir trees, black skeletons still smouldering.

The Humber pulls to a halt before the ruin of Dungavel House. Its commander takes in the consequences of Heydrich's assault. A jumble of corpses in Fallschirmjäger camouflage lie where RAF cannon fire or the Home Guard killed them. Craters pock-mark the grass lawn. A gouge runs from right to left, ending in shattered branches and the broken tailplane of the crashed Beaufighter.

The house itself is now a shell. Bullet holes perforate its stone façade. Charred furniture tumbles out of barricaded windows from gutted rooms. The roof is reduced to charcoal splinters. Brass cartridges and shrapnel from Fallschirmjäger mortar rounds litter the terrace. The north end of the building is nothing but rubble. Broken masonry, glass shards and plaster dust pour from the house's wounds.

Churchill and I stand smoking Romeo y Julieta cigars in the midst of this carnage. The armoured car's commander seems to be having trouble taking the sight in.

'About bloody time,' I shout to him.

'Let's get a drink,' says Churchill.

Churchill hauls a crate of whisky out of the pantry.

The kitchen is now a hospital with a makeshift operating table. The reconnaissance squadron's medic is triaging the survivors.

Churchill bangs the crate down on the table. 'Heroes, all of you,' he says. 'I'll organize the medals myself.'

The Home Guard take the news in silence, medals being the least of their concerns. Their sergeant and more than half of their friends are dead. The last surviving corporal takes a bottle of Macallan with his uninjured hand. 'Tears will flow in many a cottage today, sir,' he says.

Churchill nods. 'Your sacrifice will not be forgotten. The country – indeed the whole world – owes you a huge debt.'

Far away, there's an explosion, followed by the thumping beat of the armoured car's machine guns. The few remnants of the Fallschirmjäger are being hunted down.

Back on the terrace, Churchill sloshes whisky into three tin cups.

'The Beast is slain, then,' he says.

He passes the mugs to Harriman and me. Harriman smiles. He looks tired, and his immaculate suit is ruined. I hate to think what I must look like.

'What happened in your world, after my er . . . demise?' Churchill asks me.

'There was a ceasefire, and Lloyd George ran a caretaker government for a few months. We signed a peace treaty with Germany, but Labour won the election and repudiated it.'

'Good for them. Attlee's doing?'

'I believe so, sir, but I'm no politician. We fell into a "cold war" with Germany: no open conflict, but lots of covert struggle. For every resistance group we maintained in Europe, they supported an independence campaign in our colonies.'

'Why didn't that lead back to hot war?' asks Harriman.

It feels strange telling them about a future that no longer exists. Perhaps it still does exist, just in a place I can't get to. Heisenberg would know.

'We invented an incredible bomb, powerful enough to destroy a city. The threat of it prevented tensions turning into full-scale war. The Germans had the bomb too, and unstoppable rockets to deliver it. We had to keep part of our bomber force airborne round the clock. Otherwise the Nazis could have destroyed it on the ground.'

Churchill turns to Harriman. 'Our scientists are already working on the theory for such a bomb. They urge development at all possible speed. What do you think, Averell?'

'I think the President will be most interested to meet our friend here.'

A Highland Light Infantry lieutenant approaches and signals Churchill, who moves over to take his report. He chuckles the happy laugh of the victor, and shouts back to Harriman and me.

'They've found Hess.'

Hess is a sorry sight, his uniform torn and covered in mud.

Churchill, Kitty, Harriman and I are lunching on tinned ham and whisky in the undamaged lodge of Dungavel House when the Deputy Führer of the Third Reich limps into the room. He's a grave-looking fellow with deep-set eyes and bushy brows. When he catches sight of Churchill, sitting waiting for him, his knees buckle and he sinks to the carpet.

'Mr . . . Mr Prime Minister, I apologize but I can't stand. My leg is injured.'

Churchill gazes down at Hess. 'So you're the madman, are you?' he says.

'Oh, no,' Hess replies. 'I'm only his deputy.'

Churchill laughs.

Perhaps Hess still has hopes of somehow rescuing his mission. If so, the sight of a living Churchill must destroy them. He tries, of course, delineating the German peace terms with the desperate persuasiveness of a condemned man.

'Thank you, Herr Hess,' says Churchill, after hearing him out. 'I'll stop you there. My policy is victory at all costs, and those you hoped would kill me and negotiate Britain's surrender are thwarted. You have failed.'

'Mr Churchill, are you sure the Americans will save you?'

Churchill indicates Harriman. 'Averell here assures me the President will carry us through by any means possible. Already he has promised us a billion dollars' worth of tanks, aircraft and guns: enough to equip division upon division, squadron upon squadron, fleet upon fleet. With American money behind us, and Russian man-power in front, why should we negotiate?'

Hess turns from Churchill to Harriman. 'Is this true?' he asks.

Harriman nods. 'And another billion after that. And as many more billions as it takes.'

Hess limps from the room a broken man.

Churchill leafs through the papers Hess had brought with him. He passes round the maps, photos of Hess's children and personal letters. One particular piece of paper seizes his attention. I guess it's the names of the Watching Committee.

'Averell, these men are untouchable,' he says, passing the list to Harriman.

'Maybe this one?' says Harriman, pointing low down on the page. 'Perhaps we could pressure him with . . .' He glances at me and falls silent.

I crane my neck, curious about who exactly is in this bloody Watching Committee. Harriman passes the list back to Churchill. He stares at me, folds the paper, places it in an inside pocket and smiles.

'What will you do with Hess?' I ask.

'I suppose we'll say he knows that Germany is doomed and so he has abandoned ship. Hitler will claim Hess is mad, of course, and he'll be half right. He might not be insane yet, but after a few years in the Cage contemplating his failure he will be.'

'Mr Churchill, will you say Heydrich, the Fallschirmjäger and the Home Guard are crazy? Will you say that *we* are?' Kitty asks.

Churchill smiles at Kitty's naivety. 'Heydrich? Heydrich is still in Germany. Those men in the woods don't exist. They will be stripped of their uniforms and buried in unmarked graves. The Home Guard will be given medals as promised. Then they'll be called up and shipped to the Far East. Everyone involved in the aftermath of the battle will sign the Official Secrets Act. I believe I can rely on your own silence, considering the fantastical nature of your story.'

Churchill's face shows the same hard-nosed grip on things I'd seen on the Old Man's – and on Heydrich's. All powerful men seem to have it.

Maybe Heydrich was right about one thing – maybe, in the end, it is all about the Will to Power.

The debriefing takes months. I go over and over my story with a series of incredulous interrogators. I pour out every single detail I can think of: politics, technological advances, the identity of all the Soviet moles unmasked in the fifties. I even tell them who's going to win the Cup Final every year from 1941 to 1955.

Someone is going to make a lot of money betting on those results.

When Churchill decides they have everything, he invites me to his underground headquarters in Whitehall. He presents me with a Bank of England monogrammed envelope containing a generous cheque. We light cigars and drink a snifter of brandy before he raises the subject of my future.

'You realize, of course, that you can't return? You're trapped here with us,' he says.

'Yes, sir. I understood that before I left.'

'Nothing to go back for, eh?'

I have an image of Molly's calcified bones.

'No, sir.'

'And the younger you? He must be somewhere.'

'New York, seconded to British Security Coordination.'

'I'm sure he's doing excellent work. We'd better keep him there, to avoid complication. I'll authorize new identity papers for you, of course. Retirement, if you like . . . Australia or New Zealand, perhaps? Somewhere peaceful, anyway. God knows, you've earned a rest.'

'Slippers aren't my style, sir.'

Churchill peers at me over the rims of his reading glasses. 'No, I don't suppose they are. Which leads me on to the question of what to do with the Watching Committee? I already had my suspicions, but Hess had a list on his person, so now I'm certain.'

'Section 18B for them all then, sir?'

Churchill harrumphs. 'I'd like to set them swinging from a yardarm in Chatham dockyard. However, politics is a curious business and they're too powerful to arrest.'

'Tell me, sir, who's the ringleader? I could take a little extrajudicial action to send them a message.'

'You'd do that?'

'Nothing would give me greater pleasure.'

Churchill selects a single piece of paper from a folder on his desk. The gold-embossed letterhead includes an eagle, a swastika and the word Reichskanzlei. Handwritten on the page are two dozen names – the members of the Watching Committee. The name of the chairman is circled in red.

'Impossible,' I say.

'I'm afraid not.'

'But I can't kill him.'

'You begin to appreciate my dilemma,' says Churchill, picking up his cigar again.

⊕

It's good to be alive, and better still to be outside on a sunny day.

The sun reaches high in the cloudless sky. In the trees, the birds are singing. A cool breeze stirs the leaves. The road itself is deserted. Civilian cars are rare in wartime Czechoslovakia. My appreciation of the details is heightened by the hollow stomach and pumping adrenalin that precede combat. Occasional Czechs stroll past, showing no interest in the men loitering at the corner.

Three assassins who've dropped into Prague, to kill a dead man.

I'd known that the mission would be necessary ever since I arrived back in 1941. I recruited two Czechs from the Free Czechoslovak Army, named Jozef Gabčík and Jan Kubiš. Close to each other and always smiling, their English is terrible, but it's better than my Czech. We parachuted into Czechoslovakia weeks ago.

Churchill's desire to keep me alive has given me some pull with the RAF. So I've scrounged a couple of Lysander special duties aircraft to fly us out again. Of course, planning to survive and escape means the complexity of the operation is increased. The Lysanders can't fly all the way back to Britain without refuelling in France.

But I'm not getting involved in any more suicide missions.

⊕

Churchill listened to my story about Heydrich being the most dangerous Nazi leader, and the only one it's worth assassinating.

'We can't let personal feelings cloud our judgement,' he said, when I'd finished.

'No, sir.'

'The Nazi crackdown is likely to be severe.'

'All the better. Heydrich's carrot-and-stick tactics are working. If we don't stop him, he'll implement them in all the occupied territories. Production of war materials will skyrocket. If we kill him, Nazi retaliation will drive the workers back into the resistance.'

'You've killed one Heydrich already. Isn't that enough for you?'

I thought of Molly as Churchill puffed on his cigar, tapped a quarter-inch of ash into the ashtray and nodded his assent.

⊕

Churchill predicts a tough few years for Britain.

We've continued on the losing streak that convinced the Watching Committee that peace was the best option. In the desert, the advantage swings backwards and forwards, but Rommel has become a curse word in the Eighth Army. The U-boats are sinking cargo ships faster than the Clyde shipyards can construct them. The fall of

Singapore is the worst defeat in Britain's history. But the Japanese attack has 'dragged the Americans in', at least.

At the last briefing, Churchill was in a sunny mood despite the abysmal news from the Far East. The strategic picture is transformed. Hess, Heydrich and I arrived at Dungavel with the British Empire facing the might of Nazi Germany alone. Now we have powerful allies.

As the Prime Minister says, 'We're in a hole at the moment, but we fight on. We'll fend the Japanese off. We'll keep the stiletto in Hitler's back. The Russians will grind the Wehrmacht to death, whilst the Americans pay for the whole thing. I'll steer a course that brings us out of the other side of the storm intact. Battered, yes, but intact. Victory at all costs.'

I agree with him.

Victory at any cost.

⊕

The suburbs of Prague are dusty, drab affairs, even when warmed by the sun. But they offer an opportunity for an attack where German reinforcements will not be upon us in seconds. Our ambush is on U Holešovičkách at the junction with Zenklova, a couple of blocks from the Bulovka hospital. Here we'll catch fewer civilians in the crossfire. I must have learnt a little from Kitty about respect for human life.

Gabčík is waiting by a tram stop just after the bend. Kubiš is to the north, acting as lookout. Occasional horse-drawn carts and boxy grey Škodas trundle past. One of the few things I do miss about the future is the cars. I only got to drive my Jaguar once and I've got a while to wait before I get another chance.

The Protector of Bohemia and Moravia's lair in Panenské Břežany is thirty minutes' drive from his headquarters in Prague castle. SOE's spy in the villa confirmed his presence there last night. Today is his monthly conference with the collaborationist government in Prague. He'll want to give them their orders in person.

He travels to work in a black Mercedes cabriolet with the registration SS3, escorted only by his driver. Typical arrogance. Of course, he's not yet bulletproof. The Heart of Stone wasn't produced for him until the fifties. He's not bulletproof and definitely not bombproof.

The bomb is the exact shape of a thermos flask, but with more surprising contents. I twist off the Bakelite cap, arm the impact fuse and then replace the cap. Now it's live, I place it on the wall as if it's the Holy Grail.

Heydrich's chauffeur is no mug; he switches Heydrich's commute between three possible routes. Knowing this, I chose the best ambush position and waited for fate itself to bring Heydrich to me. Three times, we've staked this site out with no luck, and then dispersed to our safe houses. But I know for sure today is the day the limousine will arrive at the sharp corner we're haunting. Today is the day I complete my revenge.

I don't try to fool myself that it's anything else.

⊕

Gibson is back on ops.

The RAF offensive against Germany has new tactics and new aircraft. Group Captain Gibson is master bomber on the first thousand-bomber raid on Cologne. Climbing back into the primitive Lancaster was a shock after the Vanquish. There's a comforting familiarity about the old girl, though, with all her creaking and vibration.

It will be a few years before the back-room boys unravel the Vanquish's secrets, but already they're doing wonders: new jammers and H2S sets are coming into service, based on the ones found in Gibson's aircraft. The bomb he brought back was treated like a national treasure. Now it's in a top-secret Tube Alloys facility in the USA, where Allied boffins are working flat-out to reverse-engineer it.

Churchill hasn't told Gibson whether he'll seek to build a British Giant. The descriptions of the mechanism are, of course, almost useless. When people realize something is possible, though, even if they don't understand how, it tends to focus their minds. But Gibson suspects that research leading towards a British Giant will be discouraged. Churchill will have any eggheads who ignore the warnings 'dealt with', whatever their nationality. The consequences otherwise are too dangerous and, worse, too unpredictable.

Gibson has spent the day walking his new Labrador on the moors. It's evening and the moon is up as he returns to base. It's a bomber's moon, full and shimmering high in the sky, beckoning him back over enemy territory.

He steps out of the car and whistles the dog to heel.

$\oplus$

Prague in the summer and a Mercedes-Benz staff car.

Kubiš will drop his handkerchief when he observes the car and confirms that Heydrich is in the back. We'll hit it as it slows to navigate the bend. Thirty seconds after that, our feud will be over one way or another.

$\oplus$

Kitty had been wonderful.

We spent a blissful week recovering in a cabin in the highlands of Scotland. During the day we walked for hours across the austere rock-hewn landscape. I used the Prime Minister's name to get a Dior dress flown up to our hideaway. Each evening, Kitty wore it, and we

dined from a Fortnum and Mason hamper and made love by candle-
light. I was as gentle as possible with her. She'd seen enough brutality
for one lifetime.

I had to ask her, though. 'Did you realize that phosphorus grenade
from the Northover projector had a chance of going through the
Heart of Stone?'

'I suppose it worked because glass doesn't conduct electricity?'

I nodded as if I'd known that all along. 'Heisenberg must have
made it using Giant technology. No metal weapon could touch
Heydrich, and no human either. He had to burn – that was his vulnerability. I meant for you to fetch the grenade for me to use, you
know. It took you a lot longer than I expected.'

'The two ammunition boxes were both empty. I was about to give
up when I spotted the last unbroken phosphorus grenade in the
tower's gutter.'

'What were you thinking?'

Kitty looked embarrassed. 'I . . . he was going to kill you . . . and I
thought of Molly. She said you have to protect the ones you love.'

But I knew things had to end. On the last day, I presented Kitty with
the tickets.

'Don't send me away,' she whispered.

'I'm too old for you,' I said. 'You'd have no kind of future with me.'

Slow tears rolled down Kitty's face. She opened the envelope and
spread the Cunard Line tickets across the kitchen table, frowning.

'New York?'

'While you're there, you may want to look somebody up. He's a
young man, works for British Security Coordination. I think you and
he might be rather suited to each other. God knows, he needs someone.'

⊕

Kubiš drops the handkerchief.

Heydrich's Mercedes slows to negotiate the corner. Gabčík runs into the road raising his Sten gun. The driver swerves and Heydrich's head whips round. The car squeals to a halt opposite my hideaway. I pick up the Thermos bomb. Heydrich shouts to the driver to get the hell out of there, but the driver isn't listening. Gabčík stands in the centre of the road with his sub-machine gun levelled.

The Sten fires one round and then jams. The driver grabs his gun and Heydrich stands up in the back aiming his pistol. Gabčík drops on to one knee and pulls the magazine from the side of the Sten. He taps the base on the ground, trying to loosen the jammed rounds.

Heydrich and his driver fire at the figure crouching in front of them. They are less than fifteen yards away.

Gabčík and his useless gun are only a diversion, anyway. I lob the bomb in a high arc towards the limousine.

Too late, Heydrich spots the grenade hurtling through the air. He falls over the bodywork trying to dive away from it.

I duck back behind the wall. The effective explosive blast of the Thermos bomb is further than the distance I've thrown it.

The bomb explodes on impact.

⊕

It's another world, New York.

Kitty walks down the steps of St Patrick's Cathedral amidst the crowd from the noonday mass. On Fifth Avenue, a newsboy hands her a *New York Times* in return for three cents. The headline says:

CHURCHILL PREDICTS HUGE ALLIED DRIVE IN 1943.
CONGRESS THRILLED.
PRIME MINISTER HOLDS VICTORY IS CERTAIN.
HE GETS OVATION.

Earlier, Kitty walked into Macy's and bought a Glenn Miller record. Tears slid down her cheeks as she handed over the money. The shopgirl put her arm round her and enquired what the matter was. Kitty was unable to explain. She asked the girl if the shop had any further jazz or swing. The girl thought they might have a couple more left somewhere, what with it being so popular and all.

Across the street, towering over the cars, is a four-storey-high statue of a man carrying the world on his shoulders: Atlas, who revolted against Zeus and whose punishment was to spend eternity supporting the heavens. She looks past the statue and stares up at the International Building, counting the floors. On the thirty-fifth, she hopes, a young man is staring down at the crowd coming out of the cathedral. In his hand is a letter with a London postmark.

Kitty resolves to stay in this young, hopeful country and stop struggling with the things that are behind her.

There's a lot to forget.

She crosses Fifth Avenue and walks towards the building.

⊕

Afterwards, there isn't much left.

Fragments of the Mercedes are scattered for fifty yards: glass, shrapnel, horsehair from the seats. The bomb landed inside the limousine, and blood and body parts are everywhere. I spot the driver's head lying in the road to the right of the car.

But Heydrich has ceased to exist.

Behind me, all around me, I sense the ghostly presence of an endless army of murdered, tortured SOE heroes and heroines. I can almost hear the music. Wherever they are, Erling and Alex will be cheering. Even Reg will have a grudging smile.

This, all of this, is for them.

Gabčík lies unconscious still clutching his Sten gun. Kubiš runs past me and lifts his comrade's head in his hands. Blood flows from Gabčík's nose and ears. Kubiš picks him up.

A Škoda roars up behind us. The driver leans over and flings the passenger door open.

'For pity's sake, do I look like I've all day to hang around?' she shouts.

Kubiš hauls Gabčík into the back seat and I grab the front. I glance over at the girl behind the wheel and drink in the sight.

'And there you were worrying about getting old,' I say.

The girl is wearing a flying jacket and her dark hair is tucked up beneath a beret.

'Is it a bang on the head you've had?' she asks, glancing at me.

The way she laughs.

I remember something Kitty said one night as we lay in bed in our cabin in the Highlands.

'Poor Molly, for all her hard words she sacrificed herself to save me. Why was that?'

I don't know, but I'm going to find out.

Again I glance over at the girl driving the car. Her mouth is turned down as she concentrates on drifting through the corners, with the tyres squealing.

'I admire your courage, Miss . . .'

'Ravenhill, Molly Ravenhill.'

Epilogue

NOTED: (UNTRANSLATABLE) RECEIVED:
TRANSIENT SIGNAL ~ SPACE-TIME COORDINATES
(UNTRANSLATABLE) ~ POSSIBLE DAMAGED/MALFUNCTIONING
SURVIVOR BEACON ~ PROBE DISPATCHED.

Automated Hyperborean refugee search algorithm, Alcyone,
Pleiades Cluster, date/time outside human frame of reference

Notes

Ye may kill for yourselves, and your mates,
and your cubs as they need, and ye can;
But kill not for pleasure of killing,
and seven times never kill Man.

Rudyard Kipling, *The Law of the Jungle*

Glossary

NB: these definitions are accurate in the alternative timeline not the original timeline.

A4 Thor/ A9 Atlas/ A10 Atlantik/ A11 Germania/ A12 Europa	German ballistic missiles. Initially bombardment weapons, now used for space exploration. The manned A9 stage is capable of launching separately or stacking on a combination of A10, A11 and A12 boosters to give transcontinental or orbital capability. The full stack is capable of placing ten tonnes of cargo into orbit.
Abwehr	German military intelligence. Rival of the SD.
Adlon	Berlin's premier hotel. Located on Unter den Linden, opposite the Brandenburg Gate.
AEO	Air Electronics Officer. Aircrew responsible for electronic warfare such as jammers, warning radar, infrared flares and radar decoys.
Ahnenerbe	Nazi organization researching the anthropological and cultural history of the Aryan race. Regarded as incompetent pseudoscientists outside Germany.
AI Mk IV – Mk XI	Airborne Interception Radar used by British fighters to locate enemy aircraft.
AK-47	Soviet assault rifle, similar to the German Sturmgewehr. Much inferior in accuracy to the British Enfield Mk 9.

Arborite	Composite material made from paper and resin.
Attlee, Clement	Labour politician. Prime Minister of the UK from 1941 to 1950. Created the National Health Service and implemented the welfare state and nationalization. Consistent opponent of Nazism.
Baker Street	SOE's and later the Service's headquarters.
Beaufighter, Bristol	British two-engined, long-range heavy fighter. Obsolete by 1945.
Benzedrine	Amphetamine with euphoric, stimulant and appetite-suppressing effects. Often issued to military units in combat.
Bf-109, Messerschmitt	German single-piston-engined interceptor. Obsolete by 1944.
Bf-110, Messerschmitt	German twin-piston-engined fighter-bomber and night-fighter. Obsolete by 1944.
Black propaganda	Propaganda that purports to be from a friendly source but is actually from an enemy one. Generally more effective than simple propaganda because the listener is more receptive.
Blockleiter	Lowest political official of the Nazi party, responsible for the political supervision of a neighbourhood.
BOAC	British Overseas Airways Corporation. The 'flag-carrier' airline responsible for maintaining the British Empire's air links.
Bohr, Niels	Danish theoretical physicist and one of the fathers of quantum mechanics. Werner Heisenberg's doctoral supervisor.
Bormann, Martin	Rose to power as Rudolf Hess's private secretary. Promoted on Hess's death to head of the Reichskanzlei. De facto leader of Germany since Hitler's third heart attack, due to his manipulation of the semi-comatose Führer.

Brigadeführer	SS-Brigade Leader, equivalent to British Brigadier.
Browning hi-power	Single-action, 9 mm semi-automatic handgun.
BSC	British Security Coordination. Cover name of British Intelligence in the USA.
Buckley, Patricia	Secretary with Top Secret clearance. Recently promoted to the Service director's office.
Burgess, Guy	British spy who was actually a mole for the Soviet Union.
Canaris, Wilhelm	Head of the Abwehr, the German military intelligence service. Defected to the British in 1954.
Canberra, English Electric	British twin-jet-powered bomber able to fly at great altitude.
Churchill, Winston	British Conservative politician. Prime Minister of the UK, 1940–41. Died 1941 in an air raid.
Danzig	City and Reichsgau in West Prussia. Formed by annexing the Free City of Danzig (Polish name Gdańsk) and Polish territory.
D-Type Jaguar	Successful British racing car that won Le Mans.
Edelweisspiraten	Anti-Nazi youth group often in conflict with the Hitler-Jugend. Periodically suppressed by the Nazi authorities.
Eden, Anthony	British Conservative politician. Prime Minister from 1950 to date.
Elliott, Nicholas	MI6 officer who failed to apprehend Russian mole Guy Burgess.
Enfield M1914	British bolt-action rifle of the Great War period. Issued to the Home Guard and other rear area units in later years.
Enfield Mk 9	Innovative British assault rifle with a compact layout and 0.28 calibre ammunition. Replaced the bolt-action Lee-Enfield rifle in 1951.

Eureka beacon	Radio homing device used with a separate 'Rebecca' receiver to find range and bearing to its position. Used to locate drop zones.
F Section	Service department responsible for resistance in occupied France.
Fallschirmjäger	German paratroopers.
FANY	First Aid Nursing Yeomanry. A British all-female military unit formed in 1907 and active to the present day.
FDR	Franklin Delano Roosevelt. The 32nd President of the USA.
Flugscheibe	Flying disc. Commonly known as a flying saucer.
Franco, Francisco	Spanish general. Dictator of Spain from 1936 onwards.
Friedrich Wilhelms university	Berlin's oldest university, established in 1810, situated on the Opernplatz in the Mitte district of Berlin.
Freisler, Roland	President of the Nazi People's Court, which has jurisdiction over offences against the state.
Fuchs, Klaus	German–British theoretical physicist and spy who betrayed nuclear weapons secrets to the USSR.
Gauleiter	Leader of a regional branch of the Nazi Party. In practice the de facto ruler of a region of Germany with his decisions rubber-stamped by the de jure administration.
GCHQ	Government Communications Headquarters. British agency responsible for signals intelligence. Situated at Bletchley Park until 1951, when it moved to Cheltenham.
Gebirgstruppen	German mountain troops.
Geheime Reichsache	Secret Reich Business. Equivalent of Top Secret.

George Cross/ George Medal	Highest and second highest civil decorations of the United Kingdom. The George Cross is the civilian counterpart of the Victoria Cross. Eligible Service agents receive these medals, as they're not technically in the armed forces.
Gestapo	Geheime Staatspolizei. German secret police, responsible for suppressing 'political crime'.
Gibson, Guy	RAF officer and 'Saviour of the British Empire'.
Göring, Hermann	Commander-in-Chief of the Luftwaffe from 1933 until 1951. Also held many other prestigious positions in the Reich. Died of a gunshot wound whilst hunting with Reynard Heydrich.
Goudsmit, Samuel	Dutch atomic physicist. Now a professor at the Massachusetts Institute of Technology, USA.
Grand Slam	Non-nuclear, ten-tonne 'earthquake bomb' used by RAF Bomber Command against hardened strategic targets.
H2S	Code name of British terrain-mapping radar. by Used bombers to find their target. An extension to H2S known as Fishpond gives early warning of approaching German fighters.
Harriman, Averell	Franklin D. Roosevelt's special envoy to Britain in 1941. US ambassador to the United Kingdom, 1950 to date.
Hauptmann	Rank in the Luftwaffe. Equivalent to a British squadron leader.
He-111, Heinkel	German twin-engined medium bomber designed in the early 1930s and obsolete by 1942.
Health and Efficiency	Magazine extolling the virtues of nudism (with photos). Almost as popular as *Amateur Photographer*, and for the same reason.
Heisenberg, Werner	Germany's premier theoretical physicist and father of Germany's atom bomb.

Hess, Rudolf	Nazi Germany's Deputy Führer. Killed in an ambush by Ukrainian partisans, 1949. Germany's space station is named after the dead Nazi.
Heydrich, Reinhard	Reichsführer of the SS and Reichsprotektor of the Eastern Territories.
Himmler, Heinrich	Reichsführer of the SS, and a leading member of the Nazi Party. Died in 1954 after accidentally ingesting cyanide during a demonstration of suicide pills.
Hitler, Adolf	De jure leader of Nazi Germany. Currently gravely ill, with de facto authority assumed by Martin Bormann. Beyond occasional rumours, the public is unaware of Hitler's incapacity.
Hitler-Jugend	Compulsory Nazi group for boys from 14 to 18. SS Panzer Division 'Hitlerjugend' inducts the most fanatical boys at the age of sixteen.
Hoover, J. Edgar	Director of the Federal Bureau of Investigation of the United States, 1924 to date.
Horst-Wessel Song	Popular Nazi anthem, written by a 'martyred' storm trooper.
Hyperborea	Mythical region 'beyond' the North Pole.
Jerry	British slang term for German.
Ju-230, Junkers	German flying wing fighter-bomber. Powered by four BMW 013 turbojets mounted side by side above the trailing edge of the wing.
Ju-590, Junkers	German military transport aircraft capable of carrying up to one hundred paratroopers. Powered by four BMW 1011A turbojets.
Kaltenbrunner, Ernst	Obergruppenführer. General of Police. President of Interpol. Psychopath.
KdF-Wagen	Nazi 'strength through joy' motorcar. Buyers collect stamps in a savings book, which is then redeemed for the car.

Konzentrationslager	Concentration camp for 'anti-social elements' and other opponents of the Nazis.
Krag-Jørgensen M1930	Norwegian bolt-action sniper rifle. An improvement on the M1923 and M1925, with a heavier barrel and better sight.
Kriegsentscheidend	War Decisive. Germany's ultimate strategic priority rating.
Kripo	German criminal police, responsible for investigating 'non-political' crimes such as murder, robbery, etc.
Kübelwagen	German light all-terrain vehicle, equivalent to a Land Rover.
Lebensborn	SS programme providing financial assistance to Aryan mothers with the goal of breeding more cannon-fodder.
Lebensraum	Living space. The concept that Germany is justified in annexing territory for itself at the expense of 'inferior' peoples.
Lewis gun	British Great-War-vintage light machine gun. Obsolete by 1940.
Lloyd George, David	Liberal politician and statesman. Prime Minister of the UK 1916–22 and for six months in 1941. Died in 1945 of cancer.
Luftfaust	German shoulder-launched anti-aircraft missile.
Luger	German semi-automatic pistol. Designed by Georg Luger in 1898. Produced from 1900 to 1945.
Lysander, Westland	British special-duties aircraft capable of flying from small, unprepared airstrips such as fields. Used to recover agents from enemy territory.
Mae West	Nickname of inflatable lifejacket, named after the busty movie star, whom the devices make the wearer resemble.

Manchester Guardian	British newspaper with a centre-left, non-conformist outlook.
Marks, Leo	SOE code breaker who rose to become chief of staff of the Service.
Menzies, Stewart	Long-serving head of MI6 and the Service.
MG42	German general-purpose machine gun.
MI5	British counter-intelligence.
MI6	British intelligence. Merged with SOE to form 'the Service'.
Mills bomb	British hand grenade. In service 1915 to date.
Moisin-Nagant	Standard rifle of Soviet troops until replaced by the AK-47 assault rifle. Also used as a scoped sniper rifle.
Motor torpedo boat	Small, fast ship designed to carry torpedoes.
Northover projector	Makeshift anti-tank weapon issued to Home Guard units. Never used in anger, thank God, as it's useless.
No. 76 SIP (Self Igniting Phosphorus)	Anti-tank weapon using yellow phosphorus and benzene. In trials, caused tanks no inconvenience whatsoever. Produced in vast quantities and issued to the Home Guard.
Obergruppenführer	SS Senior Group Leader, equivalent to British lieutenant general.
Obergruppenführersaal	SS generals' hall. Meeting place for the highest ranks of the SS.
Oberstgruppenführer	SS Supreme Group Leader, equivalent to British general.
Obersturmbannführer	SS Senior Storm Command Leader, equivalent to a British lieutenant colonel.
Obersturmführer	SS Senior Storm Leader, equivalent to British lieutenant.

Oppenheimer, Robert	Professor at the University of California, Berkeley, famed for his work on cosmic rays.
Orpo	Ordnungpolizei. The uniformed police force in Nazi Germany. Responsible for maintaining public order.
Pash, Boris	Los Angeles high school teacher and US Army Reserve officer.
Peri, Andre	Captain of HMS Fidelity/La Rhin. Wanted for piracy.
Philby, Kim	British spy suspected of being a mole for the Soviet Union.
Prinz-Albrecht-Strasse	Location of the SS Berlin headquarters.
RAF	Royal Air Force. The British air force.
Rechlin airfield	Aviation testing facility, laboratory and research centre of the Luftwaffe. Equivalent to the British Farnborough.
Regia Aeronautica	Royal Air Force. The kingdom of Italy's air force.
Regia Marina	Royal Navy. The navy of the kingdom of Italy.
Reich Plan for the Domination of Europe	Nazi plan to exploit the resources of the entire European continent. Also known as the European Community.
Reichsautobahn	German motorway system.
Reichsdeutsche	A German who is a citizen of Germany (as opposed to living abroad).
Reichsführer-SS	The leader of the SS. Equivalent to a British field-marshal.
Reichsgau	German administrative area formed from the territory of occupied/annexed states, mostly in Eastern Europe.
Reichskanzlei	Reich Chancellery. Hitler's 'office' in Berlin.
Reichsmark	Currency of Nazi Germany.

Reichsmarine	German peacetime navy (renamed Kriegsmarine in wartime).
Reichsrundfunk Berlin	Radio station controlled by the Nazi Propaganda Ministry.
Reichstag	Meeting place of the German parliament. Severely damaged in a fire in 1933. Fire used to justify seizure of power by Nazis. Building demolished in 1943.
RIAF	Royal Israeli Air Force. The air force of the dominion of Israel.
Riley	A British car maker. Sister company of Morris, Wolseley and MG.
Rorke's Drift	A battle in the Anglo-Zulu War where 150 British soldiers beat off an assault by 4,000 Zulus, winning eleven Victoria Crosses.
Rotodyne, Fairey	British compound gyroplane (cross between a helicopter and a conventional aircraft). Designed and built by Fairey Aviation.
RPG-2	Russian shoulder-launched anti-tank grenade launcher.
S-Bahn	German city centre and suburban railway, primarily used by commuters.
Scholl, Hans	Major figure in the White Rose, executed by the Nazis.
Scholl, Sophie	Major figure in the White Rose, executed by the Nazis.
Scotland, Alexander	Director of 'the Cage', a British interrogation centre.
SD	Sicherheitsdienst: the intelligence service of the Nazi SS.
Section 18B	Law in the UK implemented in 1939 that authorized 'preventative detention' without trial of potential traitors.

Service, the	Intelligence and subversion agency formed from the merger of MI6 and SOE. Riven by conflict between the two factions.
SHAI (or SHA'I)	Sherut ha'Yediot ha'Artzit, Information Service. Established in 1940 as Israel's intelligence and counter-espionage arm. Officially illegal, but unofficially allied with the Service.
SOE	Special Operations Executive. British sabotage/resistance organization. Merged with MI6 to form the Service.
Speer, Albert	Adolf Hitler's chief architect and Minister for Space Exploration.
Spear of Destiny	Spear with reputed supernatural powers due to having pierced the side of Jesus as he hung on the cross. Now in Nazi Germany.
SS	Schutzstaffel, a Nazi paramilitary organization that started as Hitler's bodyguard but grew via responsibility for intelligence, security and policing to became a state-within-a-state. Has its own military force, the Waffen-SS.
SS-Gebirgs-Division	Waffen-SS mountain division.
SS-Freiwilligen-Schikompanie Norwegen	SS volunteer ski-troop formed from collaborationist Norwegians, Swedes and Danish who are expert skiers.
SS-Mann	SS man. Equivalent to a British private.
SS-Schütze	SS rifleman. Equivalent to a British private.
Stalingrad	City on the river Don where the German 6th Army was surrounded and all but destroyed.
Station 26	Glenmore Lodge, Inverness-shire, Scottish highlands. SOE Arctic warfare training centre, primarily for raids on occupied Norway.
Station IX	Service weapons research, development and production site near Welwyn Garden City.

Station XIV	Service site near Roydon, Essex, contained the Forgery section.
Sten	British sub-machine gun. Cheap but unreliable.
Stern gang	Militant Zionist group aiming to evict the British from Israel.
Sturmbannführer	SS Storm Command Leader, equivalent to British major.
Sturmgewehr-45	German assault rifle developed in the late 1940s when combat experience showed volume of fire to be more important than long-range accuracy.
Ta-183, Focke-Wulf	German jet interceptor. Its nickname, Huckebein, is a reference to a trouble-causing comic book raven called Hans Huckebein.
Thermos bomb	British No. 73 anti-tank grenade. Resembles a vacuum flask.
Thompson, Walter	Detective inspector in the Metropolitan Police. Winston Churchill's bodyguard 1921–1941.
Tube Alloys	Code-name for the British nuclear weapon project. Many of the development and production facilities were in Canada, out of range of German rockets.
Übermensch	Overman. A metaphysical concept of a superior man, perverted by the Nazis and defined in their racial terms to mean themselves.
Ultima Thule	Mythical ancient land mass to the north of Iceland and Greenland.
Untermenschen	Sub-humans. People regarded as inferior by the Nazis e.g. Jews, Gypsies, Slavs and non-Europeans.
Unterscharführer	SS Under Company Leader, equivalent to a British sergeant.
Valentine, Avro	Supersonic British airliner. Civilian version of the Avro Vanquish.

Valetta, Vickers	British twin-engine military transport aircraft of the late 1940s.
Vanquish, Avro	Supersonic British bomber, developed from the earlier Vulcan.
Vemork	Town in the county of Telemark, Norway. Site of the Wasserkraftwerk Vemork, a hydroelectric power station.
Venlo Incident	SD operation that lured MI6 into thinking there was a group of German Army officers plotting a coup d'état against Hitler. The officers assigned to help the plotters were kidnapped, and the information they gave the Nazis severely damaged MI6. Britain subsequently shunned most German resistance movements.
V-Force	Britain's nuclear deterrent force. Operated by the RAF.
Vichy	Pejorative name for collaborationist France.
von Braun, Wernher	German rocket scientist and space pioneer. The leading figure in the development of Nazi Germany's rockets.
von Manstein, Erich	German Field Marshal responsible for the relief of Stalingrad and the stabilization of the Eastern front in 1942.
Waffen-SS	Military units under the control of the SS rather than the regular German army.
Wasserfall	German surface-to-air missile developed using the same technology as the A9.
Watching Committee, the	There is no proof that this so-called committee exists. If it does exist, it cannot possibly consist of the two dozen most powerful persons in the British Empire. It's a purely ceremonial organization, which possesses no influence. Suggestions that the Watching Committee controls the British Empire are laughable. Paranoid witch hunters will not be

363

permitted to slander its members. It has no members. Because it doesn't exist.

Wehrmacht	Armed forces of Nazi Germany, including army (Heer), navy (Kriegsmarine) and air force (Luftwaffe).
Wellington, Vickers	British twin-engined medium bomber designed in the mid-1930s and obsolete by 1943.
White Rose, the	Religiously motivated non-violent resistance movement in Nazi Germany. Initially suppressed by the Gestapo in 1943. Survives underground and remains an irritant to the Nazi state.
Will to Power	The instinct to survive, grow, spread, seize and become predominant. Described by philosopher Friedrich Nietzsche as the driving force of existence.
Wunderwaffe	Wonder weapon. Group name for German next-generation weapons like rockets and jet fighters.
X-4, Ruhrstahl	First-generation German wire-guided air-to-air missile.
Z22, Zuse	Germany's most powerful computer. Claimed to be the most powerful computer in the world. Claim disputed by Britain's computer makers.

Alternative History Timeline

1939

- Nazi Germany invades Poland beginning the Second World War.
- Emergency Powers (Defence) Act passed including Defence Regulation 18B which authorizes 'preventative detention' of potential traitors.
- USA passes the policy of 'cash and carry', replacing the Neutrality Acts of 1936 and enabling Great Britain and France to buy war materiel from the USA.

1940

- Battle of France leads to French surrender and British retreat from Dunkirk.
- Widespread arrests of anti-war figures using Defence Regulation 18B.
- Hitler delivers his 'last appeal to reason' offering the British peace.
- SOE created.
- The Royal Air Force wins the Battle of Britain removing any chance of Germany's invading Britain and forcing a quick surrender.
- Franklin D. Roosevelt (Democrat) wins re-election as President of the USA.
- 'Destroyers for Bases' deal gives USA bases in Newfoundland and the Caribbean in return for fifty obsolete US destroyers.
- Tizzard Mission supplies the USA with many British technological secrets including radar, the jet engine, atomic research.

1941

- British Security Coordination operational in the USA.
- Italian Tenth Army in Libya surrenders to British.
- German 5th Light Afrika Division commanded by Erwin Rommel arrives in Libya to prevent Italian collapse.
- Lend-Lease Act passed in the USA.
- Rommel pushes the British back to the Egyptian border.
- Churchill survives parliamentary 'vote of no confidence'.
- Rudolph Hess, deputy Führer of Nazi Germany, arrives by air at Dungavel House, the estate of the Duke of Hamilton in Scotland.
- **Point Of Departure:** Hess meets several senior representatives of the 'Peace Party' of Great Britain.

NB: Alternative history from this point onwards.

1941 (cont.)

- Negotiations produce a formula for peace: Britain will leave Europe to Germany, and Germany will leave Britain to its empire.
- Churchill dies after a fluke bomb hits his residence, Ditchley House.
- The King is informed of the negotiations and approves. With Churchill dead, the King dissolves parliament and appoints David Lloyd George as caretaker Prime Minister.
- The Labour Party, with the support of some Conservatives, tables a motion of no confidence in the Lloyd George government but is defeated.
- German invasion of Crete.
- Anthony Eden resigns from parliament and tries to whip up popular discontent with the peace treaty.
- Organized resistance on Crete ceases and a ceasefire between Germany and the British Empire is declared.
- Anthony Eden is arrested under section 18B.
- Anglo-German peace treaty signed in Berlin.
- With the war over, the British cancel their purchases of war materiel from the USA.
- British Security Coordination shut down by the FBI.

- Operation Barbarossa (invasion of Russia by Germany) begins.
- General Election in the UK. Labour Party returned in a landslide on a platform of opposition to the peace treaty. Clement Attlee becomes Prime Minister.
- SOE deactivation cancelled by incoming anti-Nazi Labour government.
- The ceasefire between Germany and Britain holds, but the peace treaty is never ratified.
- The Wehrmacht approaches Moscow. Stalin deploys Siberian divisions to its defence, halting the attack.

1942

- Wannsee Conference informs heads of German government departments of their responsibility for executing the 'Final Solution of the Jewish Problem'.
- The Wehrmacht strikes south, attempting to seize the Caucasus oil fields.
- Fighting without allies, the Red Army puts up stiff resistance.
- Realizing that the stimulus of armament production is the only thing boosting the US economy out of recession, President Roosevelt tries to extend Lend-Lease to Russia. He is defeated in Congress.
- The US economy returns to slump. Unemployment hits 25 per cent.
- First gas chamber at Auschwitz becomes operational.
- Battle of Stalingrad begins.
- With intelligence on the mass murder of Jews on the Eastern Front and the extermination camps, the British offer to allow European Jews to emigrate to the British Empire.
- Encouraged by the British, the Vatican intervenes to condemn the murder of Jews.
- Clement Attlee threatens to re-enter the war. Hitler, at a critical stage of the Battle of Stalingrad and concerned by the forceful condemnation of the Final Solution by the Catholic Church, agrees to allow the emigration of the remaining Jews.
- Stalin throws his reserves into the Battle of Stalingrad. The Wehrmacht takes huge losses. A Russian counterattack succeeds in

surrounding the German 6th Army. Much of the 6th Army is destroyed in the subsequent breakout.

1943
- Transport of Jews to Auschwitz ends.
- After the disaster at Stalingrad, the advance on the Caucasus is abandoned. Field Marshal von Manstein succeeds in stabilizing the front.
- The British, fearing a renewed Nazi onslaught if the Soviet Union is defeated, work feverishly on their atomic bomb project, codenamed Tube Alloys, making good use of Jewish nuclear physicists expelled from Germany.
- Believing an atomic bomb cannot be built in time to win the war against the Soviets, Germany concentrates on its rocket programme.
- Transport of European Jews to Britain begins. Attlee announces the majority will be sent to Palestine. Others will be allowed to stay in Britain, or move elsewhere in the British Empire or the USA.
- Nearly two million Jews choose Palestine as their new home; the USA accepts half a million, Britain one hundred thousand and the rest of the British Empire four hundred thousand.
- Weakened by the heavy fighting, Germany is on the strategic defensive; unable to destroy the numerically superior Soviets, but still powerful enough to beat back any offensives. The Eastern Front is a stalemate.
- Last transport of European Jews arrives in Britain.
- First use of German A4 Thor rockets against Leningrad.
- Beria, chief of Soviet intelligence, murders Stalin and attempts to seize power.
- The Beria coup fails. Molotov becomes General Secretary of the Communist Party of the Soviet Union.
- Last transport of Jews arrives in the British Mandate of Palestine.
- Deputy Führer Hess meets Molotov to negotiate a German–Russian peace treaty, which includes Russian recognition of Germany's control of the Baltic States, the Ukraine, Belarus and Poland.

1944

- Without the power to challenge the British, the Arab nations are forced to accept the Jewish Exodus.
- Palestine is renamed Israel and becomes a dominion of the British Empire.
- Thomas Dewey (Republican) wins US Presidential Election.

1945

- First test of German A9 Atlas rocket.
- General election in the UK. Labour victory. Attlee returned to power.
- The Wehrmacht masses in the Caucasus, preparing to invade the Middle East and destroy Israel. The British are aware of German preparations.

1946

- The British 'demonstrate' the fruit of the Tube Alloys programme on an uninhabited island in the Baltic – the world's first atomic weapon.
- On learning of the British bomb, Hitler has a mild heart attack.
- The British announce a doctrine of 'containment' of Germany. Any advance by German forces towards the Middle East, across the Atlantic, or back into Russia, will be met with atomic retaliation.
- Hitler, Molotov and Dewey order crash programmes for atomic weapons.

1947

- SOE and MI6 merge to form 'the Service'. Major General Sir Stewart Menzies, ex-director of MI6, is the director of the combined service and Major General Colin Gubbins, ex-director of SOE, is the chief of staff.
- 'Vemork Operation' destroys Nazi supply of heavy water, slowing the German atomic programme.
- Attempts by German spies to discover British nuclear secrets, and British attempts to prevent German acquisition of uranium and heavy water through sabotage and covert action blamed on the Soviet

Union, bring the 'cold war' between the British and the Germans to a new level of tension.

- President Dewey agrees to free trade with the British Empire in return for Britain supplying nuclear research and materials.
- In return for British nuclear guarantees, Molotov agrees to end the Soviet Union's commitment to worldwide Communist revolution and winds up the Comintern.
- Soviet spies seek Britain's nuclear secrets with greater success than the Abwehr. Klaus Fuchs provides the Russians with much of the necessary data to build a bomb.
- First US atomic bomb tested.

1948
- First German in-service launch of A9/A10 Atlantik rocket.
- First Russian atomic bomb tested.
- Gubbins murdered by disaffected ex-MI6 officer. Leo Marks becomes chief of staff of the Service.
- Free trade leads to economic boom in the USA and the British Empire.
- Thomas Dewey re-elected as US President.

1949
- Deputy Führer Hess ambushed and killed by Ukrainian partisans.
- Nazi retaliation against Ukrainian civilians appals world opinion. Britain and the Soviet Union withdraw their ambassadors 'for consultations', raising tensions.
- Office of Deputy Führer abolished.
- Martin Bormann, Hess's private secretary, becomes head of the Nazi Party Chancellery, reporting directly to Hitler.
- Germany produces its first atomic weapon.

1950
- General election in the UK. Conservative victory. Anthony Eden becomes Prime Minister.
- Hitler has a second, more serious, heart attack. This is kept secret.

Martin Bormann restricts access to the Führer and begins to issue orders in his name.

- A German is the first man in space. Launched on three-stage A9/A10/A11 Germania rocket.
- Death of Hermann Göring in a hunting accident.

1951

- Nuclear Non-Proliferation Treaty recognizes the Big Four, Britain, Germany, Russia and the USA, as the only possessors of nuclear weapons. Except for Japan, other nations agree not to build atomic bombs.
- The Japanese, economically the weakest of the Great Powers and without much of the necessary scientific and technological base required for building an atomic bomb, continue their nuclear research.
- The USA, cut out of many of the world's markets by the Germans, Russians and Japanese, remains happy in its isolation and suspicious of involvement in world affairs.

1952

- Germany commences construction of the Rudolf Hess space station, a toroidal design, spun to provide artificial gravity.
- Hitler has third heart attack and is incapacitated. Martin Bormann becomes de facto Führer. Again, this is kept secret.
- Adlai Stevenson (Democrat) wins US presidential election.

1953

- First trial launch of A9/A10/A11/A12 Europa rocket, Germany's design for a rocket capable of reaching the moon.
- British bring Avro Vanquish, the world's first supersonic bomber, into service. The Vanquish is the world's biggest, fastest bomber and has the longest range.

1954

- General election in the UK. Conservative victory. Anthony Eden returned to power.

- Admiral Canaris defects to Britain after coming under increased suspicion of being a British agent.
- Heinrich Himmler dies. Reinhard Heydrich becomes head of the SS.

1955
- The British introduce the civilian version of the Avro Vanquish, the Valentine, on the London–Sydney route. It breaks all speed and distance records on its maiden flight.
- Events of *A Kill in the Morning.*

Factual Basis

In this story, as with any alternative history novel, I have trampled over several historical personalities in the name of entertainment. This is a work of fiction and their roles were assigned based on the requirements of drama, not fact. Below are brief notes on the real personalities and some of the concepts in the novel.

The narrator, Kitty, Molly and the Mitzi twins

The narrator, Kitty, Molly and the Mitzi twins are imaginary, although Kitty is very loosely based on Sophie Scholl, the original White Rose, and Molly is a composite of several of SOE's female agents including Violette Szabo.

Reinhard Heydrich

Czech patriots, armed by SOE, assassinated Reinhard Heydrich in 1942, possibly due to his deep suspicion of Admiral Canaris's loyalties. His subsequent career is speculation although not unreasonable in my opinion; he'd made a great success of pacifying the protectorates of Bohemia and Moravia and was seen as a huge threat by Himmler for one.

Operation Anthropoid

The description of Heydrich's assassination is based on Operation Anthropoid, a joint SOE/Czech resistance operation. Heydrich was only wounded in the real attack, but died from his injuries on 4 June 1942. Jozef Gabčík and Jan Kubiš were the real assassins and died in the aftermath of the attack.

Stewart Menzies

General Menzies was the head of British wartime intelligence and maintained control of code breaking, giving him immense power and influence in the British government. MI6 spent the war years in bureaucratic warfare with SOE and finally succeeded in absorbing and eliminating it in 1945. He retired in 1952 and died in 1968.

Leo Marks

Leo Marks was SOE's head of codes and introduced many innovations. After the war he was invited to join MI6 but refused and became a moderately successful screenwriter and playwright (his most famous film being *Peeping Tom*). He died in 2001.

SHAI

SHA'I (Sherut ha'Yediot ha'Artzit or National Information Service) was the intelligence and counter-espionage arm of the Haganah (a Jewish paramilitary organization in the British Mandate of Palestine) and the forebear of Mossad. During the Second World War, the Special Operations Executive supplied the Haganah with weapons, training and funding.

Reuven Shiloah

Reuven Shiloah was an Israeli spymaster and the first director of Mossad from 1949 to 1952. After Mossad, he was posted to the Israeli embassy in the USA. He died in 1959.

Ernst Kaltenbrunner

Kaltenbrunner was head of the SS in Austria. After Heydrich's assassination, he became chief of the Reich Main Security Office. Found guilty of war crimes and crimes against humanity at the Nuremberg Trials, he was executed in 1946.

Werner Heisenberg

Early in the Second World War, Heisenberg was involved in research into nuclear weapons. However, in 1942 the Germans concluded that nuclear weapons could not be produced in time to influence the war and deprioritized them. Heisenberg spent the rest of the war engaged in theoretical physics research. After the war, he became director of the Max Planck Institute for Physics. He died in 1976.

Nicholas Elliott

Elliott was a career intelligence officer and rose to become a director of MI6. He was sent to confront Kim Philby when the evidence that he was the mole in MI6 became overwhelming. Elliott obtained Philby's confession but could not prevent him from fleeing to Moscow. After retiring from MI6, Elliott was director of a mining company. He died in 1994.

Andre Peri

The story of La Rhin/HMS *Fidelity* in the novel is true up to 1941. In reality, Kriegsmarine U-boat U-435 torpedoed her on 30 December 1942 off the Azores. HMS *Fidelity* took 325 sailors and Royal Marines to their deaths, including her captain, Claude Andre Michel Peri.

Averell Harriman

Harriman was President Roosevelt's special envoy to Europe during the Second World War. After the war, he was US ambassador to the Soviet Union and then Britain. He was later governor of New York and a candidate for the Democratic presidential nomination. He died in 1958.

Admiral Canaris

Admiral Canaris was the head of the Abwehr, a deadly opponent of Nazism and in contact with the British. Whether he was truly a British agent or (more likely) playing his own game will probably never be known. The Gestapo arrested him after the failed attempt to assassinate Hitler in 1944. He was apparently executed just before the end of the war, although I've always wondered if the great survivor could have pulled off one last trick . . .

Guy Gibson

Guy Gibson was the first commander of the RAF's 617 Squadron 'the Dambusters'. Gibson was killed when his Pathfinder Mosquito crashed near Steenbergen in the Netherlands on 19 September 1944. 'Strawberry Blonde' is my invention, although G-George was Gibson's aircraft's call sign.

ALSOS

The ALSOS mission was a part of the Manhattan Project. It investigated German progress on nuclear energy. Samuel Goudsmit was the scientific head of the mission and Colonel Boris Pash was its commander. ALSOS captured the German nuclear project's records at the end of the Second World War and took the research personnel, including Werner Heisenberg, into custody.

Wewelsburg

Wewelsburg was Himmler's planned central ideological, pseudoscience and SS cult site. As mentioned in the text, many of the other Nazi leaders thought Himmler was a nutcase.

The real 'Obergruppenführersaal' and 'vault' are largely as described, although the vault was never fully completed as work on Wewelsburg stopped in 1943. Himmler ordered the castle destroyed in the final days of the war. It was restored later as a monument to the slave labourers from the nearby Niederhagen concentration camp who died building Himmler's folly.

Avro Vanquish

The Avro Vanquish and its civilian version the Valentine are based on plans for a supersonic Vulcan and a civilian version called the Atlantic, neither of which got off the drawing board. All the other weapons and aircraft are either real, planned or extrapolations. Some are ahead of their time, which I put down to consequences of the alternative timeline.

Flugscheibe

The Flugscheibe is based on the popular conspiracy theories about Nazi UFOs. There is some evidence that the Nazis did work on flying saucers. I suspect, though, they were probably as unsuccessful as post-war designs like the Avro Canada VZ-9 Avrocar, not the über-weapons of popular imagination. Still, it's a lot more fun to imagine all-conquering Nazi UFOs than feeble disc-shaped failures . . .

Giant

This brings us to the big one: Giant. Giant is based partly on 'die Glocke', an alleged Nazi super-weapon that supposedly disappeared at the end of the Second World War. No one knows much about it and it may not even have existed.

Vemork

The description of the Vemork raid is based on Operation Gunnerside, in which a team of SOE-trained Norwegian commandos succeeded in destroying the Norwegian heavy water production facility. Reg, Erling and Alex are imaginary characters.

FANY

FANY is a real organization, the First Aid Nursing Yeomanry. During the Second World War, many of the women in SOE were either recruited from FANY or were notionally part of it, as SOE's existence was an official secret. I've no evidence, but I find it hard to believe that the name wasn't a deliberate thing, as Molly suggests. It was officially changed in 1999 to the Princess Royal's Volunteer Corps but still seems to be used, even on the organization's own website. You couldn't make it up.

Hess's flight

Rudolf Hess flew to Scotland on 10 May 1941 intending to negotiate a peace treaty with the British Empire. There has been much speculation about his motives and whether there was a group in Britain who were prepared to negotiate with him, or whether he was tricked, deluded or insane. The true story will never be known, as the British archives have been 'weeded' and the protagonists are dead. Hess himself died in 1987 in Spandau prison, Berlin.

The Watching Committee

There was a real Watching Committee during the Second World War. It was headed by Lord Salisbury of the Cecil family, which has been one of the most influential in Britain since the sixteenth century. Its role in the removal of Neville Chamberlain as Prime Minister and the installation of Winston Churchill as Britain's war leader is not disputed. Whether it then disbanded, or merely *returned to the shadows*, is less clear . . .

Acknowledgements

I'd like to thank all the following people for their help and inspiration in the writing of this novel. All the remaining faults are my own.

- Sarah Jasmon, who showed me there *was* a theme (amongst other things).
- Jenny Sia, who tried to explain how people talk and what commas are.
- Seren Phillips, who had the courage to tell me which bits sucked.
- Gillian Barnett, who helped me get started as a novelist.
- Russell Charnock, who was always practical and supportive.
- Dave Almond, who read the very first draft.
- Antony Bircham, who was the first reader to say he 'couldn't put it down', which was a big boost.
- Kendal Aitken, who knew the universe would deliver me success if I asked it to.
- All the members of my class on the MMU Creative Writing MA, particularly Andy Dickinson, who managed to read the whole thing.
- The staff at MMU, particularly Nicholas Royle, who thought the book was a comedy, which was a lesson in humility.
- All the members of alternatehistory.com who voted *A Kill in the Morning* best story.

- Everyone on youwriteon.com, particularly Ted Smith who made *A Kill in the Morning* the YouWriteOn book of the year.
- Everyone on Quora, particularly Usman Rafi, my first reader outside the UK/USA, who reassured me *A Kill in the Morning* could work all over the world.
- Everyone who was at Lumb Bank in 2010 and Moniack Mhor in 2011/12/13 for being such a great bunch. Particularly Jo Cole, Steve Hollyman, Frank Coyle and Steve Galbraith, who all gave me useful feedback, and Myriam Frey, my German language adviser.
- Manchester Speculative Fiction Group, particularly Craig Pay, James Ridgway and Eric Steele, who all went through chapter after chapter hoping for more of Kitty.
- Terry Pratchett, for giving me my big break when *A Kill in the Morning* was shortlisted for his First Novel Award.
- Everyone at Transworld, especially my editor, Simon Taylor.
- Everyone at A. M. Heath, particularly my agent, Euan Thorneycroft.

Finally

If you enjoyed *A Kill in the Morning*, you'll be pleased to hear that every month I email a free short story to my friends and the people who love my writing. Sign up for it at:

http://graemeshimmin.com/free-story

About the Author

Graeme Shimmin was born in Manchester, and studied Physics at Durham University. His successful consultancy career enabled him to retire at 35 to an island off Donegal and start writing. He has since returned to Manchester and completed an MA in Creative Writing. The inspiration for *A Kill in the Morning* – his prizewinning first novel – came from Robert Harris's alternative history novel, *Fatherland*, and a passion for classic spy fiction.

To find out more, visit http://graemeshimmin.com.